The Wandering Heart

The Wandering Heart

Mary Malloy

A LeapSci Book
Leapfrog Science and History
Leapfrog Press
Teaticket, Massachusetts

1 - 9928

A LeapSci Book
Leapfrog Science and History

Published in 2009 in the United States by
Leapfrog Press LLC
PO Box 2110
Teaticket, MA 02536
www.leapfrogpress.com

Distributed in the United States by
Consortium Book Sales and Distribution
St. Paul, Minnesota 55114
www.cbsd.com

Cover Painting: *The Meeting on the Turret Stairs*
Frederic William Burton (1864)
Courtesy of the National Gallery of Ireland, Dublin

First Edition

Library of Congress Cataloging-in-Publication Data

Malloy, Mary, 1955-
 The wandering heart / Mary Malloy. -- 1st ed.
 p. cm.
 ISBN 978-0-9815148-5-7
 1. Women historians--Fiction. I. Title.
 PS3613.A455W36 2009
 813'.6--dc22

 2008046530

Printed in the United States of America

This book is dedicated to my mother,
Dolores Malloy,
who inspired me
first to read and then to write.

NOTE TO READERS:

This edition of *The Wandering Heart* includes a reader's guide featuring an extensive interview with the author. This section begins on page 395.

That anxious torture may I never feel,
Which, doubtful, watches o'er a wandering heart.
—Mary Tighe (1772-1810)

The Wandering Heart

Elizabeth Hatton was just nineteen years old when she threw herself off the roof of her family home. The maid, dusting in the library below, was the same age.

Elizabeth screamed as she fell as if, in midair, she'd reconsidered jumping and realized her mistake. The maid heard the scream, and then the awful sound as Elizabeth hit the flagstones of the terrace. Within a minute she was at Elizabeth's side, gently holding her hand and trying to comfort her with soft meaningless words.

She knew Elizabeth would be dead very soon; everything about her seemed broken. Head and neck, legs and arms, were all at impossible angles, and a bit of jagged bone was visible coming through her mangled calf. A pool of blood spread rapidly across the carefully cut stones under her head. Elizabeth gasped several times for breath, but seemed unable to make the air penetrate all the way to her chest. Her eyes were locked on the maid's when she made a last feeble attempt to breathe, then her pupils expanded rapidly and she went completely still.

As she reached out to close the dead eyes, the maid thought what a stupid, stupid, waste. Until this moment, she had thought Elizabeth Hatton the most fortunate of creatures. "Wouldn't I have known what to do with such a life," she thought. Elizabeth had sparkled with it: pretty, clever, beloved by her family, she seemed to have everything. She had never known want, never had to work. She could do what she wanted, go where she wanted, she had access to books and art and music. And she had thrown it all away because of a young man who was, in the maid's opinion, dull, shallow, spoiled, and stupid. All his wealth, position, and good looks could not disguise his worthlessness.

Elizabeth's last cry had been heard in the far corners of the house and now others began to emerge through the doors of the library onto the terrace. The first to arrive was Edmund. His sister's scream brought him running at full speed out of the house, but he came to an abrupt stop when he saw the horrible scene. He collapsed to his knees beside Elizabeth's body, moving his hands over her as if there might be something he could do, though he knew there was not. He hardly noticed the maid until she reached out and gently placed his dead sister's hand in his.

He looked up, directly into the eyes of the maid. In the four years she had lived in the house, this was the first time he had ever met her gaze. His grey eyes were filled with fear and a wild grief.

Looking back, the maid could not help but note how much he looked like his sister lying dead between them. To think that on this day, of all days, the brother and sister had each, for the first time, really looked at her. Had they noticed that she was, like them, a human being?

She rose to leave as others from the household arrived. Edmund touched her arm to hold her back.

"Wait," he said. "Did she say anything?"

The maid shook her head.

"May we speak later?" he asked.

She nodded.

As she went back into the house she couldn't help thinking that there would be a mess of blood and brains to clean up.

Chapter 1

The reading room in the library was Lizzie's favorite place on campus. Part of the attraction was the cathedral-like space, but mostly it was the light. Green-shaded lamps cast pools of light onto the polished wood of the tables but left much of the high-ceilinged room in a comfortable dimness. The tall windows were filled with small diamond-shaped panes of wavy glass which filtered the sunlight into a pleasant haze, but nothing viewed through these windows could be seen clearly unless you stepped right up and put your face almost against the cool surface of lead or glass. There were no sharp edges in the room. It had a spaciousness and softness which created exactly the atmosphere that Lizzie thought was most appropriate for contemplation and study. In such a room she could slip easily into the past.

In the real world, Elizabeth Manning was a history professor at St. Patrick's College in Charlestown, Massachusetts. In the big canvas book bag slung over her shoulder were papers to grade, bills to pay, an article to finish, and a letter. It was the letter which brought her here; this letter held the potential to take her across time and around the world.

Lizzie's friend, Jackie Harrigan, was head of the reading room and had an imposing perch at one end of it. Her desk was raised on a pedestal several steps above the floor to give her a view of her whole domain. Jackie raised her head when the door opened, ready to shoot her serious librarian expression at whoever entered, but she smiled when she saw her friend. The two women were the only occupants, and Lizzie consequently burst into song. She had once commented to a horrified Jackie that the acoustics of the room were better suited for singing than silence, and ever since had felt compelled to prove it on those rare occasions when they were alone there. For Jackie's benefit, Lizzie mostly sang bawdy Irish songs, and as she proceeded up the side aisle of the long room she progressed through several days of the "Seven Drunken Nights."

"Professor Manning!" Jackie scolded. "Must I remind you that this is a library?" It was her stock response to Lizzie's singing and always made Lizzie sing even louder.

The two women knew each other well enough, and saw each other often enough, that they seldom bothered to exchange pleasantries, but burst headlong into the middle of conversations. Today, Lizzie was anxious to get Jackie's opinion of the letter, and she had it out of her bag and onto the librarian's desk before either of them said hello.

"Here's something interesting," she said, "a letter from one George F. R. Hatton of Hengemont, Somerset, England." She tapped the envelope with her finger. "He has a coat of arms!"

Jackie turned the envelope around to examine it. On the shield of the crest was a heart being pierced by a long cross-shaped sword. Below it a curving ribbon held the motto *"Semper Memoriam."*

The librarian looked up at her friend. "Yuck!" she said. "A sword stabbing a heart? That's pretty graphic. It hardly seems like they need the motto there to tell you to remember it."

She pulled the contents from the envelope and quickly read the letter aloud. It was an invitation to Lizzie to come to George Hatton's home in the west of England and advise him on a collection of artifacts made by his ancestor, Lieutenant Francis Hatton of the British Royal Navy. The collection had been made on the third voyage of Captain James Cook to the Pacific Ocean. Jackie's tone changed as she read the letter.

"This is a wonderful opportunity for you, Lizzie," she said. "A Cook collection!"

Lizzie nodded. "Here's the best part," she said, pulling two photocopied pages from underneath the letter. "The guy kept a journal and it has never been published."

Jackie quickly scanned the pages. She was one of the few

people Lizzie knew who could read old handwriting as well as she did herself.

"Did you know about this when you were working on your book?"

"No!" Lizzie said emphatically. "No one did. It isn't in any bibliography, I've never even heard of it." She sighed with frustration, then took the pages from Jackie and began to point out certain passages. "It's an especially good one, too," she continued. "Francis Hatton was a wonderful writer, and a sympathetic and careful observer. I'm practically in love with him already, and I've only seen two pages."

Jackie looked again at the letter and its envelope. "Interesting that he invites you to stay at his house," she said, quoting a passage from the letter which promised Lizzie a "comfortable place to live and work" for however long she could spare for the project. "A castle perhaps?" Jackie continued, raising an eyebrow. "Or a stately home?"

Lizzie pointed to the return address, which said simply "Hengemont, Somerset."

"I think that's the name of his house," she said, beaming. "A house with a name!"

Jackie smiled and murmured under her breath about the dangers of reading too many British novels before asking her friend if she intended to accept the invitation.

"Of course," Lizzie answered quickly. "Martin and I talked about it a bit last night, and I've pretty much decided to go during the January break." She folded the pages. "I just want to find out what I can about Lieutenant Hatton before I jump off the deep end."

"Help yourself," Jackie said, gesturing toward the door to the library stacks. "You know better than anyone where the Cook material is."

Lizzie picked up her bag and was reaching for the letter when Jackie asked if she could keep it for a few minutes. "Let me see what I can find out about George Hatton while you look up his ancestor," she said.

Lizzie smiled her thanks and headed into the dusky world where the library kept the rare book collection on row after row of metal shelving. She knew exactly where to find the narrative of Captain James Cook's third voyage to the Pacific Ocean and she pulled it off the shelf on the way to her study carrel. She turned immediately to the crew list and his name jumped out at her: Francis Hatton, First Lieutenant on HMS *Resolution*. Among his shipmates were William Bligh and George Vancouver.

She began to compare the two pages from Francis Hatton's journal with the published account of the voyage. They described activities of the English expedition on the coast of British Columbia in 1778. Charming, well-written, and filled with detail, Hatton's text caught the immediacy of the exotic situations in which he found himself, and totally captivated Lizzie. She alternated between feeling a thrill of discovery and frustration that she hadn't known about this material when she was working on her dissertation and the book which resulted from it. In fact, she wondered again, why hadn't Hatton's journal ever been published? Every known scrap of manuscript material from Cook's three voyages had been pored over by scholars and publishers for two hundred years.

She had been working for half an hour when Jackie came down the spiral iron staircase with a stack of papers in her hand.

"I'm off to lunch," she said, handing them to Lizzie, "but here is some stuff on that Hatton guy. He has a rather interesting family." Beneath the letter were several photocopies topped by the title page to *Burke's Peerage*.

"You are a peach," Lizzie said. "I would never even have thought to look him up there."

"He's a Lord," Jackie said with a mock British accent.

Lizzie grinned at her friend. The two women had met in an Irish language class at St. Pat's and spent many late afternoons sharing pints of Guinness in the pub on campus. Their early relationship had been defined by tipsy explorations of the British victimization of their Hibernian ancestors, a subject Jackie returned to often.

"Thank you for warning me," Lizzie said, bowing. "I'll be sure to take my groveling clothes."

Jackie handed her the papers. "I think you'll find this very compelling reading, *mo chara*."

"Do they mention Francis Hatton's voyage with Cook?"

"Absolutely," Jackie answered. "He gets as much ink as any of them."

"So don't you think it's strange that his journal was never published?"

Jackie agreed that it was odd. "Could he have been hiding something that he didn't want made widely known?"

This had not occurred to Lizzie, and she thought it unlikely. "Like what?"

"I don't know," Jackie mused. "Maybe an affair with a Polynesian woman?"

"All the British sailors had affairs with Polynesian women!" Lizzie answered with a derisive laugh. "And I don't think they were all that embarrassed about it." She thought for another moment. "Of course they didn't usually document that kind of behavior in their *own* journals—they saved those descriptions for the actions of the *other* guys!"

The two women smiled at each other.

"Men!" Jackie sighed. "There were probably dozens of little Hattons scattered across the Pacific after the voyage."

"Well, not surprisingly, George Hatton did not choose to share that with me in my first encounter with the information," Lizzie said. "It will have to wait until I get to England and see the rest of the journal."

"Something to look forward to beyond the usual details of wind and weather," Jackie responded, turning to climb back up the stairs. "See you for lunch on Thursday," she said as she left.

Lizzie felt the small stack of pages in her hand. There wasn't time to look at them all before she had to be back in her office to meet with students.

Before she closed the volume of Cook's *Voyages,* she went back a last time to the crew list and ran her finger softly across the name "Francis Hatton, First Lieutenant." She knew already that he was a man she wanted to know better. Reading those few pages from his journal had been like the first introduction to a person who would become a fast friend. The relationship held great promise for developing into something deeper, more meaningful, even important.

She felt a tingle of excitement knowing that before long she could be living in his house, walking where he had walked, reading his private papers.

There were times when Lizzie found the past very tangible, when a connection was formed between herself and some person long dead, or some event long forgotten. Then a feeling was evoked which could not be duplicated by any other kind of experience. It was for those moments that she had become a historian, and she felt very strongly that this was the beginning of a string of those moments.

Chapter 2

As she drove home through the rush-hour traffic that afternoon, Lizzie thought of her conversation with Jackie. Her friend knew her very well, but neither she nor Lizzie herself had ever really plumbed the depths of Lizzie's conflicting feelings of attraction to and condemnation of the English aristocracy. In fact she *did* feel all the romantic possibilities that George Hatton's invitation held. She had no desire to live in the past, but she loved to vicariously luxuriate in it. Jackie would, she knew, consider any enjoyment of the Hatton experience a betrayal of her Irish heritage.

When she got home she quickly changed into sweat pants and an old shirt and went to find her husband in his studio. Over the years Lizzie had lost too many sweaters to enthusiastic painty embraces to risk going there directly, but she was eager to resume the discussion they had started the evening before about the possibility of her going to England.

"Hello, my love," Martin called to her as she opened the door to his studio. He was on a ladder, working on a canvas that covered one entire wall of the room.

She sat down in the chair that was reserved for her; it was the only flat surface in the room that was not covered with bits of paper, chalk, crayons, cups of cold coffee, photographs, tape, brushes, or tools. It occurred to Lizzie as she pondered his clutter that they might be too much alike to live together successfully. She leaned back and watched the New York skyline emerge under her husband's deft hands. She loved to watch him work and she knew that serious conversation would have to wait until his current frenzy of inspiration was spent.

It was a good view. Martin was wearing a red tee shirt and she could see the muscles of his back moving beneath it. He had a rumpled look that made her feel comfortable with him, but he also had a dark exotic handsomeness and Lizzie still felt a strong physical passion for him after almost fifteen years together. If anything, he was more handsome now at forty-five. His face was certainly more interesting and the grey that was beginning to appear in his black hair was wonderfully attractive.

As a painter, especially one who did much of his work outside, Martin was very physically fit. His arms, chest, and thighs were very muscular. He had softened somewhat around the middle over the last several years, but not as much as Lizzie had. She always meant to get more exercise but, unlike her husband, she had a completely sedentary job. She spent too many hours in a chair in front of a computer while he was going up and down ladders.

Her eyes swept from her husband to the wall of framed posters that announced the installation of various of his murals in locations all around the globe. He had come a long way from his Los Angeles upbringing and Mexican roots.

Martin finally began to back slowly down to the floor, looking at what he had just added to the painting as he did so. Lizzie could see his head turn from side to side as he scanned back and forth across the canvas. When he turned to her he was smiling.

"It looks great!" Lizzie said with real enthusiasm. The mural was a commission for a New York bank and incorporated different views of Manhattan and the boroughs. "I especially like what you've done with the bridges."

Martin stepped behind her chair and massaged her shoulders as he concentrated on his work for another several minutes. She was glad she had changed her clothes; his hands were covered with chalk and charcoal and he was inadvertently, though vigorously, transferring it to her shirt.

When he leaned down to kiss her, Lizzie knew she would now have his full attention, but only until the next moment of inspiration came. He sat down on a high stool and put his foot on the arm of her chair. She reminded him of the letter she had received the day before and Martin was immediately back into the conversation of the night before. He was not by nature suspicious, but he didn't know what to think of George Hatton or his motives.

"Why you?" he asked for at least the tenth time. "And what do you know about him?"

Lizzie had the letter in her hand. "He says that Tom Clark at the British Museum recommended me and that he has read my book."

"And how well do you know this Tom Clark?" Martin asked, pushing himself back on two legs of the stool.

Though he had never fallen, this move always made Lizzie nervous. She reached out to touch his leg, as if she might catch him by it if he fell, and explained again that she had corresponded with Tom Clark for more than a decade and had met him several times at conferences. Why he would have passed an opportunity like this on to her was mysterious, but she was self-confident enough to believe that she was qualified and deserving of the offer from George Hatton, and she told Martin so.

Martin put his feet and those of the stool firmly on the floor and leaned forward to put his arms around Lizzie. "Of course you deserve it," he said, kissing her lightly on the forehead. "It just seems like a strange thing to come out of the blue."

"This journal is absolutely genuine, though," she said, looking once again at the two pages that George Hatton had copied and sent her. They were now covered with color where Lizzie had marked several passages with highlighting pens.

"You know," she added, thoughtfully, "I've been wondering if I might have met George Hatton at some point. The name sounds so familiar."

"Hatton?" Martin asked.

She nodded.

"Isn't it your dad's middle name?"

Lizzie nodded again. "And my grandfather's, but that's not what I was thinking about."

"No relation?" Martin joked.

"Hardly!"

"Just for my peace of mind, will you call Tom Clark?" Martin asked. His eyes had been going from Lizzie to the canvas and back, and she knew that she was about to lose his attention again.

"If I do this, it would keep me from going to New York with you," she said. She liked to go with him when he installed a mural, and had planned to spend a few weeks in New York City while he finished those parts of the painting that couldn't be done in his home studio.

"Well I won't have time to do much that's fun anyway," he answered, "given where I am on the work right now and the timeframe for finishing."

He stood up and pulled a rag from his back pocket. Lizzie sighed when she saw it; it used to be part of her favorite blouse and he was using it to clean a spot off a palette before he daubed it with paint.

Martin would be spending at least three weeks in New York in January to finish the mural on site, and she had the whole month off. St. Pat's liked to keep its doors shut during January, nominally to send students off on community service projects but really to save on heating expenses.

"At least the timing is convenient," she said, standing.

Martin was already back at his ladder. He positioned it so that he could get at a spot he had been studying and then climbed to make several small strokes on the canvas. When he seemed satisfied with the changes he turned again to Lizzie.

"Maybe when I get this piece finished I can come join you for a few days in England." He perched himself on the top of the ladder as he continued. "I haven't had a chance to tell you yet, but I got an inquiry about a commission from a group in Newcastle."

Lizzie asked for the details and found that he was very interested in pursuing it. Though banks and corporate offices were his principle business—and kept the couple in very comfortable circumstances—Martin liked especially to work with community organizations, and tried to volunteer his services on at least one project every year.

He came down long enough to clean and fill his palette with paint, and then returned to the ladder. "Don't forget to call Tom Clark," he said, giving her another quick kiss before he went back to work.

Lizzie made the call the next morning. Tom Clark did not remember exactly how her name had come up in his conversation with George Hatton, nor had he seen the journal or any of the artifacts, but he knew the man and could vouch for his reputation. Lizzie called George Hatton next and agreed to come to England during her term break. He seemed genuinely pleased to hear from her, sounded perfectly civil, very English, and not at all suspicious. Lizzie considered putting Martin on the phone with him, just to reassure her husband, but decided that she would trust her instincts, and he would have to as well.

· · · · ·

Every Thursday Lizzie had lunch with her friends Jackie and Kate. It was a small ritual of gossip and female bonding that was a highlight of the week for each of them. In addition to being friends, the three women all worked at St. Patrick's College, and so their conversation generally included campus politics and the venting of professional frustrations as well as personal confidences and general news. Kate Wentworth was the captain of St. Pat's research vessel, *Brendan's Curragh,* and on this day Lizzie planned to pick her brain about some nautical details in the Hatton journal.

Their lunch venue was always the same: an Italian restaurant in Boston's North End, across the bridge from their Charlestown campus. They were well known at Geminiani's, and Rose Geminiani frequently joined them at their table. As a result, the restaurant owner knew as much about what happened at St. Pat's as did most people on campus, and was generally current on the important issues in the lives of Lizzie and her friends.

Rose was pouring them each a glass of wine when Jackie asked Lizzie if she had made the arrangements to visit her "English Lord." Kate and Rose were both interested so Lizzie explained about Francis Hatton's journal and the invitation to go to England and live in the Hatton household while she researched the mariner and his collection.

"It sounds great!" Kate said enthusiastically. "A ripping good sea yarn *and* a chance to live the good life in a stately home."

"Well the first part sounds great," Jackie countered, "but that last bit is awful! I don't see how English people can stand to live with these persistent medieval social distinctions."

Lizzie smiled. "You can't really blame George Hatton for having been born into his own family."

"I can blame him for continuing the exploitation which probably still underpins his position in society."

"Yikes!" Lizzie exclaimed. "I'm going to have to wait until I meet him before I accuse him of that particular crime."

"I still think it sounds great," Kate said, determinedly. "Lizzie can exploit the rich and powerful for a change."

They all laughed.

"And I don't really see what's wrong with it anyway," Rose added, pulling up her own chair. "What's wrong with being rich and powerful? Isn't it what we all want?"

Jackie turned to her. "Even if it is, which I'm not ready to acknowledge, isn't it better to *earn* it than inherit it?"

Rose gestured around her restaurant. "I'm working awfully hard here, and I'm not rich yet." They were laughing again when a head poked around the door of the kitchen and Rose was called away.

Jackie was now on a roll. "I don't understand why Americans continue to be so captivated by the British aristocracy more than two centuries after throwing all that out with the Revolution."

Rose returned with their lunches. "I loved Princess Diana," she said, setting the plates in front of each of the women and then sitting down again herself. "She was one of them, but look how much good she did."

"Jayzus!" Jackie said in a thick brogue. "There you have it! The power of the princess myth."

"She wasn't a myth," Rose said, grating cheese and milling pepper onto the pasta of her friends. "Diana was an actual person who did many good things, and was a victim of the aristocratic system as much as she was a symbol of it."

"A victim of what?" Jackie said incredulously.

"Of the press," Kate said, answering for Rose.

"And of palace intrigue," Rose added. "The rest of them were jealous of the attention she got."

"We know nothing about her," Jackie argued. "She was a clean slate when she came to public attention, and all the rest was carefully constructed."

"Constructed by whom?" Rose demanded.

"By the public. People projected their fantasies onto her and she then tried to live up to them. And then, of course, the press just amplified it all."

"Oh, I have to disagree," Rose said, her hands moving in wonderfully animated Italian gestures. "She was a humanitarian; just look at all her work with AIDS and land mines."

"But lots of people do many fine things and are not canonized for them," Jackie answered. "Besides, how do we know that it wasn't all a public relations campaign?"

"You are so cynical," Kate said. "Lizzie, tell her how cynical she is."

Lizzie took a bite of pasta and a sip of wine before answering. She had been pondering the "aristocracy question" for four days and wasn't ready yet to share all her thinking with her friends. About this particular aristocrat, however, she was pretty much of Jackie's way of thinking. "Well," she said, chewing and swallowing, "I don't think we actually ever heard her say much. How much were we influenced by the fact that she was extremely photogenic?"

"Oh yes, she was beautiful," Rose nodded.

"But that doesn't make her good," Jackie argued. "I mean, she seemed like a perfectly nice sort of person, willing, even inspired, to hug lepers and shake hands with people with AIDS. But each and every good action was documented by a hundred photos."

"I loved her clothes," Rose said. "I loved every article about her. I miss her since she's gone."

"*People* magazine still hasn't recovered," Jackie said with an exasperated sigh.

"On the Diana front, I'm afraid I must agree with Jackie," Lizzie said, entering the fray again. "The worship she inspired is a mystery to me. All those people when she died, crying about how they had lost a friend, how she was one of them. How was she one of them? They were all ages, races and social classes, and I don't think she represented them at all."

"So you are saying that the only people who could really have a valid connection with her were rich aristocrats?" Rose asked. "I don't think you're giving her enough credit for having a common touch."

"I just don't understand," Jackie continued, "why you, Rose, the owner of your own business, and you, Kate, a sea captain, for God's sake—both excelling in nontraditional occupations—still find yourself attracted to this whole romantic princess nonsense."

The wine was fast disappearing and the commentary came rapidly. Jackie and Rose had the opposing camps staked out, with Lizzie providing the support for Jackie, and Kate leaning toward a greater sympathy with Rose. When Jackie began to develop a list that included private helicopters and personal psychics, Lizzie felt it was time to bring the conversation back to the question that had begun the discussion.

"Okay, but what about *me*?" she asked with mock seriousness. "What about going to England and living among the swells for a month. Will it ruin me?"

"There is some danger," Jackie answered. "You like Jane Austen novels far too much for my comfort, and I know you are a sucker for history and its innate romantic possibilities."

Lizzie balked a bit, but smiled. She had been trying hard not to admit to herself that there was something very appealing about the prospect of delving into the history of an ancient English family that had not only a coat of arms, but an address that required only the name of their house and the county in which it sat. While she felt at her core that there was something fundamentally wrong about the whole idea of an aristocracy, she could not entirely cast off all the romantic notions that came from years of exposure to fairy tales, novels, movies, and the popular press.

For once, the perceptive Jackie didn't notice her hesitation. "You must behave like a spy for the little people," she continued. "Show no deference and constantly challenge the power structure!"

"Absolutely not." Kate gasped. "How rude. You must behave like the polite and civilized woman you are, and appreciate the fact that there might even be a book in this for you."

"And enjoy being pampered!" Rose added, refilling the wine glasses and gesturing for one of the waiters to take the plates. She turned back to Lizzie. "Will that gorgeous husband of yours be going with you?"

Martin often invaded their lunches when he wanted to take a break from working and all of the women knew him well.

"Maybe at the very end," Lizzie answered. "Martin is working on a commission for a bank in New York and has to spend most of his time there while I'm away."

"The best of both worlds," Kate said, raising her glass one last time. "An exotic adventure and a husband waiting at the end."

"But don't be changed by the experience!" Jackie said. She winked at Lizzie as she raised her glass. "'Semper Memoriam,' as the Hattons say! Always remember who you are."

Lizzie looked around at her friends. The four women were all in their late thirties or early forties, all born and raised in American middle-class families. Though from different parts of the country, they had grown up watching the same shows on television, listening to the same music, and using most of the same products. As friends they were a well-matched quartet for confidences. Differences of opinion were regularly, even loudly, expressed, without hurt feelings or fear of censure. They were all intelligent and self-confident, but they were not alike, and it was those differences that Lizzie celebrated as she raised her glass.

"Ladies, I believe this is the last time we will meet before the Christmas break and my removal into the luxurious den of the lion."

The four women clinked glasses. "Should I come back altered in any way, you have my permission to whip me with al dente pasta."

"I'll have it ready," Rose laughed. "Have a wonderful time."

"Take advantage of all the opportunities that present themselves," Kate added.

"And be careful," Jackie cautioned. "Don't fall for the superficial romance of the aristocratic life!"

When Lizzie turned to laugh off the warning she saw that Jackie was completely serious.

Chapter 3

When she had finally settled into her business-class seat and had a glass of champagne in her hands, Lizzie was able to think again through the hectic few weeks that had brought her finally to the flight to London. There had been little time to think about any of the Hattons, past or present, since she'd first received George's letter. She had finished up two classes, graded papers, made Christmas dinner for ten, celebrated the coming of another New Year, and stocked the kitchen for Martin—who sometimes forgot to eat when she wasn't there, especially when he was immersed in a project.

Martin had given her a book to read on the plane, *The Great Houses of England, an Illustrated Guide*, which, he said, included a description of George Hatton's home, Hengemont. She pulled it from her bag and flipped through it until she found the chapter on Somerset County, where Hengemont was the most prominent entry.

"One of the oldest homes in England to be occupied continuously by a single family, Hengemont House provides an almost textbook illustration of eight centuries of British architecture. Situated above the village of Hengeport on the Somerset coast of the Bristol Channel, the original Norman castle was built ca. 1180 by Jean d'Hautain, who accompanied Henry II to England from France, and who received the property from his royal patron. An ancient stone circle occupied the site in prehistoric times, the stones of which were incorporated into the foundation of the principal walls of the castle. The three largest stones, each reaching

twelve feet in height, are visible today framing the main
entrance to the oldest part of the house.

In 1356 and again in 1400 portions of the main tower
and the three subsidiary towers of the fortification were
pulled down and two gothic additions, one on either
side of the tower, made Hengemont a more comfortable
home for the growing Hatton family."

Beneath the description of the house was an outline plan
of the original castle, with its fortified wall meandering along
the top of a hill in a shape that was not quite square. The big
Norman tower sat solidly in the middle of the longest wall,
and smaller round towers marked each of the four places that
could be considered corners. Their locations in the drawing,
and the ruins that were indicated in an aerial photograph,
clearly showed how the topography of the hilltop had suggested the shape of the castle yard. In color plates of the current house, the three huge stones described as part of the
"ancient stone circle" that predated the house on the site were
evident around the door. The rest of the Norman stonework
was made of fairly small stones; most appeared to Lizzie to
be about the size of a man's fist, and this made it easy to
distinguish the oldest part of the building, which was from
the original castle, from the cut-stone gothic additions that
flanked it on either side.

"In 1580 the size of the house was doubled with the
addition of a wing in the Tudor style, adjoined at right
angles to the existing structure. Inigo Jones was con-
sulted on the layout of the gardens in 1623, incorporat-
ing ruined walls from the original castle fortifications.
Jones was recalled by the family in 1650 to build another wing opposite the Tudor wing, and the house at that
time took on the shape it maintains today. Running
along the back of the original Norman tower and its extensions stands the most elegant part of the house. Designed and built to the specifications of Robert Adam
in 1781, this addition includes the double staircase for
which the house is justifiably famous."

Lizzie turned the page to see the additions that grew from either end of the gothic extensions: on the left the older Tudor wing, on the right the more recent Inigo Jones wing. From what Lizzie could tell from the pictures, the place had more or less a U shape, with the open end facing the sea; the Robert Adam wing had doubled the thickness of the bottom of the U. There was a terrace and a large and lush formal garden, with beds of flowers laid in geometric patterns. It did not look like the sort of place where actual people lived in this day and age, but it had real promise as a place to stay for a month as a guest of the owner.

As she closed the book, a passage on the back cover of the dust jacket caught her attention. It was a quote from *The Awkward Age,* a novel by Henry James, describing a stately home in England, "well assured of its right to the place it took up in the world. . . ."

"Suggestive of panelled rooms, of precious mahogany, of portraits of women dead, of coloured china glimmering through glass doors, and delicate silver reflected on bared tables, the thing was one of those impressions of a particular period that it takes two centuries to produce."

Lizzie patted the book and took another sip of champagne. That was what she wanted to find in England, that sense of tangible history. That it would be found in an ancient and, she had to admit, elegant and luxurious house, was a huge bonus. She couldn't help thinking back to the conversation with her friends at Geminiani's a few weeks before, and wondered if she was justifying an attraction to wealth and nobility by couching it in scholarship.

If there was a conflict that most people of Irish ancestry shared, Lizzie thought, it was a simultaneous rejection of, and attraction to, British notions of aristocracy. In truth, she thought that most Irish peasants held a secret ambition to become English gentry. She thought of Jackie and wondered if she protested too much. Rose did not hesitate to declare that she wanted the fairy tale, and Lizzie loved and respected both of her friends, despite their positions on opposite ends of the spectrum of romantic silliness.

Martin was the only one in her immediate circle who seemed completely oblivious to the attractions of social position. He moved through life with a remarkable confidence that kept him from worrying about many of the notions that buzzed around in his wife's head. He was not impressed by wealth, fame, consequence, or possessions. He didn't scorn them; he simply didn't notice. The fact that he had, since a teenager, been able to command a hefty commission for his murals had, Lizzie acknowledged, probably provided the base for his egalitarianism, and the strange LA agglomeration of celebrities, millionaires, artists, and politicians who took notice of him early had kept him from ever experiencing self-doubt or hardship.

Her thoughts turned from her husband to her father. Lizzie had had a long conversation with him on the phone on New Year's Day. She told him she had been hired by a man named Hatton to do research in England.

"That's an interesting coincidence," he had said cheerfully. (It wasn't, however, interesting enough to ask for any further details.)

"Tell me about your grandmother's Hattons in Ireland," Lizzie pressed. She had asked him about this several times before and, as always, he professed ignorance.

"They were just poor spud farmers, Lizzie," he said.

"She never talked about her life there?"

"I think her motto was 'only remember those things that give you pleasure and forget the rest.'"

Lizzie laughed. "Well that's an interesting twist on the motto of the English Hattons! They apparently remember everything."

"It's not that she wasn't interested in history," he continued. "She was constantly reading, could talk endlessly about the ancient Romans and Greeks, about medieval Europe, the American Civil War."

He reminisced for a few minutes about things his grandmother had said or done when he was a child. She had lived with his family when he was growing up, and they had had a close relationship. "You are a lot like her," he said finally to Lizzie. "She loved history, she just didn't dwell on her own past."

Lizzie closed her eyes and tried to remember her great grandmother, now dead more than thirty-five years. She had been an ancient relic when Lizzie was a toddler, but there was still a vivid memory of crawling up into a soft and ample lap. She drifted off to sleep trying to recapture the sound of the old woman speaking, and found herself dreaming of strange soft sounds that seemed to roll around in her great grandmother's mouth before dropping off her aged tongue. The language merged with the drone of the plane engine as Lizzie slept, and in her dream, as in her childhood, she couldn't understand a single word.

• • • • •

It was six-thirty in the morning when she arrived at Heathrow Airport. Groggy and bewildered, Lizzie claimed her luggage and proceeded through the green line of customs: "Nothing to declare." Outside the gate area was a good-looking young man in his early twenties, wearing a suit and cap and holding a sign that said "Professor E. Manning." Lizzie identified herself and argued with him over who should carry which bags, eventually letting him have his way and carry everything but her purse.

"I'm Jeffrey," he said affably, slinging two of her bags over his shoulders and taking the third up under his arm. "Sir George sent me to take you to the train." He began to proceed quickly through the terminal.

"Thanks for meeting me," she called at his receding back. "I'm Lizzie."

He turned for a moment and gave her a bemused look. When he turned again to continue, he slowed his pace a bit to accommodate her but made no attempt at conversation. At the curb outside, Jeffrey opened the back door of a Bentley sedan and Lizzie crawled in as he put her luggage in the trunk.

As he slid into the driver's seat, Lizzie noticed that Jeffrey had a ponytail tucked up under his cap in back. Had the cap been less formal and on backwards he could easily have been one of her students.

"Do people call you Jeff?" she asked, giving her voice as cheery a ring as she could at that hour.

"Never," he answered.

"Oops, sorry," Lizzie said, the cheery ring gone, "you'll have to excuse my too-informal American habits."

In the front seat he adjusted the rearview mirror to look at her.

"Informal people call me Pete," he said, with a smile.

"Sorry again," Lizzie said, smiling back, "I thought you said your name was Jeffrey."

"I said my name was Jeff*ries*," he responded, with an emphasis on the final syllable, "Peter Jeffries."

He negotiated the car onto the main highway into London.

"Sir George likes us to preserve those little niceties that distinguish between the classes," he continued, "like the use of the surname only for household servants."

Lizzie leaned forward to rest her elbows on the back of the front seat on the passenger side.

"So you work for George Hatton, eh Pete?"

He smiled at her again.

"My family," he said, "has been what you would call 'in service' to the Hattons for generations."

This was a concept which Pete seemed to accept as very natural, but Lizzie found disturbing. She sat back in her seat again and pondered George Hatton, with his multigenerational family of serfs, and his desire to keep them in their place with an archaic nomenclature.

Lizzie wanted to probe more deeply into the matter, but hesitated. She didn't want to make the young man uncomfortable. Traffic was increasing as they came closer to London, and Pete's attention was drawn entirely to the road as it ceased to be a real highway and merged into city streets. As the car slowed she eased into the subject.

"So what do you do besides drive this car around London?" she asked.

"For years I helped around the farm down in Somerset," he said, glancing at her as he changed lanes, "but now that I'm at University I live in the Hatton's London house and do the odd job like this one, picking you up at the airport and transporting you to the train station."

The college professor in her surfaced. "What are you studying?"

"I'm doing a degree in business at the University of London," he said.

"And will you put that to work for the Hattons when you're finished?" she couldn't help asking.

"Oh no," he said, smiling broadly, "I'm the Jeffries that will break that chain."

Lizzie sat back again in the comfortable seat and crossed her legs.

"I guess I'm a little surprised that he lets you continue to live in his house," she said frankly.

"I said I was the Jeffries that would break the chain, not the last Jeffries to work for the Hattons," he said. "Sir George would be lost without my parents."

"Ah ha," Lizzie said, paying more attention now to the world beyond the car window as they left the light industrial sprawl of the airport and began to enter the city itself. She was silent for a few minutes but could not resist following up with Pete on a point that had been bothering her. "Excuse my American lack of class one more time, Pete," she said, "but am I also expected to refer to him as 'Sir George'?"

Pete seemed surprised by the question. "It is the form by which he is most commonly addressed," he said, steering the car through a maze of traffic barriers. "Why do you ask?" he continued. "Are you uncomfortable with these deferences to rank?"

Lizzie thought for a second, wondering how frank she should be with him. He was a stranger, he was an employee of George Hatton, but she liked him. She didn't think he was the sort of person who would call the big house to report on her as soon as she got out of the car.

"In truth," she said, choosing her words carefully, "I am somewhat uncomfortable with the whole notion of an aristocracy that is addressed differently than the rest of us."

"Well, I am too," Pete shrugged, "but in my case there is the whole parental thing. And I have nothing against Sir

George anyway," he continued. "He's always been very decent to me and my family."

"Can I call him Mr. Hatton?" she asked.

"That might work abroad, but as a guest in his house you might be the first. If not 'Sir George' then it's usually 'Lord Hatton.'"

"Lord!" Lizzie exclaimed. "That's even worse. I don't suppose I can just leap right in and call him George?"

"Well, I'm going to have to ask you not to do that because you would certainly give my mother a heart attack!" Pete said, laughing.

"I guess I can call him 'Sir' anyway," Lizzie said, "and think of it as being deferential to age and experience rather than rank."

She turned this over in her mind several times while Peter Jeffries looked amused in the rearview mirror.

"I'm sorry I won't be there when you arrive at Hengemont," he said. "This should be a very interesting meeting."

They drove on in silence for several minutes until Lizzie asked him where they were going.

"Paddington Station," Pete answered, expertly negotiating the crowded traffic of the city neighborhoods. "From there you'll take the train to Taunton, transfer to Minehead, and my father will meet you at the other end."

"I guess I won't ask him if he goes by Jeff," Lizzie joked.

Pete laughed. "He has a very good sense of humor, but strangely enough he also likes to have the distinctions of rank preserved. It solidifies his position in the household."

They approached the station and Pete pulled the car into the passenger drop-off section as Lizzie pondered his interesting remark.

"Any messages for the folks at home?" Lizzie asked.

"Heavens no," Pete said, getting out of the car and coming around to open Lizzie's door. "They'd be horrified to know that we exchanged more than two words on anything other than weather or scenery." He motioned to a porter to take Lizzie's suitcases and reached into his jacket to produce a first-class ticket to Minehead.

"Well, I've enjoyed our talk," she said, shaking his hand

firmly. "I hope we'll meet up again when I'm in London."

He removed his hat to reveal his shoulder-length ponytail and bowed with a flourish. "Likewise," he said, smiling. "It has been a pleasure."

He waved one last time as he got back into the car, and Lizzie followed the man with her bags into the station. It was a great steel Victorian cave. Lizzie paused to look at a map of the routes mounted in a glass-covered frame on the wall. Minehead was the last stop on the line headed along the south coast of the Bristol Channel. The small coastal village of Hengeport lay just beyond it.

Chapter 4

The heater on the train worked furiously, and Lizzie took off her coat and scarf and eventually stood up and wrestled with the window to lower it a bit and let some of the cold outside air into the hot compartment. She was glad that she didn't have to share the space with anyone because it was her impression that English people objected to fresh air on trains.

She settled comfortably into her seat and studied the London landscape trundling by below her. The train was on a high embankment and she could see easily onto the rooftops and into the back gardens of row upon row of brick houses. It reminded her of the opening sequence of the animated version of "Peter Pan," or of the city as described by Dickens, though now a lot cleaner. She thought about Peter Jeffries and wondered that he would share so much information with a stranger, being English and all. But Lizzie knew from past experience that she had an open face that invited confidences, and she had been just as candid with him as he had been with her, maybe more so.

As the city gave way to the suburbs, Lizzie dozed briefly, and when she woke up the countryside stretched out into the foggy distance. She had been to England several times before but never in winter, and the landscape that she knew to be verdant green in summer was bleakly grey through a light mist. She liked the movement of the train and was almost hypnotized by the repetitive pattern of field and hedge, field and hedge, field and hedge. Occasionally a village whizzed by, but so fast that she could not read the town name on the sign. She took Martin's gift from her bag and read again about the house that was her destination. None of the accompanying photographs showed it in winter. Always the grass was green, the garden in full bloom, the sea visible under a clear blue sky beyond the carefully cultivated landscape.

When she finally saw Hengemont for the first time, it was from the back seat of a Bentley identical to the one driven by young Pete Jeffries in London. She was met at the station by his father, just plain Jeffries, and she was more circumspect about engaging him in conversation than she had been with his son. They drove quickly through the village, past a charming pub and inn called the White Horse. A signboard swinging above the door showed the outline of an ungainly white horse. A moment later, as the buildings of the village gave way to farm and hedge and hillside, she saw the animal after which the pub was named, its Neolithic chalk outline scratched out from beneath the grass on a nearby slope. There were occasional farmhouses and a square-towered Norman church stretched out along the road before they entered the Hatton property.

Hengemont was huge and solid and ancient. The central tower was almost a thousand years old and Lizzie watched eagerly for it, anticipating some imprint of all those years on the big stone face of the building. She saw it first across a vast expanse of lawn, faded from the winter cold and dotted with leafless oak and chestnut trees. As they drove up a gentle slope to the great front entrance, Lizzie instantly recognized the three gigantic stones which framed it.

Jeffries handed her over to his wife, who handed her bags over to another man, whose name was not shared with Lizzie, and the three stepped into the house. The main entrance brought her directly into the cavernous great hall of the original castle. High overhead the arched ceiling was held up by enormous carved beams. On either side was a massive stone fireplace and flanking each were tapestries two stories high.

"We don't ordinarily use this door," Mrs. Jeffries explained, "but Sir George thought that you, being a historian, would like it."

"Indeed I do," Lizzie said. "It's fabulous."

High double doors opened off the room on either side. To her right Lizzie saw a grand formal dining room, and to her left a room that would, in America, probably be called the living room, though this one, with four or five different groupings of couches, chairs, and tables, reminded her more of the lobby of a fancy hotel. They continued straight ahead, finally passing through a door in a massive, though delicately carved, wooden panel. Above Lizzie recognized the gallery from which musicians would have entertained the guests in ancient days.

She was sorry that she was being hurried through this oldest part of the house, and wished that she could have stumbled on the place by herself with time to linger at each change of perspective. In her mind the very atmosphere was infused with the breath of past inhabitants, with the vibrations of the strings and horns that had once played in the space above her. She threw all hesitation to the wind and instantly adored the place.

They went through another door and dramatically changed centuries. Gone were the stone walls, carved beams, and tapestries of the medieval castle; now they were in a light and airy Georgian hall. The walls were painted in creamy pastels and a decorative plaster frieze border ran around the top of the wall and framed the doorways. Lizzie was glad that Martin had given her the book. She immediately recognized this part of the house as the work of the architect Robert Adam.

Two elaborate carved staircases dominated the room, curving up from the floor of the hall to meet on a balconied mezzanine above her. Opposite the staircase were tall glass doors, topped by an elaborate fan-shaped window with beveled glass. Lizzie could see from here out onto the stone terrace and beyond it to the garden, sloping down toward the sea. From here the outline of the house became clear. Framing the terrace on one side was the old Tudor wing, and opposite was the wing built by Inigo Jones. The fourth side of the square was open, except for some low stone ruins that must once have defined that side of the castle yard that faced the Bristol Channel.

Again there were double doors to her right and left. The ones on her right were closed, but on the left she caught a quick glimpse of a library before Mrs. Jeffries led her up the stairs. The two arcs of the staircase came up to a landing where a large painting covered almost the whole of the wall. It was of two young men, in their late teens or early twenties, and an adolescent girl. They sat in a lush landscape.

"What a lovely painting," Lizzie said, stepping slightly closer to read the brass title on the frame. *The Children of Sir John Hatton, 1773, by Thomas Gainsborough,* it said.

"He's the 'Blue Boy' painter," Mrs. Jeffries explained.

Lizzie nodded. "Is one of these boys Lieutenant Francis Hatton, who made the Cook voyage?"

"If I remember correctly, he's the one on the right," the housekeeper answered, "but we have a catalogue and I can look it up for you later."

"Thanks," Lizzie said, moving slowly along the few remaining stairs up to the next floor and gazing at the other pictures hanging above her. It pleased her that Francis Hatton looked intelligent and exuberant in the portrait.

Mrs. Jeffries showed her to her room on the second floor of the Inigo Jones wing of the house. It was at the end of a long wide hall and as they entered it Lizzie was struck by the beauty of the house's setting, which was even more dramatic from this height. Tall windows were on two sides of the room and she was drawn immediately to the windows across from the door, which faced the older Tudor wing of the house. She then turned to the windows on her right. The view was across the formal garden, barren in the winter, but giving every indication of how glorious it must be in summer. Beyond it was the ruined wall of the original castle fortifications, and beyond that fields and moors stretched out along the long slope down to the sea.

What would it be like to live here? Her imagination placed her at various locations around the house, and in various centuries of its history. She forgot that Mrs. Jeffries was still in the room until she heard her speak.

"Sir George wanted to give you some time to get settled, but will be available to meet you whenever you're ready."

Lizzie thanked her, got a tour of the room, closets, and adjoining bathroom, and told the housekeeper that she expected she would be back downstairs within a half hour.

When Mrs. Jeffries was gone, Lizzie took a few minutes to survey the room that would be her home for the next few weeks. It was extremely pleasant. The furniture was solid and heavy but the room was made to seem quite light by the expanse of windows, and by the fabric that covered the bed and the two wooden-armed chairs, an ivory silk embroidered all over with vines and small flowers. The bed had gauzy curtains, pulled back near the head, and matching fabric was at the windows. She could not help being drawn back to the view, and with each visit to the windows she took in more of the details.

The Tudor wing of the house was directly opposite across the terrace and formal garden. The surface facing Lizzie was not flat, but came forward and stepped back as projecting gabled sections of the wall alternated with areas set back into darker recesses. The windows there were mostly small, unlike the windows through which she looked. All in all, Lizzie thought, she had been placed in the more comfortable part of the house, and she appreciated the fact that her room was on the end. Beyond the Tudor wing of the house she could just see the village of Hengeport as it meandered its way down the hill to its harbor.

Mrs. Jeffries had offered to unpack Lizzie's bags for her, but she had absolutely refused, embarrassed that the housekeeper might judge the disarray of her packing and find her wardrobe inappropriate. There was a formality and stiffness to Mrs. Jeffries, almost as if she was used to a higher standard of guest. Lizzie didn't know quite what to think of her.

She opened her suitcase and sighed. When she packed for the trip she hadn't a clue what George Hatton was expecting of her. For starters, she wasn't even sure if she was going to be treated as a house guest or an employee, and Martin had been no help. When she asked him what she should pack to wear in a stately home he had suggested gowns and tiaras.

Lizzie held certain stereotypes about English people of this class getting dressed up for dinner, and it was her impression that their houses never had adequate heat or plumbing. She had decided that she would need warm clothing and that her usual wardrobe of corduroy slacks and comfortable sweaters would be fine for working during the day. Just in case things got fancy for dinner, she had packed her two nice dresses, one of which she hadn't worn in months.

Now she pulled it from her suitcase and held it in front of her as she examined herself in the long mirror on the back of the closet door. Lizzie was happy and well adjusted and had always liked the way she looked, but she had to admit that at this moment she was hopelessly unfashionable. Curvy and soft in a world that prized gaunt fitness, she also had curly hair that absolutely refused to be controlled. She had never felt comfortable wearing it short, and with each added inch of length it threatened to curl and frizz more and so she had, for years, worn it just to the length of her shoulders. Some years she had been lucky and fashionability had come her way, at other times she had simply had to wait it out, but her curly brown hair remained the same. As she ran a comb through it, she took stock, as she regularly did, of the grey that was creeping in around the edges. She would be forty years old on her next birthday.

The dress looked fine. She was, after all, here to work, not to live. George Hatton would just have to accept her as she was. She finished combing her hair, brushed her teeth, put on the dress, and retraced her steps to the staircase, lingering for a minute to look again at the portrait of Francis Hatton. His brother was darker and appeared more brooding, as if he had more responsibilities pressing on him. Their sister was a pink-cheeked girl, an apparently happy child There was another picture hanging beside the Gainsborough that seemed to show the same girl as a young woman. Lizzie didn't know if it was just a strong family resemblance, but she stood for a moment looking from the girl to the woman.

"Are you comfortable in your room, Dr. Manning?" Mrs. Jeffries asked from the bottom of the stairs.

"Yes, very comfortable, thank you," Lizzie answered. She found herself unable to resist asking, "Is this the same girl?" as she gestured between the two pictures. Mrs. Jeffries said that it was.

In her separate portrait, Francis Hatton's sister seemed more fragile, her large grey eyes intelligent but sad. Lizzie wondered what life had dealt her in the intervening years. She continued down to the bottom of the stairs.

Mrs. Jeffries did not look her directly in the eyes, but Lizzie had a feeling she was being studied by the housekeeper when she wasn't looking. She searched in the woman's face for a resemblance to the amiable young man who had picked her up at the airport and could see from the lines on Mrs. Jeffries face that she must often smile and laugh. Her face was stern enough now though, as she turned and led Lizzie toward the double doors that led to the library. "Sir George is anxious to meet you," she said.

Lizzie found herself somewhat nervous at the prospect of meeting George Hatton. She had a strong mental image of British aristocrats, derived mostly from Jane Austen novels, P.G. Wodehouse short stories, Jackie's rants, and various episodes of Monty Python, but no real experience with anyone like Sir George. She was already feeling surprisingly comfortable in the house and didn't want to lose that feeling by meeting its owner and finding him condescending, exasperating, or stupid. It was consequently a pleasant surprise to find him perfectly civil and seemingly interested in her work. He was not exactly warm, but neither was he twitty or dithering, he didn't speak with a lisp or a stutter, his handshake was firm, and he looked her right in the eye when he welcomed her to his house.

She still hadn't decided how she would address him. She didn't want to be impolite, but she was determined not to be deferential. He called her "Dr. Manning" and she, almost automatically, called him "Mr. Hatton." He raised an eyebrow slightly at that, but was too polite to comment. She invited him to call her "Lizzie," and he returned that she might call him "George, if that suited her." She said that it did and was relieved to have this first bit of discomfort behind her.

George asked Mrs. Jeffries to bring them a pot of coffee, and offered Lizzie one of two tall wing chairs situated in front of a large fireplace. As they sat down she had an opportunity to study him. If there was some indefinable yet recognizable aristocratic type, George Hatton was it. In a different time and under other circumstances, Lizzie could see how people might take it for an innate nobility. He was very tall and had an elegance about him that was hard to describe but very noticeable. His hair was perfectly white, his eyes a clear grey-blue. Though he was probably at least seventy years old, he was still a very handsome man. He was also extraordinarily polite, making every effort to make Lizzie comfortable, even telling her how much he had enjoyed her book.

They talked for several minutes about Francis Hatton and his voyage with Captain Cook. George was obviously quite proud of the connection, and Lizzie told him how excited she was about working with the objects and especially the journal.

"Those pages you sent me could not have been better chosen for convincing me to take on this project," she said.

He admitted that after reading her book he had selected those passages with her in mind. Lizzie was flattered and, for a moment, didn't know how to respond.

Mrs. Jeffries returned with coffee, saving Lizzie the necessity of having to make an immediate reply, and giving her an opportunity to watch the interaction between the master and the servant as the latter set a tray of coffee things on the table next to Lizzie's chair. George and his housekeeper seemed entirely comfortable with but respectful of each other. Lizzie tried to catch the eye of Mrs. Jeffries, but the other woman was careful not to look at her, and Lizzie made no attempt to engage her in conversation other than to thank her for the service, which George echoed.

Lizzie found herself unexpectedly liking George Hatton. Mostly it was because he was being extraordinarily cordial to her, but he was also surprising her in several ways large and small. Whatever her expectations might have been, they were not for a smart, handsome, and seemingly generous-spirited man. Had she been expecting him to be imperious or dismissive with the housekeeper on whom he depended for his comfort, she thought? A woman whom he had probably known for many years?

Now that she was actually here at Hengemont, such notions seemed ludicrous. Lizzie reminded herself sternly that it was the twenty-first century. If not for the consternation it would certainly cause George Hatton and Mrs. Jeffries, she thought she might occasionally give herself a smart slap on the cheek as a reminder.

Other thoughts still poked at her though: Pete Jeffries' comments about distinctions between classes, and the fact that Mrs. Jeffries, without exception, referred to her boss as "Sir George," and he, in turn, never called her anything but "Mrs. Jeffries," despite the fact that they probably *had* known each other for many years. And then the whole notion of servants was so antithetical to Lizzie anyway.

When she looked up, George seemed to be studying her. At least he had that in common with Mrs. Jeffries.

She picked up her cup, settled back in her chair, and asked him why Francis Hatton's journal had never been published. It was a question that had been bothering her ever since she first received George's letter. "Your ancestor was a good writer and more insightful than most of his shipmates," she said.

"Francis Hatton specifically instructed his heirs not to surrender it to the Admiralty or allow it to be published," George explained.

Lizzie thought of her conversation with Jackie. "Why didn't he want it made public?" she asked. "Are there things in it that would have embarrassed him?"

George shook his head. "Not to my mind, but it's not complete and I think he might have just hoped to finish it at some point."

"But why would he keep his heirs from publishing it? Certainly by the time it got into their hands his opportunities for finishing it were kaput."

Her host smiled at her and Lizzie wondered if she was being too informal. She was alternating between feeling very comfortable and suddenly being struck by a realization of where she was. With each jolt of awareness she felt as if her head had just hit the desk during a lecture and waked her.

She made an effort to smile back. "So why are you willing to publish it now?"

"Well," he started slowly, "two centuries have passed and there is still interest in the voyage and in this account of it. Whatever he wanted done before it was published seems now to be beyond doing."

"What do you mean, 'whatever he wanted done'? Did he put conditions on the publication?"

With a clunk, George Hatton put his coffee cup on the table which sat between their two chairs. "I'm not sure what he wanted, I suppose. I haven't actually read any conditions, I just heard from my father that Francis was unwilling to have the journal published." He poured more coffee in his cup and made a gesture with the pot to offer Lizzie a warm-up, which she accepted.

"There has always been a pretty steady stream of attention paid to Cook voyage material," Lizzie said, "but have you noticed some particular interest in Francis Hatton's account now?"

George hesitated before answering, purposefully stirring his cup and taking a sip. "My son is interested in having it come out now," he explained. "The British Museum is planning an exhibition on Captain Cook's voyages in about a year and a half, and he'd like us to participate in it."

Lizzie had heard the briefest mention of this from Tom Clark in their phone conversation a few weeks earlier. She too would be very happy to participate in such a project for the British Museum. If Francis Hatton's collection of souvenir objects was as interesting as his journal, she might be able to position herself as a guest curator for some part of the exhibition, and could certainly publish something in conjunction with it. As she mulled this, George began a rambling discourse on what he knew about Cook's third voyage to the Pacific Ocean.

Despite his keen interest in the subject, Lizzie quickly found that she knew a lot more than he did about Cook's activities, and while she would have concentrated on what he was saying if he had stuck to specific information about his ancestor, she found her attention wandering around the library.

The room pleased her enormously; it was exactly what a library should be and she could not have improved on it if she had designed it herself. It was about twice as long as it was wide, and bookshelves were on every wall from the floor to a height of about ten feet. Above them there was still enough room under the tall ceiling for a row of portraits. The line of the shelves was broken only by the fireplace, four tall gothic windows, and three sets of double doors: the pair through which she had entered, another made of glass panes, which opened onto the stone terrace, and a third which she suddenly heard George telling her hid Francis Hatton's museum "cabinet."

This information brought her full attention back to what he was saying. Lizzie had seen many "cabinets of curiosities," which were popular venues for the display of exotic artifacts in the eighteenth century. Most of the collections had long since left their original locations and been moved into museums or dispersed; it was unusual to find one still intact, especially in a private home. Until this moment Lizzie hadn't thought much about how the Hatton family would have preserved Francis Hatton's collection, but now it hit her for the first time that she might be able to see it as he had arranged it with his own hands.

The realization drew Lizzie from her chair like a magnet. Without looking away from those closed doors she rose from her chair and started toward them. George quickly put his cup down and followed her across the room. He seemed to sense that if he didn't open them first she would spring upon the doors and fling them apart, and consequently he stepped in front of her and opened them carefully, sliding the door panels neatly behind the bookcases on either side.

Francis Hatton's collection was a classic example of the late eighteenth century, displayed in a sort of giant closet with glass-fronted shelves rising from waist level up to the ceiling with rows of drawers set beneath them. Lizzie gasped with astonishment and pleasure as her eyes adjusted to the dim light and she began to discover what was lined up on the shelves.

"This was originally designed by the architect as a passage into the older wing of the house, but Francis Hatton took it over and turned it to a rather good purpose, I think."

"My goodness," Lizzie said, putting her cup of coffee on the large table that dominated that end of the room. She walked into the cabinet and tried to take it all in. Above her rose weapons, paddles, model ships, musical instruments, shoes, hats, masks, spoons, pipes, baskets, ceramic bowls, carvings, shells, stones, mounted birds, snake skins, shark's jaws, tusks and bones from numerous animals, fans, feathers—in fact anything and everything, representing every continent known in Francis Hatton's time. She opened a few of the drawers to find more of the same. Every space was crammed with artifacts, most having a label of some sort attached with a fine spidery scrawl describing what it was, where it had originated, and how it had been acquired.

Interspersed among the Polynesian clubs and the clove boats from Indonesia were a number of Northwest Coast Indian objects, including a whalebone club from Nootka Sound and a remarkable carved and painted wooden mask. George Hatton pointed out his favorite piece, a helmet with the face and claws of a bear mounted on it. On every shelf was a wonder. Lizzie asked him if the curator from the British Museum had seen the collection and George replied that he had not.

"Though I think my son Richard sent him photographs of some of the objects," he said. He turned and smiled politely at Lizzie. "We met with Thomas Clark in London a few months ago," he continued. "That's when he showed me your book and suggested that you might be able to help us figure out what to do with the collection."

Lizzie was overwhelmed by both the size and the scope of the collection and struggled to take it all in. Several of the objects were artistic masterpieces, and others were possibly the earliest known examples of their type. She could not believe that she was the first person to see it who could actually appreciate the value of the artifacts, both culturally and monetarily. It had been sitting on these shelves, essentially hidden and unknown, for over two hundred years.

"I had no idea the collection was so extensive," she said, somewhat hesitantly. "I can help you identify the North American material here, and the Polynesian, but the range of the material goes way beyond my expertise."

"Well at this point I am most interested in identifying those things that Francis Hatton collected himself on the voyage with Captain Cook," George said. He opened one of the cabinets and pulled out a wooden Australian boomerang. "Here's a piece that will interest you. It was collected on Cook's first voyage to the Pacific and given to Francis Hatton by Sir Joseph Banks, who helped arrange for his commission in the Royal Navy."

Lizzie was impressed. She took it from George and held it reverently. This was one of the first things from Australia ever seen by Europeans. She read the label pasted onto it: "Given to me by Sir Joseph Banks, July 21st, 1775. Collected by him on Captain Cook's First Voyage." Lizzie laid it down carefully and made a mental note to catalogue it with the first group of objects. As she set it on the shelf she noticed a yellow and brown plastic boomerang on the shelf behind it. She pulled it out. Written in black marker on it was a note: "To Mummy and Dad; Another treasure for the collection! John Hatton, Melbourne, Australia, September 1989."

"A joke from my youngest son," George explained. "He went out to Australia with the navy. Married an Australian girl and still lives there."

Lizzie put it back on the shelf. It was with some difficulty that she restrained her enthusiasm, not just at seeing such an important collection, but in knowing that she could be the one to bring it to the attention of the public, and of a museum and academic community that would find it remarkable.

It was incredible luck, she thought, that George Hatton had stumbled on her book at precisely the right moment. Otherwise she could not believe that such an opportunity would have come to her rather than to any number of more senior British curators and scholars. She crossed her arms and turned to look again at George.

"Again, I have to ask you why none of this was ever made public?"

"Never saw any reason to," he answered simply.

She thought it might be pressing her luck to delve deeper into this subject within her first hour of acquaintance with George, and turned back to study the collection.

"There's also correspondence in several of the drawers," George continued. A framed painting leaned against one tier of drawers, the back of the canvas facing them so that the picture wasn't visible. A manila envelope was taped to the bare brown canvas. George lifted it up by the top of the frame and leaned it against the library table so that he could show Lizzie the documents in the drawers behind it.

"There are letters about the collection in here, I think," he said, pulling one of the drawers open. It was filled almost to the top with scraps of paper. He looked at her a little sheepishly. "I had forgotten the level of disorganization in these drawers. People have just been chucking odd bits and pieces into them for about two hundred years."

"I'm pretty fast at getting through material like that," she reassured him. "It shouldn't take me too long to at least get it organized into things that are and aren't of interest for this project."

She asked him if all of the artifacts had been collected by Francis Hatton. "Except for that second boomerang," she added with a smile. She wasn't quite sure yet how much of a sense of humor he had.

He smiled back. "Don't worry. To my knowledge Johnnie's joke there is one of only a handful of things *not* collected by Francis Hatton or someone in his circle of friends and correspondents." He gestured at the crowded shelves. "Obviously he was a bit obsessive about his little hobby. I think he bothered everyone he ever met to collect things for him, but his notations seem to make clear which things were acquired by other travelers."

"The hallmark of a great collector," Lizzie responded

"I'm glad you think so," he said. "His correspondence is in some of the drawers, and then there is also the journal." He moved to a chair at the long library table and motioned to Lizzie to make herself comfortable in the adjacent one. As they sat down he asked if she was interested in taking on the project.

"Yes, very interested," she answered. "Especially if we are concentrating just on his voyage material." She folded her hands and rested them on the table as she looked again at the cabinet, trying to make a quick count of the number of Pacific pieces. Could she do the preliminary work in the weeks that she had available before classes started again?

She asked to see the journal, which had been her first

glimpse into Francis Hatton's world, and which she was anxious to read.

"I thought you'd like to see it right away," George answered. There was a carved Chinese box on the table and he put his hand on it. "This is the case in which it has always been kept," he said, opening the box and pulling a leather-bound volume from it.

He handed the book to Lizzie, who accepted it excitedly. She couldn't resist opening the front cover and turning over the marbled end paper to reveal the title page. "A Voyage to the Pacific Ocean and 'Round the World" it started. It was written in the fine legible hand that she was already coming to recognize as Francis Hatton's. She felt a thrill of anticipation.

"I look forward to spending time with this," she said, closing the book and laying her hand with a light possessive touch on the cover. She wanted to be alone when she read it. The watchful eye of his descendent could only interfere in her relationship with Francis Hatton.

She turned her attention to the painting George had leaned against the leg of the table. It was a portrait of a red-haired woman with full, lush lips and a faraway look in her eye, caught in the process of waking from sleep. One arm was stretched out toward a vanishing dream, a knight in armor whose hand was stretched out in return, but it seemed a hopeless gesture.

Lizzie smiled and leaned toward it. "Rossetti," she said. "I love his work."

George looked at it somewhat disdainfully. "I purchased it about fifteen years ago and forgot that I stored it in the cabinet." He pushed his chair back from the table and stood up. "I'll find another place for it," he said, stepping toward it.

"May I look at it first?" Lizzie asked, rising to stand beside him.

"If you like," George answered, "I'll have Jeffries hang it in your room while you're here."

"Thank you," she said with enthusiasm. "I am a fan of the Pre-Raphaelites."

"Not my cup of tea, I'm afraid," her host answered. "You're welcome to enjoy it as long as you're here."

"Why did you buy it?" Lizzie asked with genuine curiosity.

George Hatton snorted a laugh. "The model is my great-great-aunt!" He held the painting up before him. "There was a bit of a scandal attached to it and I bought it because I didn't want all that dredged up again by a public sale of the thing at auction."

"She's beautiful," Lizzie said.

"Yes, but she was wild," George said in response. "She lived with Rossetti after his wife died."

Lizzie smiled. "Ah," she said softly.

George picked up a pipe and sucked at a match through it. "What attracts you to the Pre-Raphaelites, if you don't mind my asking?"

"They have a highly romanticized view of history that amuses me," she said. Though she knew the depictions were fundamentally false, she still found them extremely compelling, and she knew that Jackie would certainly have added that to the list of things that worried her about Lizzie, had she known it.

She rested the painting carefully against the table again and found that the discussion had come to one of those strange lulls that can only be filled by turning to entirely meaningless topics. Lizzie was beginning to wish that George would soon be going and leaving her to the journal, but he made no sign of departing, and for a time they stood in uncomfortable silence.

"Where would you like to start?" he asked finally.

"With the journal," she said, sitting again and looking more closely at the carved box. She was disappointed when George sat down again too.

"Did Francis bring this box home from the voyage?" she asked, unwilling to start any actual work while he was still in the room.

"No, he shipped it from Canton on an East Indiaman to avoid having to hand it over, and it arrived back here in this box with a piece of silk and a rather cryptic letter to his sister." He leaned back, fingering his pipe. "It's rather puzzling that he didn't want it published, really. I've read it all and there is nothing very damning in it. He's a bit arrogant maybe, but God knows that was hardly a crime in the Royal Navy in the eighteenth century."

"Can I read the letter?"

"Of course," he said. "I think it's still tucked into the journal."

Lizzie carefully opened the book again and leafed through it until she saw the loose paper that was the letter.

"My Dearest Eliza," it began, "for reasons of my own, I'm sending my journal on to you from Canton. The Captain of the East India Company's ship *Cathay* has agreed to bring you this silk and the box. Look for my heart in this box, as our ancestress looked for the heart of her Crusader when he was far from home."

There followed some tender words of consolation about the recent death of their brother, and also gratitude for what she must be doing to comfort their father at such a hard time. He promised that his return was not far off and signed the letter, "Your affectionate brother, Francis."

Lizzie leafed through the journal, reading the entries at the top of each page: "Ship *Resolution* Rounding Good Hope," said several, "On the Coast of New Zealand," said others. She saw titles for Tahiti and the Sandwich Islands, and finally "Ship *Resolution* on the Northwest Coast." The last entry was dated April 14, 1778, and the ship was at Nootka Sound.

"Why did he stop keeping the journal?" she wondered aloud, flipping through at least sixty more sheets of clean white paper left in the book before any more were used.

George Hatton shrugged that he had no better idea than she.

She took a magnifying lens from her purse and looked along the binding edge of the paper at the last sheet that contained an entry. A number of pages had been cleanly cut out, as if with a razor.

"George?" she said, gesturing to it and leaning the book toward him.

He bent nearer to look.

Lizzie pointed to the book. "Who cut the pages out?" she asked.

He was puzzled. "Cut out?" he said, pulling a pair of glasses from his pocket and staring intently at where she was pointing. "I never noticed that," he murmured, standing to get closer to the journal. "My grandfather first showed me this journal when I was a child and he lamented the fact that the voyage was interrupted. He never noticed any pages missing and he had been looking at it since he was a boy in the nineteenth century." He sat down again, clearly perplexed.

Lizzie went back to the letter. "What does this mean?" she asked, reading aloud from the letter, "Look for my heart in this box, as our ancestress looked for the heart of her Crusader."

He dismissed it as family folklore, though Lizzie felt that there was something more to it which he was unwilling to share with her. She didn't press the subject however; it didn't seem like anything she needed to know to begin the job at hand anyway.

"Well, I might as well get started with the work," she said.

George gave her permission to set up a temporary office on the big table in the library, and to use the phone for Internet access. Lizzie went back to her room to get the carry-on case that held her computer equipment and then returned to the library and set up a working space with her laptop computer, printer, and portable scanner. She also had a digital camera that would allow her to photograph the objects in the collection and put them, along with whatever documentation existed about them, directly into her computer. This process would save her a lot of time in transcribing documents and describing artifacts.

The actual work seemed to interest George less than talking about it, and he finally began to make motions that he would leave Lizzie alone in the library. "Supper is at seven," he said as he left. "Mrs. Jeffries will give you a fifteen-minute warning in case you lose track of the time."

When she felt that she had gotten herself organized enough to make a good start the following morning, Lizzie took a break and called Martin to tell him that she had arrived safely.

"I was hoping you'd call," he said. "What's it like there?"

"The house is fabulous," she said. "Just like in the book

only grander, if you can believe it. Thanks for that book, by the way. It really gave me a good introduction to the place."

"And what's *he* like?"

"He's not exactly a regular guy, but I like him," she said. "And he's smart—he loves my book."

On the other end of the line she heard Martin's laugh.

"I miss you," she said.

"I know, sweetheart. I miss you too."

She hadn't noticed that it was dark outside until she hung up. There were several lamps in the library, as well as two large chandeliers filled with scores of tiny bulbs, and the fire, which was still crackling away. She walked to the dark windows and looked out across the stone terrace at the winter remnants of the garden. There had been no real sunset, no blaze of red or orange, just a silver streak of light left on the horizon.

"Dinner is in fifteen minutes, Dr. Manning."

Lizzie jumped when Mrs. Jeffries spoke to her from the open door.

"Thank you," she said. "Where do I go?"

"Straight across the hall," Mrs. Jeffries answered, pointing past the double staircase that dominated the foyer of the Adam wing of the house.

The housekeeper seemed to be looking at her as if she was a great puzzle and Lizzie wondered if there was something odd about her appearance, or if the other woman was waiting for her to move in response to her announcement. She began to be uncomfortable under Mrs. Jeffries' scrutiny, like a specimen in a Petri dish, until the other woman seemed to realize with a start that she was being rude and turned to leave the room.

"Thanks again," Lizzie called after her. She wondered how long the other woman had been standing at the door watching her before speaking.

After dinner Lizzie found that the time difference and two days of travel were catching up with her, so she made her excuses and went to her room. She stood for a few minutes at the tall windows looking down the dark expanse to the sea below. She could barely make out the outline of the ruined stone wall in the distance and she became frustrated trying to mentally reconstruct the look of the original fortifications in the darkness.

"I hope there will be time to explore it all while I am here," she said to herself as she got into bed. As she turned to pull the chain on the lamp near her bed she noticed that the Rossetti painting was on the wall near the door.

That night she had a dream. She was standing on the terrace at Hengemont; the garden was in full bloom. Beyond the garden, and the stone wall, and green fields dotted with sheep, lay the sea. A big square-rigger moved along under full sail. The sailor was returning home.

Lizzie turned in her bed and woke. She knew where she was; she was at George Hatton's big rambling ancestral home, Hengemont. The house was absolutely silent and she was wide awake.

She had closed the curtains that faced the other wing of the house but left them open on the side facing down the slope to the Bristol Channel. She sat up in bed and looked out at the night sky, perfectly clear and scattered with stars. According to the clock it was 4:30 in the morning and the room was quite chilly. She got up and pulled on the robe that had fallen to the floor at the foot of the bed and then opened the door out into the hall.

A soft lamp glowed on a small table about halfway down the long hall, but the passage was otherwise empty and dark. Lizzie closed the door and went back to stand for a moment at the windows facing the sea. There was a lighthouse at Porlock Weir that blinked twice and then was dark, then blinked twice again and was dark. She counted the seconds between each double flash, a habit from her research days when she had spent several weeks sailing off the coast of Alaska. Eight seconds.

There were a few lights visible in the tiny village of Hengeport twinkling through the trees that stood between it and the house. She pulled the curtains back slightly from the other set of windows and looked across the courtyard to Hengemont's Tudor wing; it was totally dark.

Lizzie crawled back into bed, taking with her the book that Martin had given her. In her dream she had seen the house as it looked in the book, surrounded by the bloom of summer, and not as she could actually see it in the chilly grayness of winter. She smiled to herself. She had always been very impressionable in her dreams and she enjoyed it when they cast a soft and romantic spell, as this one had.

How many people had crossed this patch of earth, she thought. How many lives lived, loves felt, tears dropped. She looked again at pictures of the house until she fell back to sleep with the light on and the book open.

Chapter 5

Lizzie slept soundly until almost eight the next morning and woke feeling that she had beaten the worst of the time change. Nobody had said anything about breakfast, so she decided to just go down to the library and start working. Mrs. Jeffries heard her as she came down the stairs.

"Did you sleep well, Dr. Manning?" she asked.

"Yes, very well," Lizzie answered.

"Would you like a full breakfast?"

"No, thank you. I don't usually have much in the morning."

"Can I bring some tea to the library?"

"Would coffee be possible?"

"Of course," Mrs. Jeffries said. She looked up at Lizzie and when Lizzie smiled at her, she smiled back.

Lizzie still had the strange discomfort of not quite knowing how to behave with Mrs. Jeffries. After all, the woman wasn't *her* servant. Was it crossing some line of protocol to want to be friendly, even familiar with her? And even if it was, should that matter, Lizzie wondered? She didn't have to abide by any master/servant nonsense. But what were Mrs. Jeffries' expectations of guests? Since she was the stranger, Lizzie thought she should be open and friendly but not aggressively so until she better understood the domestic landscape.

The library beckoned and Lizzie was eager to get to work. The temporary office that she had set up the previous day lay before her on the big table and the room was filled with sunlight. Lizzie felt a buzz of satisfaction as she settled into her new work space. This will be a very nice way to spend the month of January, she thought happily. Through the tall windows she could see a layer of frost on the terrace, but she was comfortable inside. A big fire was already roaring in the grate at the other end of the room.

She decided to start right away with a transcription of the journal, which would, she thought, serve as the basis for any book or exhibit that might follow. It was her practice to begin with a thorough description of the document, so she entered:

> Shipboard Journal of Francis Hatton, entitled: "A Voyage to the Pacific Ocean and 'Round the World on HMS *Resolution,* Under the Command of Captain James Cook, R.N., by Francis Hatton, Lieutenant, 1776, 1777, 1778. . . ."

There was a blank space at the end of the title, where Francis Hatton had apparently intended to fill in the subsequent year of the voyage, but had never done so. Lizzie continued:

> A manuscript in the collection of Sir George Hatton, a descendent of the journal keeper, Hengemont House, Hengeport, Somerset, England. The record begins with the departure from Portsmouth on July 12, 1776, and ends abruptly on April 14, 1778, while at Nootka Sound; a number of pages are then cut out at the binding. Numerous blank pages follow. In the back...

She turned the journal over to see if Francis Hatton had entered anything on the last pages. There she found a "List of Artefacts for My Cabinet at Hengemont." It was a wonderful discovery, exactly the kind of thing that she had always hoped to find while working on her dissertation, but had never been so lucky as to locate. She began typing again. There were a number of things from the "Sandwich Islands" or Hawaii, including a feathered helmet and a necklace made of a sperm whale's tooth and human hair. She glanced up to the cabinet and saw them on the shelves, then moved on to the Northwest Coast Indian objects, typing furiously.

> A mask representing a wooden-lipped woman, and two of the wooden lips.

A bone club from Nootka Sound, curiously carved.

A hat woven of rushes representing their manner of hunting whales.

A whaling harpoon with the tip some kind of hard shell.

A garment made from the fibres of the trunk of a tree.

A hat or cap in the form of a bear's face.

Except for the cedar bark garment, which had likely disintegrated over two centuries, Lizzie looked to each item in the cabinet as she read the description. It was an extraordinary collection. The mask, especially, was really a work of art. Finely carved and painted, it had a wonderfully expressive face.

There were two additional entries but they had been crossed out. Lizzie studied them under her magnifying lens, held them up to the light at different angles, and even took the journal over to the window to see if direct sunlight would help expose the writing underneath the inky scratches, but try as she might she could not decipher what had been written originally on the last two lines. She went to the cabinet with the book in her hand and ticked off each item on the list against the objects that she saw. There didn't seem to be anything in the collection from either Hawaii or the Northwest Coast that was not on the list.

During the course of the morning Mrs. Jeffries came in with a pot of coffee and some scones with jam. Lizzie took a break and enjoyed just being in such a lovely room. She tried to picture Francis Hatton in this very room, looking at his cabinet and handling his artifacts.

Soon after she had returned to work in earnest, George came in to check on her progress. She showed him the list in the back of the book and her enthusiasm over it infected him. When she asked him if he could decipher the crossed-out entries he looked at them for several minutes, borrowing Lizzie's magnifying lens again and giving it a thorough examination, but without success.

They broke for lunch in midday and talked more about the project, and after a full afternoon of work, Lizzie was once more surprised when Mrs. Jeffries came to call her to dinner. Unlike the day before, when she had arrived in the library in the afternoon, with the lamps lit and the fire roaring, today no one had disturbed her to turn on the lights or feed the fire and the room had grown decidedly gloomy. Lizzie was working at the table with a single lamp that threw a pool of light onto her computer and the journal she was transcribing, but the room was otherwise quite dark.

"My goodness," Mrs. Jeffries said, throwing the switch to turn on the chandeliers, "you'll ruin your eyes working in the dark like this."

"I didn't even notice," Lizzie explained. She had been so absorbed in Francis Hatton's journal that she hadn't noticed either the passage of time or the loss of light. She closed the book and turned to Mrs. Jeffries. "It's really interesting work."

Mrs. Jeffries took a few steps toward Lizzie.

"Do you mind if I ask what you're working on?"

"Not at all," Lizzie said, pleased at the request. She gave a quick outline of her project.

"So you're only working on the man who collected the things in the cabinet?"

Lizzie answered that she was.

"So that's why you were interested in the Gainsborough painting," Mrs. Jeffries said, almost to herself. She looked up at Lizzie. "I thought you might be here to look into the history of the women in the family."

Mrs. Jeffries seemed to read the confusion on Lizzie's face; she hesitated before speaking again.

"Well, dinner will be ready very soon," she said finally, turning and walking ahead of Lizzie across the hall to the family dining room.

Maybe Mrs. Jeffries was shy, Lizzie thought. She didn't like to think that her behavior was based on some expectation placed on servants to be distant or obsequious. As she developed the thought more, she wondered if perhaps the housekeeper was still feeling out Lizzie's position in the household, just as she was herself.

Dinner passed quickly. George was interested in knowing

her progress, but not intrusively so. Mrs. Jeffries brought food to the table, but never spoke conversationally to Lizzie when George was present.

Lizzie found herself missing her husband's company and went from the dining room back to the library to call him at the end of the meal.

"How's the work going?" Martin asked.

Lizzie described Francis Hatton's journal and told her husband how she felt she was really getting to know this man, dead for almost two centuries.

"Should I be jealous of old Frank?"

She laughed. "You know, I started to think of him as Frank today."

"Then it must be a great journal," Martin said. "If you like him so much from such a distance of time."

"Not to mention social class," Lizzie added.

"Yes please," he said, *"Not* to mention it." They laughed. "I don't want you to think that we need to rely on the weather to have a conversation, but it snowed hard here today, almost eight inches. I never left the house."

"Are you getting plenty to eat?"

"Of course," he said. "Why do you always worry so much about me when you're not here?"

"I like to think that you need me."

"Rest assured I do," he said. "I don't need you to feed me, necessarily, but I sure am missing you."

She hung up the phone and went into the hall beyond the library. There was no sign of Mrs. Jeffries or George, or any sound except the ticking of clocks. Lizzie wondered if she might sneak for a few minutes back into the medieval hall through which she had come the day before. It lay just beyond the hallway that she was in; Robert Adam had designed this extension so that it backed on the original structure of the house, the square Norman tower. She passed beneath the double staircase and pulled open two sets of doors. The first was in the Georgian style of the newer wing, with painted wood and plaster friezes surrounding the casing of the door. Beyond it was a short passage through the thick stone wall of the original castle tower and another door, a massive ancient oak door, covered with the square iron heads of numerous hand-forged nails.

Lizzie pushed on the door, which creaked loudly on its iron hinges. She stopped for a moment and looked around again. She hadn't been invited to make herself at home in the house, though she certainly was beginning to feel very comfortable in it. She didn't know when she might cross over the line and invade someone's privacy—George's or the Jeffries', or that of some occupant not currently at home. In truth, she didn't even know if there were other people in the house. There was at least one other servant, the man she had seen when she arrived. Were there other family members who might want to avoid strangers, that she didn't know about? Lizzie spun the question out to include the odd folks secreted away somewhere in garrets or cellars—mad aunts or ex-wives, or bonded servants all but enslaved and sweating on those toils that made the Hattons rich.

It occurred to her that she would be embarrassed if she were found walking around the dark house. She slowly pulled the door closed and quietly retraced her steps to the big staircase. She climbed up to the landing and stared at the Gainsborough painting of Francis Hatton and his siblings. The portrait was larger than life size, and as Lizzie stepped up to look at it closely she found that her eyes were on a level with his, as he sat comfortably in his painted rural landscape.

"Frank," she whispered, "you and I are going to be great friends."

She continued on to her room and after a hot bath fell sound asleep.

• • • • •

Over the next few days, Lizzie settled into a pattern of work. She felt remarkably comfortable in those parts of the grand old house through which she walked each day, loved the library as a work space, and found George an intelligent sounding board for each new discovery. She didn't often have the opportunity to discuss work-in-progress in this way, and she enjoyed the process. That George made no attempt to direct the course of her work, or really to do much more than praise what she was doing, made his comments especially valuable. He was generally able to answer Lizzie's questions about his family history, and when he was not, he knew where to find the books that could.

Mrs. Jeffries kept up a regular supply of hot coffee and small snacks and Lizzie would frequently take breaks from her transcription to sip and munch and ponder the delights of playing the aristocrat. She would often stand at the tall windows that faced across the terrace. The cold landscape beyond made her glad to be inside, but she also tried to picture the garden in other seasons, and enjoyed daydreaming about the house in other centuries.

During one of her reveries, as she leaned against the tall back of her chair, Lizzie felt eyes on her and turned softly to find Mrs. Jeffries watching her from the doorway. She smiled at the housekeeper who smiled back, embarrassed, and asked if she needed anything.

"I enjoyed meeting your son in London," Lizzie said, hoping to finally engage the older woman in a real conversation. Except for the brief exchange about her work, it seemed that, during the whole time Lizzie had been at Hengemont, they had talked only about whether or not Lizzie wanted to eat or drink something.

"Peter told me that you and he talked," she said.

"I liked him very much," Lizzie continued. She added what she knew about the competitive nature of the program at the University of London, and commended Peter Jeffries' obvious talent and effort.

"I believe you are a professor?"

Lizzie responded that she was, and Mrs. Jeffries asked her some additional questions about where she was from in the U.S.

"Are you married?" she asked.

Lizzie answered that she was.

"So is Manning your married name?"

"No, my husband's name is Sanchez." With women of her mother's generation, Lizzie often felt that some explanation was necessary for not taking Martin's name, but Mrs. Jeffries didn't seem to require such an explanation, or even, Lizzie thought, to be interested.

"Your ancestors," Mrs. Jeffries continued, "were they English or Irish?"

"All four of my grandparents were born in America, but my great-grandparents were from Ireland," Lizzie answered, somewhat surprised by Mrs. Jeffries' curiosity.

The housekeeper seemed to sense Lizzie's surprise. "My grandmother was a Manning," she said, by way of explanation. "She came from Ireland with her sister over a hundred years ago. They worked in this house."

"Maybe we're related," Lizzie said, pleased to make a friendly connection

Mrs. Jeffries continued to press her for information for a few more minutes. Did she know what part of Ireland her Manning ancestor had come from? Was it a man or a woman? Lizzie was unable to answer most of her questions. She had asked these very same things of her father just before she left for England, and of her grandfather a decade or so earlier. His mother, he said, had always given him excuses rather than information. Her husband had died just before they were to emigrate, she had two tickets for the transatlantic passage and had redeemed one to support herself for a time on her arrival in New York, before she got a job working as a domestic servant. Her son, Lizzie's grandfather, was born shortly thereafter. Lizzie had spent some time trying to identify what ship she came on, but had never had any luck. This was very much in contrast to the other side of her family. For her mother's grandparents Lizzie had birth certificates, immigration data, and oral histories.

She thought of the dream she had had on the plane coming over. Her father's grandmother had lived to be a hundred, and Lizzie had some hazy memories of the old woman from when she was a small child. She had a brogue so thick that as a little girl Lizzie was often completely mystified by what she was saying, and occasionally the old lady lapsed into a tongue that even her son couldn't understand.

"She spoke Irish," Lizzie heard herself say to Mrs. Jeffries.

"So she was from the west of Ireland?"

"That was always my understanding."

"What was her name?"

"I'm named for her," Lizzie answered. "She was Elizabeth Manning—also called Lizzie."

The housekeeper nodded to herself. She seemed about to say something more, but George's arrival at the library door silenced her. She looked at her watch, made a comment about lunch, and left the room.

• • • • •

On her fourth morning at Hengemont, Lizzie was feeling herself very productive. She had entered Francis Hatton's list of artifacts into her computer, but before she actually opened the cabinet and examined each of them she was determined to finish transcribing the journal so that she could print it out and have a working copy. Years of research and writing had made her a fast and accurate typist, and since the young sailor's penmanship was generally quite legible she worked at a rapid pace. George Hatton stopped in once in the middle of the morning to see how she was getting along and then left her alone until lunchtime.

The *Resolution* had already rounded the Cape of Good Hope and was on the coast of New Zealand when a noisy party entered the house and interrupted Lizzie's momentum. A few moments later an energetic girl burst into the library where Lizzie sat, fingers poised over the keyboard of her computer. Each stopped her activity as their eyes locked, the little girl seeming surprised and embarrassed, Lizzie being only startled. She smiled at the girl and said hello.

Lizzie was a sucker for cute little red-haired girls, and this was a particularly wonderful example of the species. Freckle-faced and strawberry-haired, with her straight hair pulled back by a black headband and from there falling loose down her back, she was at that wonderful big-toothed age. She had grey-blue eyes that reminded Lizzie of George Hatton's. The girl's curiosity soon overtook her fear and she approached Lizzie at the table where she sat.

"Are you the American?"

"Yes I am," she said, holding out her hand to the girl. "I'm Lizzie."

"I'm Lily Hatton," the girl said seriously, shaking Lizzie's hand.

"Do you live here at Hengemont?" Lizzie asked her.

Lily shook her head. "Most of the time I live in London," she answered, "but on holidays and weekends I live with my dad in Bristol." She skipped around the table, dragging her hand along the wood. "Sometimes we stay here though," she added, "with my grandfather."

In the hallway beyond the library door Lizzie heard the sound of men in conversation and soon after George entered the room, followed by a man who was introduced as his son, Edmund. Lizzie had thought when she met George Hatton that he must have been extremely attractive as a young man, and his son seemed to stand before her as a demonstration of what he might have looked like thirty years earlier. Edmund had the same height and build as his father, and shared the same remarkable grey-blue eye color that was evident in all three generations of Hattons in the room. His hair was about as dark as it could get and still be considered blond, though lighter streaks of grey were scattered throughout.

It was in his bearing that Edmund Hatton least resembled his father. He did not have the same aristocratic elegance, though he seemed self-assured and intelligent. He wore jeans and a pullover sweater, had several days' growth of beard, and had a comfortable and friendly demeanor that made Lizzie like him instantly.

They shook hands and then he put his hand gently on the head of the little girl. "I see you've met my daughter Lily," he said.

Lily asked for further explanation of what Lizzie was doing in the house.

"I'm a history teacher," Lizzie answered. "And I study the stories of interesting families like yours."

The four of them chatted comfortably for about fifteen minutes, and Lizzie found Lily to be a perceptive and intelligent nine-year-old with a wonderful sense of humor. When they moved to the dining room for lunch, Edmund asked Lizzie about the work she was doing and made suggestions about places to look in the house for additional papers that might be tucked away. George told him about the missing logbook pages, and Edmund expressed an interest in seeing what Lizzie had found so far. When they were finished with their meal, Lizzie returned with Edmund to the library, while George and Lily chatted on about school and her life in London.

Edmund was clearly very knowledgeable about his ancestor's voyage. He had read the journal more than once, as well as the official narrative of the voyage and all of the other journals that had been published. As they spoke of the collection, Lizzie realized that he was not only smart and well informed, but keenly interested in the period.

"Have you read my book?" she joked.

"Indeed I have," he answered with a smile.

Lizzie was somewhat embarrassed. She hadn't been seeking his interest or approval, but she found herself pleased.

After an hour of conversation about Francis Hatton and his voyage, Edmund asked Lizzie how she liked the house.

"It's extraordinary," Lizzie said. Now it was her turn to be the student and she asked him several questions about the layout of the original castle and the subsequent additions. At one point they rose from the table so that he could point out some of the features of the old castle grounds in the garden.

When Lily and George came to find them, Edmund was asking Lizzie if she'd had a chance to look around the house and grounds and she replied that she had not.

"Dad," Edmund scolded, jokingly, "you're not being a very good host. Don't forget that Professor Manning is a historian and will not only be interested, but can probably tell us a thing or two that we don't know."

"Please," she said, "call me Lizzie. 'Professor Manning' seems to be putting unreasonably grandiose expectations of my expertise into your head."

"You're the best guide," George said to Edmund. "Why don't you show her around?"

Edmund agreed that he would, and they spoke for a few minutes about his schedule.

"I have to get back to Bristol this evening," he explained, "but Lily wants time to visit with her friends in Hengeport before she goes back to London, so we'll be back in a couple of days. Can you wait till then to tour the house?"

Lizzie answered that she could and as they said their good-byes, she found herself looking forward to their next meeting.

When she retired to her room after dinner, Lizzie flung open the tall windows facing down to the sea. The air was bitter cold. There was almost a balcony beyond the windows, but it was so narrow that she thought it must have been made more for the look of the house from the outside than for the use of the guests on the inside. There was no room for her to step outside, but she leaned on the stone railing and admired the view of the village lights until it became too cold.

She found herself thinking about Edmund Hatton. It was a long time since she had met anyone so interesting. There was nothing romantic or sexual about her attraction to him. She had a happy marriage and he had a daughter, so he must also have a wife. Still, if this were a romance novel, Edmund would be the perfect hero. Lizzie laughed out loud as she thought it. She turned back the covers and climbed into bed. She was in a situation that had all the classic elements: a big old stately home in the English countryside, a handsome aristocrat, and herself as a spunky and intelligent heroine. Except that she also had her husband at home, a job to do, and a philosophical aversion to the whole notion of an aristocracy in the twenty-first century.

Chapter 6

For the first time, Lizzie woke early enough to join George for breakfast. She told him how much she had enjoyed meeting Edmund and Lily the day before.

"Your granddaughter is a wonderful girl."

"Yes she is," George said with pride. "Smart as a whip, just like her father."

"Edmund said that he's a physician?"

George spread marmalade onto his toast and nodded. "Has a practice in Bristol," he said. "Runs a clinic there."

Lizzie couldn't help thinking that someone with the Hatton connections could certainly have done better than that and George seemed to read her mind. He gave her a brief history of Edmund's medical career, which included several years volunteering with various international charitable organizations.

Lizzie asked George about his other children. She already knew there was a son John in Australia, and her host told her about his third son, Richard.

"The oldest," he said. "He's a financial man in London."

"He's the one who was with you when you visited Tom Clark at the British Museum?"

"Yes, and he is keenly interested in seeing us get the collection organized to make it accessible to them."

"Is he a history buff?"

George laughed. "No, I don't think anyone would ever accuse him of that. He is more interested in the social and political connections that it will bring him. Those things are valuable in his business."

Lizzie appreciated his frankness. It explained why the

Hattons had finally opened up access to the collection after having kept it secreted away for so many years. She had also wondered how a family like the Hattons supported their anachronistic lifestyle in the modern world, and the fact that Richard, who must be the heir to Hengemont, was some sort of banker or broker made sense to her. A big fortune could be used to generate its own money.

They had a few more minutes of conversation on family topics before Lizzie felt that it was time to get to work.

"I must resume my voyage with your ancestor out to the Pacific Ocean," she said to George as she rose from the table.

"I can't wait to hear the outcome of your adventure," George said. "If you need anything from me today, I'll be working up in my own study. Have Mrs. Jeffries give me a call."

She thanked him for the offer and they each went off to their projects, Lizzie settling in with the journal to finish transcribing the text.

The first part of the voyage was just as she knew it from having read the journals of a number of Hatton's shipmates and the official narrative published by the British Admiralty.

The Royal Navy ships *Resolution,* under the command of Captain James Cook, and *Discovery,* under the command of Captain James King, departed from Portsmouth on the twelfth of July, 1776, just a week after the American colonists claimed their independence. Cook and his men would have known nothing of the news across the Atlantic at that time, though a few future American citizens were among the crew.

The ships sailed south, rounding the Cape of Good Hope at the end of November, midsummer in the southern hemisphere. They touched at Tasmania, then New Zealand, and then headed north into the Pacific. Their mission was to seek a passage across the top of the North American continent back to the Atlantic Ocean. In February 1778, to their surprise and delight, they stumbled upon a group of islands, which Cook named the Sandwich Islands after one of his patrons. Francis Hatton's descriptions of Hawaiian people and of the lush landscape in which they lived were filled with enthusiastic detail. Lizzie loved Francis Hatton; he had few of the pretensions she expected of an upper-class Brit, and even fewer of the stereotypes that most eighteenth-century mariners held of the native people they encountered on a voyage.

She found herself laughing at his wonderful prose as he described his comical attempts to communicate with people with whom he had no common language, and where even sign language was riddled with cross-cultural confusion. "Frank," as she now regularly found herself calling him, knew that the girls he was trying to impress were laughing at his antics, and he laughed at them himself. He was an avid collector and Lizzie loved that about him. He had a keen eye for cultural details, an open but detailed manner of describing them, and a fair hand for sketching houses, people, plants, animals, and artifacts. He delighted in what he considered his "conquests"—every time an object came into his collection he meticulously detailed the circumstances of acquisition and as much as he could tell about the thing, without knowing the language.

Lizzie found herself looking frequently up to the cabinet, where most of these objects were sitting quietly. Every now and then she stood up and walked over to open the glass-fronted cases to look more closely at the fish hook, carved drum, gourd rattle, or bark cloth being described. It was a wonderful day. By dinner time she was able to report to George Hatton that there was a tremendous amount of information in the journal about the Hawaiian collection and that it would make a very good exhibition and catalogue.

She called Martin that night to report on her progress. He was leaving for New York the next day and for at least a week it would be difficult to reach him during hours that were convenient in both their time zones.

"All is well in my world!" she declared, "except for the absence of you, of course."

"So the work remains interesting?"

"It isn't just that the collection is large," Lizzie explained, "but that dear old Frank described almost every piece." Her enthusiasm was obvious even across the Atlantic, and she expounded on the relationship between the journal and the artifacts in some detail to her husband. "It is a truly extraordinary assemblage of stuff. I still can't believe that I am the first person to get a chance to work with it like this."

"Now that you know him better, has George explained why he chose to bestow this honor on you?"

"That, I think, was luck," she said. "One of his sons is some kind of an investment guy in London. He wants to be a player at the British Museum and is using this collection as his ticket in." Lizzie told Martin how George had accompanied his son on a visit to meet Tom Clark at the museum, had seen a number of different books on similar subjects and had liked hers. "The rest is history!" she concluded.

"Well, I hope my time in New York will be as productive," he said.

Lizzie realized that she had been doing most of the talking. "I hope so too," she said. "Are you excited about going?"

"Nah," he admitted. "I think it's going to be a good mural, but I'm starting to hate these bank jobs. They bring in the money, but they don't excite me like the community projects."

They spoke for several minutes about the potential projects that Martin was considering and the one that interested him most was the one in Newcastle. It was apparent to Lizzie that he had been thinking about it seriously in the few days she had been away. The possibility that he would join her in England was now a probability.

"Though it doesn't seem quite fair that you will be in a stately home while I'm holed up in a coal town," he joked.

"Oh come now," she argued, "you'd much rather be in a coal mine than a castle."

"I'm missing you," he said.

She kissed her hand and touched the phone. "Me too."

• • • • •

Lizzie knew that she would marry Martin the first time she saw his picture. At the time she was a graduate student at Berkeley, with a part-time job in the office of the Anthropology Department. Among her other menial tasks, she sorted the mail and opened up the general announcements that weren't addressed to anyone in particular. That day as she leaned against the metal cabinet with its dymo-labeled cubbyholes, she slid her forefinger under the tape that sealed a single sheet of folded paper; it was an announcement of an upcoming campus lecture series.

As the paper opened, she was immediately drawn to the picture of the third speaker on the list, identified as "Martin Sanchez, Mexican-American Artist." There was just something about him that captivated her. Instead of posting the flyer on the departmental bulletin board, she slipped it into her backpack. When she got back to her room, she cut the picture out and tacked it to the edge of the bookshelf above her typewriter and stared at it for a long time. The lecture wasn't for six weeks, and according to his biography Martin Sanchez lived in Los Angeles, so there was nothing for Lizzie to do but wait.

Jean Marie, her roommate, was clearly puzzled. "Who is that guy anyway?" she asked on several occasions. But Lizzie never seemed inclined to answer. She looked at the picture often. Medieval European royalty had exchanged miniature paintings to sell themselves to prospective mates, she thought, and she would have agreed to marry Martin Sanchez from this picture.

When he finally came to San Francisco to talk about his work, Lizzie was completely bowled over. He was funny and smart and she loved his paintings. At that time he was selling himself as a barrio boy, whose astonishing graffiti was discovered by an art critic for the *L. A. Times*. Lizzie found him exotic and romantic, hung on every word at his lecture, and studied each slide carefully.

Even then, his work had consisted almost entirely of murals. In the last slide he showed the sketches for a new work, which would be a neighborhood project in San Francisco. When the lights came up Martin turned and looked directly at Lizzie and each felt a jolt. Though the audience around her was applauding, Lizzie felt as if she were in a vacuum, her eyes locked on his. When the time came for questions, he suddenly seemed uncomfortable, shaken. He looked relieved when the professor who had introduced him thanked him and invited the crowd to wine and cheese in the lobby. His eyes sought Lizzie's again and she smiled. They continued to exchange looks through the interminable reception. Finally, after twenty minutes of chit-chat with strangers, he approached her and introduced himself.

"I know who you are," she said, offering her hand, which, to her surprise, he kissed softly. "I'm Elizabeth Manning."

"Elizabeth?" he asked.

"Well, Lizzie," she stammered. She felt that she was appearing foolish, girly, stupid. She had said "Elizabeth" because she wanted to appear more elegant; that attempt was now shot to hell.

"I feel like I know you," he said.

She slept with him that night. She had never before slept with any man, and he seemed pleased and surprised that she was a virgin. For the next four days, Lizzie and Martin hardly left his hotel room except when he was scheduled to meet with people about his project. They talked about everything. About themselves and their families, about books and movies, plans and dreams. Lizzie was not as surprised to find herself completely absorbed in him, as she was to find that the feeling was mutual. She was madly in love and so was he.

Lizzie often laughed to herself as she thought of all that she had learned of him since. In fact, it *had* been graffiti that had gotten him noticed, but Lizzie had subsequently learned of his comfortable middle-class upbringing in Glendale. His father was the director of the Parks Department and his mother was a librarian at Herbert Hoover High School. While his father had immigrated from Mexico with his own parents when he was still a child, Martin's mother's family had been in California for generations. Today, Martin objected to being labeled a "Mexican-American artist." Though proud of his roots, he wanted now to be defined by his work and, with ever-growing acclaim, he was. Lizzie was proud of him, loved him, and felt confident in his love for her.

Before she drifted off to sleep, Lizzie tried to imagine Martin at Hengemont and it was an oddly jarring mental picture— as if the page from one book had somehow been mistakenly bound into another on a completely different topic. It wasn't that he wouldn't love the place. The paintings alone would thrill him, she knew. And yet, she felt that he just didn't belong here. How strange, then, that she should feel that she did.

Chapter 7

Francis Hatton's journal held Lizzie's total attention for several days. She was glad that she was so completely charmed by his prose. If this had been like most seafaring journals—a straightforward account of wind, weather, location, and sail handling—it could never have gripped her imagination the way it did.

On the day that she turned to the last portion of the journal she announced her intention to George and to Mrs. Jeffries to work straight through the day and hoped she would not be interrupted. This was the part of the voyage of greatest interest to her, the Northwest Coast of the North American continent. It was where she had grown up, and it was a geographical region that she knew not only through historical documents but from firsthand experience. As she read Hatton's text she could picture each location.

The *Resolution* proceeded from Hawaii to the coast of North America in late winter, 1778. On the seventh of March the crew sighted land which Cook called "Cape Foul Weather," giving an indication of the impossibility of doing anything more than logging its position at 44° 55' North Latitude and 135° 54' Longitude West of Greenwich.

On the twelfth, Cook named Cape Gregory, after the Pope whose feast day was celebrated on that day. Francis Hatton made the first of several comments in his journal about his captain's propensity to name landfalls after saints from the Roman Catholic calendar, though Gregory had been useful to mariners by correcting the calendar, and Hatton thought that must be the reason. Stormy weather drove the ships off the coast for ten days, and when they sighted land again it was at Cape Flattery. This was a place well known to Lizzie. Her family had been going there for years, whenever her father felt compelled to see the sea—a compulsion inherited by all of his children. Cape Flattery was at the northwest corner of Washington State and marks the southern entrance to the Strait of Juan de Fuca, though Cook and his crew failed to see the great channel leading inshore.

A week later the ships dropped anchor in Nootka Sound on the west coast of Vancouver Island. There they stayed for a month, making needed repairs to the ships and trading extensively with the natives. Frank Hatton was in his element here. He quickly became friendly with a boy about fourteen years old, teaching him English and learning from him as much of the language of Nootka Sound as he could collect. Lizzie read through three full pages of vocabulary lists where translations of simple words were given including body parts, numbers up to ten, fish, furs, and other goods traded. There was also the naturalist's zeal for specific plants and animals, some of which were clearly unfamiliar to Hatton, and, of course, there were native words for all the collectibles like "mask," "rattle," "club," "arrow."

"I have seen here," wrote Hatton in a burst of enthusiasm, "pine, cypress, strawberry, raspberry, currants, alder, wild roses, leeks, mosses & ferns too numerous to count, also numerous specimens of the animal kingdom, some seen live, and others observed through tracks or through furs, claws, and teeth included among the accouterments of the Indians." Another list followed noting the common occurrence in the region of raccoons, bears, deer, foxes, wolves, whales, porpoises, seals, sea otters, and a number of birds including crows, ravens, magpies, gulls, ducks, swans, sandpipers, plovers, and Lizzie's favorite, a "large brown eagle with a white head and tail." Fish and insects were likewise documented. Lizzie was impressed. The descriptions took her from the ancient comfort of Hengemont to the coast of British Columbia.

Hatton collected everything he could, and wrote warmly of the young man who helped him in his endeavors and whose name he gave as "something resembling Tatooshtikus."

When the Englishmen had been at Nootka Sound for about two weeks, a party of visitors arrived from further north and Tatooshtikus introduced Frank Hatton to a young chief by the name of Eltatsy, with whom Hatton also developed a very friendly relationship. But on April 14 it all ended abruptly. At that point the pages were cut from the journal and no more information was to be had.

Lizzie closed the journal in frustration. What had happened to the rest of it?

As she could go no further with the journal itself, Lizzie decided to concentrate for the rest of the day on cataloging the manuscripts in the drawers of the cabinet. It might be that the missing pages had become separated from the journal, but still survived and were somewhere else in the house. The first drawer she pulled out was filled almost to the top with loose papers that gave the impression that they had been dumped in randomly over many years. Lizzie opened each drawer in turn, collecting the odds and ends of paper and the miscellaneous souvenirs of many generations that filled them, and placed the contents in neat piles on the table.

Several piles were devoted to receipts for repairs, renovations, or additions to the house, and to new furnishings or decorations. There were invitations to parties, weddings, and other social events, including a number at court, that dated from the time of Francis Hatton right down to the 1950s. There was a whole drawer full of calling cards, many of which were engraved with the names of the most prominent people of five generations of British art and politics. There were postcards from all over the world, and letters, mostly bound into neat bundles and tied with ribbon.

The last drawer contained odds and ends of broken toys, thin pieces of veneer, and bits of ivory, wood, and mother-of-pearl that looked like they must have come from the decorative inlay of furniture. There was a small disc of abalone shell that might have once been part of a Northwest Coast Indian artifact and Lizzie held it carefully as she looked at the objects in the cabinet above her. The whalebone club from Nootka Sound was missing a piece of its elaborate abalone inlay; she opened the door of the case and laid the disc on the shelf near the club. When she came back to the artifacts she would put it in an envelope, attach it to the club, and flag it for the conservator at the British Museum. She poked through the remaining fragments in the drawer, but nothing else looked at all familiar.

When the drawers had been emptied of their papers, Lizzie made herself comfortable at the table and took stock of the piles before her. She turned first to the receipts. These she thought would have little relevance to her current project and she would be able to get through them quickly. Many of them were actually related to the building or outfitting of the cabinet. There were small scraps of paper on which an illiterate carpenter or glazer had left his mark of "x" in lieu of a signature, and there were some notes of exchanges of things collected by Francis Hatton for things collected by friends or acquaintances. Mostly these related to coins and medals, and Lizzie quickly saw that none of the ethnographic artifacts collected by Hatton on his voyage had been traded away. She heaved a sigh of relief; she would not have to track down things that long ago had entered other collections.

The bundles of letters were tackled next. Most were personal correspondence of a sort that would have interested Lizzie were she not on a specific mission—including love letters from three different centuries. The last bunch to be examined was the correspondence between Francis Hatton and his father, Sir John Hatton, which George had told her about. They were mostly chatty letters from son to father, filled with descriptions of places visited along the route of the voyage. Lizzie assumed these must have been sent from Canton at the same time that Frank sent the box with the journal to his sister. She wondered why he hadn't addressed the journal to his father, as the two of them obviously had a very open and affectionate relationship. She turned over another page to find a letter edged in black. It was the notice to Frank Hatton of the death of his older brother Richard, and it included a plea for his return at the earliest possible moment, even though his father knew that that time had to be at least several months away. "At such a time as this," it concluded, "it is painful but necessary to remind you that your obligations to your family take on a new prospect. You are now the heir to the title and property of Hengemont, and your place is here."

Frank's response was very moving. He gently comforted his father on the loss of Richard, and told him that even if he left the *Resolution* and returned on one of the East India Company vessels then in Canton, it could only speed his return by a few weeks or months and, given the death of his captain, James Cook, he felt obliged to see his voyage through to the end.

Lizzie turned over the last page and paused a few minutes before wrapping the papers back into their bundle and tying the faded ribbon around it. She looked into the cabinet again. It seemed that Frank Hatton had come home and concentrated his efforts on his collection, as his change in circumstances would certainly have prevented him from making another voyage.

She worked her way quickly through pile after pile of papers, refilling the drawers as she went along. As there had clearly been no organizational principle in their arrangement, she made no attempt to retain the original location of the papers she had transferred to the library table as she put them back in the cabinet. She filled the lowest drawers with things that she had surveyed and knew that she wouldn't need on this project. She paid the greatest attention to the documents that were related to Francis Hatton, but the other piles were shaping up as well. Correspondence, bills, scraps of poetry, household inventories, instructions to servants, invitations, all came into her hand in a random order and were shuffled into organizing piles.

There was one intriguing scrap of paper, obviously very old, on which someone had written with a quill in heavy black ink:

𝔚𝔥𝔢𝔯𝔢 𝔦𝔰 𝔥𝔦𝔰 𝔥𝔢𝔞𝔯𝔱?

Except for its age it didn't seem to hold any value, and it certainly wasn't pertinent to Francis Hatton, Lizzie thought as she set it aside. From the paper and the penmanship she thought it was probably a few centuries older than Francis Hatton's day. She smiled as she touched the paper. Some bastard must have done something terribly wrong to warrant such a documentation of his heartlessness. She could picture some ruffed Elizabethan getting his marching orders from a similarly ruffed woman, perhaps standing in this very house.

As she went through the loose manuscripts she found a small piece of stationery engraved with the name "Elizabeth Hatton" and the address "Hengemont." It was covered with sentence fragments written in a trembling hand, among which appeared the question "Where is his heart?"

"The women in this family appear to have been very unlucky in love," Lizzie thought to herself as she quickly divided papers by subject matter.

There were two bits of mediocre poetry, each asking the question again: "Where is his heart?" Lizzie began to wonder if it was some family lore connected with the sword-pierced heart on the Hatton crest. Maybe it was referring to honor or family duty or something other than love. She pulled out the piece of old stationery again and the scrap of paper on which she had originally seen the question, and decided to form them into a pile of their own.

Francis Hatton had also mentioned a heart in his letter to his sister, she thought. She opened the journal and unfolded the letter. "Look for my heart in this box, as our ancestress looked for the heart of her Crusader," she read softly. She looked inside the box again, but once the journal had been removed it was empty. She sat back in her chair and stretched her legs out to rest her feet on the long bar of the table. George Hatton had known what the heart reference meant, but hadn't wanted to share it with her. It was a puzzle, but not one that she could solve now. She put the scraps of paper into the box with the journal and letter and moved back to the piles of bills, receipts, and correspondence that had come out of the cabinet drawers.

As the afternoon turned to early evening she remembered to turn the lights on, and at one point Mr. Jeffries came in and asked if she would like him to build up the fire. In the course of their casual conversation she was pleased to learn that George's son was expected for dinner. Lizzie wrapped up the rest of her work quickly and went to her room to change. She hadn't expected Edmund to return until the next day and had planned to dress up a bit before she saw him again.

When Lizzie came back downstairs, George was in the library with another man, but it wasn't Edmund. If Edmund was a more-relaxed version of his father, this man was a stiffer and haughtier model of the handsome Hatton male approaching middle age. He was impeccably groomed, clean shaven with an angular face that was not softened by his expression. His eyes were bluer than those of his father and brother. They landed on Lizzie for a moment, before dismissing her and moving back to the papers that surrounded her computer.

George introduced Lizzie to his son Richard, who waved at her with the back of his hand without looking at her again. He had a drink in one hand, and with the other he pushed around the letters between Francis Hatton and his father, which he had untied from their bundle. He had obviously gone through several of the piles of papers that she had organized, dispersing them across the table. Lizzie fumed at his rudeness and crossed the room to reclaim her workspace, giving some effort to keeping her anger in check and maintaining a calm and professional demeanor. George sensed she was upset and called to his son.

"Richard," he said, "Don't undo any of Lizzie's hard work." He started to describe what Lizzie had found in the journal to his son, who now turned to look hard at Lizzie. She returned what she felt was a rude and condescending stare, taking stock of him while George continued to talk as if the two of them had just met on the friendliest of terms.

The younger man stiffened when he heard Lizzie refer to his father as "George," and made no attempt to disguise his surprise and irritation when he learned that Lizzie would join them for dinner. There had been a time, before Lizzie arrived at Hengemont, when she wondered if George Hatton was intending to treat her as a guest or as the hired help, and she had been pleased to be received and treated so graciously. Richard Hatton apparently had a different idea about what her role was, or should be, in the household.

The contrast between the atmosphere around the dining table that night and the afternoon she had spent there with Edmund and Lily could not have been more pronounced. Richard Hatton positively bristled with hostility and Lizzie was at a loss to understand the source of it. He was everything his brother was not: imperious, stuffy, arrogant. The hour and a half spent at the table was agony for Lizzie, clearly uncomfortable for George, and a trial which Richard made no attempt to disguise by polite behavior, preferring instead an exaggerated and dramatic stiffness and silence.

Mrs. Jeffries exchanged a look with Lizzie at one point, and then quickly looked away as she moved wordlessly around the table, serving and clearing dishes. Her husband brought out the big tray with coffee, which his wife then poured. It was obvious that there could be few if any secrets in the Hatton family that were not well known to the couple who worked for and lived with them. Lizzie looked to see if either George or Richard Hatton had any notion of this. George often thanked the Jeffries for a helpful action, but Richard never acknowledged either of them, except in gestures indicating when he wanted something more or wanted something taken away. Lizzie could appreciate that George had a relationship with the couple that was apparently built on trust and reliance. Richard, on the other hand, treated them like necessary parts of the background machinery that made him comfortable, not unlike good pieces of furniture. As the meal progressed she liked George more, Richard less, and was determined to get to know the Jeffries, especially Mrs. Jeffries, better.

When she went to her room that night, she once again threw the windows open, breathed deeply and tried hard to relax. She was used to being liked by almost everyone. It was unusual enough for someone to dislike her, unheard of for them to make such a display of it, and she condemned Richard Hatton for his unwarranted rudeness. The whole episode left her feeling tight inside and unable to sleep for several hours. Only the interesting nature of Francis Hatton's voyage, and the promised return of Edmund the next day, made it worth spending that night at Hengemont.

• • • • •

The next morning brought new insults. Lizzie skipped breakfast in order to avoid having to spend another uncomfortable meal with Richard, and found him, to her chagrin, once again in the library looking at the correspondence of Francis Hatton.

"You seem to have made yourself quite at home here," he said, looking over her computer and other equipment and even picking up some of her file folders. He asked her several questions about her work that sounded more like demands for information, and he seemed not at all pleased with her answers.

"Have you been in touch with Mr. Clark at the British Museum about what you are doing here?"

"Not yet," she responded coolly. "I'm waiting until I am completely familiar with the collection."

"I'd like you to be in touch with him immediately," Richard said. "Make sure he knows everything you're doing." He opened one of the file folders and began to go through the papers.

Lizzie was livid. From across the table she pulled the folder back and closed it. "Excuse me," she said coldly, "but I'll have a report ready for your father within a few days, and I'll contact Tom Clark when I have assembled information that will be useful to him."

George arrived at that moment and seemed embarrassed by his son's rude behavior. "Now Richard," he began, "Lizzie has my complete confidence. . . ."

Richard cut him off. "That's all well and good, Father. But she must understand that everything she finds here, all information, all documents, all artifacts, belong to us, and that her final results must all be approved."

Lizzie was speechless with anger and frustration, and contemplated quitting the whole enterprise at that moment and marching from the room. She wondered how long Richard was going to stay at Hengemont, and how much he planned to meddle in her project. George took him aside and after nodding at Lizzie, led him from the room. She sat down at the table and laid her hands on the smooth surface, once again trying to relax herself through controlled breathing. Her eyes were closed and she didn't open them again until she heard Mrs. Jeffries set a tray on the other end of the table.

Silent and efficient as ever, the housekeeper had brought a

pot of coffee and some toast and scones for Lizzie's breakfast. They smiled at each other.

"Dr. Manning, . . ." Mrs. Jeffries began.

"Since we are practically related," Lizzie joked, "may we be less formal?"

"When we are alone you may call me Helen," Mrs. Jeffries responded warmly.

"Thank you, Helen," Lizzie said with a sigh of relief. "The 'distinctions between classes,' as your son Peter described them, are beginning to wear on me a bit."

"Well, if you are thinking about Richard Hatton," Helen Jeffries responded, "he is a snotty twit and always has been." She smiled at Lizzie conspiratorially. "I see that my bluntness surprises you," she continued, "but if I'm not mistaken, we are pretty much of a mind on this."

"Pretty much," Lizzie said. She felt better at that moment than she had in the last two days.

Helen Jeffries continued. "There's no denying it. Even Sir George knows it. But to make up for it, the good doctor, Edmund, is a real human being, and that's the truth."

"Well Helen," Lizzie said, toasting her with a cup of coffee, "I'd say we are pretty much of a mind on that too."

• • • • •

As Richard was now nowhere to be seen, and as she and Helen Jeffries were well on the way to becoming chums, Lizzie's morning passed more pleasantly than she had expected. Edmund arrived before lunch and he and his father stopped into the library where George, as if no uncomfortable exchanges had taken place at this very table two times in the last twelve hours, asked Lizzie to bring them up to date on her work. She was able to report that she had made real progress in her inventory of the loose manuscripts. The incomplete text of the journal was frustrating, but there was plenty of material for an interesting book and the artifacts would make for an important and visually compelling exhibit.

Richard joined them for lunch, and it quickly became obvious that there had been no thaw in the frozen nature of his reception of her at the family table. Edmund chided him on his silence, but eventually just ignored him, leading Lizzie to believe that Richard might often be in a snit over one thing or another. As Lizzie was now uncomfortable talking about the voyage project in front of Richard, and as George seemed still somewhat embarrassed by his oldest son's earlier behavior, the bulk of the responsibility for conversing fell on Edmund, who was able to provide the animation and interest that his brother lacked. He began to explain an interesting and somewhat perplexing case that had come into his office the day before. Lizzie was keenly interested in medicine and for an amateur had a very broad knowledge of the subject. Her college roommate once bought her a subscription to the *New England Journal of Medicine* as a joke gift and Lizzie had never let the subscription lapse. In fact, Edmund's case reminded her of an article she had read there about two years earlier.

Edmund was impressed. "You're the second person to cite that article to me today," he said. "The other was a London specialist."

Lizzie smiled. "I have an extremely unpredictable and arcane body of knowledge," she said.

"I should say so," Edmund said.

"And I've always been interested in medicine."

"Did you ever consider becoming a doctor?" George asked her.

"For about two months, until my first college chemistry grades came back," she answered with a laugh.

The lunch passed quickly, despite the iceberg that sat unmovable in the midst of their otherwise happy party. They moved from the dining room back to the library, and Lizzie showed Edmund the Northwest Coast artifacts that she thought were most interesting. As she and George had already talked about many of them, he drifted off before the conversation ended and Richard, after silently fuming at his brother's back for several minutes, also left the room.

Lizzie had liked Edmund right from their first meeting, but now she also felt a growing respect and a gratitude that he would go to such extraordinary lengths to make her feel welcome. As they sat side by side at the table, she felt her affection for him deepen. As an adult, she had not often met people with whom she felt she could develop the kind of fast friendship that had marked her relationships in high school and college. In fact, the women who formed her lunch circle were almost the only really close friends she had made since then. She had many friendly and collegial relationships that had developed over the years, but the close and intimate bond that defined the true friend and confidante was one that did not often occur, and she valued it when she encountered it. Edmund was warm and open. Whether he felt the same way about her as she felt about him she could not say, but at this moment it felt good just to sit beside him.

He was interested in the Northwest Coast Indian artifacts, and Lizzie pulled them off the shelf one at a time and set them on the table where they looked at them carefully. She still felt the mask was the most important, and as she held it in her hand she pointed out several of the features that made it a masterpiece.

"Look at the way the carver has centered the grain of the wood around this cheekbone," she said, touching it softly.

"It's beautiful," Edmund said.

"One of the best I've ever seen," Lizzie said. "I actually think I may know of one or two other masks carved by the same artist." She had already, she explained, e-mailed one of her museum friends back in Boston, requesting pictures from two American collections that she could compare it to.

They talked about art and the conversation naturally evolved to the other works on exhibit in the house. "I love that big Gainsborough of Frank and his siblings on the landing of the staircase," Lizzie said.

"Frank?" Edmund asked with a laugh.

Lizzie blushed. "I feel like I know him pretty well," she said, grinning sheepishly. "I hope he doesn't mind that I've become so familiar."

"Have you seen the other portrait of your old pal Frank?" Edmund asked, returning her smile.

"No," Lizzie said with surprise. "I didn't know there was another one, and anyway I'm waiting for our tour tomorrow."

Edmund was apologetic. "That case that we were talking

about, the one you seem to understand so well despite your sorry grades in chemistry. . . ."

She held up her hand, "Please," she said, "no more. Just give me the bad news."

"That case requires my attendance again tomorrow." He seemed genuinely sorry. "Can you wait until the day after?"

Lizzie was disappointed. She wanted to spend more time with him, but she managed to respond graciously. "Of course," she said, "I have plenty to do here until your return."

When they parted soon after, Edmund kissed Lizzie on the cheek and gave her a quick hug. She thought about it as she walked up the stairs to the landing. She liked him a great deal and he was on her mind when she stopped to look again at Francis Hatton in the Gainsborough painting. Was there a resemblance between Edmund and his ancestor? For the first time it occurred to her that she could detect one.

Chapter 8

The fact that Edmund was becoming her friend did not lessen Lizzie's anxiety about Richard. As long as he remained in the house, she could not entirely relax or feel comfortable. She wanted to talk to Martin, but he was in New York and she had been unable to catch him.

Both of the Hatton brothers left in the course of the next morning and Lizzie found herself relieved to be rid of Richard but regretting Edmund's departure. She could finally return to her work with some concentration, however, and that she did as soon as the door closed behind them.

She went directly to the library and found the mask they had been discussing the day before still lying on the table. She picked it up again. It was always exciting for her to hold such a work of art in her hand, and this was one was particularly powerful. The eyelids were carefully carved, with only the pupils cut out for the wearer to see through. The eyebrows and lips were in the squarish style of Haida or Tlingit art, but the nose was so realistic it led her to believe that it might be a portrait of an actual person. Lizzie carefully returned it to the shelf and turned her attention to the Hawaiian artifacts.

There was a Polynesian adze made from the shell of a giant clam. Lizzie had seen these tools before, when she worked at the Boston Museum of Natural History, and she checked carefully to make sure that the blade was still securely attached to the handle before she picked it up to move it to the table to be photographed. A piece of vellum was sitting underneath the heavy shell blade to protect the varnish of the shelf. Lizzie measured and photographed the adze, scanned the attached label and returned it to the shelf.

As she moved the vellum into place beneath it, she saw that the underside had a message of some sort written on it. She went back to her computer and got a sheet of printer paper, which she folded into a square about the same size as the vellum. She replaced the original protective sheet with her improvised one and took the vellum out to see if it had more information about the adze.

She had seen old manuscripts written on tanned animal skins in the rare documents collections of several libraries, but this was the first time she had ever held one in her hand. It had grown stiff with age, its corners rolling inward. The ink was very black, the letters difficult to distinguish and the language archaic. With some effort Lizzie managed to make a best guess of what it said.

For love and for honour they did dye
Purer passion betwixt woman and man was ne'er else upon the earth
But where is that heart wich he did pledge upon the tower wall?
Not sham stone that stood for it in colour only
But that wich beat within his chest
Or, barred by death
Unbeating, within gold casket she could hold against her breast
—E.dH. Anno 1382

It would have been entirely meaningless had she not seen similar references to a heartless man two days earlier. Instead of returning it to its original location, Lizzie opened the carved box and put it under the journal with the other documents that seemed to be on the same theme.

She continued to document Francis Hatton's cabinet, taking each object from its shelf, photographing and measuring it, and typing a description into her computer. It really was a wonderful collection. From the Northwest Coast and the Polynesian Islands alone, there were more than fifty items. She turned to a Hawaiian feathered helmet, a real treasure in both artistic and monetary terms. It had lost a number of feathers over the last two centuries—the cost of keeping it in the English climate. Lizzie was pleased to see that most of the lost feathers had been collected and folded into a piece of paper that sat on the shelf. As she unfolded the paper she caught her breath. Beneath the tiny red and yellow feathers she could see writing. It was another poem. She carefully poured the feathers onto a clean sheet of paper and read.

It was for love that she died
And he for honour
Could one know a greater love?
But where is his heart?
Where is his heart?
Can she rest without it?
Knowing, can I?

It was so similar to the other poems that Lizzie could not resist pulling them out again. She laid the piece of vellum and the now unfolded piece of paper side by side. The subject was clearly the same, but there was no way that they could have been written by the same person or even at the same time. In fact, they were probably written several hundred years apart, if Lizzie could trust her judgment about the paper and the penmanship. It was very puzzling. And what about that scrap of paper with the question on it? She put that next to them as well. "Where is his heart?" it asked. It was the same question asked in each of the poems but again in a different hand and from a different era.

Maybe it was the poetic references to heartlessness, but as she worked through the day Lizzie couldn't get the phrase from Francis Hatton's letter to his sister out of her head: "Look for my heart in this box, as our ancestress looked for the heart of her Crusader." She read the letter again and then looked hard at the box which had contained the logbook, as it sat on the table in front of her. It was covered with Chinese carvings, made of some aromatic wood—probably camphor or sandalwood. The top showed two lovers in an ornate and flowery garden, though maybe it was meant to show siblings, Francis Hatton and his sister Eliza. She sat down at the table and pulled the box toward her so that she could examine it more closely.

"Look for my heart in this box," she murmured.

The front edge of the box was carved with leaves and flowers surrounding the Hatton family crest—the heart pierced by the sword, and bounded by the motto "Numquam Dediscum." There was something strange here, she thought. She and Jackie had talked about the motto on the Hatton family crest and this wasn't it. She opened her briefcase and pulled out her original letter from George; there was the crest embossed on his stationery, identical except for the motto, "Semper Memoriam."

Lizzie had spent the requisite years studying Latin at her Catholic school, and if she remembered correctly, "Numquam Dediscum" would be something like "Never Forget," while "Semper Memoriam" was, as Jackie had pointed out several times, "Always Remember." They meant almost the same thing really, so why would Francis Hatton have changed it? She looked again to the top of the museum cabinet where the crest was carved again. There was the motto, "Semper Memoriam," but "Numquam Dediscum" was also worked into the carving on the front of the cabinet, in a frieze border of vines and flowers that ran along the boundary between the upper glass cases and the lower bank of drawers.

Lizzie examined the box again, running her thumb along the crest. There was something peculiar about the carving, almost a movement there. Certainly Eliza Hatton would have recognized something strange as well. Suddenly the front of the box sprang open and Lizzie jumped back, startled, into her seat. She looked around sheepishly, hoping that no one had heard her unintentional oath, and preparing to explain how reading shipboard journals always made her swear like a sailor. She was also preparing to describe how she had broken the box when she realized that it was not broken. The front was hinged and she had pressed on a spring latch that was set behind the heart of the crest. "Look for my heart in this box," she thought. "Very clever."

In a compartment hidden beneath the floor of the box and behind the hinged front was a sheaf of papers. Lizzie pulled out the missing pages of the logbook, a few loose letters, and a small disk wrapped in silk. She set them all on the table and stared at them for several minutes before reaching forward to push at the silk, now brittle with age, but still a bright sky blue. It would have fallen away had Lizzie pushed at it hard enough with the eraser of her outstretched pencil, but she finally recovered her composure enough to realize that it would require more care to unwrap the contents if she wanted to preserve the silk that covered it. Inside was the small oval portrait of a young woman, probably just a teenager. Lizzie thought she might be Francis Hatton's sister, whose portrait was on the landing of the big staircase.

She turned to the papers, a quick glance telling her that the log entries picked up exactly after the last one in the bound book. There were also two letters and a poem. The poem being the shortest text, she read it quickly first.

A maiden and a knight upon a tower
A pledge of love between them spoken
His heart with her would lie by passion's power
The promise then he sealed with a token
A ruby stone, a rock-hard heart would memory be
Of him and of his love while she
Alone and waiting through the year
Would learn the news that death had claimed her dear
And what of his heart? Of which this stone by agonizing memory
Made her depend, and not upon his heart—nor he
Eliza H. 1780

Why was this secreted away? Lizzie wondered. It wasn't all that different from ones she had found in the drawers. She laid it aside and picked up the first letter.

May the 3rd, 1778

My Dearest Eliza,

An incident occurred today in which you played a part. You will readily recognize that this letter is written on your birthday. I dressed with special care this morning, thinking of you, half a world away at Hengemont, now a woman of eighteen years. In your honour I wore about my neck the miniature portrait that you gave me upon my departure. It captures not only your features, but also your spirit, and I look at it often when I think of you and home.

Today it caught the attention of a young native chief of my acquaintance. This man, Eltatsy by name, has become something of a friend after several weeks of contact and negotiation. He wears a woven blanket or robe that is quite the most impressive work of craftsmanship that I have seen since leaving England. You know me well enough to believe that I pressed him pretty hard to part with it for my collection, but he never wavered, no matter what I offered him and, in truth, I have gone pretty high.

Today he came aboard the ship and saw your miniature around my neck. He showed great interest and through gestures and what little bits we have each learned of the other's language, I attempted to explain to him the importance to me of this small painting, that more than being just an object, it represented for me something priceless, my dear sister. I untied the ribbon on which it hung and let him hold it in his hand as a gesture of friendship. He then took off his robe and let me look at it quite closely. He offered, in jest, to exchange it for your portrait, knowing that I would not accept such a trade. At that moment, for the first time, I understood how important that article was to him. Until then, I had always believed that there had to be a price at which he would finally part with it.

Now I must tell you something that your brother did which you will not find very gallant. You know that I had another miniature with me, that of your friend Margaret Gurney. Don't think too ill of me Eliza, but I sent down to my cabin for it and offered Miss Gurney's portrait to Eltatsy for the blanket. She is not as pretty as you, but the picture is really very nice. Eltatsy laughed in a friendly sort of way as he put his robe around his shoulders and handed me back your picture.

He was wearing a really splendid hat, a wooden helmet covered with the face of a bear. This was also something I had offered him a good price for on several occasions. Now he offered me the hat in exchange for Miss Gurney's miniature. We each had refused to part with the most precious article in our possession, but were willing to sacrifice a lesser gift—though still very meaningful and valuable—as a token of the friendship we have developed. This wonderful artefact will take prize of place in my cabinet when I return.

Again, I must beg that you will not think less of me, dear sister, for parting with Miss Gurney's portrait. I know that you and father have high hopes for a marriage between us, and it still may come off when I return home. It will depend on how much she likes my collection!

This was altogether a wonderful day. Though this letter may not come into your hands until you are even another year older, I hope it will bring to you the joy I felt in celebrating your birthday so far from home.

Your loving brother,
Francis

Lizzie reached for the miniature portrait lying on the table in front of her and picked it up. This was the very object that Francis Hatton and the Native Chief Eltatsy had handled and admired that day, more than two hundred years ago. The face that looked up at her was not only very pretty, but had a sweetness that made the subject seem good humored and likeable. No wonder Francis Hatton had loved her so dearly. And what a good brother he must have been. Had Eliza received this letter? Lizzie remembered the portrait of her on the stairs. The expression there was so different that she would hardly have taken them for the same person.

Why had this letter been hidden away? Lizzie turned to the next letter, which had no date and seemed almost to have been written in a different hand. The writing was much larger and,

Lizzie thought, shakier. Blots of ink were everywhere on the page. Lizzie felt powerfully that it contained bad news.

"Dearest Sister," she read, "Disaster! Disaster!"

The letter had obviously been written in a state of extreme emotion. It described the death of Captain Cook at the hands of the Hawaiians, and the loss to disease of his successor, Captain Clerk. Francis Hatton seemed to feel that he had to bear some of the responsibility for these tragedies, for having committed some terrible sin. Lizzie raced through the letter trying to grasp what had happened. The details, he said, would be found in these pages from his journal. She hurriedly turned to them.

The first one was dated April 16, 1778, two days after the last entry in the bound journal. The ship was still at Nootka Sound. Francis Hatton was still happily writing about his work with his effervescent teenaged assistant Tatooshtikus, and was actively negotiating with the other officers and the local chief, Maquinna, to bring him along on the northbound cruise when they departed Nootka Sound.

There were several entries in which Hatton commented on the level of artistry exhibited on the Northwest Coast, which exceeded anything he had ever seen on his voyage "or even among the finest cabinets in Europe visited in my earlier travels."

While the relationship with Tatooshtikus was jovial and paternalistic, Hatton's feelings for the visiting Eltatsy were completely different. Lizzie could sense his real respect and regard.

> April the 16th, 1778: Today I saw the most beautiful
> blanket or robe. Words can hardly describe the fine
> quality of the weaving and the intricate pattern of this
> remarkable thing—I must call it a work of art, for it is
> certainly the finest example of Indian handicraft I have
> yet seen. This blanket adorned the person of Eltatsy,
> a young chief of the visitors from the northern tribe.
> He is a man of great height and would be thought
> handsome, I think, even in England. His manners
> are friendly yet have a kind of elegance that make his

noble birth apparent, even among Savages. Through Tatooshtikus, but even more through gestures of the hand and expressions of the eyes and face, I communicated with him at some length. Eventually, of course, I offered to buy the blanket, but no amount of buttons, blades, or blankets of ours would purchase it. He also wears an extraordinary hat or helmet with an actual specimen of a bear's face mounted onto a carved wooden helmet; no inducement would make him part with that either. His wife was with him, as ugly as he was handsome, disfigured by a wooden disk inserted in her underlip, and she was quite shrewish in demanding that I stop asking for the blanket in her presence. According to Tatooshtikus the blanket is a symbol of Eltatsy's high rank, and the figure woven into it is a bear—his family crest. I think the blanket and helmet may be a uniform of sort, by which other people on the Coast may recognize his lineage and position.

Lizzie was not surprised to read Hatton's disgust at seeing the wooden labret that extended the lower lip of Eltatsy's wife, a high-ranking Tlingit Indian woman. As the lip ornament was not worn by the women of Nootka Sound, this was the first time it was observed by the Englishmen, and Hatton's comments were consistent with those Lizzie had seen dozens of times in other shipboard sources. The woven robe worn by Eltatsy was, Lizzie recognized instantly, a ceremonial dancing blanket, originating among the people from the Tlingit village of Chilkat on the coast of Alaska. These blankets were such extraordinary examples of the artistic skill of the women of that region that Lizzie was not surprised Hatton was so taken with it.

Over the next several days Hatton pressed Eltatsy for the item. On the seventeenth he wrote that he had again tried to "convince him to sell me his blanket. I am determined to have it at any price, though he has already refused tobacco, mirrors, rum. I will soon run the risk of offering more than the Captain has allowed for private trade. (In truth, I already have.)"

On the twenty-sixth the ships left Nootka Sound to proceed north with Tatooshtikus aboard. He informed Hatton that they would meet up with Eltatsy again when they got near his village and that Hatton could then continue the bartering process which the young native boy, and most of Hatton's shipmates, found a very comical game.

On the third of May they entered a large channel, which Cook named "Cross Sound" to honor the feast day of the Holy Cross. Hatton was full of expectations as a number of canoes came toward them. Standing in the prow of one was Eltatsy, wearing his ceremonial regalia, singing a welcoming song, and powdering the surface of the water with handfuls of downy white feathers. The ships each fired a canon in salute, and soon Eltatsy and a number of important individuals from the local tribe were on board the *Resolution*. Eltatsy introduced an older man to the Englishmen, whom Captain Cook and Frank Hatton took to be his father, and whose name was given in Hatton's journal as "Whooner."

At one point in the festivities, Cook turned to Hatton and said, "I am sorry Mr. Hatton, but in the interests of diplomacy I forbid you asking this good gentleman to strip and give you his clothing!" Hatton thought it a fine joke, but was pleased to see that everyone on board recognized Whooner's outfit as a truly remarkable work of art. In addition to a robe like Eltatsy's, though "with a somewhat different design," Whooner wore a large head ornament made of feathers and strips of bark. Just above his face was mounted a small carving, a wooden face, perfectly formed, and set into a frame inlaid with pieces of abalone shell. Hatton described it as "the most remarkable bit of carving I have ever seen."

Hatton and Eltatsy soon renewed their friendship, and now Hatton found that Tatooshtikus was more of a hindrance than a help. It was becoming increasingly clear that his language was not the same as that spoken by the people at Cross Sound, though Eltatsy had a good workable knowledge of the language of Nootka Sound and was infinitely patient with both Hatton and Tatooshtikus.

Many jokes and banter were exchanged about Eltatsy's blanket, and the trade of items described in Hatton's letter to his sister took place. When the ships departed, it was with good feelings on all sides. They left Tatooshtikus behind for Eltatsy to convey back home on his next visit there. Hatton wrote eloquently of his fondness for Eltatsy, and of his appreciation for having developed a "friend among Savages."

Lizzie turned over the next page of the log to find the writing dark and blotted. It almost looked as if Frank Hatton had wept onto the page, and he had carefully drawn a thick black line around the first entry.

> May the 4th, 1778, 11 p.m. It is my sad responsibility to report the death of the estimable Eltatsy. After a day spent in commerce with every appearance of good fellowship, our ships weighed anchor at about 3:00 p.m. to beat out of Cross Sound. Within a half hour, a thick fog settled upon us and we began to fire our cannons in an effort to determine where the shoreline was by using the echo from the land to indicate our distance from it. One of the gunners, by habit, loaded shot into a gun and, by a horrible accident, our friend was struck and killed, along with everyone in his canoe. As the fog lifted and we saw what had been done, our remorse was great. Everyone on board thought well of this man, but I think that I felt him a friend most of all.

> May the 6th, 1778: Fog keeps us within this canal for another day. Today the captain sent some small boats to scout further up the inlet to see if there is a passage there out to the Northeast—I commanded one boat. As we made soundings around several rocky outcroppings, I saw that one had a number of small wooden huts built upon it, very unlike the large habitations of the local people. As I looked, the clouds began to break and a ray of sunlight hit the topmost hut perched on the pinnacle of the rock. Hanging on one wall was Eltatsy's blanket, or one identical to it. It seemed a sign that I should get one of these remarkable weavings after all, perhaps as a tribute to him. I ordered the men to pull in close that I might explore this island a bit. I think they

knew my real purpose—my collection is the source of some amusement onboard. The climb to the top of the rock was not easy, but it was eminently worthwhile. The huts were clearly not living places, but seemed rather areas for storage or for the careful discard of important objects. A number of them had blankets like Eltatsy's, now decayed by time and the elements.

On one of them I found the bear blanket hanging in all its glory. It may be that since Eltatsy is dead, his wife is superstitious about retaining this garment. If that be so, I thought to myself, then may not the blanket be more carefully kept in my cabinet at home, than out here exposed to the wind, rain, and salt air?

Thinking that I might provide a more fitting memorial for the man we had inadvertently killed, I removed and folded the blanket. Before leaving with it, I was determined to see what other treasures might be contained within the hut and, as there was no door, I pried off two of the planks to look inside. There I saw a most remarkable box, carved and painted with a design similar to that woven on the blanket—I thought I could make out some of the elements of the bear motif that Tatooshtikus had pointed out to me. The lid was tied on with a very intricate series of knots in a cedar bark cord. As they appeared to be something of pair, I determined I must take the box as well as the blanket. Had it been any larger I could not have carried it by myself, but it was, fortunately, of a size that I could remove. I placed the folded blanket on the top and made my way back to the boat, where again the men made some jokes about my collecting, but I was now so pleased with my acquisitions that I let them have some sport at my expense. We sounded somewhat further up the canal, but reached water too shallow for the ships and returned to our vessel to inform the Captain.

There were a number of entries for the passage along the Aleutian Islands and attempts to get north through the Bering Straits and thence to the coast of Russian Asia. Cold weather and ice dominated several entries, and though Hatton talked about his collection, and speculated about what was in the box, he waited to open it until warmer weather would give him more privacy by allowing him to send the lieutenants who shared his cabin up on deck when they were not on watch.

It wasn't until the ship once more turned south for Hawaii that he spoke about the box again. Lizzie scanned the entries quickly; she had a sense of foreboding about what was to come. Though Francis Hatton had not realized what he had taken when he removed that box from the island, Lizzie was fully aware. Even if she had not suspected it from his second letter to his sister, she had read enough Northwest Coast Indian anthropology to know that he had robbed a grave of its occupant. In the entry dated New Year's Day, 1779, Francis Hatton made the same discovery.

> January the 1st, 1779—A smooth crossing thus far back to the Sandwich Islands and the men are very much looking forward to the women they met there before and to the fresh provisions such a stop will afford us. I am in hopes of getting one of the feathered capes I saw there but could not procure on our last visit. Today when my shipmates are on watch I will open the box from the "Blanket Island." There is too little room in the cabin when the three of us are here, and they complain enough as it is about the amount of space my collection consumes. I hope it might contain a few good masks and maybe some weaponry. It is my intention to return it to its original state after I have opened it, so this sketch is intended to document the tying of the cord around it."

In the middle of the page was a good sketch of a Northwest Coast Indian bentwood box. Lizzie could see where Hatton had drawn the claws and teeth that marked a bear in the bold iconographic style of the Tlingit Indians. His sketch noted with a sailor's precision the location and formation of the knots on the cord that bound the box. In the next entry his handwriting was dramatically poorer. Lizzie knew what he had discovered.

2:00 p.m.—As I have so carefully described what I have found and collected up to this point, honour requires that I do so now as well, though I wish my discovery of today could be forgotten and the box returned swiftly to its resting place on the island in Cross Sound. In short, I found inside it the partially cremated remains of a man—there was no mistaking the long bones of the leg and the portions of the skull and jaw that were immediately apparent upon opening the box. I am, in fact, convinced it is the mortal remains of the very El-tatsy who refused to sell me the blanket now stowed beneath my bunk, because his honour was somehow bound up in it. To have so capriciously robbed a grave is unforgivable in any case, but how much more so in mine, whose family has for centuries been cursed by thoughts of a corpse that could not be buried in the family tomb. What will Eltatsy's widow think when she finds his grave empty? Oh horrible day.

January the 5th, 1779—I considered for a time today throwing the blanket and the box overboard, and giving Eltatsy a sea burial, as I would myself wish were I to die now. But as that was not *his* wish, nor the wish of his family, I cannot do so. The box must be returned, of that there is no doubt in my mind, and I am determined that it must be done. "Semper Memoriam" has been my family motto since my Crusader ancestor failed to return from the Holy Land as promised. "Numquam Dediscum" will now be my motto until this task is completed. According to my best calculations the burial island is located some forty-five miles up Cross Sound from the cape denominated "Cape Bingham" by Capt. Cook, and determined by Mr. Bligh to lie at 57° 57' north and 123° 21' west of Greenwich. It is a small rocky outcropping, the highest of several such rocks or islets which lie in a group behind a pleasant island near to the north side of the inlet. Eltatsy's village lies beyond it another few miles. It would be impossible to convince Captain Cook to alter our course at this point in our cruise, so my plan now is to return to this ocean on the very next expedition that leaves England after our return.

Shorter and shorter entries followed and Hatton's handwriting deteriorated until Lizzie had a hard time deciphering what was on the page. The man was clearly in agony over his actions and Lizzie felt terrible for him.

January the 26th, 1779. No one in the crew must ever know of the corpse beneath my bunk. The luck of the voyage has turned, and I fear that I may have brought the Jonah on board, yet I feel a sacred duty to return it to the place from which it was taken.

Feb 14—Disaster! There could be no worse news to report. The excellent Captain James Cook is dead, killed by the very Sandwich Islanders who were so civilized and hospitable on our last voyage. Captain Clerk takes his place in command.

April—Clerk now is also dead. What a sorry turn of events has come to this ship. I cannot but wonder if some of the responsibility does not lie with me. My shipmates are worried for my health and my sanity— I cannot confess my guilt to any man on board and the weight is awesome. God willing Captain King will bring us safe back to England.

That was the last entry. Lizzie knew how the voyage ended. Captain King returned safely in 1780, and the publication of the official narrative of the voyage four years later first introduced the world to the value of sea otter pelts from the Northwest Coast in the marketplace at Canton. A number of ships followed in the wake of Cook's voyage, pioneering a transpacific trade from England and America. Had Francis Hatton returned with the blanket and the box on one of those voyages? The death of his brother and his altered circumstances upon his return would seem to argue against it. Lizzie had no doubt now as to the identity of the two artifacts crossed off Hatton's list; the only question remaining was whether they had been returned to their original resting place.

She had been to Alaska several times in the course of researching her dissertation and she knew Cross Sound was the passage north of Chichagof Island, lying along Alaska's "inside passage." She and Martin had been there on the Alaska ferry on a trip to see nearby Glacier Bay. During the course of her research Lizzie had scanned several nautical charts into a special software program so that she could edit them on her computer and add information from shipboard logbooks. Now she opened the file and brought Cross Sound up onto the screen.

With her finger she traced a passage into the sound, reading Hatton's description aloud. Cape Bingham was clearly marked. Forty-five miles east brought her past the entrance to Glacier Bay and into a channel called Icy Strait. Just off the north bank was an island called "Pleasant Island," which had rocky outcroppings to the south and east. The "Porpoise Islands" on the east looked especially promising to Lizzie as a location for Hatton's "Blanket Island." There had once been a Tlingit village on the adjacent coast, which was marked on Lizzie's chart as "Old Hoonah (abandoned)." Across Icy Strait to the south was the newer village of Hoonah, which had replaced it.

"Hoonah," she whispered. Hatton's "Whooner" must have been the chief of Hoonah. She tried to remember what the village had looked like when she stopped there briefly on the ferry. She thought there was a cannery and a lot of fishing boats, with the usual stuff that accompanied them—a gas station, motel, cafe, etc. She also thought there was a longhouse and some totem poles there.

"What a different world from this," she thought to herself as she closed her computer, laid the papers on the table in front of her and sat back in her chair. She looked around the comfortable and elegant room in which she sat. The leather bindings of the books were rich and soft, slightly faded over the years into mellow reds and golds and greens. The oak table had been rubbed for three centuries by soft cloth in rough hands.

What led young Francis Hatton to leave behind this solid and comfortable existence for the discomfort of the ship and the unknown world of the Pacific Ocean? Lizzie shivered as she thought of what it must have been like to encounter the "Icy Straits" of the Alaska coast in April and May. She could almost hear the sound of ice crunching against the wooden planks of the unheated ship.

And then to have had such a horrible experience. She really sympathized with him. His passion for collecting had caused him to steal something that clearly did not belong to him, but his response seemed out of proportion to the crime. It was, after all, obviously an accident that he had stolen a corpse rather than a box of masks or weapons as he thought. Lizzie even doubted that the corpse was that of Eltatsy, as the two days between Eltatsy's death and Hatton's discovery hardly seemed enough time for the burial rituals and cremation to have taken place. The crest on the blanket and the box were certainly consistent with the corpse being someone in Eltatsy's lineage, however. Would Hatton have been as horrified had he thought the corpse was that of a stranger rather than of his new friend? In any case, his response was entirely out of character for an English Navy man of the eighteenth century. That he showed any consideration at all for the feelings and beliefs of a Native American was not consistent with the behavior of most of his fellow countrymen.

Lizzie wondered even more why Francis Hatton would expect his sister to understand, even share in his shame and remorse. "To have so capriciously robbed a grave is unforgivable in any case," he had written, "but how much more so in mine, whose family has for centuries been cursed by thoughts of a corpse that could not be buried in the family tomb."

The several papers with the insistent question "Where is his heart?" lay strewn across the table. She picked them up one after another. They had the same kind of urgency, almost horror, as Francis Hatton's letter.

Helen Jeffries made a sound near the door of the library and Lizzie jumped with surprise, her heart beating rapidly.

She looked up at the housekeeper.

"Helen," she said, pushing her chair back from the table, "you startled me."

"Sorry, Miss, I came to tell you that lunch would be ready in about fifteen minutes.

"I thought you were going to call me Lizzie when we were alone."

Helen smiled at her, crossed the room and came to stand near Lizzie's chair. The scraps of poetry caught her eye and she reached out to pick one up, then set it down and quickly picked up another.

"What are these?" she asked.

Lizzie sensed an urgency in Helen's voice and answered that she didn't know. "I found them when I was going through the papers in the cabinet," she said, watching curiously as Helen picked up one after another of the papers. "Do you know what they are?"

"No," Helen answered, "but I don't like them."

"Don't like them?" Lizzie responded with astonishment. "Why not?"

"They are all by Hatton girls aren't they?"

"I suppose so," Lizzie said.

"They weren't sane," Helen said bluntly. "They all suffered from some sort of curse." She seemed really upset and turned to look directly at Lizzie. "I thought you said your research didn't include them."

Lizzie stood up and put a reassuring hand on Helen's shoulder.

"These are all things I found by accident," she explained. "I thought they were interesting, but they aren't the subject of my research." She couldn't understand why Helen was acting so strangely. She took the paper which Helen still held, gathered the rest of the poems into a stack, placed them back in the carved box and closed the lid.

There was no chance at that moment for Lizzie to ask Helen what, in particular, bothered her about the poems or about the "Hatton girls" having written them, because George arrived looking to escort Lizzie to lunch.

In her enthusiasm to show George her discovery of the

morning, Lizzie pushed Helen's concerns, and her curiosity about the poems, into the background.

"I found the missing pages from the journal!" she said excitedly.

She sat down again and when George sat beside her she passed them to him and he began to read.

"What about lunch?" Helen asked. "Will you be wanting it later?"

George's first inclination was to abandon lunch altogether, but then he asked her to bring whatever was portable to them in the library.

For the next three hours Lizzie and George talked through each of the new pages. She was able to point out to him on her computer chart exactly where the ship was for each entry, and he moved as quickly as he could from one page to the next without losing sight of the important details.

His excitement turned to something like regret when he read the last pages that Francis Hatton had written, and his letters to his sister. It was clear to Lizzie that the missing journal pages took him completely by surprise and he was visibly disturbed by the thought of Eltatsy's stolen corpse. George didn't elaborate, but Lizzie thought he might be unnerved by the thought that it was somewhere in the house. She was still surprised, though, when he asked her the very question she was about to ask him.

"Where is it?"

"I don't know," she said. "It's certainly not in the cabinet."

"I had no idea," he said shaking his head. "I have never heard even a hint of this before."

Lizzie described to him what she thought the box and blanket looked like, and even showed him some pictures of similar objects from the pile of catalogues of Northwest Coast Indian artifacts that she had brought with her as a working library.

"Have you ever seen anything like either of these anywhere in the house?"

He was certain that he hadn't.

Helen had been in and out of the room with lunch and Lizzie had an idea that she had followed at least some of the conversation. She asked George if she might show the pictures to the housekeeper in case she had seen them.

"That's a good idea," he said. "Mrs. Jeffries is more familiar than I am with some of the odd nooks and crannies of the house."

Helen looked closely at the pictures and listened to Lizzie's description of the two items and, like George, was emphatic in her answer that she had never encountered either of them, but promised to keep them in mind as she went through the house.

As Helen left the room, Lizzie turned back to George. "Did Francis Hatton ever make another voyage?" she asked.

George was thoughtful. "I certainly don't remember ever hearing about another voyage."

"You have a very complete collection of voyage narratives," Lizzie said, gesturing up to one of the bookshelves behind him. She had discovered this collection on her second day at Hengemont and had been meaning to look at them more carefully. "There weren't all that many British voyages to the North Pacific in the next decade," she continued. "And it's unlikely Francis could have returned to the Northwest Coast except on one of the voyages you have documented here. I'll take a little time today and see if I can find any indication that he ever returned the corpse."

George took off his glasses and wiped them with his handkerchief. "You've been working so hard," he said, "I'm sorry that it is too cold for walking outside. You are welcome any time you need a break to have Jeffries drive you into the village or down to the harbor."

Lizzie thanked him. "Edmund told me he'd give me a personalized tour around the house and grounds when he comes back, and I've been waiting for that."

George stood to go. "Well, he should be back tomorrow, and then you really should get out of the house."

He looked tired, and less poised than Lizzie had ever seen him. She couldn't help reaching out and giving him an affectionate pat on the arm. "Thanks," she said again, "but I'm doing just fine."

Chapter 9

George seemed not to want to talk to Lizzie any further that day about her discovery and sent his regrets that he would be not be joining her for dinner, preferring to take a tray in his own room.

Lizzie was surprised and somewhat miffed. Having found the new journal pages, she understood why Francis Hatton had wanted to keep it from being published, and she wanted to know more about what he might have said in his will regarding the subject. She wondered if George was now feeling some hesitation about seeing the project through to the end, and was worried that her expectations of enhancing her own career through a publication of Francis Hatton's collection and journal might be dashed.

All these things raced through her mind as Helen still stood near her, having just delivered George's message.

"Would you like to join me and Henry in the kitchen for dinner?" Helen asked her. (It was the first time that anyone had acknowledged to Lizzie that "Jeffries" had a first name.) She welcomed the invitation and found herself in a new part of the house for the first time since her arrival more than a week earlier.

The kitchen was set behind the informal dining room in which she had taken her meals with George, and was obviously in a much older part of the house. It had a huge stone fireplace, a legacy of the days when the meals had been cooked over open flames. Set into it at various levels were small ovens for baking bread and keeping food warm, now made obsolete by the big gas range that stood in a corner of the kitchen. The room was enormous, with long tables for preparing food and high banks of glass-fronted cupboards filled with row upon row of dishes and serving pieces. It was obvious that very large parties could be served from this kitchen.

A small pine table near the fireplace was set for four. Lizzie knew that there was at least one other man who worked at Hengemont, but she hadn't seen him since her arrival, when he had carried her luggage in from the car. Now she was finally introduced to Bob Moran who, Henry Jeffries said, managed the "outdoor affairs" of the Hattons.

Outside of George Hatton's presence, the three were talkative and amusing. Henry Jeffries had a wry sense of humor, Helen smiled easily, and Bob, who had the broadest English accent Lizzie had ever heard, told story after story about communicative dogs, eccentric farm machinery, and remarkable examples of oddly shaped vegetables that he had encountered over his sixty-plus years. The food was the very same food served on the Hattons' table, and Lizzie felt more comfortable than she had at any meal eaten in the house.

After dinner, the two men retired from the kitchen and Lizzie helped Helen clean up the dishes. For the first time that evening, talk turned to the Hattons. Though she suspected that the family was often the topic of conversation around their table when they were alone, the servants were very careful not to discuss their employers in her presence. Helen, however, had now clearly left both her discomfort and much of her discretion behind, and Lizzie took it as a compliment to herself. She knew the housekeeper was far too loyal and discreet ever to gossip about the Hattons with outsiders.

Helen asked how Lizzie's work was going, hoped that Richard's presence in the house hadn't been too awful for her, and shared Lizzie's high opinion for Edmund. About George they were each more circumspect. Lizzie respected him but hadn't really warmed to him, and she wasn't sure that Helen Jeffries, after sharing a house with him for many decades, had either.

"How long have you worked for the Hattons?" Lizzie asked, wondering just how far back the relationship extended.

"I was born in this house and have always lived here," Helen replied.

This took Lizzie by surprise. Though she had suspected the older woman had been here a long time, she was unprepared for the fact that Helen Jeffries had spent her whole life at Hengemont. They finished the dishes and Helen prepared a pot of tea and brought it back to the table, where Lizzie joined her.

"I told you that my grandmother came here as a servant more than a hundred years ago," she explained, sensing Lizzie's interest. "There were lots of Irish girls working here then. My grandmother and her sister were only fifteen and sixteen when they arrived, still with the hay in their hair and speaking mostly Irish."

Helen's grandmother had married a local fisherman in Hengeport, bore nine children, and come back to work in the house in middle age, eventually becoming the head housekeeper. Most of her children had worked for the Hattons, and her daughter—Helen's mother—had also become the housekeeper.

Helen described to Lizzie how much Hengemont had changed in the years since her grandmother first arrived in the last decades of the nineteenth century. There had been some twenty servants working in the house then, several men who kept the grounds, and a few hundred engaged in the agricultural enterprises of the estate, almost all in positions that were now gone. The Hattons and Bob Moran were all that were left at the house, except for a few teenagers from Hengeport who came in part time to help with the housekeeping and yard work.

"But the house isn't any smaller," Lizzie commented. "It must be an enormous job for you and Henry to do the work formerly done by twenty." She could have added that neither of them was young, either, but held her tongue. The Jeffries must each be close to seventy—and maybe older.

"Most of the house isn't in use now," Helen explained. "There used to be grand parties, continuous guests, and meals and entertaining in the big rooms at the front of the house. Now all we do is dust them. When there is the occasional party, I can get extra help from the village."

The two women continued to talk for almost two hours.

Lizzie was curious about George's financial situation and asked Helen how the Hattons supported themselves. She couldn't help but wonder how an old family continued to live in such style without a pretty big influx of cash.

There had been some very hard times in the first half of the twentieth century, Helen told her. Farm land in Somerset and real estate in London had been sold, some of it, she thought, quite valuable. In the last few decades much of the family's fortune seemed to have been recovered through investments.

"That's what Richard does," she said. "He moves the money around and has made piles of it."

"And Edmund works."

"Yes, he does. But I think he would have become a doctor in any case. He certainly isn't in it for the money, and second sons. . . ." She left the sentence hanging, as if it was obvious what happened to younger children in an aristocratic household.

The conversation turned again to the two Irish sisters, and when Helen began once more to prod her for details about her great grandmother, Lizzie felt that she couldn't carry the pretense of a familial relationship any farther. She was growing too fond of the older woman.

"I don't think my great grandmother could be related to your grandmother," she said softly. "Manning was her married name, not her maiden name."

Helen gave her a look that was hard to read. "And what was her maiden name?"

Lizzie felt slightly uncomfortable giving the answer. "I'm not completely sure," she said, "but I think it was Hatton." She gave Helen a wry smile. "Now that is a weird coincidence, isn't it?"

Helen looked very thoughtful. It seemed that she might have more to say on the subject, but couldn't easily formulate her thoughts or questions. Lizzie felt, in any case, that she should wrap up the evening; the Jeffries were very early risers. She brought the tea dishes to the sink. Helen got up to see her out of the kitchen, and Lizzie impulsively kissed her on the cheek.

"Thank you," she said. "I can't tell you how much I enjoyed the evening."

"Maybe you'll join us again," Helen answered.

"I'd like that."

As she was leaving, Helen said her name again.

Lizzie turned around and waited for her to speak.

"Lizzie," she started again, "We talked earlier about those Hatton girls who wrote the poems I saw today. . . ." She hesitated again. "What is your interest in them?"

"Only curiosity," Lizzie answered. She could tell that Helen was really concerned. "I wondered if they could be related to something Francis Hatton said in a letter to his sister, but couldn't find any real connection."

Helen nodded and seemed satisfied.

"Why do you ask?" Lizzie continued.

"I just think that you need to be careful about following down any path that makes you identify yourself too closely with them."

Lizzie was completely perplexed by this. "Why would I?" she said.

"It's an inherited thing, I think."

"What is?" Lizzie demanded in a stronger tone than she intended.

Helen immediately backed away. "I don't know," she stammered. "I can't really give you any more information. I don't understand what happened to them, I just worry about you getting involved in it."

Lizzie liked Helen, but was losing patience with the vague gothic quality of the present conversation and again said a warm good night to the woman before leaving.

As she left the kitchen and passed through the Hattons' family dining room to the grand hallway with its elaborate parquet floor and double staircase, Lizzie felt the change of station in a very pronounced way. She wondered if the Jeffries felt it each time they moved from their part of the house to George's.

Helen's comments nagged at her. The woman clearly had suspicions about something, but could not commit to just saying outright what they were. Her implication seemed to be that she thought Lizzie might not only be related to herself, but also to the Hattons. The coincidence of the two names was certainly strange, and Lizzie couldn't deny that there was surprising satisfaction in contemplating a relationship to this house.

On her second night at Hengemont she had tried to sneak into the medieval hall, but thought that she would be embarrassed if found there. Now she felt a strong desire to see it again, and more comfortable about the distant whereabouts of both George and the Jeffries, and also with her own place as a guest if she encountered any of them. She went boldly and directly to the doors beneath the double staircase and opened both sets, first those that exited the Georgian hallway, and then the big oak door into the medieval hall beyond it.

Except for two small night lights, the massive room was dark. Her steps echoed on the stone floor as she went to a lamp on a table along one wall and turned it on. The light barely penetrated to the ends of the room; this was a space designed to be lit by dozens of torches.

Lizzie walked to the center of the hall and looked in each direction. Her eyes scanned up the tapestries that dominated two of the walls, and across to the musicians' gallery above where she had come into the room. The details of the carving along its front face were obscured in the dim light.

What would it be like to know a thousand years of your own family's history? It was a powerful notion for Lizzie, more powerful than a connection to wealth or position. To be one of *these* Hattons, rather than one of *her* Hattons—who couldn't remember back two generations—that would be something.

· · · · ·

Despite the excitement of having found the missing pages to Francis Hatton's logbook, Lizzie did not feel that she had a clear direction of where to take the project next. Francis Hatton's story was disturbing, and his response so poignantly sad. George's response had also taken her by surprise. His discomposure the afternoon before, when he learned about the corpse of the young Chief Eltatsy, had kept her from asking about other references in Hatton's text, especially his odd reference to another corpse "that could not be buried in the family tomb."

By the middle of the morning, George had made no appearance and Helen informed Lizzie that he would not be coming down to lunch. Despite their warm exchange in the Jeffries' kitchen the night before, Helen was all business again this day, as she offered to bring Lizzie a tray in the library.

The day was spent transcribing and studying the missing pages of the journal, and Lizzie looked forward with eager anticipation to Edmund's return. He would, she felt, be her best source of information for solving the puzzles in the text, especially since his father seemed to be avoiding the subject.

When she heard the sound of his arrival in the hall, she collected the papers and returned them to their hidden compartment in the box so that she and Edmund could share the whole experience of discovery. The latch on the box was just snapping shut when the wrong brother entered the room. It was Richard.

Lizzie felt a knot form in her stomach, the bile well up in the back of her throat. She nodded at him curtly, he ignored her, and she turned back to her work. The atmosphere in the room could not have been more uncomfortable. Richard poured himself a drink and sat in one of the wing chairs opposite the fireplace. Lizzie could sense his clenched jaw moving tensely back and forth. Once again she asked herself where the hostility toward her could possibly come from, and there seemed two possible explanations. The first was that he was just an arrogant son-of-a-bitch who disdained anyone below his class, a "snotty twit," as Helen had called him. The second possibility was that he did not think she was either important enough or smart enough to put the material from Captain Cook's voyage into a package that would be publishable or exhibitable by the British Museum. According to Tom Clark, George had made the decision to hire her, apparently without hesitation and without consulting his son, when he saw her book. Admittedly there were a number of scholars better known in the field than Lizzie—including Tom Clark himself—who must have been preferable to the snobbish Richard.

After several minutes of tense silence, George arrived. He was obviously surprised to see his son. "Mrs. Jeffries just told me you were here, Richard," he said. "I didn't expect to see you back again this winter."

"I'm still concerned about this British Museum project."

Lizzie gave George a little wave of greeting and turned back to her computer, though her attention was focused behind rather than in front of her. She didn't think that there was any physical exchange of greeting between the two men, not even a handshake; certainly there was not any sort of embrace.

"Have you asked Lizzie about her progress?" George asked his son.

Richard drained his drink and set the glass on the table beside him.

"No," he said cooly, "she's your employee, not mine. I thought it was best to ask you."

Lizzie was hoping that George would put Richard in his place, but to her disappointment he once again acted as if there was nothing amiss in the relationship between Richard and herself.

"She's found some wonderful things, Richard," he babbled, "and she's shared everything with me." He brought the decanter of brandy and two more glasses to the table. "Let's have a drink," he said, "and then Lizzie you can show Richard what you found yesterday."

He poured the drinks and Lizzie took a gulp. She felt the heat of anger retreat and be replaced with the flush of alcohol. She forced herself to calmly show Richard the missing logbook pages.

He read them without any change of expression. "Interesting," he said, "but I don't think you should include any of this in an exhibition or book."

Lizzie was speechless for several seconds before she was able to sputter a response. "What?" she said, shocked by his response. "It's the best part of the story. It should definitely be included."

"I don't think so," Richard responded, clearly working hard to control his rising anger. "You weren't hired to expose our ancestor as a thief and a grave robber."

"I thought I was hired to find out what Francis Hatton did on his Pacific Voyage and describe it."

George finally began to show his son that he was upset by the direction of the conversation.

"I don't see what your problem is Richard. This happened more than two hundred years ago, and there is every indication that Francis was filled with remorse for his actions."

"I just don't like it," he said.

"Well, this whole conversation is premature anyway, because Lizzie hasn't finished her research."

Lizzie sat silently through the exchange, wishing she was home in Boston or anywhere besides this room.

George turned to her. "Lizzie, my dear," he said politely, "you go ahead with the work as you see fit. When you have finished your research we'll have a chance to look at everything together and decide what to do next."

"Thank you, George." She replaced the papers in the box and closed the latch, turned off her computer, picked up all of her file folders and, clutching them in her arms, excused herself and went to her room.

• • • • •

Lizzie sat in her room for more than an hour fuming. She wiped at tears of frustration as they welled up in her eyes, determined not to let them roll down her cheeks and start her sobbing. She would not give Richard the satisfaction of making her cry.

Her earlier analysis of Richard's hostility and what lay beneath it seemed somewhat more understandable after his recent outburst. He was both a snotty twit *and* unimpressed with her credentials. She had never thought that another scholar would do a better job than herself, and she did not think that Tom Clark or any other potential candidate for the job (almost certainly male and English) would bow to Richard's ridiculous demands to hide information once it had been uncovered. His expectation that he would be able to control the story once he made it public was completely arrogant and unrealistic. And why would he want to?

George had said that Richard hoped to enhance his position on the London cultural scene through the presentation of Francis Hatton's collection and journal. Lizzie figured that the Hatton name was old enough and distinguished enough to put Richard in the right social circles, but perhaps new money and foreign money, which he would want to attract for his investment business, required that he bring himself to attention with the sort of splash and cachet that was assured with a big new exhibition that had the Hatton name at its center. If that were the case, she thought, then he would want his family to appear noble and important, and the corpse of Eltatsy could come back to haunt him.

Lizzie did not return downstairs again until Helen came to tell her that dinner was almost ready and that Edmund had arrived. His presence would, Lizzie knew, lighten the mood in the house. Unfortunately, when she got to the dining room, only Richard was there.

"Do you always eat your meals with my father, Miss Manning?" he asked peevishly.

"Yes, of course," she answered, "and I would prefer it if you would call me Dr. Manning."

"Just what are your intentions here?" he demanded.

"I'm here to work on a project for your father and then leave," she answered, matching his tone. "What's your point?"

"Well, I've seen secretaries set their sights on their employers in the past," he said, "and all this 'Lizzie' and 'George' business seems more than casual."

"Oh for God's sake," she said. "Grow up."

"I guess you're finally noticing that I would be a rather old son for you."

"Thank you so much for pointing that out," she said with mock seriousness. "My husband and I were considering adopting an upper-class twit, but now that I notice, you *are* too old for consideration."

Edmund had entered the room behind his brother and now he laughed out loud. "Touché, Lizzie," he said. "And for God's sake, Dick, don't be such an ass!" He smiled at Lizzie and she relaxed a bit.

George arrived to hear the last exchange and ordered Richard to apologize, which he did in the most perfunctory manner. "So you're married," he said, as if a superficial attempt at civility would make up for his horrendous rudeness. "And where is Mr. Manning?"

Edmund came and graciously took Lizzie's arm and lavished consideration on her during the meal to make up for his brother's cross behavior. After dinner, the two of them went to the library where Lizzie showed him her discoveries of the previous day. His response was exactly what Lizzie expected and wished for: enthusiasm, regret, sympathy for both Francis Hatton and for the family of Eltatsy, and curiosity about what had happened. He had none of his brother's concern about reputation, no hesitation that the story should be told as found, no doubts about Lizzie's judgment in handling the information.

Edmund and Lizzie were admiring the miniature when George and Richard joined them. They were deep in conversation, but Lizzie heard George shush his son as they entered the room.

"Enough!" he said angrily, "I won't have it discussed further."

"But is it her maiden name or her married name?" she heard Richard whisper.

Lizzie and Edmund pretended to be engrossed by the tiny portrait that they were putting back into the Chinese box, but the tension in the air was palpable. George resorted once again to liquor as the cure for the room's bad temper. In addition to whiskey, brandy, and sherry, he even offered to order up some tea or coffee from Mrs. Jeffries.

"What do you fancy, Lizzie? We have some liqueurs in the salon, if you would prefer one of them."

"Actually, I'd prefer wine, if there is still some left from dinner," she said.

"I think there was," George said graciously. "Richard, would you please go see?"

Richard made a bow to his father and left the room. When he returned several minutes later he had a bottle in his hand and offered to pour for Lizzie. She thanked him, the four acted civilly for ten minutes, and then Richard departed for his own room; George followed soon after.

Lizzie took advantage of the time alone with Edmund to return one more time to Francis Hatton's letter to his sister.

"What's going on here?" she asked, pointing to the passage about the Crusader.

Edmund poured himself another drink and held up the bottle of wine to Lizzie. She nodded and he filled her glass again as well.

"Sit here by the fire," he said, "and I will tell you a story."

Always somewhat susceptible to the effects of alcohol, Lizzie seldom drank this much. After two glasses of wine at dinner, this now made her fourth for the evening. She was finding it particularly potent, but it was also giving her a nice buzz; she felt slightly flirtatious with Edmund and, most important, Richard was entirely gone from her thoughts. She stretched herself out comfortably in her chair as Edmund began to speak.

"One of my ancestors, whose name I can't remember, lived in this house in the middle of the thirteenth century," Edmund began. "He had two sons, Richard and John. Richard, the oldest, was engaged to marry a young woman named Elizabeth something-or-other."

He stood beside the fireplace and Lizzie looked up at him.

"The last name doesn't matter," he explained before continuing. "Elizabeth came to Hengemont to meet her husband-to-be and ended up falling madly in love with his younger brother."

"A scandal," Lizzie said, "and true love. Good elements of a story."

Edmund nodded and continued. "But John, the younger son, was pledged to go on a Crusade with his father, and anyway the fair young maiden was supposed to marry Richard, and so it didn't make any sense for her to change horses as it were."

Lizzie made a snort of laughter. "Excellent metaphor," she said. She was really feeling the effect of the wine, but did not decline when Edmund drained what was left of the bottle into her glass.

"As luck would have it, Elizabeth had a younger sister with her, and she was pretty cute too, and eventually Richard was persuaded to marry her."

"Just like that?"

"Well, actually I think the father of these two girls had a substantial amount of cash on hand, and I think that the father of the boys needed it to make his Crusade."

"Aha!" she said. "Then this is not really a story of true love."

"Oh, as I have always heard it, between Elizabeth and John it could not have been more powerful."

"This story is fairly canonical in your family then?"

"In what way?"

"It gets told the same way generation after generation without elaboration?"

Edmund paused a moment. "I'm not sure about that," he said, "but I believe the details have remained basically the same for many centuries."

"Who told it to you?"

"My Aunt Bette, my father's younger sister."

"Okay," Lizzie said. "Go on then, the two sisters married the two brothers."

"Yes, Elizabeth married John, and her sister Margaret married Richard. There was feasting and a tournament with games of war, etc., and then John and his father set out to go to the Crusades."

"This must have been terrible for the new bride Elizabeth."

"Devastating! She thought that their marriage would keep him from going. She tried everything to make him stay, but John's father was adamant, and now that he had all the money he needed to pay his troops and such, he was determined to leave the very day after the weddings."

Lizzie stared into the embers of the fire as Edmund described how Elizabeth pleaded with her new husband, how he, still just a teenager, struggled with his father to stay with his new bride, but in the end was forced to tell her that he had to go.

"The house then consisted of just the central stone tower and some outlying walls," Edmund continued, "and the two of them went up to the roof. There they wept together, then made love, and then he made a stupid promise that he would come back."

"Why was it so stupid?"

"Because almost no one came back from the Crusades, including him, of course." He paused for a moment and finished his brandy. "It turned out that Elizabeth had become pregnant from that one night of lovemaking. Richard and Margaret were also pretty fertile young people, and within a year there were two babies at Hengemont, a son for Elizabeth and a daughter for her sister. But Margaret died in childbirth."

Lizzie listened with heightened concentration to the end.

"Richard thought that he and Elizabeth should now marry, but she insisted that she had to wait for John."

"Was he still alive?"

"No."

"Was there proof?"

"Yes, I think so."

"And how does her story end?"

"She killed herself."

This was not what Lizzie had been expecting. Edmund's romantic and somewhat jocular story had suddenly taken a turn that made her profoundly sad.

"She went up to the top of the tower and threw herself off," he said softly. "Years later the son of Elizabeth and John married his cousin, the daughter of Richard and Margaret, and *their* son was my ancestor."

"This is a very sad story Edmund."

"Yes, it is."

"I thought it was going to be a romance."

"Romances are often sad."

The last log of any size on the fire broke apart and fell onto the grate. Edmund put his glass on the table and began turning out the lights around the room. Lizzie wobbled a bit as she stood up.

"Do you need help getting to your room?" he asked.

"No, but thanks. Five glasses of wine is way over my limit though, and I'll probably suffer for it tomorrow." They walked together to the door of the library and up the staircase.

"Lizzie," he said earnestly. "I really want to apologize for Richard. He is such an ass sometimes."

"Why?" she asked. "Do you think he made Elizabeth kill herself?"

Edmund laughed softly. "No, you silly woman. Richard, my brother!"

Lizzie was startled for a moment and then burst into almost hysterical laughter. "See what a good storyteller you are," she joked. "I forgot all about him."

He put his arm around her as they reached the staircase. "Are you sure you don't need help?"

She shook her head. "Will I see you tomorrow?"

"If you are up early enough. I have rounds at the clinic and have to be back to Bristol by noon."

"When am I going to get my long-promised tour?"

He slapped his head. "Oh damn," he said apologetically, "You're still waiting for me to see the house?"

She nodded, disappointed that he seemed to have forgotten.

"This weekend without fail," he promised, lifting his hand up in a pledge.

He removed the steadying arm from her shoulders and they moved up the stairs, separating with a chaste kiss on the landing before he went up the opposite staircase, toward the older wing of the house.

She held tightly onto the railing as it wound its way around to form the balcony. It was a long drop to the floor beneath. Opposite her was the big painting of Francis Hatton and his siblings, and the three of them seemed to move a bit within the frame. Lizzie felt dizzy and nauseous, and chided herself for taking that last glass of wine as she moved unsteadily down the long hall and around the corner to her room.

That night she had a dream of falling in love with Edmund. There were vivid, swirling images. They were dancing, they were at a party surrounded by chattering guests, they were running up stone steps, hand in hand.

The stairs went round and round, turning a tight corkscrew around a center stone pillar. There were narrow windows above every dozen or so steps, sending a shaft of light that brightly illuminated their passage for a moment, which then grew dimmer and dimmer until the first hint of the next window could be seen, and then they were suddenly in another shaft of light. She began to pant a bit, but he encouraged her. "We're almost there," he said, squeezing her hand. Finally they burst through the door at the top. The bright light blinded her for a moment and then, as her eyes adjusted, the whole countryside swept away beneath her. She reached up to straighten her hair, it was caught up in loops of braids, one circling each ear. As the wind caught softly at her dress, she looked down and felt the deep green velvet.

He pulled her toward him and she put her hand up to touch his face, his hair, his beard. He leaned down to kiss her for the first time. His lips were soft and warm, his tongue moved gently across her mouth. His hands explored her body and she reciprocated, stroking and pulling at odd male garments.

When they were naked, she lay upon the cold stones of the tower's floor and he lay upon her. The sex was quick and hard and left her breathless. In the distance a bell chimed the hour three times. By the third bell, she could no longer feel his weight upon her. The sun faded and the stone began to feel colder until she was shivering.

Lizzie woke with a start. She had no idea where she was, but a clock was chiming just above her head and she was lying on something hard and cold. She felt around her and found the edges of two cut stones with a line of mortar between them.

Her eyes finally began to pick dim patches of light out of the darkness and she sat up. She was wearing her usual nightwear, one of Martin's undershirts and a pair of panties. It took her several minutes to realize that she was in the great medieval hall of Hengemont's Norman tower. She stood up, very unsteadily, and went to one of the chairs that stood along the wall. It had a velvet seat and as she sat on it she thought momentarily about the dream. She had been wearing a velvet dress.

Lizzie trembled violently from a combination of cold and fear. She had no idea how she had gotten to this part of the house. She had never experienced anything like this before and it was terrifying. When she was fully conscious, the enormity of her situation overwhelmed her. She moved quickly to return to her room, hoping that no one would see her along the way. She went from the medieval hall through the door into the Adam wing. She looked carefully in all directions and then moved quickly up the staircase. She wrestled to pull her shirt down to cover herself, but it was too short for real success, and she could not even cover her panties. All the residents of the all the paintings seemed to watch her disapprovingly as she slunk down the hall, stopping frequently to listen for any sounds. When she finally came to her own room she raced into the water closet and vomited.

Her warm bed was so welcome that she pulled the covers over her head; she was still shivering and now she also began to cry uncontrollably. She had no idea what had happened to her.

Chapter 10

Lizzie was exhausted when she woke. She felt like she had been running all night. The sun streamed through the window and when she looked at the clock on the bedside table she couldn't believe it was ten-thirty. What must they think of her downstairs? She lay motionless for another ten minutes, covering her eyes with her arm.

Had she actually left her bed last night? Or was that part of an elaborate dream? At this moment she didn't know for sure. She shivered as she remembered the moment she woke, half naked in the middle of the great medieval hall, and then worked hard to convince herself that it hadn't actually happened.

When she sat up, her head throbbed so hard that tears rolled down her cheeks. "What is happening?" she thought, standing with some difficulty, and then holding on to the bed as she circled around it to the bathroom door. She took four aspirin and sat again on the bed. She had never had a reaction like this from alcohol. She rubbed her temples with her hands, squeezed her eyes tightly shut, and breathed slowly, in and out, in and out. When she opened her eyes she thought that she felt somewhat better. The aspirin must be starting to work.

On the wall opposite her, another woman was rising from her bed. Lizzie hadn't taken the time to look closely at the Rossetti painting since it had appeared in her room. Now she rose slowly and walked over to it. Inside the frame a woman lay in a room not unlike the one in which Lizzie stood. Around her the sheets and bedspread were tousled as if she had tossed and turned all night—or had passionate sex, Lizzie thought.

The woman rested on one arm; the other reached out to a knight in armor who was vanishing as she woke; he reached back, a gold chain in his hand. The signature was "Rossetti, PRB."

Lizzie knew Dante Gabriel Rossetti and his Pre-Raphaelite Brotherhood. This sort of subject matter was common for them. There were lots of knights and ladies in their paintings and poetry, many references to Arthurian legend, and a rather romantic view of death. There was a brass marker on the frame that Lizzie had to polish up with the hem of her shirt to read. It said "'Elizabeth Wakes from the Dream' by Dante Gabriel Rossetti, 1872." She shivered at the coincidence.

Feeling well enough to go downstairs, Lizzie dressed, brushed her teeth, and went slowly down the hall to the staircase. She tried hard not to think about making the trip in the opposite direction in the middle of the night before, and averted her glance from the accusing portraits. Francis Hatton seemed happy enough in his picture, though, and Lizzie mentally blew him a kiss as she rounded the landing of the stairs.

There was no sign of anyone downstairs. The library was empty, though there was a pot of coffee as usual. She poured a cup and went to her place at the library table. There were two notes with her name on them, one from George and one from Edmund, each expressing regret at missing her before leaving the house. Edmund said that he had waited as long as he could for her, and hoped she was well.

As she sat down at her computer, Helen appeared.

"Are you feeling all right this morning?" she asked.

Lizzie put her elbows on the table and rested her cheek in her palm. "Oh Helen," she said. "I had a terrible night."

Helen pulled up the chair beside her and put her hand on Lizzie's forehead. "Are you ill?" she asked with concern.

"I drank too much wine, I think," she said hesitantly. She wondered if she could be completely honest with Helen about what had happened to her and decided that she could not. She knew that Helen was harboring very odd suspicions about her family background, and she did not want to compound them by adding more fodder to a flame of mistaken identity.

Helen offered to make her a light meal, and Lizzie accepted. "I think that tea would be the thing this morning," she said, eyeing the cup of coffee on the table in front of her.

Helen gave her arm an affectionate pat. "I'll bring you a breakfast tray, Lizzie, and you must promise me to eat something."

Lizzie turned her computer on and stared at the screen. What should she work on today? She leaned back in her chair and closed her eyes, thinking about the dream. In it she had willingly had passionate sex with Edmund Hatton.

"Hard at work, are we?" Richard's voice brought her bolt upright in her chair. He came to the table, poured himself a cup of coffee from the pot, and sat in one of the chairs opposite her.

She met his arrogant stare. His eyes were intensely blue, with none of the grey shading that marked those of Edmund, George, and Lily. His face was impassive, never flinching or changing expression as he sipped coffee from his cup. Lizzie noticed that he didn't hold his pinkie up, and wondered why she thought he would. Finally she could stand the silence no longer.

"Have I done something to offend you?" she asked bluntly.

"Why do you ask that?" he said with mock politeness.

Lizzie smiled at him, a smile that she hoped was menacing, like a tiger greeting a wildebeest. "I don't know," she said, "you just seem so disappointed to find me here."

"My dear Dr. Manning," he said, smiling back with the very look Lizzie had been trying to achieve. "Or may I call you Lizzie?" he continued. "Everyone else around here seems to. If I'm not mistaken, I think I even heard our Mrs. Jeffries refer to you in that informal American way."

Lizzie tried her menacing smile again. "I guess I just have that effect on people."

"I guess that's it," he said obsequiously.

There was an uncomfortable moment of silence which Lizzie was determined not to break.

"So," Richard said finally, "how is your work going?"

"Very well, thank you."

"What will you be working on today?"

Lizzie hardly knew how to respond. She sensed that he really was interested in knowing what was happening with her research, but didn't trust her to inform him about it with any candor. If that was his notion, Lizzie thought, it wasn't far off. She gave him a brief overview of the obvious material, not mentioning the new pages from the journal or the conversation of the day before, until Helen arrived again with her tea.

"Ah Mrs. Jeffries," he said, watching from his chair as the housekeeper wrestled the heavy tray onto the table. "We were just talking about you."

"I've brought Professor Manning some toast and tea. Would you like some?"

"No, as you know, I breakfasted at the normal time. But I would be happy to share Lizzie's tea."

Both women looked at him suspiciously, then shared a look between themselves.

"Let me pour," Richard continued, "I love to play the mother." He pulled the teapot and cups toward him. "Lizzie, what do you take in your tea?"

He made a show of being polite as Helen left the room and Lizzie organized her papers to begin work. When Richard had given her the cup of tea, she asked him if he really wanted a report on her research.

"No," he said, still maintaining his rigid air of politeness. "I just didn't want to leave again without feeling that we had an understanding between us."

"And do we?"

"Not exactly, but at least you know I'm speaking to you."

Lizzie tried out her smile again. "Thank you, I am so much more comfortable now."

With that he gave her a dramatic bow and left the room. Lizzie sat still and silent for several minutes. It was clear that Richard still didn't like her, but at least he wasn't going to continue to undermine her publicly. What his private plans were she couldn't say.

She took her cup of tea to the window, where she looked out along the old line of the castle grounds as she drank. The glass panels of the tall French doors to the terrace were cold enough to fog up as she breathed on them, and when she leaned unsteadily against one of them, she shivered. She moved over to where the fire was burning low in the grate and sank into one of the comfortable chairs in front of it. She thought about the story that Edmund had told her the night before. In the flames she sought out the images of Elizabeth and John, their encounter on the tower. She drained her cup and set it on the small table. The tournament was starting.

She sat in a wooden stand erected for the day, surveying the crowd and waiting for him to appear. Her lover. She remembered the feel of him from the night before on the tower. The touch of his hand, the thrust of his hips. She blushed at the thought of what had happened.

From the elevated height of the stand she looked out across the castle yard, teeming with people, and over the far wall and tower. The land sloped down to the sea.

Finally she saw him. He was covered from head to toe with chain mail, over which was draped a belted cloth tunic; it was the color of rust and was covered with white crosses— the badge of the Crusader. He was in earnest conversation with his similarly clad father. Around them, armed men checked their shields, swords, and lances in preparation for the fight.

He looked up to her and smiled. Her heart melted. He wore a new heraldic device on his shield and leather epaulets. It was a castle tower; below it ran a wave of the sea, and on top of it were two hearts. He bowed his lance to her and she felt a surge of love. "John," she said.

Helen woke her softly. "Lizzie, dear," she said. "Lizzie, let us help you up to your room."

She opened her eyes to see Helen's worried look. Beyond her, Lizzie could see Henry standing at the door with a similar worried expression on his face.

The housekeeper stroked her hair and talked to her in the most gentle tones.

"What's the matter?" Lizzie said, sitting up.

"You were making such sounds that we were afraid you were ill," Helen said with concern.

Lizzie took Helen's hand and rose unsteadily from the chair. "As a matter of fact, I don't think that I am entirely well," she said. "But I can't spend the whole day sleeping."

Henry took a few steps into the room and stopped, looking to his wife for a clue as to whether he was needed. Lizzie smiled at him and waved him off.

"Thanks, Henry," she said, "but I'm not going to go back to bed quite yet."

Helen tried to convince her otherwise, but Lizzie was adamant. She moved across the room back to the library table, leaning unsteadily on Helen. The room rocked back and forth with the same motion she had felt after getting off a ship from a sea voyage. Lizzie held on to the edge of the table and sat down hard in one of the chairs around it. She looked at the remains of her breakfast and felt slightly nauseous.

"I'm rather embarrassed about this, Helen," she said, pushing the tray away from her. "But I seem to have a full-blown hangover from my over-indulgence last night."

"You'll feel better in bed."

"If I go back to bed and sleep all day then I will revert to North American time," Lizzie said emphatically. "It's important that I try to get some work done today."

Helen seemed for a moment like she might try to argue, but then assented. She instructed Lizzie to call her instantly if she needed anything, then took the tray and left Lizzie to her work.

The winter sun pierced the windows with streaks of bright light and Lizzie closed her eyes and tried to concentrate. The short nap had not been refreshing. The dream was, in fact, as vivid as any she could remember. It had been meticulously detailed and she was surprised at how much of that detail she could remember. Colors were vibrant, she had actually felt the motion of air against her face, the heat of the sun, the smell of dirt and sweat and horses. Why, she wondered, would she dream about a tournament? She knew nothing about arms and armor and yet, if pressed, she felt that she could describe pretty accurately what kind of equipment was used at this particular imaginary joust.

The previous night she had dreamed of Edmund, she was

certain of that, and it had been overtly sexual. This afternoon she had called her lover John. She rolled it all over and over in her mind. The story that Edmund had told her had obviously influenced her more than she knew at the time. That story, in combination with the Rossetti painting, the book that Martin had given her, and the age and eminence of Hengemont must have all come together in this strange dream, she thought. But still, it was much more detailed, emotional, and somehow startling, than any she had ever had in the past. It was hard to shake.

The brightness of the sun was hurting her eyes and she moved to the other side of the table so that her back was to it. Now she could see the rays picking out details in the room, which jumped out at her. She closed her eyes again and ordered herself to concentrate. She looked again at the pages that had been cut from Francis Hatton's journal and at the miniature of his sister Eliza.

"Concentrate," she told herself, "concentrate. Think of the job."

Without the bentwood box and the Chilkat blanket, the central artifacts on which she would logically focus an exhibit or book were missing. She sat back in her chair and stretched her legs out so that her feet could rest on the long supporting bar that ran under the table. She looked around the room.

The doors to the cabinet were open and she stared into it intently, trying to take it in as if she were seeing it for the first time. What would Francis Hatton have done with two sizable objects that he wanted to hide? Would he have destroyed them? Lizzie couldn't imagine that. He clearly wanted to return them. Had he done so? There didn't seem to be any evidence of that, but she needed to go over the documents related to subsequent voyages to the Pacific. Would he have put them somewhere else in the house? If so, Lizzie was probably out of luck because the house was huge and George had not invited her to go exploring. Somehow she couldn't imagine that Francis Hatton would have just stuck them anywhere. He was so careful about the cabinet.

They weren't in the glass-fronted cases; she could see everything in them from where she sat. The drawers were clearly too shallow for the box, though the folded blanket could have fit in one of them, but she had already been through all of them and hadn't seen it. Between the upper cases and the lower drawers was the decorative carved border with the crest and the intriguing mottoes that had led her to discover the hidden panel in the journal's box.

She put her feet flat on the floor again and pulled the box toward her. The carving on it was Chinese, while the carving on the cabinet was clearly not Chinese. Lizzie didn't know very much about different styles of European cabinetry, but the carving on the cabinet seemed consistent with the decoration she could see around the rest of this wing of the house, mostly borders in carved wood or molded plaster.

The cabinet frieze had one panel on it, though, on which the carver seemed to have copied the design from the front of the Chinese box, though he had given it a distinctly European finish. Lizzie rose and went over to look more closely at it, bringing her magnifying lens with her. The carving was at waist level and she bent over with the magnifying glass to study it. There were the same leaves and flowers, family crest and alternative motto: "Numquam Dediscum."

"On the box," she said softly, running her hand over the carving, "the secret panel opened when I pressed right here."

Lizzie pressed and a portion of the border on the cabinet sprang open. She stood perfectly still for almost a minute, then turned around and looked behind her. The Jeffries were nowhere to be seen, and she was pretty certain that Richard was gone. There was a tall clock in the library and another beyond it in the hallway, and for the first time she heard their ticking as two distinct sounds, but otherwise it was perfectly still. She put her hand into the space behind the panel and pulled out the contents. She already knew that it wasn't the artifacts she was seeking because the space wasn't big enough. What she did find was a small flat case, a diary of some sort, and a key. Lizzie was excited by the last item. Was it possible that there was another panel hidden somewhere where she might find the carved box and the blanket? She brought them all over to the table.

The small diary was inscribed "Bette Hatton" on the title

page and was filled with pages of writing in a tiny script. There were several loose papers tucked inside it, including a long letter on stationery from the Victoria and Albert Museum. As Lizzie stacked up the rest of the papers she found one on vellum that resembled the poem she had found, but this one was in French. There was another poem as well, of unknown age, and similar in theme to the ones she had already found. There was something disquieting about them, but Lizzie set them aside and turned to the small tooled-leather case that had also been behind the pane.

It was small enough that Lizzie could hold it in one hand. There were bronze hinges on each of the two outside edges, and a gold-colored clasp in the center, which she easily unfastened. As she opened it from the center, she found that she was looking at a medieval triptych—three miniature paintings set into side-by-side panels. She gasped at the beauty of it; the colors were unbelievably vibrant and the small size made each part of the thing seem jewel-like. Each of the paintings was only about five or six inches high but the detail was remarkable. The center painting at twice the width of those on either side was still only about five inches across, yet it was filled with people and action.

The panel on the left showed a romantic scene of two lovers, their hands clasped together, standing on some sort of crenellated tower. "Courtly love," she thought. The middle panel was a celebration of some sort with knights and ladies. The right-hand panel was the lovers again, but not so happy this time. She had her hands at her face, obviously weeping; he held out a necklace to her with a red stone at the end of a long chain. It looked like a large ruby.

It was the story of Elizabeth and John, she realized, and the central panel showed a tournament. As she looked at the details her hands began to tremble violently. This was the tournament about which she had just dreamed. Lizzie dropped the thing on the table, as if it had suddenly shocked her.

She shook her head in disbelief, sat down, stood up, sat down again, and eventually picked up the triptych and carried it to the window to look more closely at the tiny paintings. There was no question. If she had described her dream to an artist, in all its vivid detail, it could not be more similar to the picture she now held in her hand. Lizzie felt the blood drain from her face. The tournament was the very one she had seen in her dream. Was the encounter of the lovers on the tower her encounter with her dream lover? For a moment she thought she would surely faint.

She sat down again and pressed her fingertips against her closed eyes and rubbed gently. There must be an explanation, she told herself. Absolutely unwilling to believe that she was experiencing some supernatural phenomenon, she wracked her brain, trying to think of when she might have encountered this picture, or something like it. Could it have been reproduced in one of the Hatton historical materials she had examined, maybe even without realizing it? She was disconcerted, if not actually scared. The coincidence that she would discover a painting of a scene immediately after dreaming about it was one she could hardly begin to fathom. Except that she was in this house, and this house held this story.

The acrid taste of bile rose into her mouth and Lizzie ran from the library. She very nearly vomited onto Robert Adam's parquet floor as she ran to the bathroom tucked under the curved staircase, but she made it just in time. When there was nothing left in her stomach, she pulled the chain on the toilet to flush it, closed the lid, and turned to sit on it. She wiped the beads of sweat from her forehead with a piece of toilet paper and sat there for nearly ten minutes, until she finally felt composed enough to return to the library.

The solution to her dilemma was apparent. If she was to believe that she had subconsciously picked up facts and images and woven them together from her own knowledge and imagination, then she could deal with it best by identifying the sources.

She went back to the library and looked again at the triptych. On closer examination the tournament scene was not, in fact, identical to the one in her dream. She breathed slowly in and out. The knight looked the same, but then he looked the same in the Rossetti painting, and she had studied that painting this very morning. Maybe Rossetti had seen this triptych, she thought. And she, having seen the Rossetti, filled in the rest. She felt better. She commanded herself to be rational and accept this explanation. She turned to the letter typed on stationary of the Victoria and Albert Museum.

December 29, 1964
Miss Elizabeth Hatton
Grosvenor Square
London

Dear Miss Hatton,

I return, by courier, the triptych which you left for me to examine last week. It received a great deal of interest among my colleagues since unknown pieces of this early date and of such charm and artistry do not often walk in the door unexpectedly.

As you know from the work I did at Hengemont a dozen years ago, my own field of expertise is portraiture, and though you expressed a belief that this was an ancestral portrait ca. 1250, I must tell you that my colleagues and I have reached a different conclusion. Works of this sort, showing secular scenes, began to be popular in France and Flanders in the late fourteenth and early fifteenth century; such a work would have been unheard of in England at the earlier date. The regular contact across the channel by Norman families in medieval times makes a French origin for this piece very likely.

Several clues help us establish a timeframe within the painting itself. The clothing is our best indication of the period when the artist flourished (as opposed to the date of the action depicted). In the twelfth and thirteenth centuries, for instance, most of the paintings which survive are biblical scenes, but the subjects wear medieval European

clothing, which we can use to establish a date. If you look at the women
in your triptych you will see that they
wear high-waisted gowns with long, draped
sleeves. Their elaborate headdresses are
very distinctive. Similarly the short tunics of the men, with their padded and
pleated bodices and full sleeves, indicate the reign of Henry IV.

The great exceptions here are the
knights and the most prominent woman in
the central panel. My colleagues and I
found your family's oral history to be as-
tonishingly accurate in this matter. The
bride wears a costume which you will instantly see is not similar to that of her
companions, and it <u>does</u> originate in the
middle thirteenth century. Mr. Hastings, a
curator in the arms and armour department
here at the V&A, tells me that the armour
is also consistent with that date, and
with the Crusade of that time. The depiction here is, he says, clearly that of
a "Joust à plaisance" or joust of peace.
(Earlier tournaments had occasionally
become so violent that young men were
killed at home before having a chance to
go off to be killed in the Crusades!)

I believe that your triptych is meant
to be a depiction of specific people and
events of the middle thirteenth century,
but painted about 150-200 years later,
probably a commission by someone in your
family to capture those earlier incidents while the memory of them was still
actively being recounted. The artist attempted accuracy with the central figures,
but then had to depend on his own experience and knowledge to fill in the other
details.

If you would like to see similar medieval secular works, I invite you to meet

with me at the V&A where I would be happy
to show you some of our own treasures of
the period. The Devonshire Tapestry (ca.
1425-50) is particularly interesting. Other such scenes of garden parties, daily
life, weddings, tournaments, and settings
of courtly love, can be seen in a number
of illustrated manuscripts in our collection and at the British Library.

   I hope you enjoyed a most happy holiday
season and I look forward to serving you
again if the occasion arises.

Mr. C.H.F. Wells
Keeper of British Portraits
Victoria and Albert Museum

Lizzie took the triptych over to the light of the window
again, and brought her magnifying lens to get a better look
at the details. She wanted to see those clues mentioned by the
author of the letter. Yes, she could see what he had mentioned
about the clothing. In the left panel the young woman wore a
dark green gown, belted just under her breasts with a red sash.
A small ruff of golden fur lined the collar of the dress and the
openings of the sleeves, which dropped from just below her
shoulders almost to her knees. Her hair was gathered up over
her ears in elaborate braids, over which she wore a white veil
that had obviously been stiffened in some way around the face
to give it a specific shape. Her lover wore a knee-length tunic
that hung in multiple pleats from a square yoke. Around his
waist was a leather belt, and he wore soft-looking boots that
came up to his knees and then rolled over into large cuffs. His
hair was short, his head uncovered. They wore similar, though
not identical, clothing in the tiny painting on the right.

   In the central panel were numerous people wearing similar
clothing, though there were also young men with embarrass-
ingly short tunics that did not even reach their hips. Most of
the men wore tights and codpieces and pointed shoes. Some
of the women wore veils hanging from unbelievably elaborate
headgear. Lizzie tried to imagine what they were made from

and could only conclude that they were padded fabric formed into rolls and buns that were worn on both sides of the head. Everywhere were long slashed sleeves, or cuffs that hung almost to the ground. The overall effect was very festive.

The knights in the foreground wore full suits of chain mail, including hoods that fit over the head and around the face, and mittens that covered the hands. Over the chain mail was draped a belted rust-colored tunic covered with white crosses. Shields, swords, and lances were in abundance. In the stands, musicians held long horns.

Lizzie angled her magnifying lens to look closely at the two central figures. As the letter said, the young woman was dressed in a distinctively different manner as she stood in the stands staring straight ahead of her. She appeared to be wearing a blue dress with tight-fitting long sleeves; a row of fastenings was just visible from elbow to cuff. Over that she wore another looser dress of a silvery color, almost a shift. It had no sleeves, and in fact the arm holes were so large that they extended down to her hips, and the whole thing was fasted with a gold cord slung low around her waist. Instead of the elaborate headdress of the women around her, she wore a small embroidered cap with a long sheer veil hanging from the back of it. A matching piece of fabric circled her face, passing under her chin and then disappearing up under the cap, where it must have been fastened in some way that Lizzie couldn't see.

Her lover also stood staring straight ahead, his armor matching that of his comrades in every way except that he carried a shield with a heraldic device and wore epaulets with the same figure on it. This was the crest that Lizzie had seen in the Rossetti painting and later dreamed about. At the top were two side-by-side red hearts. Below them, in the center of the shield, a row of up-and-down blocks represented the crenellated battlements at the top of a castle tower. Below that, a wavy blue line represented the ocean's waves. It occurred to Lizzie as she stared at it that this was not the Hatton family crest, with its sword-pierced heart.

Lizzie looked at each part of the triptych through her magnifying glass until her eyes hurt. Then she set it upright on the table and stared at it some more, trying to get the essence of the whole picture. For a moment she glanced out the window, across the formal garden and the sloping hill, down across the old ruin of the castle wall to the water. Her eyes jerked back to the wall and Lizzie felt a shiver run from her lower back up her spine to her neck. In the scene of the tournament, could she discern bits of the Hengemont landscape? Before the other wings of the house were built, and while the walls around the castle yard were still standing, this tournament had probably happened right here, almost seven hundred and fifty years before. Lizzie saw that her bare arms were covered with goose bumps and she rubbed them lightly.

She stepped over to the tall French doors and tried to see more closely, her hand resting on the bronze handle of the door. She looked at the ruins at the far end of the garden. Could she make out in them the outline of the castle walls from the triptych? She tried not to think about the fact that she had seen such a scene in her dream as well. The door handle sank under the weight of her hand and the door swung open. Lizzie stepped outside. The air was chilly and she ran her hands up and down her arms again. She told herself that she was excited, not scared. She closed her eyes and captured again the sensations of her dream: the sound of armor clanking, the beat of horses' hooves, the voices of ladies in a crowd. When she opened her eyes she realized again that this was similar, but not identical, to her dream. She wished she had a better sense of what the landscape had looked like in the age of the Crusades.

She thought of the book Martin had given her. Very quickly she ran to her room and grabbed a jacket and the book. There was still time before the light faded for her to go again to the garden and see if she could trace the outline of the original castle. She opened the book to the description of the original structure and walked with it down to the ruin.

Here were the remains of a small tower and a wall. This would have been the northwest tower shown in the artist's rendering of the original fortifications. Lizzie followed the wall back toward the house. The family's church, which she had seen when Henry Jeffries drove her here from Minehead, was visible through a cast-iron gate in the wall and Lizzie stepped up to it, prepared to go through and follow the path on the other side, but the gate was locked. It was bitter cold and the sky was beginning to darken. Lizzie felt a weight of sadness as she looked at the church and the tombstones surrounding it. All those people she was coming to know were there, she thought. She made her way slowly back to the house and plopped herself back into her chair.

The triptych was still standing up on the table and she looked at it again, and at the papers scattered around it. The poems were a mystery. She sat upright again, and spread them out in front of her, including the one written by Francis Hatton's sister, which was with the logbook pages. From the box where she had been consolidating them over the last few days, she took the other examples and laid them out as well. Placed alongside one another, they made an astonishing display.

The handwriting was all different, the papers were different, the poetic styles ranged from stilted to effusive. There were nine total. Two were on vellum, including the one in French. Another was on parchment, several were on heavy rag paper, and one was typed. They shared certain references to a love affair and a central question: "Where is his heart?" It seemed impossible, but Lizzie had to conclude that they were written many years, in fact many centuries apart. Four had a signature of some sort, and where it was distinguishable the names were similar, either the initials "E.H." or some form of "E. d'H." or "Elizabeth Hatton," the same name that appeared engraved on the stationery. Three had dates: 1382, 1780, 1887.

There was something so strange in this small pile of papers that it made Lizzie's hand shake slightly as she touched them. One by one she placed them on her scanner and created a computer file, as if by converting them into high-tech bits of data she could somehow dispel her discomfort. She tried to organize them chronologically, guessing the order in which they had been written based on her previous experience with manuscripts, but she quickly realized that her own field of expertise was too limited to material from the late eighteenth century to the present. She just couldn't be sure about anything other than that the French poem on vellum was probably the oldest and the typewritten text the most recent.

Who could she ask about this, she wondered? And was this really any of her business anyway? It certainly was beyond the scope of the project for which George Hatton had hired her. Did he know what these things were about? She looked again at the triptych lying on the table in front of her. It was an artistic masterpiece and certainly genuine. It had to be enormously valuable. Did George know it was hidden in that compartment?

Before she spoke to him about it, Lizzie decided to send a quick e-mail message to Jackie back at the St. Pat's College library. Maybe she would be able to find someone to date the manuscripts by their penmanship and poetry.

"Mo chara," she wrote,

> A mystery has emerged here at the stately home
> of Sir George Hatton. (I have managed to dodge *that*
> bullet, by the way. I have so far been able to be polite
> without being deferential to his Lordship!) I've been
> trying to process several centuries' worth of miscel-
> laneous papers. I'm not sure whether you, as my
> model librarian, would find it a dream-come-true or
> a nightmare, but there is certainly plenty of stuff here
> to intrigue and challenge an amateur archivist such as
> myself.
>
> For instance, what do you think of the attached? If
> I'm not mistaken, they range across several hundred
> years, yet seem remarkably similar in sentiment. Can
> you give me a sense of the dates of these? Under the
> image of each I have written a brief description of the
> paper. The handwritings are so distinctive that there
> must be a clue to the age there. What do you think?

> I await your thoughts with thanks.
> A chara,
> Lizzie :)

> P.S. Can you translate the French one for me, or find
> someone who can?

Lizzie sent the e-mail with her new file of scanned images attached. She had just finished reorganizing the material when George appeared at the library door. He wanted her to know he was back, he told her.

She stood up, shoving the small bits of paper into a file folder and laying it on top of the triptych. She wasn't ready to talk to him about it yet.

He offered her a drink, but she refused.

"I want to apologize to you about Richard," George stammered.

Lizzie had not thought even once about George's rude son since he left. "Please don't worry about it," she said. "We talked more civilly before he left."

Her host looked somewhat relieved. "It was uncharacteristic of him to be so loutish," he said.

Lizzie was not convinced that this was true and she made no response.

"It's very important to me that *you* do this project, Lizzie."

"Thank you, George. I appreciate that and I'll try to do a good job for you."

"I have no doubts about your abilities," he continued.

"How much will Richard be involved?" she asked hesitantly.

"He won't be involved in your part at all," George said emphatically. He offered her his arm to escort her to dinner, and she took it. His polite concern kept the conversation superficial, which was just as well. Lizzie didn't want to have to admit that she hadn't thought even once about Francis Hatton that day, and she wanted to think about her new discoveries for a bit before she asked George about them.

Chapter 11

Lizzie tried to go through some of the Pacific Ocean voyage narratives the next day, but she eventually lost interest and returned to her room to get her coat so that she could walk outside. On the way, she paused to look again at the large portrait of Francis Hatton with his brother and sister that stood on the central staircase of the house. Next to it was the portrait that Helen had told her was of the sister when she was a bit older. There was something remarkable about the sweet, pensive face of Eliza Hatton as Joshua Reynolds had painted her. Her auburn hair was swept up rather gently to the top of her head and several small flowers were woven into the soft curls. She held a straw bonnet in her left hand against her waist. There was a delicate lace scarf wrapped around her shoulders, which she held closed with her right hand. Just below that hand Lizzie thought she could see a necklace.

She couldn't be sure, but it looked very much like the gold-chained ruby she had seen illustrated in the triptych. She walked up and down several stairs, trying to get a better angle from which to see the details, but the details weren't there. The artist had suggested it, without actually showing it with any detail. It suddenly struck Lizzie that the Rossetti painting might have the same necklace and she went quickly to her room to look at it again.

There it was. There could be no mistaking it. The knight held a necklace out to the waking Elizabeth: the gold chain dangled from his hand, but in his palm was a red jewel or something like it.

Rossetti's knight wore the same armor and the same heraldic device that she had seen on her lover in the dream and later in the triptych. It must have been the source of it, she thought again, though she hadn't really taken the time to look closely at the painting until this moment. She viewed it from various distances, and from several different places in the room. Finally she took it from the wall and brought it over to the window, in the process remembering the manila envelope she had seen taped to the back of the canvas when George moved it in the library a few days before. She leaned it carefully against the wall and looked again at the envelope. The stiff old tape that held it to the canvas gave way easily as Lizzie slipped her finger under it. Inside were two pages of text typed on the letterhead of a London art gallery, and several folded newspaper articles.

"Wicked Ways of Well-to-Do Women!" read one of the headlines. The article was dated August 10, 1979, and described the partying, lurid affairs, exhibitionism, and drug use of several upper-class British girls and women. The newspaper was one of the English tabloids that published a picture of a topless woman every day. The text on Page One was entirely gossip; where it "continued on pg. 16A," Lizzie was surprised to see the Rossetti painting reproduced as an illustration.

"Naughty Daughter of Hengemont Manor Lord," was the caption.

> Lady Elizabeth Hatton, whose father, Sir John, was Lord of the Manor at Hengemont in Somerset, was one of the naughty misses of a century ago. She was a wild child at school, and a handful at home. Lady Elizabeth ran away to London at the tender age of eighteen and joined in on the fun and games of the 'Pre-Raphaelite Brotherhood,' a group of artistic geniuses who flaunted convention or anything that hinted at propriety.

Lizzie groaned.

The other two articles were no better. She unfolded the typed sheets and read a description of the painting as it was to appear in an auction catalogue.

"Rare and Valuable Painting by Dante Gabriel Rossetti," was the title.

Elizabeth Wakes from the Dream, 1868
by Dante Gabriel Rossetti (1828-1882)

The London-born Dante Gabriel Rossetti was a member of the group of artists known as the Pre-Raphaelite Brotherhood, formed in 1848 by Rossetti, William Holman Hunt, and John Everett Millais, under the influence of Ford Maddox Brown.

The artist William Morris, who joined the circle at a later date, introduced Rossetti to the subject of this painting, Lady Elizabeth Hatton, in 1867. Having lost his wife of two years in 1862, Rossetti was in a period of depression and failing health. Miss Hatton was, according to Morris, "haunted by remarkable dreams that brought on a melancholy state." Her tragic demeanor made her attractive to Rossetti, still mourning the loss of his wife, and he asked her to sit for this painting.

In 1870 Rossetti had the coffin of his young bride exhumed in order to recover and publish a volume of his poetry he had buried with her corpse. The resulting publicity and the poor critical response to the work sent a despondent Rossetti retreating to the countryside where he shared a home at Kelmscott with Morris. Miss Hatton was invited to join them and thereafter remained at Rossetti's side. She lived at his London home at 16 Cheyne Walk during his period of virtual isolation in 1877, and was with him at Birchington-on-Sea when he died in April, 1882. Miss Hatton returned to Rossetti's London house and lived there until her death in 1930 at the age of eighty-one.

There was more information on who had owned the painting, where it had been exhibited in the years since it was painted, and some quotations from reviewers who, for the most part, considered it to be among Rossetti's strongest work. He had certainly captured something in the expression of the sitter, Lizzie thought as she returned the envelope to the back of the canvas and hung the painting back on the wall.

Whatever fear she had felt earlier that there might be something to her dreams beyond her own fertile imagination began to fade. Here was the knight she had seen. She had always had an active imagination and a tendency to be suggestible. Suddenly a flood of memories came to mind of earlier dreams influenced by landscapes through which she traveled, by work she had done, and by books, movies, and television.

Lizzie decided to go back to work. She had already lost too much time on other things than the project for which she'd been hired. As she went downstairs, though, she couldn't help looking one more time at Eliza Hatton's portrait, and she wondered if there were others with the same jewel. "Okay," she told herself, "give it a few more hours just to put the whole thing behind you."

She found George looking for her in the library when she returned and gave him an update on where she stood with the project.

"I've transcribed the whole of the journal," she told him, "and it really is remarkable, one of the most detailed and interesting I've ever encountered."

"Including the pages that were removed from it?"

Lizzie told him that even without those missing pages it would be an important record of Cook's voyage; with them, it showed the humanity and complexity of Francis Hatton in exceptionally moving terms.

"And the objects?" he asked her.

"I've photographed and catalogued all of the artifacts that he collected in the Pacific," she said. "Logically, that would be the focus of a book or exhibit since his journal doesn't record the Asian or Indian Ocean parts of the voyage." She glanced up into the cabinet. "And he seemed to have lost his passion for collecting things on the return voyage, after he discovered Eltatsy's corpse. There are a few things from Indonesia that I would include, but the rest of the stuff seems to have been given to him by other people and not collected first hand."

They talked about how she would write up the material. George did not object to including the Eltatsy material. Neither of them mentioned Richard or his objections, though

Lizzie thought they were probably both thinking in that direction. She prodded him gently about the reference to the other corpse in Francis's letter to Eliza, but once again George declared ignorance or disinterest with an affected naiveté that was nonetheless quite firm.

"So what is left to do?" George asked her.

Lizzie had been wondering how to answer this question, especially since her interest had wandered somewhat in the last few days.

"Before I can write my own text, I need to fill in the biographical details about Francis's life, and especially to look at the subsequent voyages to the Pacific, to see if he was on one, or found a way to return the burial box and the Chilkat blanket." She paused for a moment. "Without knowing what happened to those items, there is a real hole in the story," she said finally.

George nodded. He seemed pleased with her progress and felt that she had accomplished a lot in a short period of time. "You've been working on this pretty hard since you got here," he said. "It hardly seems like you've left the library."

It was the perfect opening. Lizzie asked him if she could take a few hours that afternoon and look more closely at the collection of Hatton family pictures hanging around the house.

"Of course," he answered. "I'm sorry that I didn't think to offer that suggestion myself. Mrs. Jeffries has a catalogue of the paintings and can show you around." He called his housekeeper on the intercom and asked her to join them with the book.

"In the summertime, we open portions of the house to the public and Mrs. Jeffries is our tour guide," he explained. "The collection really is quite good. The Victoria and Albert Museum sent someone here to inventory the paintings about forty-five years ago so that they could be included in a big compendium of British art, and we benefitted by getting a catalogue for our own purposes."

"Do you mind if I take some pictures for my research?" Lizzie asked.

George agreed, apologizing again that he had never shown

her Francis Hatton's portrait. "Be sure to have Mrs. Jeffries point it out to you," he said.

"I've seen that Gainsborough portrait with his brother and sister," Lizzie said, "but Edmund mentioned that there was another one."

"And it has the boomerang in it."

Lizzie was surprised and pleased by the information. "Eighteenth-century portraits with ethnographic artifacts that can still be identified are very rare," she told George. Her enthusiasm for her subject matter was returning. "And I'm anxious to see what Francis looked like at an older age."

"He's not much older than in the other painting," George explained. "But it shows him at the age of the voyage." He invited her to make herself quite at home in any part of the house that interested her, an offer which he had never made before.

Helen was waiting for them to finish their conversation, and George turned and gestured for her to join them, instructing her to show Lizzie any portraits that interested her and especially "the Navy Room." He poured himself a glass of sherry and settled into one of the fireplace chairs with a newspaper as they left the room.

"Do you want the standard tour?" Helen asked, "or do you want to see the closets with the skeletons?"

"Skeletons please."

"Any place in particular that you would like to start?"

"Let's begin with that big Gainsborough on the landing."

They proceeded to the stairs and Helen handed Lizzie the catalogue as they talked. She read the description: *The Children of Sir John Hatton*, 1773, by Thomas Gainsborough," it said, echoing the title on the frame. The names and dates of each followed: "Richard (1750-80), Francis (1755-1845), Elizabeth (1760-81)." There was then some biographical information about Gainsborough and his prodigious output of portraits and landscapes.

The sketch on which this painting was based had been done here at Hengemont, when the artist lived nearby at Bath. A year later he had moved to London and become enormously fashionable. Lizzie was disappointed that there was not much information about the subjects of the painting. The three young aristocrats were painted sitting on and around a broken stone wall. Several tall trees were immediately behind them, and in the distance the ground sloped down to the edge of a large body of water.

"If you step up the last few stairs there," Helen said, "and look out the big window, you can see where they were posing."

"Thanks," Lizzie said, her reverie broken. "I'd like to do that in a minute." She looked again at the adjacent portrait of the girl, standing alone. The catalogue said it was painted by Sir Joshua Reynolds in London in 1781, the year the sitter died a tragic death.

"She died so young," Lizzie murmured.

"She jumped off the roof of this wing of the house as it was being constructed. . . ." Helen started the explanation without emotion, as if she had told the story a hundred times before to tourists, but as the words came out she seemed to become conscious of their meaning and trailed off into silence.

Lizzie was stunned. "She committed suicide?"

The housekeeper nodded and gave her a meaningful look. "Leapt from the scaffolding as I understand it."

Eliza, Frank Hatton's beloved sister, had committed suicide, just as that older Elizabeth had. Lizzie looked again at the date, 1781. He must have been here at the time. What could have happened?

"Do you know why?" she asked.

Helen shook her head. "But I told you already that many of these Hatton girls were cursed with madness."

Lizzie tried hard to keep from imagining Eliza's broken body laying on the stones of the terrace, her brother kneeling beside her, insane with grief. She turned back to the Gainsborough. "And the older brother died rather young too, didn't he?" Lizzie looked again at the catalogue; Richard Hatton had been thirty years old.

"Yes, and without a son," Helen said. "That's why your Lieutenant there, his brother, left the Navy and became Lord of the Manor." She seemed pleased to bring the conversation back to Francis Hatton.

"Of course," Lizzie said softly. In the portrait the three seemed at ease, as if problems could not touch their lives of wealth and position. Eight years later two of them would be dead.

"The older brother," Lizzie continued, "how did he die?"

"I'm not exactly sure, but I believe it was some contagious disease," Helen answered. "It was he that worked on the design of this wing with the architect Robert Adam," she continued. "He had great plans for Hengemont, and he and his father dedicated an enormous amount of time and money to it."

"How terrible for the parents to lose two children in two years."

"I believe the mother was dead more than ten years by that time, and the father did not long survive the daughter."

"And all these tragedies began while the younger son was still in the Pacific."

Helen was silent, as if acknowledgement was unnecessary.

"But Francis certainly lived to a ripe old age," Lizzie added, looking again at the handsome face of the young man. He would have been eighteen years old at the time of this portrait.

"Aye, and there's another picture of him." Helen added that in the other portrait Francis Hatton was wearing his uniform. Lizzie knew it must be the picture George and Edmund had mentioned. She expressed her desire to see it next, but before they left the staircase asked if Helen could tell what was under Eliza Hatton's hand in the Reynolds' portrait.

The housekeeper did what Lizzie had done a few hours earlier, walking up two stairs and then down two stairs to see if she could get a better perspective. "You know," she said, "for all his fame, I find that Reynolds was not all that clear on the details, excepting the faces."

"Do you think it could be a ruby necklace?" Lizzie asked.

"It certainly could be," Helen answered. "In several of the other pictures there are women wearing such a stone." Again, her sentence lapsed into sudden silence, as if she had caught herself in an explanation that took her by surprise.

Lizzie felt a tingle of excitement. "After we see Lieutenant

Hatton in his uniform," she asked, trying to make her voice sound casual, "would you mind pointing out those paintings to me?" She sensed that Helen was becoming alarmed at her interest and looked up to find the housekeeper looking at her with a motherly concern.

"Lizzie," she started.

"Yes?"

"May I ask again why you want to know about these women?"

Lizzie was starting to lose patience with this recurring theme of Helen's. "I've already told you it is simply curiosity at what seems to be an interesting story," she said, trying not to sound exasperated.

"You don't fear that you are falling into something dangerous here?"

Lizzie thought about the two vivid dreams she had had, but was able to give Helen a reassuring smile as she shook her head and asked to continue the tour.

Helen agreed. She led Lizzie down the hall to the room directly above the library, where they found the life-sized portrait of Lieutenant Francis Hatton in the blue-coated uniform of the Royal Navy. It had been painted in 1775, the year before he departed on his voyage to the Pacific. The catalogue explained that the artist, Nathaniel Dance, painted numerous portraits of naval officers in the late eighteenth century, including a famous one of Captain Cook, the commander of the expedition on which Francis Hatton made his collection.

This was a very different Francis than the one in the Gainsborough portrait on the main staircase. Then, Frank had been eighteen, posing with his brother and sister. Now, at twenty, he looked as if he had made the transition from boy to man and was bound on the great adventure of his life. His eyes seemed to shine in anticipation and his lips were almost breaking into a smile. He stood beside a table on which sat a chart, a telescope, a large shell, and the boomerang, which Lizzie recognized from his cabinet—the gift of Joseph Banks from the first Cook expedition. Through a window behind him two ships were visible in a harbor. He looked straight out from the portrait into Lizzie's eyes. His hair was soft and curling, long enough on the sides to touch the embroidered collar of his uniform, and pulled into a ponytail in the back. Lizzie thought she could detect a resemblance to Edmund.

Next to the portrait of Francis was one of his uncle, also a naval officer, and also painted by Dance. Though painted in the same decade, the two men were clearly from different generations. The older man wore a white wig, curled up along the bottom edge. Where Frank was lithe, this man was bluff and heavy. He leaned one hand on a sword and looked down to the right corner of the painting. Behind him a red curtain was swept back to reveal a large frigate, probably the vessel he commanded when this portrait was painted.

These two paintings were in a large hall which Helen told Lizzie was called the "Navy Gallery." In addition to the pictures, the room had a number of ship models, dozens of swords, some uniforms on mannequins with numerous additional hats mounted around them, and even two small cannons. So many Hatton men had been officers in the Royal Navy that their portraits covered the walls almost from floor to ceiling, with gaps filled in only occasionally by the unusually stern-looking women who were presumably their wives. Lizzie began to leaf through the printed guide to identify some of them, and Helen explained that the female portraits were only placed in this hall if they had been painted as the other half of a pair of matching portraits with their naval husbands.

"You could write a history of changes in Royal Navy uniforms across the centuries and illustrate it with the pictures in this room," Lizzie said to Helen.

"You could," she answered. "And of hairdos too."

Lizzie nodded her agreement. They strolled along the length of the room. Sometimes the subject of a portrait was depicted standing on a ship, his hand upon the railing, the planking of the deck visible beneath his buckled shoes. Sometimes the sailor was unaccountably shown standing in a pastoral landscape of meadows, hills, and trees, but in the distance a ship was in a harbor and in the man's hand was a telescope, as if he was just itching to finish posing, turn around, and check out the seafaring activity behind him.

A few of the men were depicted leaning on anchors; several

held their uniform hats in one hand, a sword in the other. One of them wore a cape that was gathered up into one hand across his waist. His other hand, just visible beneath the cape, rested on the hilt of a sword. A few of the pictures had more than one subject, usually a pair of brothers in matching uniforms. One showed a father in the uniform of a captain, examining a small ship model with his sailor-suited son.

The paintings were hung in roughly chronological order, and Lizzie was fascinated as she watched long wigs be replaced by hair that grew and was cut as decades passed. Facial hair ranged from clean-shaven to full beards, with every possible combination of sideburns, moustaches, and beards in between. Uniform collars and cuffs showed a full range of evolution. Some collars rose up to mid cheek, others were invisible beneath a row of gold braid or embroidery. Cuffs went from simple and unadorned to large and elegant, folded back all the way to the elbow and elaborately secured with rows of buttons. Scarves of black or white alternated with ruffled cravats for covering the necks of the uniformed men in the pictures. There were sashes and epaulets, loops of gold braid, and medals galore, some hanging on ribbons around the neck, others pinned to the chest. Several of the Hatton officers wore the Star of the Garter—the highest rank one could achieve in England.

Lizzie spent a bit of time examining the models and a case of navigating instruments in the center of the room. Several of the same instruments could be seen in the paintings where the subject, like Frank Hatton, exhibited them nearby or held them in a gloved hand. There were globes and charts, sextants and telescopes.

"It's a fabulous collection!" Lizzie said with enthusiasm.

Helen nodded.

As they headed to the far end of the room, Lizzie saw two framed photographs, one from each of the two World Wars, and each with a pair of brothers. In the more recent one, two handsome young men wearing the white dress uniforms of the period looked confidently into the camera. They had small fair moustaches, ruddy cheeks, and straight white teeth. Lizzie wondered where they were today.

The photographs reminded Lizzie that she wanted to document some of the portraits with her own camera. She asked Helen if she would mind waiting while she ran to her room to get it. Lizzie made a quick trip down the hall and around the corner to her own room and was back within five minutes. She snapped a picture of the large Naval painting of Francis Hatton and then asked again about the necklace. She already knew of three portraits in which it appeared, but were there others?

Helen looked at her watch and then leafed through the catalogue. "If you don't mind, Lizzie," she said, "I'll tell you which ones I think are worth looking at, and let you stroll around a bit on your own. I have some other things I need to do today." She seemed torn between needing to be elsewhere and worrying about leaving Lizzie on her own. "Are you sure you'll be okay?"

When Lizzie assured her that she would, Helen laid the catalogue on one of the exhibit cases and opened it to a floor plan of the house. "It should be pretty clear where you are if you use this as a guide," she said, turning the booklet so that Lizzie could see it as she pointed out the pertinent spots. "Two of the paintings are in the Tudor wing of the house, one upstairs and one downstairs." She nodded toward the far door of the room they stood in. "You'll get to it most easily by continuing straight on through there."

She described a route through the house and traced it with her finger on the diagram. It would take Lizzie to the end of the Tudor wing on the floor they were on. At the end of that wing she could go downstairs and then double back on the ground floor. That would bring her to the west end of the old gothic extension on the west side of the tower. Helen called the large room there the "salon," and told her there were several large portraits hanging there, including, she thought, one of a woman wearing a similar necklace.

Lizzie thanked her for her help. "You're sure it's no problem for me to be wandering around on my own?" she asked.

Helen assured her that all of the places she mentioned were "more or less public" areas of the house. "You won't need to go poking into any of the family's private rooms," she said, though as soon as she said it she seemed to have another thought. "Though, now that I think of it," she said slowly, "there is a picture in Sir George's study of his sister, and if I'm not mistaken she is also wearing a ruby necklace."

Lizzie remembered that Edmund had told her that his father's younger sister, Bette, had first related to him the story of Elizabeth and John.

"Do you think I could see the picture?"

"Well if we go in quickly, I don't think Sir George will mind," Helen answered, "and it's right on the way. He keeps his rooms in the Tudor wing."

Lizzie followed the housekeeper through the door at the far end of the Navy Gallery and into the room beyond it. She hadn't yet been in the Tudor wing of the house and the feeling was very different. The ceilings were lower, the exposed beams carved and dark. The walls were covered with a similarly dark-stained carved paneling. George Hatton's study was in the first room they came to. It faced into the courtyard at the corner of the building. It was an old-fashioned man's sort of room, with leather chairs and heavy furniture; the big leather-topped mahogany desk was neatly organized, with papers filed into all the various cubbyholes. The windows were made up of small diamonds of leaded glass set into arched stone casements. The room was smaller and darker than Lizzie would have expected the owner of the house to choose as his sanctuary, especially with such a large and diverse selection, but she liked the room and liked him more for having chosen it. Helen sensed her curiosity.

"Sir George moved back into this part of the house after his wife died," she said. "This and the adjoining room were his as a child."

Such private information made Lizzie feel a bit like an intruder, and she was glad to turn her attention to the framed picture Helen held out to her. It was a color photograph taken in the garden at Hengemont on an autumn day and was inscribed across the lower right corner, "To George—A great brother. All my love, Bette."

The girl in the picture had long straight strawberry-blond hair, parted in the middle and falling almost to her waist.

Lizzie loved her outfit; as a girl she had been a big fan of mod Londoners, and Bette's clothes in this picture were just the sort of thing that Mary Quant had designed and Twiggy had worn in the late sixties. Lizzie was too young then to be mod, but she remembered her older sisters trying hard to get their mother to let them wear something just like this. Bette's short dress was covered with a design of large flowers in pink, green, and white. She wore textured tights on her slim legs, and white leather boots up to her knees. In one hand she held a white leather hat with a clear plastic visor, and around her neck she wore several strings of large and small beads, and the ruby necklace.

"I didn't expect her to be so young," Lizzie said, handing the picture back. "Where is she now?"

"She died long ago," Helen said sadly, looking at the girl in the picture as she placed it back on the top of George's desk. "Not long after this was taken I think."

Lizzie noticed there were other family photographs there. One showed George with a woman who must have been his late wife. Others showed the two of them with three boys in different stages of growth, and another showed a larger extended family, the boys now husbands and fathers with their own families. She recognized Edmund through the whole series. She wanted to step up and look more closely at his wife, but Helen was leading the way out of the room and Lizzie knew it would be unseemly to stay and probe the family's personal business in this way.

As they stood together in the hallway, Helen hesitated, then said one last thing to Lizzie about the Hatton women.

"I know this is an interesting story, Lizzie," she said, "but there is some danger for women with Hatton blood and I hope you will be careful."

Lizzie looked as closely as she could at Helen in the dim light. The woman had finally said what she had wanted to say for several days.

"And you think I'm susceptible?" Lizzie asked.

"I do."

"Because I have ancestors named Hatton?"

Helen nodded.

Lizzie tried to laugh off Helen's concerns, though she knew the older woman was completely serious. She stepped forward and kissed her on the cheek.

"Thanks Helen," she said. "I will be careful."

Helen was thoughtful for a moment as she looked at Lizzie, but finally seemed somewhat relieved, at least at having said her piece.

"This is a dark hallway for picture viewing," Helen said, pointing the way for Lizzie as she pulled the door to George's room closed behind her, "but I think the picture that will interest you on this floor is fortunately near one of the lamps."

After double-checking to be sure that Lizzie was oriented on the floor plan and knew where she was going, Helen disappeared through a door in the paneling that Lizzie hadn't even noticed. She looked down the long hallway. About halfway down were two recessed areas where windows allowed daylight in, but most of the way was lit by wall sconces that must have been made originally for candles and were, over the years, converted first to gas fixtures and then to electricity. Now they had little flame-shaped bulbs that flickered and gave a very inadequate light. A few narrow tables had been added over the years and a more modern lamp sat on each of them.

Helen had indicated that there was an interesting portrait near the first of the tables on the right. Lizzie moved slowly, occasionally reaching out to touch the paneling, which looked satiny-smooth. The doors, all closed and surprisingly short, came at irregular intervals, each set into a carved casement with a gothic arch. There were some pictures hanging here and there but it was too dark to see them clearly.

When she finally came to the table indicated by Mrs. Jeffries, Lizzie paused and looked more closely at a matching set of six small portraits. According to the catalogue, they were the "Six children of Sir Richard Hattin, 1520." Five of them were boys, ranging in age from about ten to mid-twenties, and all of them had the Hatton coat of arms painted above their heads in the upper left corner of the painting. Over their shoulders in the right corner was a legend giving their name. The last painting Lizzie came to was the one she sought and

fortunately it was nearest to the table. By moving the lampshade slightly, she was able to bring the painting clearly into
view. It was quite small, only about the size of a book. The
carved frame seemed massive on the small painting; Lizzie
guessed that the frame had an area of wood that was at least
equal to the square inches of canvas.

It took a few minutes for her eyes to adjust from the darkness of the hall to the pool of light that now flooded the painting. The subject looked young and very petite and was shown
from the waist up, sitting in a dusky interior. The name "Elizabeth Hattin" and the date 1520 were written in a dark gold
script, as if on the wall behind her. She wore a dark dress with
an inset of embroidery below the square neckline. The bodice
was quite flat, the sleeves puffed out with some additional
material that was set beneath a slash in the fabric, and then
retied with small gold cords. Her face was small and delicate,
and appeared very pale against the darkness of the paneling
behind her. Her auburn hair was parted in the middle and
combed under a headpiece that rose to a gentle ridge above
her forehead and had a short dark veil attached. The gold
chain was around her neck, the ruby dangling from her long
fingers as she held it up for the viewer. There was no artist's
signature and the catalogue identified it only as "Sixteenth
Century English School."

Lizzie was glad she had a digital camera, because she knew
it would be hard to get a good picture here. She tried to angle
the lampshade and position herself so that the flash of the
camera wouldn't reflect off the paint of the portrait. After
three attempts, the image in her viewer was clear enough to
make her feel that she had at least documented the painting
for her growing collection—though what the collection was
for was not yet clear.

She reached the halfway point of the hallway, where the
architect had sacrificed the rooms that otherwise would have
appeared on either side of the hall in order to bring some natural light into the gloomy atmosphere. A gabled window was
on either side of the corridor and it was consequently a large,
light, and airy space; even the ceiling was higher here. This
was the feature that gave this wing of the house the unique

silhouette Lizzie had noticed from her own room across the courtyard, with sections stepped back from the main wall of the house.

She walked to the window on that side and looked across to find the windows of her own room, then crossed to the other side of the hall and looked out over the scattered fields toward the town of Hengeport and the sea. There was the small, square-towered Norman church that she had seen from the gate in the garden. This wing of the house blocked the view of it from both her room and the library, so she was glad to get such a good view of it from here. Gravestones circled it on all sides. Frank Hatton and his sister were probably buried there, and she was determined to get there before she left.

She continued to the end of the hall and found the steep and rather narrow staircase that was indicated on the floor plan.

On the ground floor she found that there was no central hallway, but rather a series of three large rooms, each the full width of the wing and consequently well lit with windows on opposite walls. At one time these must have been parlors or dining rooms, but Lizzie wasn't sure how the various wings of the house had been used when they were built. The Hattons were clearly a large family in Tudor times, if the six children depicted upstairs were any indication. She passed from the first room into the second. They were sparsely furnished and there was a museum feeling to this part of the house. Identical paneling, flooring, and lighting fixtures were in each of the rooms, and each had a large fireplace and several gigantic paintings.

In the second room Lizzie quickly identified the painting that Helen had sent her here to see. It was taller than life size and again was part of a set, described in the catalogue as three siblings. On one side of the young woman's portrait was a painting of a handsome young man, on the other that of an adolescent boy. Lizzie stepped up close to the central painting to read the label: "Lady Elizabeth Hatton, 1601, by Robert Peake." She then stepped back to the middle of the room to get the full effect. It was a very striking portrait.

Lizzie had to wonder if the young woman was as beautiful

as she was painted, or if Mr. Peake had given her a gift in the portrait, but she was stunning. She had reddish-brown hair pulled straight back from her face and fixed on top of her head in an elaborate sculpture of curls that incorporated a delicate gold net that looked a bit like a halo. Her elegant gown was thick with embroidery. Behind her head a stiff, lace-edged collar spread out like a fan. The neckline had a triangle cut out of it with its top point at her throat and the bottom edge just low enough to suggest cleavage, without actually showing any. The ruby of the necklace rested in that space, one of several gems that she wore in addition to several long strands of pearls, but it was unmistakable. Lizzie snapped a picture of it, then turned around and took in the whole of the room. There were several chairs with high, carved wooden backs and she went to sit in one of them.

When she had been in the medieval hall a few nights before, she had felt the powerful feeling of history, but not so strongly the attraction of wealth. In this room she wondered what it would be like to live like the woman in Peake's portrait. Helen clearly thought Lizzie was related to this family, and Lizzie couldn't resist indulging in the fantasy, if only for the several minutes that she sat in this room. To be relieved of all financial burdens, to have all the unpleasant tasks of life taken care of by others, to wear such clothes. She stood and imagined herself in such a gown. It must have been terribly uncomfortable she thought. The stiff bodice bound her breasts tightly, the large skirts weighed a ton! She smiled to herself; perhaps it was not such a comfortable life after all.

She proceeded on through the last room of the Tudor wing and into the older gothic wing that joined it at right angles, then took out the floor plan to see where she was. On the floor above, she had reached this spot from the Navy Gallery, which was above the library, but on this floor Francis Hatton's cabinet had been built into the doorway that would originally have provided access from here to the Adam wing of the house, and consequently she could only proceed on to the big salon. She had formerly glimpsed this room from the other end when she first came into the house and had thought then that it resembled a hotel lobby. This was the first time she had actually been in the room and it was much more subtle than she had acknowledged at first.

This was part of the first addition made to the original castle, and though it had been extensively restored in the Victorian period, it still had several of the original gothic features. A huge stone fireplace was at the center of the longest wall; opposite it was a bank of windows, which must have been quite tiny when first built, but had been enlarged over time and now gave the room a spacious and airy feeling. The difference between this and the dark tight quarters of the Tudor part of the building was remarkable.

There were three large tapestries in this room, and several paintings. Lizzie gravitated to the only portrait of a young woman, and again referred to the catalogue to see who the subject was.

"This is becoming a bit familiar," she said to herself as she read the entry in the catalogue: "*Lady Elizabeth Hatton at Nineteen*, painted in 1717 by Godfrey Kneller." This young woman stood looking back at the viewer over her shoulder, her elaborate red and gold gown falling in pleats from an embroidered band that stretched between her small shoulders. She appeared to be wearing a wig, and the jewel and chain were woven into it, along with a strand of pearls and several ribbons; the point of the ruby just touched the top of her forehead. Lizzie took a picture of the painting and then proceeded into the central medieval hall.

She shivered a bit when she thought of finding herself there the night before last. She took a deep breath and determined to study the tapestries in the hall and concentrate her efforts on looking at the swords, spears, and shields mounted high on the wall in decorative patterns, and at faded banners hung on angled poles from the musicians' gallery. There were only a few minutes left before dinner to look into the big formal dining room across the hall from the salon, and then she hurried back to her room to change her clothes. As she went up the big staircase she looked again at the Gainsborough and Reynolds portraits. She took a picture of Eliza Hatton, then went to her room where she put the camera into the drawer of the bedside table. Tomorrow she would load all of the pictures into her computer and print out copies so that she could compare them.

"And then what?" Lizzie asked herself. "What am I going to do with them?"

When she returned to her room again after dinner she went once more to the windows. It had become her habit to stand here each evening before going to bed. Orion was high up in the sky, followed by the bright light of its companion star, Sirius. There were still lights on all over the house, several of them in windows high up on a third floor. "Those must belong to the Jeffries," Lizzie thought. Across in the Tudor wing she could now identify George's study, which had a lamp burning, and the center hall on the second floor, where there was also a light.

Where did Edmund sleep when he was at Hengemont, she wondered?

Chapter 12

The next day Lizzie rose very early and dressed carefully. She was feeling somewhat agitated. She felt that she had had another disturbing dream, but could not remember any details. Edmund would be her companion today and she had been thinking about him a great deal, seeking his likeness in portraits of his ancestors.

She managed to get to the library without Helen's notice. When she turned on her computer, a response from Jackie was waiting.

> Showed those manuscripts you forwarded to your old mentor in the English Dept., Prof. Brandon. In the attachment you'll find the notes we made about possible dates, etc. These are our top-of-the head reactions, but as I sensed a note of urgency underneath your jovial tone a quick response seemed desirable. Andy and I will continue to look at them though. This is a very strange and interesting collection. That French piece is rather garbled (and a really old style of French!). It seems to be some sort of ode to a dead lover, and anxiety over the whereabouts of his corpse. I'm going to stop over to the French department with it and get you a more exact translation.

Lizzie opened the attached file and printed a copy. It was her scanned images of the manuscript poems, now organized chronologically and covered with notes from Jackie and from Andy Brandon, whose nearly illegible scrawl she had long ago learned to decipher. With the poems three to a page the text was too small to read easily, so she printed out a file with each poem on a separate page and laid them out in the order suggested by her colleagues, placing the manuscript poems over the scanned image on each page.

On the one in French, Andy had scrawled "definitely the oldest, probably late thirteenth or early fourteenth century" and Jackie had added "I agree" and her initials. The other vellum document came next, with its date of 1382. The single line "Where is his heart?" was considered by both Andy and Jackie to be from the Tudor period, though they did not agree on a precise date and Lizzie could only conclude from their rambling commentary back and forth that it was from between 1500 and 1600, which she wrote quickly on the printout.

On the piece of paper that had been used to hold the feathers from the Hawaiian helmet, Andy had written "ca. 1700," and again Jackie wrote and initialed "I agree." Eliza's poem from 1780 was next in the order, followed by the two poems which Lizzie had found rather mediocre upon first reading, but on a second time through found both pain and passion in them. One was "early to mid nineteenth century" according to Jackie and Andy, the other had the date 1887 written by the author on the bottom of the page. As she picked up the more recent of the two to lay it on top of its printed image, Lizzie noticed a faded line on the reverse side in pencil. "Written on the occasion of the death of my beloved niece, Elizabeth— October 17, 1887." Lizzie laid it gently down again.

Across the last item seen by her friends in Boston, Jackie had written in her neat librarian's hand: "The font used on this stationery was popular at the end of the nineteenth century." Lizzie wondered if the author of this poem was the niece memorialized in the last poem, which lay next to it on the table.

She hadn't sent Jackie the typescript poem, but she placed it in the lineup as well. The text reminded her of the "Beat" poets of the fifties and sixties. "What is a man?" it started. "And what is a woman?" A series of other questions followed: "What is love?" "Is love real?" An interesting follow-up comparison between a man's heart and his penis made the whole question of which organ he was missing all the more intriguing.

Lizzie put her palms on the edge of the table and leaned over the bits of paper now arranged before her. She looked from one to the other and back again. There seemed to be one from every century from the thirteenth to the middle of the twentieth. They were all by women and they all seemed to be named Elizabeth Hatton, or something similar. It hit her suddenly that the portraits were also all of women with that name. She ran back to her room to get her camera, and quickly snapped a picture of the Rossetti painting while she was there.

When she returned to the library her heart was beating fast and the hair on her arms was standing up. She slipped the disk from the camera into her computer and hit the print button. As the photographs began to roll out of her printer, she went again to the cabinet and took out the triptych. The letter said it was a "depiction of specific people and events of the middle thirteenth century, but painted about 150-200 years later." She decided to put it first in the sequence she was building. She wasn't sure whether the woman in it was the one who wrote the oldest poem or not, but she placed the two poems on vellum next to the triptych, the one in French first, the one in the old-style English next.

There were two portraits of Elizabeths wearing the ruby necklace from the reign of the Tudors, dated 1520 and 1601. Either of these women could have written that enigmatic line "Where is his heart?" but Lizzie didn't know which one. Jackie and Andy had left a span of dates that included them both.

The poem from "ca. 1700" Lizzie paired up with the portrait hanging in the salon, which was painted by Kneller and dated 1717. Francis Hatton's sister Eliza was easy to match between poem and portrait.

Helen stopped in at about seven-thirty, surprised to find Lizzie up and working so early.

"Do you want breakfast or coffee?" she asked as she came into the room.

Lizzie stood to block Helen's view of the table. She knew

that she might find the assemblage of photos and poems placed together on the table evidence that Lizzie had fallen prey to the "Hatton family curse," and she simply did not want to engage in that conversation again.

"Thanks for the offer," Lizzie said, trying to sound casual, "but I'm good till lunch." She waited for Helen to leave before she turned her attention back to the items on the table.

The next painting in order was the Rossetti, the subject of which must also have been the author of the poem dedicated to the dead niece. If the information in the material that went along with the painting was correct, this Elizabeth Hatton was the only one of the group to live past her twenties, and her poem had been written when she was thirty-four. Instead of wearing the ruby in the painting, she was reaching for it as it was clutched in the hand of the vanishing knight. There was no picture of the young woman who had been memorialized by her aunt, but she must have been the owner of the engraved stationery.

The last items referred to George's sister who had undoubtedly composed the typewritten poem and must also have been the author of the diary.

"I wonder what happened to her," Lizzie thought. Helen had said that she had also died young.

Lizzie had no idea what any of it meant, but it obviously meant something. Time passed quickly as she went over and over the links between the women, until she heard voices in the hall and Helen returned to tell her that Edmund and Lily had arrived and would soon be joining George for lunch. Lizzie glanced at her watch; it was eleven-thirty. She had spent more than four hours in frenzied activity and hadn't once thought about Francis Hatton.

Lily's clear voice rang through the hall. Lizzie quickly gathered up the triptych, diary, and manuscript poems and returned them to their hiding place in the cabinet. The computer printouts she slipped into a file folder. She wasn't ready to share all this with either Edmund or George. They probably knew about it already anyway, and it was not the history she had been hired to write. She was closing her files and shutting down her computer when Lily came into the library.

Lizzie couldn't resist grabbing her into a warm hug, and Lily hugged back.

The two of them strolled hand in hand from the library into the hall and from there into the medieval part of the house, the big room that had been Lizzie's first interior glimpse of Hengemont and which she had only been in a few times since. Her midnight excursion there was now seeming more and more like a dream and less and less frightening.

"I love this room," Lily said.

"Why do you love it so much?"

"Because it's so old!"

"That is exactly why I love it too," Lizzie exclaimed, squeezing the little girl's hand. They talked for several minutes about history, as Lily pointed out her favorite things in the big medieval hall, and they continued their conversation as they went to join George and Edmund for lunch.

"There you are!" George called out to Lily. "I hope you weren't bothering Dr. Manning."

"Not at all," Lizzie said. "She is a very knowledgeable guide to the house."

George asked Lizzie if she was finding the research interesting today. She was embarrassed by the question. She was finding her work today exceedingly interesting, but it was not the work he thought she was doing.

The atmosphere at lunch was warm and lively. Lizzie felt herself drawn into conversation by turns with each of the Hattons. Again she couldn't help but notice how attractive Edmund was, not just physically, but as a person. He had good relationships with his father and daughter, was obviously very smart, and if his father's reports were correct also had a social conscience and a generous spirit. She blushed when she thought about the dream she had had about him, but kept up an animated exchange with him all through the meal.

Edmund offered to refill Lizzie's coffee cup and poured one for himself as well. "You've probably noticed that my father drinks tea," he said smiling, "but I've been converted to American ways."

"I believe morning coffee to be our greatest gift to the English people," Lizzie said as she thanked him.

"And as a gesture of thanks for all my countrymen, I shall finally give you the tour of the house and grounds that I have been promising."

"But it's too cold today for the outside part of your tour," George said. He looked at Lizzie.

"I've already put it off too many times," Edmund began, "and if we don't do it today I don't know when I'll get back to do it." He looked at Lizzie. "We'll start inside and if it gets any warmer move outside later."

George seemed to think it was a good plan, and he explained to Lizzie that he and Lily would be gone for the rest of the day. "We're going into Bath to visit an old friend of mine."

Edmund seemed like such a good dad, Lizzie thought as she watched him bundle his daughter up for her car trip through the snowy countryside. When the good-byes had finally been said, the house seemed quiet. Edmund heaved a mock sigh of relief and they began their tour.

Hengemont was a very different place as seen through the eyes of Edmund Hatton, who had grown up there and obviously loved the old house. No catalogue or floor plan could capture the life of the place as he did. As he pointed out portraits, he told Lizzie amusing anecdotes about his ancestors. He had a good knowledge of his family history without letting pride in his genealogy make him prejudiced in an examination of it. They shared personal information as they moved from room to room. She told him about her teaching, and about Martin's work as an artist. He described some of the traveling he had done, working as a volunteer physician in Africa. Lizzie learned that Edmund was divorced from Lily's mother. She was again impressed with both his intelligence and his good humor and the time passed quickly.

They spent a fair bit of time in the Navy Gallery, and when they went from there into the Tudor wing, Lizzie asked him about the panel through which Helen had disappeared on her earlier tour. He showed her the catch disguised behind a border of the paneling and the door swung silently open. Behind it was a narrow staircase going up and down.

"Above us are the Jeffries' rooms," he said. "Below us the big Tudor galleries."

"Was this designed as some kind of secret passage?" she asked, intrigued.

"Are you picturing Jacobites hiding here during the Rebellion?"

She smiled with delight. "No, I was hoping it might be priests lying low with the relics of saints during Henry VIII's destruction of the monasteries," she answered. "Or pirates coming up from the Bristol Channel to store their booty."

Edmund laughed. "I'm sorry to tell you it is not as intriguing as either of those options. There are passages all over the house that were built to allow the servants to get around without being seen."

Lizzie lost her jovial tone. "Really?"

He answered her with more seriousness. "Not only in the house. There is a tunnel that runs from outside the wall of the estate directly to the kitchen. It made it possible for servants to come and go without passing through the garden."

She thought about this for several moments, remembering how much she had felt the change of station just going from the kitchen into the dining room. The idea that the Hattons had gone to such elaborate efforts to keep their servants from cluttering up the landscape was absolutely disgusting to her.

"Was this an invention unique to Hengemont?" she asked.

He shook his head. "All of the big old houses have them," he said, sensing her discomfort. "It's not the proudest part of the family history, but it made for some very interesting games of hide-and-seek with my brothers."

He nudged her gently with his arm in an attempt to restore her good humor, and looked at her with a smile so warm that Lizzie could not help smiling back.

"Do you want to see the best of the secret passages?" he offered.

When she accepted, he led her back to the big double staircase in the Adam wing of the house. Though she had gone up and down it several times each day during her stay at Hengemont, she had never noticed a door there, well-disguised in the paneling. It opened onto another set of stairs, much steeper and narrower than the public one. Edmund found the light switch and led her up behind the wall on which the Gainsborough painting hung.

"This wing of the house was attached directly to the old Norman tower," he explained, pointing out the small round stones that formed one wall of the staircase.

One of the niches that had formed a window in the original tower had been widened into a doorway at the top of the stairs, and they passed into the musicians' gallery above the main medieval hall.

Lizzie couldn't help recalling her first dream as she looked down onto the stone floor below her. It had begun with a climb up to the top of the Norman tower with Edmund. She wobbled a bit, then blushed when she saw that he was looking at her.

"Are you all right?" he asked.

"Steep climb," she said. "I'm just a little out of breath."

"Do you want to sit down for a minute?"

She shook her head and then asked, somewhat nervously, "Can you get up to the top of the tower from here?"

He showed her the door that led to the next set of stairs. A sturdy iron bar had been mounted on it and was secured with a padlock. "I don't know where the key is," he said apologetically. "I'll run down and ask Mrs. Jeffries about it if you want me to, but it's kind of a cold and snowy day to go up on the roof."

She shook her head again and tried to smile. He led her back down the stairs, explaining as they went that he hadn't been up on the roof since he was a boy. They went back to the library and he pointed out some of the features visible across the terrace. The sun was low in the sky and it was snowing lightly; they decided to put off the tour of the grounds until the next day.

"I'd love to see the church if that's possible."

He told her there was a monument there to Francis Hatton and she expressed her eagerness to see it. They settled into the chairs in front of the fireplace and he offered to pour her a drink.

"Only club soda," she said. "The last time we sat here drinking I suffered for it the next day."

They spent the evening talking about the various places

to which they had traveled, of Alaska and Africa, and of the nature of the world in their time. There was no talk of a past that did not include themselves. When they parted he gave her a quick kiss on the lips and it felt very natural.

• • • • •

It was very late, past midnight, but Lizzie could not sleep. The three scenes from the triptych were stuck in her head like a bad song that could not be dispelled. She put on her bathrobe and tiptoed downstairs. Throughout the house there were small lights on and she was able to get to the library without difficulty. She went to the cabinet and took the triptych and Bette's diary back to her room.

Sitting on the bed, Lizzie once again looked carefully at the triptych. She had to angle the shade of her lamp to illuminate it and when the light was just right, the bright reds, blues, yellows, and gold sparkled with the reflected light. The details of the faces, though tiny, were wonderful and filled with expression. Lizzie pulled out her magnifying glass and studied each panel again, starting with the meeting of the lovers on the castle tower.

"This has to be the Norman part of this house," she thought, rising and going to the window. Most of the time when she had looked out the window she'd concentrated her gaze downhill toward the sea, but now she looked back in the other direction. The moon was almost full, bright white, and high in the sky across the Bristol Channel. The outline of the castle was illuminated perfectly. Lizzie held the small painting next to the window at eye level and looked from it to the silhouette of the castle roof. There was no doubt that the meeting between the lovers depicted in the painting was set on that tower. She felt a thrill of discovery followed by another, tinged with fear, at the memory of her own dream, which had also been set there.

She went back to the bed and pulled out Bette's diary. She had until now avoided looking at it. Now she scanned a few entries in the middle; they were filled with romantic and sexual fantasies. Lizzie closed the book. It felt like an invasion of privacy, but she rationalized that this was what historians did—invade the privacy of dead people. Her curiosity was so great that she knew she would be unable to concentrate on the business at hand if she didn't put this mystery behind her. She opened the diary again.

"I write this at the advice of Doctor Stuart," it began, "but whether I will actually ever share its contents with him or not is uncertain. It is becoming increasingly clear that my family thinks I am mentally ill."

Lizzie closed the book again. This really was a very personal chronicle and the woman who wrote it had lived in her own lifetime. That safe distance of centuries or even decades was missing. There was no excuse that she was a historian doing research; this was prying, uninvited, into someone else's painful secrets. She sat for several minutes and then opened it again.

Where to begin is always a problem. I think I've always been sad, but things are worse now. Maybe I should start with those strange poems I found. I was playing in great-great-grandfather's little museum and discovered the secret hiding place behind the carving. There was a ruby there. I took it to Mrs. Hastings and asked if I could wear it. She said it was probably glass if I found it in the cabinet. She even made a joke that it was probably something that Francis Hatton got from some Indian maharajah or the Shah of Persia. There were other things hidden with it, including the poems.

Bette then described what she had found in the cabinet, which was basically what Lizzie had found there, except that Lizzie hadn't seen the necklace. Bette described the triptych, the poem in French, and some, though not all, of the other bits of verse, along with the necklace.

I thought these things were interesting and I took the little painting and the necklace to Father in his study and asked him what they were. He seemed very surprised that I had found them. He had never seen them before, but he told me that he knew what they were.

178 • Mary Malloy

In a sidebar directed to "Dr. Stuart if you ever read this," Bette noted that this was one of the most memorable conversations she ever had with her father. "Ever since my two oldest brothers died in the war," she wrote, "he does not seem to want to show affection to his other children."

John Hatton told his daughter that he had learned the story from his great-aunt, an eccentric old woman who came to see him at his Oxford University lodgings on his twenty-first birthday. He was, at that time, the last male Hatton. His two older brothers had been killed in World War I and he had not yet married and had his own children

Lizzie thought of the two photographs she had seen in the Naval Gallery. Was it possible that both pairs of brothers had been killed? What a tragedy that would have been for Bette's father, who would have had to face the loss not just of his brothers, but of his sons. Thinking about the man, Lizzie remembered that he was also George's father. She had not recognized George as one of the young men in the World War II photo. Were those his brothers? Lizzie remembered that when they were in the Naval Gallery during their tour, she and Edmund had talked only of Francis Hatton. Would it be intruding to ask him about those men who were so much closer?

Chapter 13

Lizzie had promised George that she would try to find out if Frank Hatton could have made another voyage to the Pacific to return the corpse of Eltatsy and the blanket, and she was determined to spend some time on the question the next morning before breakfast. The snow had stopped and the sun was just peeking over the horizon. She hoped that she would be able to finally get a tour of the old castle grounds of Hengemont and visit the family church with Edmund.

The library had a first-class collection of voyage narratives, and Lizzie pulled down the volumes for the voyages of Captains Dixon, Meares, and Vancouver. If Francis Hatton had returned to the Northwest Coast, those would have been the likeliest opportunities. She scanned the crew lists of the first two volumes; no Hatton. As she opened the first edition of *Vancouver's Voyages* a letter fell out. Lizzie stooped to pick it up and found that it was signed by George Vancouver himself. It was addressed to Francis Hatton, dated March 23, 1790.

Dear Friend,

Your letter of the 14th inst. gave me great pleasure. To sail again with a shipmate such as yourself would be just the thing to insure the voyage would pass with both humour and honour. I was somewhat surprised by your request to come along as all word received of you of late has painted you rather the gentleman farmer than the salt, but you are certainly not the first man called back to the sea from a pleasurable life ashore and I suspect it is the opportunity to add to your splendid cabinet that really draws you.

Let me know what I can do to encourage your participation in this enterprise. You could not have given me more promising news as I make the final preparations for this voyage.

Fair winds old friend,
George Vancouver, R.N.

The signature had been scratched with a quill and Lizzie ran her thumb across it. George Vancouver. He had touched the same paper that she now held in her hand. She momentarily reached across time. Outside, the sun was beginning to show itself with force. Lizzie opened the first volume of the published narrative of Vancouver's voyage and scanned the crew list printed in the first pages. Francis Hatton was not there, though according to this letter he clearly intended to go on the voyage. She needed a good biography of the man and now she scoured the shelves in earnest for a family genealogy of the type written for aristocratic families in the nineteenth century and packed with the sort of details she was looking for. It didn't take long to locate *The Hattons of Hengemont* on a shelf too high to reach.

The library was equipped with a chair whose top could be pushed back to form a step ladder. Lizzie loved this special piece of library furniture and had explored several high shelves just to be able to use it. Now she pulled out the Hatton genealogy and turned around to make her way back down to the big table. For a moment she glanced out the window, across the formal garden and the sloping hill down to the sea. The sun was starting to pick out the details of the stone wall at the end of the garden.

Even this slight elevation made a difference in the view and Lizzie felt a twinge like static electricity at the base of her skull. It was the view she had seen in her dream as she sat in the wooden stands at the tournament. The heavy book wobbled in her hand and she turned and sat on the top step of the ladder, clutching the book as if it would keep her from falling. For a moment she thought that she might faint. She closed her eyes and saw again the landscape from her dream, smelled the odors, heard the sounds.

She sat quite still for several minutes, breathing heavily. Then she climbed slowly down the ladder, still clutching the book. It was the same powerful sense of *déjà vu* she had felt upon seeing the triptych. She felt a confusion of centuries, as if she was, waking and sleeping, moving through time, from the medieval world of her dreams to the seagoing career of Francis Hatton to the present. Once again she attempted to rationalize and justify things that she did not actually believe could be rationalized and justified. She spoke purposefully to herself again about the sources of the images, and willed herself to move on. She opened the book and breathed deeply.

Even though she felt, strangely, that she knew Francis Hatton's personality and character rather well from having read his journal and letters, Lizzie knew almost nothing about the details of his life either before or after the voyage. Now she dedicated herself to sketching them in.

Quickly leafing through descriptions of the early generations of Hattons, Lizzie found her way to the chapter on Francis. Not everyone in the family had his or her own chapter, but Frank's adventure on the Cook voyage made him one of the more famous members of the family. As the second son of Sir John Hatton, Francis Hatton had not been raised with any expectation of inheriting the family title or property. He had gone to Oxford and served a stint as a midshipman in the Royal Navy. Traveling through Europe on a "grand tour," he was captivated by the various collections regularly visited by young men like himself. On his return to England he visited the Royal Academy in London, expressing an interest in learning more about the new science of Natural History. Through a series of connections and coincidences he found himself introduced to Sir Joseph Banks, one of the most influential members of the Royal Society, and a man who had risen to prominence after accompanying Captain James Cook on his first voyage to the Pacific Ocean.

It was Banks who encouraged Francis Hatton to enlist for the voyage then being planned, Cook's third visit to the Pacific. The Hatton family had strong ties to the Royal Navy and, with Frank's earlier service as a midshipmen, there was no difficulty in arranging a commission and fixing him with an appointment to the ship *Resolution*. Between the time he enlisted and the time the voyage commenced, he had several months to apply himself to navigation and take the examinations that allowed him to enter the ship's crew with the rank of lieutenant. The biography gave an extensive description of the voyage, which Lizzie skimmed quickly, noting that Hatton's collecting tendencies were always considered an important part of his identity. He was famous for his museum cabinet.

Upon the death of his brother, he unexpectedly became heir to the family titles and fortune; he returned to Hengemont at the age of twenty-five in 1780. There he discovered his sister suffering from something the biography called a "decline of spirits," which Lizzie thought must have been depression or something like it. The book was becoming very frustrating now that she wanted something more than facts delivered in the most polite and politic manner possible. The author of *The Hattons of Hengemont* was clearly not going to interpret for her what life was like in the house in the years following Frank Hatton's return.

There was a mention of Frank's marriage to Margaret Gurney on New Year's Day, 1781. Lizzie smiled. Had he ever told her that he'd traded her miniature for the bear helmet?

One full page of the book was then devoted to the building project that the Hattons, father and sons, undertook with the architect Robert Adam. The library in which she sat was constructed at that time, along with the cabinet, though most of the fame of the wing was concentrated on the foyer and staircase that backed the old medieval hall.

In 1781, as the work on the new addition was being completed, and before the exterior scaffolding was removed, Eliza Hatton climbed to the top of it and threw herself onto the stone terrace below. John Hatton had a stroke when he learned about it and died the following year.

Even though Lizzie already knew the facts from Helen Jeffries, she felt the tears well up as she read.

The terrace on which Eliza died lay just beyond the window in front of her, the window that she had looked through with such pleasure every day as she worked here at this table. Her eyes were drawn to the terrace. The stones looked hard and cold. Lizzie could not keep herself from wondering exactly where it had happened. Had Eliza's blood soaked into the stones? Was there any trace of those molecules after more than two centuries? A tear slid down Lizzie's cheek and she wiped it away. She tried to tell herself that this was *history* and she was a historian. These people were not her friends, or her family; they were her subject matter. With difficulty she finished her notes. Frank lived to be ninety years old, dying in 1845 and leaving behind several children and grandchildren.

Lizzie closed the book. She sat motionless, scanning the room with its tall shelves of books and the prominent museum cabinet. She felt agitated, sad about these people who had died so long ago, worried about them even.

George was surprised to find her working so early when he passed by the library door on his way to breakfast. Lizzie rose and joined him, taking out a tissue and pretending to blow her nose as she wiped her eyes. Edmund and his daughter were already at the table.

Lily was her usual effervescent self, amused this morning that both she and Lizzie were named Elizabeth. "I'm named for my grandmother," Lily explained, "my mum's mum."

"My grandfather used to tell me that I was named after his mother," Lizzie answered, "but my mother tells me that I'm really named after Elizabeth Bennet in the novel *Pride and Prejudice.*"

"She named you after someone in a book?"

"Well, it's her favorite book," Lizzie explained.

They talked for several more minutes about books that they both liked, until Edmund interrupted to ask Lizzie if she wanted to take their tour around the grounds. "The weather is much better today," he said.

Lily was going to a party at the home of a friend in the village, and left right after breakfast. Edmund and George saw her off while Lizzie went back to her room for her coat. When she arrived back in the library, she reminded Edmund that she wanted to see the church as well as the grounds, and he fished in his pocket for a key which he held up.

"I remembered," he said. "We are ready to go."

They started their tour in the old medieval hall. Edmund

showed Lizzie the interior features that survived from the Norman castle, and then proceeded out through the main front door, as he pointed out the three big stones that framed it.

"You see here how the house got its name," he explained. "The stone circle, or 'henge' that stood here in prehistoric times was dismantled and the stones incorporated into the castle. As it sits on this hilltop it was the henge on the 'mont' or mountain, and consequently became Hengemont."

Edmund was able to point out to Lizzie where each of the other nine known stones were in the foundation, and gave her a general idea of where archaeologists thought the circle had stood.

"This area is rich in prehistoric sites," he added. "Was the weather clear enough to see the white horse on the hillside coming from Minehead?"

Lizzie told him that it was and that she had seen the horse. Edmund pointed out the gothic additions to the front of the house and they then went back inside, through the main hall and into the foyer of the Robert Adam wing. From here they went out to the terrace as Edmund gave Lizzie a rundown of the construction of the various additions to the house. The general outline was pretty much as she had read about it in Martin's book, but Edmund was able to add numerous details. Their conversation was easy and comfortable, and occasionally they stood close enough for their arms to touch as they looked at one or another of the details of the house.

As they went down the terrace steps into the garden, and from there down the slope toward the gate to the church, Edmund described the footprint of the original stone walls. He touched Lizzie on the arm to get her attention before motioning around the outline of the old castle keep.

"There was a passage along the connecting walls right around the whole compound," he said as he pointed out the castle yard, from the church down to the harbor, and back up the slope again. "The connection was broken with the building of the first additions in the late fourteenth century."

From where they stood they could see the original roofline of the tower as it stood up squarely behind Robert Adam's elegant Georgian addition.

"What a great view it must be from there," Lizzie said, looking at the top of the tower.

"Well as you know from the story I told you, it was a favorite place for romantic trysts back in medieval times."

Standing here in the bright sunshine, the images from her dreams seemed very distant. She studied the crenellated roofline. "Can we go up there?" she asked, surprised to hear herself asking the question.

"You know I thought you might be interested in that," Edmund answered, smiling at her. "When I got the keys to the gate and the church from Mrs. Jeffries I asked her for the roof key as well. She says it's been lost for years."

"When were you up there last?"

"I think I was about eight or nine. My Aunt Bette took me up there."

They stood silently for a moment as Lizzie took in the prospect from every angle around her, and then Edmund gestured toward the gate and the church beyond it. Without thinking about the action, she slipped her arm through his as they walked across the garden and he, with equal comfort, rested his hand upon her arm.

"The chapel was built by the first member of my family to live in England," he said as they walked. When they reached the gate, he took the key from his pocket and opened it. They passed along the path through the churchyard to the big oak door of the church and Edmund produced another key to open it.

Inside it was cool and dark. Light filtered in through tall narrow windows and Lizzie's eyes gradually adjusted. She had been in a number of churches of this vintage in England, and she couldn't help feeling that this was a particularly wonderful example. Each generation had added its own details and monuments, and changes and additions had been made over the years, but the resulting clash of styles was not so jarring as it often seemed in other churches.

Near the door were two matching monuments commemorating local men lost in the two world wars. As Lizzie scanned the names she noticed that each list had two men named Hatton. She thought again of the photographs she had seen in the

Navy Room, and of Bette's description of her uncles and her brothers. These were those young men. Like Francis Hatton they had served in the Royal Navy—one had been a Lieutenant on the *Hood,* sunk by the *Bismarck.*

Below the two plaques was a quotation from a poem by Rudyard Kipling: "If blood be the price of admiralty, Lord God we ha' paid in full!" Lizzie blinked back tears. She turned from the monument and smiled sheepishly at Edmund.

"These are long lists for a small village," she said softly, gesturing to the war memorial. She wanted to add something about the impact on his own family, but her emotions were suddenly so close to the surface that she feared a deep discussion might result in a flood of tears. Edmund looked at her with an expression that Lizzie thought lay somewhere between pity and exasperation. She grinned back sheepishly.

They circled around the church and Edmund pointed out interesting features here and there, speaking in a low voice. Lizzie was impressed with his knowledge of architecture and history, and the Hatton family monuments were like a textbook of memorial styles through the centuries. It wasn't like other tours, however; Edmund was no disinterested stranger. Though his descriptions were always in the third person, Lizzie couldn't help thinking that these were the graves of his own family.

They stopped at a remarkable Elizabethan alabaster carving of a ship. A man in armor, with a ruff around his neck and his hands clasped in prayer, was being lowered by two comrades into the sea.

"He died on a voyage to Portugal," Edmund said from behind her. "He was on a diplomatic mission and was buried at sea." A woman carved from similar stone was kneeling in prayer before it. Edmund pointed her out as the wife of the sailor.

They looked at other monuments and finally stopped at the one that memorialized Francis Hatton. It was a marble oval, inlaid with a mosaic map of the world. The route of Hatton's voyage was shown in colored stones.

"It's strange," Lizzie said, looking at it, "but I almost feel like I know him. I've read so much of his writing now, and his personality just infuses it. He's a very easy man to like."

Edmund let her study it for several minutes.

"If I were you, I think I would derive a great deal of comfort from a place like this," Lizzie said hesitantly, turning to face him.

"What do you mean?" Edmund asked.

"I don't know," she stammered. "It just seems that there is a sense of belonging or something." She paused before a monument of three marble men, each resting casually on an elbow, their full-length effigies mounted one above the other, each looking into the space above her.

"Three brothers who died young," Edmund murmured. They walked in silence toward the front of the church. "More than thirty generations of my family are buried here," he said when he spoke again, "and I guess there is a certain sense of comfort in that." He paused before a small and simple plaque in the wall: "Jane Merrill Hatton, 1932-1994".

It had to be the memorial for his mother, she thought, wondering where the actual grave was, and moving forward without speaking.

"One is constantly reminded of all the tragedies in the family by a place like this, however," he said finally, glancing around at the dozens of graves. "I don't know if it's true in every family, but there do seem to be an awful lot of Hattons who died young or tragically, and I am reminded of that every time I come in here."

"That is, of course, the other side of the coin," Lizzie said philosophically. "I have always rather regretted not having a family burial place, because it seemed that there was such a sense of history in it." She paused and looked at him. "But there is a lot of tragedy in the past."

"We like to think of it as a unique feature of our own lives?"

Lizzie responded with a nod and slight smile.

As they reached the transept of the church, Edmund pointed out the oldest Norman features, and in the gloom Lizzie saw several full-length tomb chests with carved effigies on the top. The light filtered through a stained glass window and fell with an orange glow on the oldest of them. In marble, stone, and alabaster, the medieval Hattons lay head-to-foot around the wall of the north transept, each in a set-back cell with a gothic arch. Edmund pointed out the ancestor who had come from Normandy with Henry II, and his heirs. Many were carved wearing the armor they carried into battle.

As they reached the fourth niche along the wall, Lizzie stopped short. The couple lying side by side before her were the lovers from the triptych.

The painting that showed the two of them in the "clothing appropriate to their own time" was taken directly from this carving. The knight wore the Crusader armor that Lizzie knew from the triptych, the Rossetti painting, and her dream. The chapel suddenly felt clammy and Lizzie shivered slightly as she moved toward the tomb.

The effigy of the pair had been carved flat but was mounted at an angle that allowed both of the lovers to be seen from the floor of the church. Nonetheless, Lizzie stepped up the two steps that would allow her to stand directly beside the carving and look closely at the details. The faces were beautifully carved, the clothing wonderfully detailed. The stone was now almost entirely grey, but it was possible here and there to see slight vestiges of paint on them and Lizzie realized that the triptych artist had depicted their clothes in the colors that must still have been visible on the carving in the middle of the fifteenth century.

On the tunic of the knight she could just barely see the rust-colored background covered with small white crosses. His shield and epaulets showed the same heraldic device she had noticed in the triptych and the Rossetti painting: two hearts atop a battlement, with the waves of the sea beneath. Along the edge of the stone were their names: Jean d'Hautain and Elizabeth Pintard d'Hautain.

She reached out her hand and tentatively touched the face of the knight. His eyes were closed, the stone cool.

"John," she whispered softly.

Edmund came up to stand beside her. Lizzie was suddenly flustered.

"What is it?" Edmund asked.

She cleared her throat, trying to sound calm. "I recognize these two as John and Elizabeth from the story you told me," she said. "Do you know the little medieval painting of the jousting scene that's in the cabinet? Two of the figures were taken directly from this carving."

Edmund shook his head. "I'm sorry to say that there are probably lots of things in the house that have escaped my attention; that doesn't even sound familiar."

They were standing so close that Lizzie could feel the contour of his arm through her sweater. Through the whole of the day they had often touched each other and the contact was casual, easy. But now, standing in front of these two lovers, Lizzie felt for the first time that there was the potential for something more. She thought again of her dream and the passion that had filled it. The image of Edmund's mouth on hers, his tongue on her lips, his body lying naked on her own. She felt herself flush from her core to the roots of her hair and was relieved that the dim light of the chapel disguised it from her companion.

She stepped back. Commanding herself to think of other things she turned her thought to the paintings that she had examined so closely the day before. Looking around the chapel she thought about the women wearing the ruby. Where were those women anyway?

"Where is the woman from the Rossetti painting?" she asked Edmund.

"My goodness, you have been getting through the collection very thoroughly," he answered. He turned his back to the Crusader effigy and stepped down the few stairs to the stone floor of the church. "If I remember the story correctly," he continued, "she requested to be buried with him. I think they are down in Brighton or someplace."

Lizzie thought for a moment. It was possible that the other young women had married and consequently been buried with the families of their husbands. The fact that their graves were not immediately obvious here shouldn't be such a mystery. But, she thought, at least one had died single in the late nineteenth century. Her aunt had written a poem for her. Where was she? And where was Eliza, Frank's sister? She had also been single and died young. Lizzie could no longer resist asking Edmund about those women.

"I found some interesting scraps of poetry in Francis Hatton's cabinet," she started.

Edmund turned to her.

"They were all written by young women, and. . . ." Lizzie felt her voice catch in her throat and coughed. "I don't want to sound too morbid," she continued, somewhat haltingly, "but I can't help wondering what happened to them. Where is Francis's sister Eliza, for instance?"

Edmund looked at her intently. "I'm beginning to see the danger of hiring a historian to poke through the family papers," he said. "One then has to face the prospect that she might find an old skeleton."

Lizzie tried to make a joke. "But that's the problem," she said, "there don't seem to be enough old skeletons." She immediately regretted the tastelessness of the remark, but Edmund seemed to take it in stride.

"Ouch," he said. "I guess I deserved that, but this is getting to be a rather unseemly conversation to have in a mausoleum."

"Sorry," Lizzie said softly, "I don't mean to make light of it. I just find it intriguing."

Edmund was thoughtful for a moment and then led her over to the south transept of the chapel. "I don't see any reason to keep it a secret," he said, "though it has always been treated that way." He gestured to Lizzie to help him move one of the pews back and pointed to a series of marked stones set into the floor. "These women all committed suicide quite young. They couldn't be buried in the consecrated church so they are buried in an adjacent burial ground."

Lizzie looked at the stones. There were ten of them, small bricks engraved with names and dates, laid into the floor of the church in a row. Except for one man, named Edmund, who had lived in the late nineteenth century, each of the stones had the name Elizabeth Hatton, or one of the versions she recognized from the paintings and poetry. The earliest set of dates was 1234-1254, the most recent 1868-1887. There was at least one in every century from the thirteenth to the nineteenth.

These were the authors of the poetry. The women in the paintings.

"Whoa!" Lizzie said, grabbing unsteadily at the back of the pew.

She was building a file of these women, and here they all were. She plopped herself into the pew and fumbled in her purse for a Kleenex to wipe her forehead.

"Are you all right?" Edmund asked with concern. He sat beside her.

Lizzie felt her heart pounding. She knew her face was flushed but when she reached up to touch her temple with her fingertips it was cold and clammy. She attempted a smile.

"This is really, really weird," she said.

Edmund put his arm around her and waited for her to explain.

Lizzie did not know how even to formulate a logical question, let alone an explanation about how she had made links between these women through such disparate sources. In a disorganized jumble she begin to spill the information out to Edmund: the poems, the paintings, her correspondence with Jackie and Professor Brandon back in Boston, the ruby.

"Wait a minute," Edmund said, pulling his arm back and folding his hands in his lap. "When you say you found 'scraps of poetry,' what are we talking about here?"

More coherently now, Lizzie described her discoveries in detail, then explained how she had linked almost every poem to a painting.

"There is no marker here except the one for that man Edmund," she said, pointing to the one stone that didn't fit into her file, "that I don't have some document for, either a text or a painting." She had hoped that by saying it out loud, and sharing it with Edmund, she could dissipate the strangeness of the experience; but it was not so. If anything, the extraordinary coincidence that brought all the threads together was even more astonishing when she put it into words.

Edmund was silent for a long time as he processed the information. Lizzie pondered the stones at their feet.

"My God," he said at last, "I hardly know how to respond. I thought I knew all about these women, but I never saw any of that stuff you describe."

"Surely you've seen the paintings. . . ."

"Well, of course I've *seen* them, but I never consciously linked any of them to these girls, I never noticed any ruby, and I've never seen the poems." He paused and put his arm along the back of the pew behind Lizzie. "Why did you make this file you're talking about?"

"Total coincidence!" she insisted. "I found the poems, noticed that they were very similar but written generations apart and I just got curious. Then I found the triptych and started to notice the ruby everywhere, so I began very casually to assemble the file. Purely as an academic exercise," she added.

After another period of silence it occurred to Lizzie that these were not simply abstract ideas to Edmund. They were his relations.

"I'm sorry," she said. "Your response to Francis's actions seemed interested and concerned, but you didn't seem to take it personally. I begin to forget that this is your family."

"It's not that," he said after a moment's silence. "Francis behaved like a human being. He made mistakes and he regretted them. There's nothing to be embarrassed about in being descended from him." He paused again. "But these women. . . ." He fumbled for words. "It's hard to explain."

Lizzie did not know what to say in response. She touched her forehead again; now it felt hot. "You know," she said, finally, "I think I may have a fever."

Edmund rested his hand lightly against her cheek. "You do feel a bit warm," he said. He asked if she wanted to go back to the house.

"Could we just sit here for another minute?" she asked.

He nodded. "Of course."

She had a bottle of water in her purse and she pulled it out and took several sips.

"I'm sorry I can't let this go," she said. "But how did they die?"

"I think in every case they jumped from the roof."

"Hence the padlock?"

Edmund nodded. "The survivors of these girls went to some rather extraordinary lengths to remove access to the highest parts of the house." He touched one of the stones with the toe of his boot. "The stone steps that went up the corners of the original tower, as well as most of the walls of the fortification, were actually torn down by angry, grief-stricken fathers." His eyes met Lizzie's.

She looked down at the stone where Edmund's boot lay: "Elizabeth Hatton, 1760-1781." It was Frank's sister, Eliza. Helen said that she had jumped from the scaffolding as they were building the Adam wing of the house. Not two hours ago, Lizzie had walked across the very spot on the terrace where she died. She took another long drink of the water.

"I'm sorry, Edmund," she said when she had emptied the bottle, "but I want to ask you another personal question about your family."

He nodded, touching her shoulder softly with his hand.

"Your father's sister," she stammered. "Is she buried here?"

"Bette?" he asked.

She nodded.

"Bette's not dead," he said. "Why did you think she was?"

"Helen Jeffries told me."

Edmund smiled and stroked his beard. "I suppose Mrs. Jeffries thinks she is protecting the family honor," he said wryly.

Lizzie turned slightly to catch his eye.

"My aunt Bette is in a convent in France," he said matter-of-factly.

"She's a nun?" Lizzie asked with surprise.

Edmund laughed. "Oh no, it's not as bad as that! She's just loony!"

Lizzie smiled. "I know this is none of my business," she said apologetically. "But, as you said earlier, poking around in people's papers makes one more curious than is polite."

"Did you find papers that belonged to Bette?" he asked.

"I found a poem comparing a man's heart to his penis," she said.

Edmund laughed again. "That sounds like the Bette I remember," he said warmly, "though that's not why she was committed." He shifted a bit and moved his feet back underneath the pew on which they sat. "She was a wonderful aunt when I was a boy. Beautiful and full of life, but in her early twenties she turned dark and became suicidal, just like these women." He paused before turning again to Lizzie and continuing. "I had just gone away to school at the time, so I must have been about thirteen years old, and nobody would really tell me what happened to her when I came home on holiday. I finally learned, much later, that she was committed to a mental institution in London, and after several years was transferred to this convent in France."

Edmund explained that Bette had become so obsessed with the story of Elizabeth and John that she had gradually assumed Elizabeth Pintard d'Hautain's identity. "She was a good student in French," he said, "and started to speak it almost exclusively. She also wore a sort of modified medieval costume, which made people mistake her for a nun. Eventually my father thought it was best to find a community of kind people who could take care of her."

Lizzie was still curious, but she knew it would be rude to question him further on the subject. She didn't tell him that she had read some of Bette's diary. "I'm sorry," she said. "It's a sad story."

He nodded.

They were silent for a few minutes.

"Who put these stones here?" Lizzie asked eventually.

"I'm not positive," he answered, "but I think it was the woman from the Rossetti painting."

Lizzie asked him if he would be offended if she copied down the information from the stones and he shook his head. She pulled a notebook from her purse and quickly took the name and dates from each. He then offered her a hand to help her to her feet, and she helped him move the pew back into its place.

It was snowing softly again when they left the church. As they walked through the churchyard, Lizzie tried to read the names on some of the gravestones, but she was getting a terrible headache and it was hard to focus. Edmund saw that she was unsteady and slipped his arm through hers as they walked.

"Who are all these people?" she asked gesturing at the headstones.

"People who lived in the community," he answered softly.

"Not your family?"

Edmund led her through the gate and out onto the path that would lead them back to the Hengemont grounds. "I suppose some of them are, but I think my family is mostly buried inside the chapel."

Lizzie wanted to ask him where the women were, but hesitated. As if sensing her thoughts, he pointed to a separate area of the churchyard, just beyond the original wall. A large oak was surrounded by stone slabs and the area was enclosed by its own low stone wall.

"Why did your family persist in naming girls Elizabeth?" she asked. "It almost seems like it was a sort of curse."

Edmund shrugged his shoulders. "In my own case, I simply didn't take it very seriously," he said. "I didn't really want to name my daughter Elizabeth, but it was my ex-wife's mother's name and she insisted. I went along thinking it wouldn't make a difference."

Lizzie felt a bit of a breeze and shivered. She had forgotten that Lily's name was also Elizabeth. She couldn't help making the leap to the fact that it was also her own name. Is that why Helen had been so concerned about her?

When she looked up at him, Edmund smiled ironically. "You know," he said, "my father was more angry at me for naming my daughter Elizabeth than he has ever been at any other time in my life."

Chapter 14

As they came in through the terrace doors into the library Edmund turned to Lizzie.

"Are you up for lunch?" he asked.

She wasn't feeling hungry, but something hot to drink sounded good. "Maybe some coffee and something light?"

Even as she said it, Helen Jeffries was at the door, offering to bring those very items.

Lizzie looked at Edmund and smiled. He laughed. "I used to try to trick Mrs. Jeffries with my comings and goings, but she cannot be fooled."

As they took off their coats, Lizzie could not stop thinking of those two rows of memorial stones, and the young women they represented.

"Not to be too morbid," she said finally, "but there do seem to have been an inordinate number of young girls with emotional problems in your family."

"You do get right to the point, don't you," Edmund responded, with better humor than the comment deserved.

Lizzie realized her rudeness and apologized. "It's really none of my business," she said quickly, "but I can't stop thinking about them."

"No, it's all right," he answered. "I've actually tried to look at the suicides as clinically as possible. I even wrote a paper about them in medical school."

Her interest was piqued. "And did you draw any conclusions?" she asked. "Were you able to form a diagnosis?"

"No, not exactly. There was clearly a family tendency toward depression and, at least in Bette's case, something more serious. Bette is a schizophrenic, in addition to having taken

LSD and other drugs in the sixties. But I think there was drug use in some of the other cases as well. In fact, I think that even going back to medieval times the women in my family may have had hallucinations brought on by drugs."

"In medieval times?" Lizzie responded with complete surprise.

He nodded. "It wasn't uncommon then for women to put drops of belladonna in their eyes to make their pupils dilate. They thought it made them more attractive."

Lizzie gave a gasp of surprise.

"Belladonna," he continued, "means 'beautiful woman,' but it can be a hallucinogen, and the state of pharmacology then was imprecise enough that people didn't always know what they were brewing. They used different parts of the plant, prepared it in different ways, and regularly had disastrous side effects."

"But how could you possibly know all this?" she asked. Her mind was racing back over the evidence that she had seen. "The first one was more than seven hundred years ago. What sort of proof could survive?" She was silent for a moment and then asked again, "How could you possibly know?"

"I'm not the first person in my family to be interested in medicine," Edmund explained. "There is an extraordinary collection of medical texts in this library that go back to the time the house was built." He stood up and walked to the corner bookshelves that ran between the doors to the hall and the terrace. Lizzie had concentrated so intently on the voyage narratives that she had never looked at the books in this section. She rose and followed as he began to pull books off the shelf and laid them on a small table nearby. "A few of them are in Arabic, brought back from the Crusades, several are in Old and Middle English, and even more are in Latin."

Lizzie picked them up as Edmund laid them down. The authors were Bartholomaeus Anglicus, John of Trevisa, and Wynkyn de Worde. One Latin text, *Causae et Curae,* was by Hildegard of Bingen; Lizzie recognized the name as that of a composer of a number of extraordinary pieces for women's voices. She had sung them in college.

There was a small volume in dark leather covered with

gold-tooled Arabic script. Lizzie picked it up carefully and opened it from the back. There, someone had long ago written the title in Roman letters with an old-fashioned hand: "Uniform ti Qanun fi al-tibb; The Canon of Medicine of Avicenna, ca. 1000."

"This is extraordinary," she said. She picked up another one and read the title *Liber de Proprietatibus Rerum*.

Edmund looked over her shoulder and translated, "On the properties of things. I always loved that title," he added. "It tells about heaven and earth, angels, animals, rocks, plants, anything and everything." He took the book from her hands and carried it and the others back to the bigger table. "It's a keystone in the history of medicine, and I paid special attention in my Latin classes just so I would be able to read it."

They sat in the same chairs they had earlier taken to look at Francis Hatton's journal, and Edmund took over Lizzie's role as the expert as they talked about the early medical texts. He obviously loved these particular books, each a carefully transcribed manuscript, painstakingly written by hand centuries before the printing press.

"Here's the earliest known medical text in English," he said, showing her a volume with neat, but undecipherable, script. "Old, old, English," he laughed, seeing the puzzled look on her face. *"The Leechbook of Bald.* I love the title; it says something about the state of medicine in the age of Alfred the Great."

Lizzie was impressed at the age and condition of the book.

"The most important one for understanding what happened in my family is this one," Edmund continued, carefully opening the most innocuous-looking book on the table. It had no title stamped in gold on the old leather, and it had obviously been read many times, as the binding was coming apart at the edges. Inside, the thick paper was covered with rows of black ink.

"It was compiled by one of my ancestors," Edmund explained, "a woman who grew herbs, compiled careful recipes for preparing them, and collected anecdotes about their use."

Lizzie leaned over to look at the book, and asked who the author was.

"Margaret Hatton," Edmund answered. "She kept this book between 1425 and 1460, more than five hundred years ago. It gave me my first introduction to the drugs in use in medieval times."

"When you say 'drugs,'" Lizzie asked, "do you mean herbs?"

"Where do you think drugs come from?" he responded. "Aren't you the one who reads *The New England Journal of Medicine*?"

She shrugged and smiled. "That was a stupid question, I guess, but I was trying to get a sense of what kind of medical arsenal someone like Margaret Hatton had in the fifteenth century. You say that belladonna was a hallucinogen, but how common was it?"

"It grew wild all over this part of England. You can still see it along roads and walls, and it's common in the hedges." He looked surprised at her ignorance. "Don't you know it? It's also called nightshade—has a white flower and a green berry."

Lizzie shook her head.

"Well, it's easy to cultivate, and Margaret Hatton certainly had it in her garden, along with henbane, monkshood, and mandrake, all very powerful drugs." He began to leaf through the book. "Of course she also used garlic, basil, chamomile, and the more exotic spices that she got from travelers to warmer climates—cinnamon, cloves, cardamon, nutmeg, mace."

He found the page he was looking for. "Here," he said, pointing out a passage. "This is her description of mandrake root."

Lizzie pulled the book toward her and read with some difficulty. The handwriting was very careful, but the language was archaic. Margaret Hatton was describing the powerful effects of mandrake; it could be used to anesthetize someone enough to perform a surgical procedure, including amputation, and it could "staunch ye flowe of bludde." But an overdose could lead to madness, she cautioned, and she did not recommend it as a love potion, though others had used it as such. "Thus did Richard doom Elizabeth," was the final line.

"This is in reference to that very first Richard and Elizabeth?"

He nodded. "As I interpret this, he gave her mandrake as a love potion to convince her to marry him." He closed the book and folded his hands together. "Mandrake is in the same general family as belladonna, they both contain certain alkaloids that have important medical properties, but as I said, despite old Margaret's care at writing down the recipe, it was simply impossible to control dosages before the advent of modern laboratory equipment."

Lizzie took the book from under Edmund's hands and began to turn at random to various pages. "She wrote this two hundred years after the event, though."

"Yes, but the story is still being told in my family today, and we have many more distractions. She was more than five hundred years closer to it."

Lizzie could not help but notice how careful and precise each entry in the book was.

"I am impressed that Margaret Hatton was trying to understand things from a scientific perspective."

"I was too." Edmund leaned back in his chair and was thoughtful for a moment. "My brother Richard and I once collected belladonna berries and extracted the seeds," he admitted. "We prepared it using a recipe in this book."

Lizzie was surprised at the abruptness of his comment. "Did you do anything with it?" she asked.

"I didn't, but I think Dick actually took it several times for its hallucinogenic effect."

Lizzie didn't say anything. She was thinking about Bette Hatton. After a minute she looked at Edmund, and it seemed as if he might have been thinking about her too.

"I know it was stupid of Dick," he said. "But it's one of the reasons why, when I got to medical school, I decided to look into these 'herbs' more carefully."

There was another moment of silence as Lizzie digested all the information Edmund had given her.

"So the women in your family who took them, took them for medicinal purposes?"

He nodded. "I believe so."

"And not just to make themselves more beautiful?"

"I was being too flip when I said that," he responded.

"This is, in fact, quite serious. Most of these girls were probably suffering from depression and all of its attendant symptoms, including digestive problems, and their families were most likely trying to help them by giving them one of these compounds."

"In modern terms, what's in them?" she asked.

"Scopolamine, which was an important anesthetic and is still used to prevent sea sickness; atropine, one of the first drugs used to treat Parkinson's disease; and hyoscyamine, which controls spasms in the gastrointestinal tract." He began to gather up the books and put them in a pile. "All useful and important. But, because of the side effects, all compounds that are now made synthetically."

Helen arrived with lunch and the two continued their conversation about medieval pharmacology as they ate. When they finished, Edmund went to call his office and Lizzie stood for several minutes at the tall windows, looking across the terrace. She thought again of Eliza and felt a chill. She rubbed her arms and looked at her watch. It was three-thirty. In the distance a bell rang and a few minutes later Helen appeared again with a package for Lizzie.

"It's from Richard," Lizzie said with surprise, reading the note. "He apologizes for having been so beastly, and says he wishes me luck on my research." She opened the package to find a small box of fine chocolates. She offered one to Helen, who declined, but took one for herself. She lingered over it as she turned back to the window. She was feeling somewhat warmer, though the terrace stones looked harder and colder than they had even a few minutes earlier.

Lizzie shivered. She went to her computer and began to add the information from the memorial stones to her growing file on the Hatton women.

The scrap of paper from her notebook seemed to recede into the desk as she read it, her scribbled writing almost to come loose from the paper and move around on its own. The name repeated itself over and over: Elizabeth Hatton, Elizabeth Hatton, Elizabeth Hatton. The dates of birth and death swirled on the page.

Edmund came in and began speaking, but at first she couldn't make out the language.

"My God, you're white as a sheet," was the first thing he said that she could understand. He came to sit in the chair beside her and reached for her hand. "Your pulse is racing," he said.

Lizzie's head throbbed, though it cleared enough to make her embarrassed. She had prodded too deeply into the subject of these suicides during the day. She felt that Edmund was near the end of his patience with her on the subject. She withdrew her hand.

"Thanks," she said, "but I'm really fine."

He looked worried. "You look exhausted."

She told him that she hadn't been sleeping well the last several nights.

He looked at her again closely. "Bed is probably the best place for you."

She mumbled her agreement, and began to rise from her chair but felt very unsteady. He took her arm.

"Would you like me to give you something to help you sleep?" he asked.

Ordinarily, she would never have found it necessary, but she was feeling so jittery and unnerved that she assented.

"Have you taken valium before?" he asked.

"No. I don't remember ever taking any kind of sedative."

"Are you allergic to any drugs?"

She shook her head. "Not that I know of."

"It's usually a pretty good bet," he said. "I'll call down to the chemist and have them send over a few tablets." He left to make the call and Lizzie sat down again. The paper on the table seemed solid enough. She put it into the file folder with the poems and shut off her computer. She was able to stand more steadily now.

"You look a little better," Edmund said when he returned. "Can you make it up to your room?"

"Of course," she said. "Please stop worrying."

He couldn't resist attempting to take her arm, but she shook him off.

"If you want to go up and get into bed," he said, "I'll bring the prescription up when it comes."

"Thanks," Lizzie said. She forced herself to walk steadily to the library door, into the hall, and up the stairs.

There were the portraits again. Eliza's sad eyes followed her as she reached the landing. Lizzie was glad that she was going to have some pharmaceutical help getting to sleep that night.

When she got to her room she slipped into her nightgown and robe, trying to make herself presentable to receive a visitor in her bedroom. Bette's diary was still lying on her night table and she picked it up again. It would be stupid to start working at this point, especially since she was sure the valium would probably knock her out pretty quickly. She thought she would just read a bit before Edmund arrived, and she was feeling better now that she was could lie down.

The fact that she now knew that Bette wasn't dead made reading her diary seem like even more of an intrusion into her privacy, but Lizzie thought that there might also be an explanation of some of the family's tragic history. She leafed through it until she found a passage that seemed to be relevant. There was "a story that must be told," Bette wrote. "My aunt wrote it down for my father, and I will copy it here."

Though Bette occasionally had a wonderfully idiomatic sixties turn-of-phrase, the story she related was written with stylish grace and with flashes of wit. It was the same story that Edmund had told her, about a Norman woman named Elizabeth Pintard who arrived at Hengemont in the middle of the thirteenth century to marry the heir to the d'Hautains, another Norman family. Before she was introduced to her intended husband, the young bride-to-be accidentally met his brother, John, in a chance encounter on the roof of the castle, and fell instantly in love.

Bette described that first encounter with potent romantic imagery, and was almost pornographic in her depiction of their next encounter on the tower, as newlyweds. When they met there a third time to say good-bye, Elizabeth made her husband promise that he would come back and John promised he would, that "his heart was hers," as Bette put it.

John gave Elizabeth a heart-shaped ruby. This, he said, was in token of his heart until that day when he would come back to her. This ruby, exchanged in love seven hundred and fifty years before, was the very stone that Bette had discovered in the compartment secreted in Francis Hatton's cabinet, and that all those Hatton women had worn through the years. Lizzie picked up the triptych again. Clearly this was the story told in the three paintings.

In the triptych there were several knights in evidence, one wearing a crown over his helmet. Lizzie wondered who he might be. There was no mistaking which one was John d'Hautain, the hero of the story. He was the knight in the effigy on the tomb. And Elizabeth Pintard d'Hautain was the woman who lay beside him. Lizzie went back to Bette's diary.

Bette admitted that she had dropped acid several times the year before and was occasionally having mild hallucinations, which she described as flashbacks. They presented themselves as extremely vivid colors, motions in inanimate objects, a heightened sense of taste, and acute hearing. She wrote endlessly of sexual encounters; she was obviously very promiscuous, but there was no love or joy in it. Her depression was palpable in her writing, and Lizzie felt very sad reading it.

Edmund's knock startled her. She had forgotten that she was expecting him. Lizzie quickly closed Bette's diary, fastened the latch on the triptych case, and placed everything she had taken from the cabinet into the drawer of the bedside table. She crossed the room and let Edmund in. Helen was with him and she brought a tray with a pot of tea, a little pitcher of water, and the box of chocolates that Richard had sent.

"My goodness this is good service," Lizzie said. "I wish you were my doctor at home."

"This is the service that I give to house guests," Edmund said with a smile. "I never treat my patients this well." He gave her the prescription and a glass of water. "Take one of these now," he said. "The other is in case you need it tomorrow night."

Lizzie took the pill as instructed.

"Will you be down for dinner?" Helen asked.

"I don't think so, thanks."

"Should I bring you a tray?"

"No thank you," Lizzie answered. "I expect I might sleep right on through it, but I will have another chocolate." She offered one to Edmund. "This was a rather nice gesture on your brother's part," she said.

He agreed that the gesture was unexpectedly thoughtful, but refused the chocolate. "Like most of the Hattons, I am allergic to the stuff," he explained.

"That's unfortunate," Lizzie said, popping one into her mouth. "It is possibly the best medicine of all." She asked him to make her excuses to his father and Lily.

He smiled at her. "Of course. I hope you're recovered in the morning."

When he and Helen were gone, Lizzie got back into bed and returned to Bette's diary.

> My father told me that his great-aunt made him promise that he would tell this story to his daughter if he had one, and that now he had done his duty. He told me this story without emotion.
>
> I asked if he would take me up to the roof and show me where those two lovers met. He told me I could get the key and go there myself. I said the story he told me was so romantic. He said "Death isn't romantic."
> My father has no fear of the past. This kind of thing doesn't scare him—though he told me his aunt was scared when she told it to him. Told him to take it seriously, but he doesn't. "War is serious," he told me. "Human beings are dangerous. Germans are dangerous. Your own government can be dangerous," he said, "but the past can't hurt you."
> I'm sorry that I can't remember my brothers who mean so much to him. I'm sorry that my mother died when I was so young. I can't help thinking that it was somehow my fault, though George once told me I shouldn't think like that. Our parents were too old to have another baby, he said, but wanted to replace their sons that died. That didn't make me feel better.

"What is love?" she wrote repeatedly, and "What is the

relationship between love and sex?" There were questions about the faithfulness of men, and a comment on the suffering of women that resulted when promises were broken.

"I have been wondering a lot about sex," she wrote, "and why I don't like it much, especially because other women seem to."

> I guess the real problem is that I have never been in love. Not really in love—deeply, madly in love. Not Elizabeth's kind of love where you would actually die because you couldn't be with the object of your affection. I wish I could feel that. To feel those hands, those lips.

Lizzie began to find the subsequent entries frightening. Bette's breakdown was becoming apparent. More and more she identified with her ancestress, Elizabeth d'Hautain, who had pledged a profound devotion and had subsequently been shattered by her lover's death. Eventually Bette began to go to the roof on an almost daily basis.

> October 19, 1965—I went up there again today just as the sun was setting. I felt so alone. I actually climbed up on the wall and looked down at the ground. The trees below me in the garden looked lovely, just at the peak of their autumn colours. I have decided to keep the key.

> October 25, 1965—George arrived today. He left Jane and the boys in London. I think my father called him down here to cheer me. He is such a good fellow, really. We went for a long walk and talked for hours. He took my picture in the garden.
>
> When I think about love, I can't help thinking back to a time when George was home on a school holiday. He came into my room one evening, bursting to tell someone that he was in love. She was a woman he met at Oxford. "So brilliant, so beautiful," he said. A few days later he screwed up his courage and told our father.
>
> For the next few days they were completely silent.

Finally I heard my father tell George he must end it. "She is not suitable," he said. Within a few months he was married to Jane.

Today I asked George about that woman from college. He laughed. I asked him if he had really loved her and he said yes. No hesitation at all, just "yes." I asked him if he had had sex with her and he actually blushed. "I don't think that's the kind of thing I should be discussing with my little sister," he said.

I asked him why he didn't marry her. He said that because she was a Catholic, father said he couldn't. I don't think George was ever in love with Jane in the same way. She was just more "suitable."

What's wrong with men? Even the good ones can be asses.

George returned to London and Bette went back to the roof. She began to see a local doctor for some kind of therapy on a weekly basis, which soon became daily, and eventually the doctor became so concerned that he convinced her father that she should go into a hospital in London.

Father says I have to go away. I know they are planning to put me in an institution. If only there was a woman I could talk to. I wish my mum was alive, but even she probably would not understand what is wrong with me. I wish Elizabeth d'Hautain could come through time and tell me what it was like to love John. I wish father's great-aunt Elizabeth could come through time and tell me what to do. Unlike father, I would appreciate all the things she had to share. He keeps asking me where the key to the roof is. They watch me all the time. They let me go to the library, but practically nowhere else. I feel like a prisoner now. Why are men so heartless? If one cannot have real love, then is life worth living?

Lizzie felt nauseous as she read it. There was now something undeniably scary about the poems, the portraits, the gravestones, the dreams. What had happened to all those girls?

Lizzie snapped the book shut and tossed it onto the bed-side table. She had to get up to move the tray from the bed to the dresser; then she took a sip of water, turned out the light, and walked to the window. The moon was just rising, a bit fuller than the night before, cold and stark white. She shivered in her thin nightgown.

Across the courtyard she could see the yellow glow of a lamp in the end room of the Tudor wing. Was that Edmund's room, she wondered? Edmund, whom she was beginning to find so fascinating. Was he a heart breaker like his great-great-great-great-grandfather? Lizzie still felt slightly sick, her stomach in a knot. Her arms were covered with goose bumps, her teeth chattering with the cold. She climbed back into the bed and pulled the comforter up to her chin. She was still feeling agitated. Why wasn't the valium working? Even as she asked herself the question, she drifted off to sleep.

Lizzie was surprised when she woke again. For the first time since she had been at Hengemont, she felt hot in her room. The sheets were damp from perspiration and she wondered again if she might have a fever. She heard the chime of a clock from the hall and looked at her watch on the table to confirm the time; two in the morning. The valium did not seem to be working. Lizzie found the bottle of pills and read the label. It seemed like it was too early to take another one and she decided against it. She didn't think she would be able to sleep, but it came quickly when she closed her eyes.

She was again on the tower when she saw him. He was covered from head to toe with chain mail. Over it he wore the rust-colored tunic; the white crosses that covered it were picked up by the moonlight—the badge of the Crusader.

"Don't go," she whispered.

He raised her chin with his fingers and kissed her gently on the lips. He had kissed her before as they stood at this spot. Again the gentle kiss was followed by one more passion-ate. His lips were full and soft, but pressed hard against her own. His mouth was slightly open and as it moved over her own she felt his teeth against her lower lip, the movement of his tongue. She felt a warmth inside despite the coolness of the evening and the cold stone of the tower against which she was leaning. She pulled his body tight against her and felt the armor beneath his tunic.

She wept.

"Wife," he said softly, "Love."

She moved her hand up to rest it against his cheek.

"I'll wait for you," she said.

He picked up his shield. She recoiled slightly at the sight of it. His helmet rested on the stone wall behind her. She turned to pick it up and give it to him. In the polished surface she caught a glimpse of herself, reflected back.

Lizzie's body jerked and she woke. The reflection had not been of her own face, but of the face of the woman on the tomb.

She felt physically sick. Sitting up, she turned on the light and rubbed her eyes hard with the backs of her hands. She wondered what effect the drug was having.

It had been so strange to see that face, impassive and staring, exactly as it looked in the triptych. At least this time she knew the source of the image. She looked again at the bottle of valium and decided to take another one. There was no reason why she should be having these vivid dreams and waking up if the drug would give her a good night's sleep. She poured herself a glass of water from the pitcher Edmund had brought and took another of the pills.

When she finally fell asleep again it was still fitful, filled with dreams that were less vivid, though no less disturbing, than those she had had earlier.

She was moving through the house, looking for her lover, desperate to find him. She made her way up to the roof, but he wasn't there. She felt rather than knew that he was dead and her despair was terrible. She cried out in anguish, tears came in a torrent.

A cold mist came up from the sea and soaked through her dress. She was cold. Her bare feet were chilled by the icy stone. She thought of her lover lying cold and dead in a big stone tomb.

She understood now why they had all died. Who could live with such despair? She climbed up onto the stone wall in front of her and looked down at the courtyard far below. The ground would race up to meet her and in a moment she would join him in the frozen grave. She would wrap her dead arms around his cold body and put her lips softly against his.

Chapter 15

L izzie," she heard softly, almost a whisper, "Lizzie, hold very still."

Edmund was behind her and slipped his arm around her waist. She touched his hand, which held her firmly, and turned slightly.

"John?" she asked.

With a swift motion Edmund pulled her off the wall and they fell to the stone deck of the roof. Lizzie struggled to wake up. Her nightgown was soaking wet and she was shivering. The white moon was almost directly overhead.

"Where am I?" she mumbled.

"You're on the roof of the tower," Edmund said. He spoke softly, stroking her face with a gentle motion, but still holding her firmly with his other arm.

"The roof?" she asked.

"Yes," he said gently.

"What are we doing on the roof?"

"I saw you from my window, and I was afraid you were going to jump."

"How did I get here?"

"I don't know."

Lizzie shook now with cold, but was too confused to be frightened. Could she actually have jumped, she wondered? She mumbled the question to Edmund.

He assured her she was safe, rocking her gently for several minutes. Her nightgown clung damply to every curve but she felt no embarrassment. Finally Edmund stood and helped her to her feet. She immediately felt nauseous and turned away from Edmund to vomit onto the stones of the roof.

212 • Mary Malloy

"Sorry," she said, embarrassed. She wiped at her mouth with the hem of her nightgown.

"Here," he said taking off his robe and wrapping it around her, "wear this until we get inside."

They went through a thick door and down a steep set of stairs. Edmund's arm was tight around her shoulders and Lizzie leaned hard against him, unable to support her own weight. When they got to the bottom of the stairs they passed through a door into the musicians' gallery and from there found their way onto the landing of the big central staircase. Helen was hurrying toward them from the floor below.

"Is everything all right, Dr. Hatton?" she asked with concern.

"Everything's just fine," he answered, "but Dr. Manning isn't feeling well."

"Can I help?"

"No thank you," he said, "I'm just going to bring her back to her room. You go back to bed."

"All right then," she said, looking back at them as she turned to go.

From the opposite direction George now approached them, tying a robe over his pajamas and shuffling to get his feet into sheepskin slippers.

"What's happening?" he asked.

"I found Lizzie on the roof," his son answered. "I think she was having a bad reaction to a prescription I gave her."

"How did she get onto the roof?"

"I don't know yet."

George pushed Lizzie's hair back from her face and tried to get her attention. "Lizzie, dear," he said several times.

Lizzie finally rose to a level of consciousness that allowed her to acknowledge his address. "Hi George," she whispered.

George continued to look at her, taking in her wet nightgown under Edmund's robe. For the first time Lizzie noticed that Edmund was wearing boxer shorts with an old tee shirt. The two of them were both barefoot.

George looked puzzled. "Lizzie," he pressed, "what happened?"

"Dad, let me get her out of these wet clothes and then we can find out," Edmund said as he moved toward Lizzie's room. When they got there George stood outside the door while Edmund took Lizzie into her room, found her a pair of sweat pants and a shirt and helped her into them.

"Isn't this a little intimate?" she said as he pulled her shirt down over her head.

"It's all right," he said, "I'm a doctor."

She snorted a laugh. She seemed to have no will to act or sense of reality. It was as if all this were just part of another dream. She heard George knocking at the door.

"Edmund," he whispered loudly.

Edmund went to the door and opened it a crack. Lizzie fell back on the bed. She heard George tell Edmund not to let her go back to sleep, the two of them should come down and meet him in the library. Edmund tried to argue, but his father was adamant.

"Get her dressed and get downstairs," he said.

Lizzie was finally regaining her faculties and rising to a state of wakefulness. She had a feeling she was in trouble. George wanted to speak to her. The triptych was still in the bedside table and it occurred to her that he might be mad she had taken it from the library. She grabbed it from the drawer of the table and went downstairs with Edmund.

The seriousness of her situation was beginning to sink in as Lizzie reached the library with Edmund and saw George pacing back and forth in front of the fireplace. She had actually been up on the roof of the house, seemingly ready to jump. She had never sleepwalked before she came to Hengemont, and all this had been done entirely without consciousness. She prepared herself for George's anger and was surprised when he spoke very softly and kindly to her.

"Lizzie, my dear," he said. "Can you tell me now what happened?"

He guided her into one of the armchairs by the fireplace. Lizzie noticed that Edmund was wearing his robe again and had put on a pair of her socks. She looked down at her feet; she was wearing a matching pair. She was beginning to feel quite warm.

"Man oh man," she sighed. "This is the weirdest thing that has ever happened to me."

Edmund knelt beside her chair with his medical kit. He took her pulse, looked at her pupils with a small flashlight—which made her cringe in pain—and then began to tie a rubber tourniquet around her arm.

"What are you giving me now?" she asked as she saw a syringe in his hand.

"I'm not giving you anything, Lizzie," he answered softly. "I'm taking a sample of your blood." He finished and held a swab on the puncture, then put a small bandage over it.

"You don't ordinarily walk in your sleep?" Edmund asked.

She shook her head and said emphatically, "I've *never* done it before I came to this house!"

Helen appeared at the door, her expression filled with concern. George asked her to bring a pot of tea; she hesitated for a moment before leaving again.

Edmund was ready to ask Lizzie another question, but George held his hand up to silence him. "This isn't ordinary sleepwalking," he said to his son. "She had to have a key to get onto the roof, and even I don't know where it was."

Lizzie roused herself. "I think it must be the key I found in the cabinet."

"You found a key in the cabinet."

She nodded.

"How did you know it went to the padlock on the roof?"

"I didn't," she said slowly, trying to remember how she even got up to the roof door, let alone unlocked a padlock with a key. She could not recollect any of it. "I was thinking about the roof because of the story of Elizabeth and John."

Edmund began again to ask her a question, but again was silenced by his father.

"How do you know about Elizabeth and John?" he asked.

"Edmund told me. I found a little painting that showed their story," she explained, handing the triptych to George, "and then I found a bunch of poems about them."

George looked at the triptych. "Where did you find this?"

"In the cabinet," Lizzie answered, "behind the panel."

"What panel?"

Edmund helped Lizzie rise to her feet and she led the two men over to the cabinet. She pressed the carving and the door sprang open.

"I discovered this a few days ago," she said. "This series of writings on the same theme of a lost lover, a heartless man, written over a period of seven hundred years. And these are the authors," she said, going to the table and opening one of her file folders. She spread out the photographs she had taken of the various portraits of women wearing the necklace, then put the triptych and the poems alongside them.

"Do you see the necklace he is handing her in this painting from medieval times?" she asked them. "It's the same one that all these women in your family are wearing over the next seven hundred years."

She turned to Edmund. "These are the women who committed suicide, whose memorial stones you showed me in the church this afternoon." She ran a hand through her damp hair. "I guess I must have somehow gotten caught up in this same weird obsession they had."

Helen arrived with tea and the three of them were silent as cups were poured and passed around. As Lizzie drank her tea she felt gradually stronger and more in control. She sat down again at the table and watched as the two men passed the poems and the photographs back and forth between them. She realized that Bette's diary was still in her room, but decided against telling them about it. As much as she had felt like an intruder reading Bette's private thoughts, she knew that Bette's brother and nephew would feel it even more.

George was incredulous as he looked at the material she had gathered. Edmund was less so after their discussion in the church.

"I knew something," George said hesitantly. "Though I never saw all this. . . ." He gestured across the papers, then folded his hands on the table in front of them. He cleared his throat and spoke again softly. "I have, however, seen the symptoms Lizzie exhibited tonight."

"Bette?" Lizzie asked softly.

"Yes, Bette," he answered. "My sister. I saw her often in this necklace," he continued. "She was wearing it when we found her up on the roof more than thirty years ago. She had a total nervous breakdown and had to be institutionalized."

"Where is the necklace now?" Lizzie asked.

"She still has it," George answered. "Wears it to this day. Calls it her heart." He picked up the triptych. "And this, I've never seen it before. I didn't know such a thing existed."

"You didn't know about that panel then?" Lizzie asked, nodding back toward the cabinet.

He shook his head.

"And then there were these vivid dreams. . . ." Lizzie stopped. They would think she was really a fool if she started in on the dreams.

George's tea cup rattled against its saucer as he went to place it on the table. "Dreams?" he said. His voice was choked. "You had dreams?"

Had Lizzie not already been frightened by the experience, the look on George's face would have sent her there. Neither of them could speak, or look at the other.

Edmund suggested that they should all go back to bed and revisit the conversation in the morning. George stopped him.

"I'm sorry," he said, "but Lizzie can't stay here anymore." He turned to her. "I'm sorry my dear," he continued, "but I think you're in danger staying in this house. Obviously there is something that happened to these women and it is happening to you."

"Wait a minute," Edmund interrupted. "You're not suggesting that this is some sort of contagious paranoia?"

"Well look at the evidence," his father said, nodding at the documents on the table. "It's happened at least ten times before."

"Yes, but all of those women were related by blood," he said. "As a doctor I'm willing to believe that there might be some inherited tendency toward mental illness, but not that just by reading these poems Lizzie would catch it." He turned to Lizzie. "I think you've probably had some sort of reaction to the sedative."

Lizzie interrupted. "Whatever caused it, and it was probably my own impressionable imagination, I feel much better now."

"That may be so," George said, "but I'm sorry that I no longer feel comfortable having you stay in this house." He avoided Lizzie's eye. "I guess the best thing to do would be to get you packed and back to Boston."

"Wait," Lizzie said. "Don't you want me to finish up the Francis Hatton project?"

George shook his head. "I don't think you realize the seriousness of this," he said. "I think that you may be in some danger."

"Has there ever been anyone outside your family that suffered from this problem, whatever it is?"

"No," he said slowly, "but I am still concerned about your safety and well-being."

"I would like to finish the project, George," she said after thinking for a moment or two. "It's interesting, it will help my career, and I can do a good job on it." She looked up, trying to gauge his expression. "I can finish up the work here in the next few days, and then I'll go on to London to do the rest of the research that needs to be done there." She poured herself another cup of tea.

"You can't sleep in the house," George said firmly. "Not under any circumstance."

"I can stay at the White Horse Inn," she answered, just as firmly. "I can walk back and forth." There was an uncomfortable pause. "Please," she continued softly, "to go now without understanding fully what is happening to me would leave me very frustrated."

"But you would be alive," he said.

Edmund looked uncomfortable throughout the exchange between them, but now he said, "Let her stay, Father. I'll work with her here at the house to make sure nothing happens."

George Hatton was thoughtful for a moment, and then nodded. "All right," he said, "two days here and then go to London." He began to leave the room, but turned one last time. "I hope you understand," he said, "I'm only worried about your safety."

Lizzie nodded. "I know," she said, "and I appreciate it."

When he was gone, she turned to Edmund. "And thank you, too," she said.

Edmund was still drinking a cup of tea. "Moving out is probably not a bad idea, given my father's state of discomfort," he said. "But I don't see any need to look for supernatural reasons for your episode here. Sedatives can cause idiosyncratic reactions such as you experienced." He said he felt a need to apologize for having prescribed it, but explained that he had never before had a patient react like this to valium.

She admitted to him that she had taken both pills. "The dreams were so vivid. . . ."

He shook his head at her.

"For a smart woman, you can do stupid things," he said. "But I'm glad you told me."

"Do you think it is what caused the sleepwalking?"

"It wasn't exactly sleepwalking," he said. "I think it would best be described as some sort of 'fugue state.'" He explained to her that he had read of people who got into their cars and drove long distances, only to arrive at the other end with no memory of having left their house. He reassured her there was no reason to think that she would ever experience anything like it again.

She liked that explanation. It didn't explain how she had arrived in the medieval hall a few nights earlier, but she had already made herself more comfortable by convincing herself that that episode was a dream.

As they talked, she packed up her computer and Edmund offered to take it out to his car while she got her clothes together. She went back to her room and quickly packed her things. Bette's diary was still on the bedside table and she tucked it into her carrying case. She went to the window, probably for the last time, she realized, and looked back at the roof. She shuddered and turned to face the opposite direction. The very first light of dawn was creeping over the horizon.

Helen knocked as she was finishing her packing and when Lizzie invited her in, hovered around her like some sort of mother animal watching a cub with one eye and a stalking tiger with the other.

"I'm not sure what is happening here, Helen, but I acknowledge that you tried to warn me and I did not take you seriously," Lizzie said. She went to Helen and put her arms around her, hugging her tightly. "Thank you," she said.

"I can't say that I really understand what is happening either," Helen answered. "I just want to be assured that you are completely well."

With some effort, Lizzie convinced her that she was. It took more effort to convince her that she could make it to Edmund's car without leaning on her. Henry arrived to take her bags, and Lizzie followed the Jeffries from the room.

When she came down the stairs, Lizzie stopped again on the landing and looked at the painting of an innocent Francis and Eliza. As she said her temporary good-byes to them and to Hengemont she found herself feeling tumultuous conflicting emotions. On the one hand she had come to love the house and its occupants. On the other hand, it was just plain creepy.

• • • • •

Edmund made the arrangements for her room at the White Horse, which was cramped but comfortable. It had a four-poster bed, on which she placed her briefcase and books, and a small desk where she set her computer.

When her bags were delivered she asked Edmund to stay with her for a few minutes.

"Thank you for saving me," she said. She felt suddenly shy and awkward around him.

"It was my pleasure," he said with a sort of gallant bow.

"How did you happen to see me on the roof?"

"A sound woke me. I think you may have cried out," he said. "I opened the window and heard you crying." He came to stand beside her and put his arm around her.

"Are you really okay now?" he asked.

She nodded and laid her head against his shoulder. They stood together in a gentle embrace for several minutes, Edmund resting his cheek against her forehead. Then Lizzie pulled away and turned toward the window.

"Now that I am thinking a little more clearly, I have to tell you that tonight was not the only sleepwalking incident this week."

"No?"

"No, that night that Richard came, I woke up in the main hall."

"Why didn't you tell me this earlier?"

"Because I wasn't sure if it was a dream or not, and I had too much wine that night." She closed her eyes. "Maybe I have a virus or something, because I've been throwing up too."

"Not just tonight."

"No, after that first strange episode, and one other time when I fell asleep in the library and had a very vivid dream."

"Were you drinking?"

Lizzie thought about this for a moment. "Only tea, I think." She continued to look out the window. "I'm sorry I can't see either Hengemont or the sea from here," she said. "I was getting spoiled in that wonderful room."

"It is a good view," he said. "My room is in the opposite wing but in the same corner position."

She turned. "I wondered if it was your light that I saw last night."

They looked at each other for a long time. Lizzie was not exactly sure if she was fully capable of controlling her behavior at this moment. She wondered what Edmund's thoughts were on the subject. Under the circumstances, she knew that he would be professional with her. He had, after all, prescribed the drug that might be responsible for the whole nightmarish episode.

He very gently kissed her on the lips. She put her hand upon his cheek; his beard was just as soft as she had imagined.

"Get some rest," he said, pulling back, "and I will see you later when we're both recovered from last night's experience." He left quickly and in only a few minutes she could see him through the window as he got into his car and drove away.

Lizzie was filled with alternating bouts of relief and anxiety.

She felt that her life was out of control. She couldn't believe that she had actually climbed to a precipice without any consciousness of the act.

Chapter 16

After several hours of sleep, Lizzie woke to find her perspective returning. She was unsure at first whether the incidents of the night before had been a dream, but she was clearly not at Hengemont. She was, however, alive and well, and tucked into a warm bed. What had happened with Edmund, she wondered, and how far would she have gone had he shown an inclination to pursue her? Certainly they had shared a very intense emotional experience. He had saved her life, she thought with gratitude, and that was powerfully romantic.

She had no suicidal feelings or desire to harm herself, nor even a fear of having felt such feelings. They were totally absent. In fact she was anxious to get back to work. Not, however, at Hengemont, not yet. She called and talked to George.

"I'm so glad you called, Lizzie," he said anxiously. "I have been so worried. Are you all right?"

Lizzie tried to sound jovial. "Yes," she said, "and I'm feeling somewhat embarrassed at having hauled the household out of bed in the middle of the night."

"Don't worry about that," he assured her, adding that she should not, however, underestimate the danger to herself if she stayed.

"I know," she said. "In fact, George, I think I'll just hang out here at the White Horse for the rest of the day and come back to wrap up at the house tomorrow. Will that inconvenience Edmund too much?"

"Not at all. He's still asleep, and probably needs it just as much as you."

"I'm sure he does," Lizzie said. "I'll see you tomorrow George."

She hung up the phone, then picked it up again and called room service for breakfast and coffee. For some reason she was especially hungry this morning.

"I'm sorry, miss," she was told, "but we stop serving breakfast at eleven a.m."

Lizzie looked at the clock. It was almost three in the afternoon.

"Sorry, I had no idea it was so late," she apologized. She was convinced that the girl on the other end of the line must think her completely crazy. "Still having some jet lag," she mumbled as an explanation. She ordered a pot of coffee and whatever the daily special was for lunch.

Lizzie hung up the phone and turned on her computer. The cursor blinked at her. What was it she wanted most to know, she wondered? It seemed that the first thing she should do is make an integrated file of the women. She already had a file on the poems and paintings, and now she should compare it to the list she had made of the stones in the church. She didn't have to look very hard to find a correspondence between the two.

Room service arrived and as she ate her sandwich she made a list that incorporated all the information she had gathered from the poems, the paintings, and the gravestones. It was twelve names long, each name followed by the evidence that linked that particular woman to the others. The fact that Bette had heard the story of the first woman from her father, and that he had heard it from his great-aunt, meant that there must be a pretty strong oral tradition in the Hatton family as well. She wondered if George would be willing to talk about it at some point.

When she finished the list she sat and looked at it for a long time, draining the pot of coffee in the process.

1. Elizabeth Pintard d'Hautain, 1234-1254 (medieval tomb with effigy in the Hatton church; her story is depicted in the triptych and was told to Bette by her father)

2. Elizabeth d'Hautain, 1273-1292 (must have written

the poem in French; no portrait)

3. Elizabeth Hautain, 1356-1382 (wrote the middle-English poem on vellum dated 1382 and probably had the triptych made; no portrait)

4. Elizabeth Hattin, 1499-1520 (she's the one in the "English School" painting wearing the headgear; may have written the one-line question)

5. Elizabeth Hatton, 1583-1602 (the other contender for the one-line question and the subject of the painting by Robert Peake)

6. Elizabeth Hatton, 1698-1719 ("It was for love that she did die" poem, and portrait by Kneller)

7. Elizabeth Hatton, 1760-1781 ("Eliza"—Frank Hatton's sister; painting and poem)

8. Elizabeth Hatton, 1812-1830 (not a great poet and no portrait)

9. Elizabeth Hatton, 1848-1930 (friend/lover of Rossetti and subject of his painting; wrote the poem for her niece; not buried at Hengemont church, but probably responsible for the memorial stones for the others there)

10. Elizabeth Hatton, 1868-1887 (the subject of her aunt's poem, and the owner of the stationery; no portrait)

11. Bette

12.

Her pen paused above the last number on the list. She considered putting her own name there, but decided against it. She already knew everything she needed to know about herself. Then she thought about Lily and wondered if she should be on the list. Her name was also Elizabeth Hatton, but as far as Lizzie knew, she didn't even know the story at this point.

The strangest thing about the list was still the first woman on it. She had apparently leapt to her death from the tower when she learned that her lover was dead. How had her story been passed on? The other question that was bothering Lizzie was why poor old John was still being condemned centuries later for being heartless. If he was killed in the Crusades, which Lizzie assumed he must have been, then why would all these women have persisted with the question, "Where is his heart?" Surely a man dead in battle had to be forgiven for not returning, even if he had foolishly promised to do so.

She wished she had taken the Hatton genealogy from Hengemont because now she wanted to put those ten dead women into some sort of larger historical perspective. If she could make this seem like an ordinary research project, she thought, then she could remove herself personally and emotionally from the picture.

It suddenly occurred to her that she had a sheaf of photocopied pages from *Burke's Peerage* which her friend Jackie had given her at the college library before she left Boston. That now seemed like months ago.

Lizzie crossed to the bed and rummaged through her papers until she found what she was looking for. It was six pages long and in a tiny typeface, but it gave a history of the Hatton family. She went back to the bed, sat back against the pile of pillows, and read it, full of curiosity and anticipation.

> The first member of this distinguished family arrived in England from Normandy in the company of King Henry II in 1153. Born, like his patron, in Le Mans, and of a similar age, Jean d'Hautain grew up with the young prince and remained his friend as long as he lived. (The name, d'Hautain, meaning "haughty," is said to have been received from his royal friend as a jovial commentary on the young man's pride of dress and fastidious personal habits.) In 1165 Jean d'Hautain married the Lady Matilda de Vere, who waited on Queen Eleanor; a son and heir, Henry, was born in 1168. Jean d'Hautain was elevated to the rank of Baron by his king in 1169, and received lands in Somerset where he built a castle, Hengemont, in 1180.

Lizzie read quickly through the next portion: Henry's son, Alun, was "summoned by King John to attend parliament." There was only a passing mention of the marriage of Alun's two sons, Richard and John, to sisters by the name of Pintard. Alun and his son John were mostly acknowledged for being among several men in the family who died in various Crusades, in their case in a battle fought in Mansoura, Egypt, in 1250. Lizzie made a note of the name of the place and the date in her file on Elizabeth and John.

Their son, Jean-Alun, "having distinguished himself in the Scottish wars of Edward, was one of the three hundred persons of eminence knighted by that monarch at Westminster." He married his cousin Catherine.

At some point the family name was changed from the French "d'Hautain" to "Hattin" or "Hatton," both spellings being used, somewhat interchangeably, until about 1700, when the latter spelling was settled on. According to *Burke's*, the name was not just an Anglicization of the earlier Norman-French name, but was specifically chosen to honor the men of the family killed in the Crusades. On one of the twin peaks called the "Horns of Hattin," Christ is said to have given his Sermon on the Mount. Below this point in 1187, at the village of Hattin, Henry II's Crusading army was massacred by the great Saladin, and the remnant of the true cross carried by the Europeans was lost.

A son born in 1360 had gone into the Navy, the first of many to do so. He served under John of Gaunt and became an admiral. This association, and *his* son's career fighting in the "French wars of Henry VI," put the family strongly into the Lancastrian camp during the Wars of the Roses. Two brothers born in 1440 and 1441 consequently found themselves on the wrong side of the war when Edward IV came to power, and were executed at Sarum by order of the king in May 1466.

The political power of the family seemed to put their heads constantly in danger. Another Hatton was executed in 1556 for having conspired against Queen Mary in favor of her sister, the Princess Elizabeth. When Elizabeth came to the throne, the family's honors were again restored. In the next two centuries Hattons could be found in the House of Lords, in the Royal Navy, as bishops and public servants; one was Lord of the Exchequer, another Ambassador to Portugal. They often circulated very close to the Royal Family. Francis Hatton's participation in Captain Cook's third voyage was a highlight of the family's adventures in the eighteenth century.

Through the various European wars the Hattons offered

up son after son, attaining many honors, but devastating the family tree in the process. Mostly they were in the Royal Navy, but there were several entries that listed other military service, like "Edmund R.G. Hatton, K.G., served in the Zulu War 1879, in the Nile Expedition 1884-5, in the Sudan Expedition 1885-6, and on the N.W. Frontier of India 1897-8." Lizzie could not help but notice that *Burke's Peerage* seemed little interested in suicidal girls, and none of them were mentioned.

The two oldest sons of the family were killed in World War I naval actions, a phenomenon repeated with the same tragic details in World War II. As the only surviving son after the war, George Hatton, whom she had now come to know so well, inherited the family title and property

Burke's appended an extensive family tree and Lizzie ran her finger down page after page of Richards, Johns, and Edmunds in the Hatton family. The girls weren't listed and she decided to make her own version of the family tree, adding the Elizabeths who died young, and leaving out all other children who weren't either heirs to Hengemont or known to her through some part of the story.

Hatton Family Tree

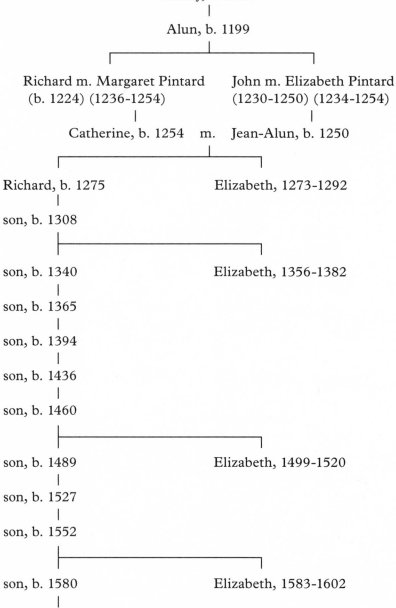

Jean d'Hautain, 1133-1183 m. Matilda de Vere, 1143-1190

Henry, b. 1168

Alun, b. 1199

Richard m. Margaret Pintard   John m. Elizabeth Pintard
(b. 1224) (1236-1254)   (1230-1250) (1234-1254)

Catherine, b. 1254 m. Jean-Alun, b. 1250

Richard, b. 1275   Elizabeth, 1273-1292

son, b. 1308

son, b. 1340   Elizabeth, 1356-1382

son, b. 1365

son, b. 1394

son, b. 1436

son, b. 1460

son, b. 1489   Elizabeth, 1499-1520

son, b. 1527

son, b. 1552

son, b. 1580   Elizabeth, 1583-1602

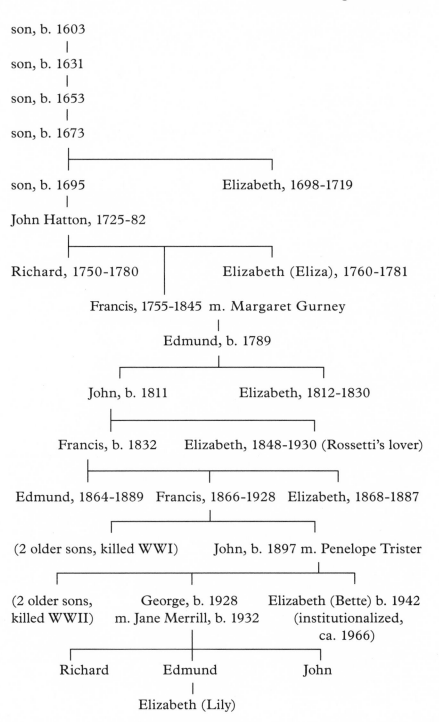

son, b. 1603
|
son, b. 1631
|
son, b. 1653
|
son, b. 1673
|
son, b. 1695   Elizabeth, 1698-1719
|
John Hatton, 1725-82

Richard, 1750-1780   Elizabeth (Eliza), 1760-1781

Francis, 1755-1845 m. Margaret Gurney
|
Edmund, b. 1789

John, b. 1811   Elizabeth, 1812-1830

Francis, b. 1832   Elizabeth, 1848-1930 (Rossetti's lover)

Edmund, 1864-1889 Francis, 1866-1928 Elizabeth, 1868-1887

(2 older sons, killed WWI)   John, b. 1897 m. Penelope Trister

(2 older sons,   George, b. 1928   Elizabeth (Bette) b. 1942
killed WWII)   m. Jane Merrill, b. 1932   (institutionalized,
                                                ca. 1966)

Richard   Edmund   John

Elizabeth (Lily)

The book had been published before Edmund and his brothers were born, so Lizzie added their names at the bottom without dates. The three were probably all born in the fifties or early sixties, she thought. Lily was the last Hatton that Lizzie knew of.

She put down the papers and rubbed her eyes. It was just after eight o'clock and she hoped that she could catch Martin back at home. The phone rang twice and she heard his familiar voice.

"Hello, darling," she said, lying back on the bed again. "I'm glad you're home. I really miss you."

"You better," he replied, "because I'm miserable without you."

Lizzie asked about his trip to New York and they chatted for a few minutes before Martin asked her what was wrong.

"You sound upset, Liz, what's the matter?"

"Oh Martin," she said, her voice choking, "the strangest things have been happening to me." She described the poems she had found. "You know the strangest thing though?"

He waited at the other end.

"There were a number of girls who killed themselves by jumping off the tower here." She paused again, trying to think of how to tell him what had happened to her.

"Yes," he said, "what about them?"

"Well, *they* wrote the poems. They all became obsessed with this family story about a hopeless medieval love affair." She didn't know what to say next.

"Lizzie," Martin said with some urgency, "what's wrong."

"Well, strangely enough, last night I sleepwalked up to the roof."

"What?"

"I ended up on the roof without having any memory of going there."

She tried to explain that she had been having trouble sleeping, had become agitated about the suicides, and that George Hatton's son, who was a doctor, had given her a sedative to which she had a weird reaction. She spoke very quickly, and breathlessly, ending with a somewhat garbled description of a "fugue state."

There was a silence of several seconds when she finished. She expected her husband to ask her if she was still sane. Instead he said, "You must get out of that house immediately."

Martin had always been more superstitious than she, but the fervor of his response took her by surprise.

"I've already moved out," she said matter-of-factly. "I'm now at the White Horse Inn in Hengeport village."

"What are your plans?" he asked with concern.

"I finish at the house tomorrow and then I'm going up to London."

"Are you okay working there? I'm not so sure you should go back at all."

"No, I'm okay," she assured him. "My host is concerned enough about my sanity that I don't think he's going to let me out of his sight."

"I don't think you take these things seriously enough Lizzie," Martin said. "There are things out there in the world that we don't really understand."

Lizzie tried to lighten the tone of the conversation. "Well, when we hang up you can call the Psychic Friends Network and ask them what I should do."

Her husband was not amused. "Those people aren't really psychic," he said. "But you may be. Please take this seriously and be careful."

"I will," she said soberly. "I wish you were here. I could use a hug."

"I don't suppose you want to come home until you know more about what's happening?" he asked. "Or are you going to force me to chase you over there?"

"You know me so well, dear Martin. When can you get here?"

"I'll make the arrangements and meet you in London in a few days," he said. "I was planning to come next week anyway, but I'll change my ticket."

"Thanks, darling," she said. "I feel better already."

"And I feel worse."

"I'm perfectly fine."

"Call me tomorrow night and let me know what's happening.

I'll have made my travel arrangements by then and I'll meet you soon after in London."

They said their goodbyes and Lizzie hung up the phone. She was feeling very anxious and now Martin knew it. She was also feeling guilty about her growing attachment to Edmund.

Lizzie could no longer deny that she was powerfully attracted to Edmund Hatton. Why wouldn't she be, she thought? He was kind, intelligent, handsome, and rich; he had a wry wit but wasn't overtly funny like Martin. At first she had thought he might have an English reserve, but he had definitely warmed to her, as she had to him.

When they first met they had shaken hands, then exchanged light kisses on the cheek, which evolved into warm hugs. But something had happened recently that she had a hard time reconciling. Now they kissed on the lips, and the friendly hugs had somehow turned into something longer and tighter, something more like an embrace.

She certainly loved Martin, and there was a profound guilt in all of this. Guilt and fear and curiosity and excitement. How far would she go with it? To commit adultery with Edmund would, she knew, mean the end of her marriage to Martin, and that she did not want. Still, Edmund's arms felt very good around her, his warm, soft lips fit well against her own. When she was expecting him, she found herself feeling not only a sense of anticipation, but something physical as well, some surge of energy, which she tried very hard to cover with a patina of nonchalance.

She hadn't actually felt like this in many years. Occasionally she found men she encountered sexy and attractive, but she had thought that this high-school-crush response was years behind her. She liked the comparison though. It allowed her to think there might be some hormonal rationalization for her feelings and actions, but did not lessen the feelings of anxiety, desire, and the various fears: fear of rejection, fear of acceptance, fear of misunderstanding, fear of change, fear of sameness.

For now, she told herself, her first priority must be to protect Martin and her relationship with him. Even though she hadn't really *done* anything wrong, she had *felt* things that now stood between them. It was the first time in the whole of their relationship that she had ever failed to share something important with him.

Chapter 17

The Norman chapel in which the Hattons were buried was not the only church in Hengeport. When the Church of England took over the properties of the Catholic Church in the sixteenth century there continued to be a small local population that practiced Catholicism, secretly at first, but with greater openness as the various monarchs came and went, dragging the country back and forth with them from Protestantism to Catholicism and back. In the middle of the nineteenth century, the first wave of a flood of Irish immigrants came to the area to fish, to work in new factories that were beginning to dot the landscape, and to enter the employment of the Hattons, either as domestic or agricultural labor. Within a few decades a new Catholic church had been built in the neighborhood and Lizzie passed it as she walked the next morning from the White Horse Inn to Hengemont. It was a plain brick structure, with none of the Norman solidness or the gothic impressiveness of the older church at the edge of the estate.

As she stood pondering it the door opened and a man came out. He wore a priest's collar, a rubber apron, gloves, and Wellington boots. He was carrying a bucket in one hand and a mop in the other. He saw Lizzie and waved, leaning the mop against the wall and calling out a greeting.

Lizzie saw there was no way to avoid a chat with the priest. He introduced himself as Father Folan, and Lizzie was surprised to hear his Irish accent. Being an active and curious small-town pastor, he already knew who she was and what she was doing at Hengemont

"So how is your work going?" he asked, after their preliminary introductions were finished.

Lizzie explained to him a little about the Francis Hatton collection from the Pacific Ocean. The priest was friendly and comfortable and seemed very interested in the project.

"You know," he said, after thinking for a minute, "there may be something related to him in our little document collection here." He turned and gestured for her to follow him into the side door of the church. "I remember something about the man being on a voyage with Captain Cook."

Lizzie was completely astonished. They arrived in his crowded study behind the altar and Father Folan took down an old metal file box with a rusted key in the lock and a peeling paper label that said "Hengemont." Inside were a number of leather-bound ledger books of the kind used as ships' logs or estate account books, and several loose papers.

"I'm surprised," she admitted. "I never expected to find anything relevant here."

From behind the next door Lizzie heard the whistle of a kettle.

"I just put some water on for tea," the priest explained. "May I offer you a cup?"

Lizzie nodded. As he stepped out of the room she took off her coat and looked around at the shelves crowded with books, boxes, and loose papers. Father Folan returned with a small tray on which he had put two cups, a teapot, milk, sugar, and a small plate of cookies. He served Lizzie and then turned to one of the ledger books. It was bulging with manuscript letters pasted to each page, which he turned over quickly until he came to the one he sought.

"This is it," he said. "I remembered that there was something here signed by Lieutenant Francis Hatton. It struck me as odd enough when I saw it, because by his time the family was firmly in the Church of England and it seemed strange that he would request a Catholic priest to come down to his own church."

"It does seem strange," Lizzie responded. "What did he want, absolution?" She knew how seriously he had taken his transgression with Eltatsy's corpse. Could it have driven him to the local priest? The Anglican vicar would have been in the employ of his family.

236 • Mary Malloy

Father Folan interrupted her thoughts with a little chuckle. "Nothing so radical as that," he said, "but odd nonetheless. Here it is." He pointed to the signature of Francis Hatton, which Lizzie recognized from his letters. "He is requesting a priest to come to their church for the opening of a tomb in 1781."

Lizzie looked at the letter with puzzlement. "A grisly bit of business," she said, "but I can't see why he would need the help of a priest to do it."

"Because the corpse had been buried as a Catholic and there was clearly some family superstition involved in the whole business," he said. He read the letter again, and then looked at another page attached to it with a pin and written in another hand. "This is a sort of report from the priest," Father Folan said, detaching the second piece of paper. "They opened up one of the Crusader tombs in the church. Apparently the sister of Lieutenant Hatton was unstable and had become obsessed with knowing if your man, the Crusader, was in fact interred there. Her brother had the tomb opened at her insistence."

Lizzie felt goose bumps rising on her arms. "And was he there?" she asked.

"No," the old priest answered, shoving his glasses up onto his head and holding the paper close to his face. "The strange thing is that the sarcophagus was so clean that it was apparent to them all that neither the Crusader nor his wife had ever been buried there, though the effigies of both were carved on the lid, and the inscription indicated the tomb was built for them."

Lizzie was trying very hard to maintain a nonchalant tone. "Well, it had been over five hundred years by then," she said. "Maybe they had just completely deteriorated into dust."

"The priest here is pretty clear that he had been called to witness the removal of other twelfth and thirteenth-century corpses from local tombs and that there was always some remnant of bones, teeth, clothing, or something. He was convinced there had never been any bodies buried in that sarcophagus." He looked back at Lizzie. "Certainly his experience in these matters was much greater than mine." He patted her hand as he saw her wan complexion. "I've read some of his other papers and I have no doubts about the trustworthiness of his comments."

"What happened to them?" she asked, hoping the priest had additional information somewhere in his file.

"Well, the Crusader may, in fact, never have returned from the Holy Land," he answered. "There's something else here. I sent to Rome for it." He reached up to a high shelf and pulled down another box in which Lizzie could see old papers bound up with string, and one impressive large roll of vellum.

"When I was a young priest in Ireland," Father Folan continued, "I heard that at the time of the Reformation a number of priests fled from England to Rome, taking their parish documents with them. When they told me I would be assigned to Hengeport, I wrote to the Vatican to see if they had anything that should be returned to this parish and I got this file." He pulled several bundles out of the box and laid them on the table. "Most of them are in very old Latin, and I'm still struggling with the translations." He removed the roll of vellum from the box with care; two ribbons were wrapped around it.

"Here it is," he said, "from the time of the Crusades." He unrolled the scroll; the ribbons each had a flat disk attached to them. "Wax seals," he said to Lizzie as he picked up first one and then the other. Lizzie pulled her chair in close. One of the seals she recognized: the three lions of the crown of England.

"It's the old seal of the king," she said.

Father Folan nodded. "Indeed it is," he answered, "the seal of Richard the First—Richard the Lionhearted, and here's his mark," he said, pointing at the "Rex" scrolled at the bottom of the vellum document. "No wait," he said, looking more closely, "that's not an 'R' for 'Richard.' What is it?"

He fumbled about with his glasses until Lizzie reached into her bag and pulled out her flexible plastic magnifying square. She passed it to the priest and he nodded his thanks. She was so impatient to look at the paper that she was tempted to squeeze in beside him, but she remained silent until he raised his face and looked at her.

"It's an 'H'," he said finally, "with the Roman numeral for three."

"Henry the third," they said simultaneously.

Father Folan winked at her. "It was a number of years before they began to add the symbols of the other countries they plundered, Ireland foremost, of course," he said, "but also France, Scotland, and Wales."

He picked up the other seal. "Ah, look at this," he said. Lizzie obeyed, examining the hard red disk closely. The impression was still remarkably clear: a horse with two riders, each wearing armor and carrying a shield.

"Do you recognize the arms?" Father Folan asked.

She shook her head.

"If I'm not mistaken," the priest said, looking at it again under the magnifier, "it's the seal of the Knights Templar, the great warrior priests of the Crusades."

"What does the document say?" Lizzie asked, her excitement tinged with nervousness.

"Well, as I said, it's a very old-fashioned Latin," he said, pushing his glasses up to the top of his head again and lowering his face almost to the page to take advantage of her magnifying glass. "It appears to be a contract between King Henry and the Knights Templar for the care of a young English knight, John the Proud, and, in the case of his death, their agreement to send his remains back to his bride in England; for which services William Longespèe, the Earl of Salisbury, will leave some amount of money that I can't translate."

"Without embalming, how did they propose to transport a corpse from the Holy Land to England?"

"I'm sorry, my translation may not be entirely accurate, and there is sort of a mixture of Latin and French here. They talk of sending his 'coeurs,' which I first took to mean his corpse, but on second thought it may actually refer to his 'coeur,' his heart."

She had heard about heart burials, but couldn't imagine how they would have been managed in medieval times and, despite her morbid curiosity, couldn't ask about it without cringing.

"I heard a rumor you are a doctor," the priest said. "Surely the idea of removing a heart from a corpse can't be entirely alien to you."

"I'm not that kind of doctor," she replied. "I can solve your history problems, but not your medical ones."

"Well, if you were a doctor in the Middle Ages you would not have had the luxury of making such distinctions. Everyone had a pretty conversational knowledge of blood and body parts, and it wouldn't have been unheard of to send young John the Proud's heart back in lieu of his entire body."

She asked him again if he knew how it would have been preserved.

"I think they tried to dry or mummify it with salt or hot sand, and then packed it into some sort of small casket. Certainly the body parts of saints were sent all over Europe in jeweled 'reliquaries' or relic carriers. For the Knights Templar it would all have been in a day's work."

He continued to study the document, now pulling a small Latin dictionary down from the shelf behind him.

"Who is this 'John the Proud'?" Lizzie asked.

"I was just trying to figure that out," he said, thumbing through his dictionary. "They give the name as 'Celsum,' which could be 'proud' or 'lofty' or 'haughty,' or even just mean that he was very tall. I'm not sure."

"What would it be in French?"

"Maybe 'fier' or 'hautain.'"

"That's the original name of the Hattons," Lizzie exclaimed, "d'Hautain, the first one came over with the Normans." Her words caught in her throat.

"Where is his heart?" she thought.

When the question had been asked, it was in reference to his actual heart!

While she had been sipping tea and munching cookies, they had been talking about *his* heart, *the* heart. She tried to keep her hands from rattling the cup against the saucer.

Father Folan, his face deep in his dictionary and the manuscript, did not seem to notice her consternation.

"Of course," he nodded, "John the Proud, Jean d'Hautain, John Hatton, that would be the reason this contract came back to this church. In the thirteenth century there probably wasn't anyone living at the castle who could read it, so they would have brought it to the priest."

"But the heart never came back or it would have been in that sarcophagus in the church down the road," Lizzie pressed. "So maybe John the Proud didn't die then after all, or maybe the Knights Templar took advantage of the distance and simply kept the money." Lizzie stood up now and began to pace around the small room, trying to fit the pieces together.

Father Folan rolled up the document. "Oh I don't think the Knights Templar would have reneged on a contract signed by the king. Though they were destroyed by torture and disgusting lies in the end, their success depended on their honor. If Hatton, or 'd'Hautain' as he was apparently called in Norman times, had died in their care, I'm positive the Templars would have tried to live up to their agreement."

"So where is his heart?"

Lizzie had asked the question and now she repeated it. "Where is his heart?"

She sat down again by Father Folan. "Where was this contract made?"

The priest scanned the signature area again. "The document was signed in London, but the reference here to the Earl of Salisbury implies that he was the one responsible for the delivery of the heart to the right person."

"Who's the Earl of Salisbury?"

"I'm sorry, my dear, but I have no idea."

She sat down again. If Father Folan had noticed her agitation, he was polite enough not to mention it, turning instead to other documents in the ledger of the Hatton family and leafing through them. He stopped at a letter and read it several times before turning the whole volume toward Lizzie.

"Here's something that may interest you," he said, "if only for the coincidence of being about a young woman with your same name."

Lizzie tried to gather her thoughts together and show interest. Father Folan pointed out a letter dated June 14, 1888. She pulled the heavy volume toward her and read.

Dear Father,

I am writing to you on behalf of one of my parishioners, Lizzy Manning. She worked until recently on the Hengemont estate and said that she would be known to you. Miss Manning is with child and says that the father is Edmund Hatton, the heir of Hengemont Manor. She knows that a marriage between them is out of the question. She cannot go back to her family in Ireland. It is her plan to emigrate to America and to say that she is a widow. For this she needs money, and it seems that young Hatton should pay her expenses for a time.

Would you be so good as to approach him on her behalf? She thinks £50 should be enough to pay her passage and get her settled in America. Confidentially between us, I think she deserves a good deal more, and Hatton is certainly being relieved of his responsibilities with very little inconvenience to himself. Please urge him to do what he thinks is right. A boat leaves from here in a fortnight for New York and Miss Manning is hoping to book passage. Let us know at your earliest convenience if Hatton is willing to do his duty.

Father John Sullivan,
St. Joseph's Parish
Liverpool

P.S. I hope you will not be too quick to dismiss or condemn this girl for the predicament in which she finds herself. She seems a very good girl, proud and independent and believes herself in love with this young man. She is making a great sacrifice on his behalf and it is probably more than he deserves.

On the bottom of the letter was a note in another hand indicating that £300 had been sent via courier to Liverpool.

Lizzie sat dumbstruck. This was what Helen Jeffries had been hinting at with all her questions and meaningful looks.

This was Helen's great-aunt and also, in Helen's mind, Lizzie's great grandmother. But was that really possible? Lizzie's thoughts tumbled back and forth from what she knew to what she could deduce, and from there to speculation, imagination, and desire.

She knew enough of her own family history to know that her great grandmother had immigrated through Ellis Island in the 1880s and that her grandfather had been born shortly after in New York City. Lizzie's grandfather had told her more than once that his father died before he was born, in a shipboard accident en route from Ireland to England. His mother was not on the same ship, having gone ahead to Liverpool to arrange their passage to the U.S. while her husband wrapped up business at home. She was, consequently, left pregnant and a widow at the age of twenty and had emigrated under those difficult circumstances.

Was it possible that the pregnant girl described in this letter *was* her great grandmother? If so, then none of her grandfather's history was true except the voyage to America and his own birth. She closed the big book slowly and set it on top of a jumble of papers on the priest's desk.

She sank back in her chair. Surely Helen could not know more about Lizzie's identity than she did herself. There were plenty of Elizabeth Mannings in the world. The Boston Public Library alone had six of them in its computer, a fact that had created certain glitches in Lizzie's records over the years. There was no reason to think that the name had not been just as common a hundred and twenty years ago. Even the coincidence of two pregnant women of that name getting on a Liverpool ship at roughly the same time could be explained by the large numbers of Irish and English immigrants heading across the Atlantic to New York. They were the two biggest ports involved in the immigrant business. Manning was a common enough name in both countries, and Elizabeth was certainly a popular name for girls.

But there had always been in the stories she heard from her father and grandfather that glaring gap in information, that inability to know the whole story; something was always missing or held back.

She began to grapple with the very strong possibility that the Hatton's family history was now *her* family history. Her mind was racing. First she thought about her dad. What would it do to him to learn that his father was the illegitimate son of a British aristocrat who had rejected his pregnant grandmother? She knew he would hate it. Her thoughts then went quickly to Edmund. Her conflicting thoughts about him had a historical echo in the last century in characters with their very same names! This was a coincidence that she could hardly even articulate. Scariest of all, she might now be in a direct line of descent for an obsessive madness that had caused nine women to commit suicide, and she not only knew she was susceptible, but feared she already had the disease.

Father Folan had been silent as she worked rapidly through these thoughts, none of them pleasant. Now she looked up at him and he spoke.

"You look like you've had something of a shock," he said, dragging her back to the present. "I'll heat up the water again and we can have another cup of tea."

She nodded. "Yes, please. If it's no trouble." Her voice was hoarse.

She opened the ledger and read the letter again several times. Though she needed to check the passenger lists to be sure, she was becoming more and more convinced that she was as much a descendent of Elizabeth Pintard as was Eliza or Bette or anyone else who had succumbed to the obsession. She looked through the rest of the letters in the book; nothing else pertained to the woman who might have been her great grandmother. There was, however, a card announcing the death of Edmund Hatton in 1889 at the age of twenty-five. She wondered if that other Lizzie Manning had ever known.

Father Folan returned with the teapot.

"I take it, then, that this is not just a coincidence with the names," he said gently.

Lizzie shook her head as he poured her a hot cup. "There is a very good possibility that that woman was my great grandmother," she said.

"And you knew nothing about this?"

"This probably makes me look very dense," she said, "because the hints were all around me. Helen Jeffries, the house-keeper at Hengemont, practically hit me over the head with it on more than one occasion."

"And why didn't you take the hint?"

Lizzie thought about this for a moment. Her comfortable sense of who she was had been shaken by this new knowledge. She tried to explain it to the priest.

"It seemed impossible," she said. "Two of the people I have loved best in the world, my father and grandfather, never admitted of such a possibility." She brushed at a tear as it slid down her cheek. "We have always celebrated our Irishness, reviled people like the Hattons as exploiters, reveled in our oppression. For forty years that has been a central part of my identity." There was a pause as she caught at a sob in her throat. "I hardly know what to think. Did they lie to me?"

Father Folan asked her if she really thought that was possible and she shook her head.

"No," she said thinking about each of the men in turn. "I don't think they knew. I don't think she ever told them."

"And do you blame her for that?"

She shook her head again. The priest was so nice that she found herself telling him everything that she knew about her great grandmother. "I guess it was just too hard in those days to acknowledge an illegitimate baby," she said sadly. "There were always gaps in the story about where exactly she came from and what the relationship was between the Mannings and the Hattons in her background."

She sipped the tea and thought about how hard it must have been for that other Lizzie Manning; she had kept her secret for the rest of her life.

Father Folan broke her train of thought. "I must admit to you," he said slowly, "that I knew something about all this before you arrived here this morning."

Lizzie looked up at him, confused by the comment.

"Helen Jeffries has expressed her concerns about you to me on more than one occasion over the last month," he said. "She doesn't know about this document, but I remembered having seen it on an earlier perusal of the ledger."

"Is that why you invited me in? Just to show it to me?"

He shook his head and smiled. "No. One is seldom able to lay such plans. I didn't know if she was right about the relationship or not, and you sounded like an interesting woman, so I was hoping at some point you'd come around." He chuckled and patted her on the hand. "And if you did, then I thought I'd just slip it over to you casually to let you have a look."

Lizzie didn't know how to respond. The priest was a cipher to her; he was taking the situation with too little seriousness and too much joviality for her taste. She sat glumly as he continued to grin at her, until finally she began to wonder if *she* was taking it all too seriously.

She asked if he had had a similar motive with the material about Francis Hatton and John d'Hautain.

"No," he said with enthusiasm. "That was just a wonderful bonus! Who knew anyone would ever be interested in that stuff!"

Now she could not resist smiling at him. As grisly as the information was, the discovery of it *was* exciting. In many ways she saw that he was a kindred soul. The time would come she knew, and hopefully not far from now, when she would find herself telling this whole story with a humorous spin.

Father Folan patted her hand again, seeing in her expression the trend of her thoughts. "Well then," he said warmly, "this will change your relationship to the Hattons."

Lizzie had been thinking that very thought, and remembered that George was expecting her. Draining her teacup, Lizzie rose and shook hands again with the priest. "I was due at Hengemont ages ago," she said, "and I really need to get up there." She picked up her bag. "Thank you for a most interesting morning."

"Mo chara," he said, "good luck on your quest."

Lizzie smiled at his comfortable use of the Gaelic word for friend, which she and Jackie had adopted a few years earlier. Her world of Boston and Saint Pat's seemed very far away.

Chapter 18

Lizzie entered the house now with very different feelings than she'd had on that first day. It was hard to believe that less than three weeks had passed. The large portraits on either side of the main hall took on new meaning as she looked at them for a resemblance to herself or her family. Certainly her own pale complexion and wide-set eyes were everywhere, though they had always been there and she had never thought it meaningful before. Now, with her new knowledge, she thought several times that she saw something in the shape of a nose or the fullness of a lip to remind her of her father or one of her siblings. As her hand ran along the polished railing of the staircase she thought of ancestors that had passed the same way for centuries. She felt a glow, not quite of pride, but of knowingness, and her interest in Hengemont and its history was suddenly more tangible.

Helen walked beside her. The two women had said very little beyond hellos when Lizzie returned. Helen was worried about Lizzie and the bizarre circumstances under which she had left the house. Lizzie was waiting for the right moment to begin, in earnest, the conversation Helen had been wanting to have with her since she first arrived. As she looked at her friend, Lizzie was reminded that she wasn't just a descendent of the Hatton's, but of their maid as well.

"I hope you are all right, Lizzie," Helen started.

Lizzie could not resist hugging the woman. "Let's talk later," she said.

Helen agreed. "Sir George is expecting you," she said. "I'll tell him you've arrived."

Lizzie went to the library, where the pile of poems and the

pictures were still on the table where they had left them on that awful night; she leafed through them again. Including herself, twelve women had sought John d'Hautain's heart. Nine had killed themselves and one, after a suicide attempt, had been institutionalized for mental illness for more than thirty years. That left herself and the subject of Rossetti's painting.

Lizzie looked again at the photograph of that painting. This woman had left Hengemont and formed a relationship with a real man. A man who, admittedly, was as obsessed with love and death as she was, but who still had a beating heart through most of their years together. And yet she had also clearly felt the obsession at some time. It was the subject of the painting, and it was the subject of her poem.

"*Her* poem," Lizzie murmured as she turned to it. It had been written not in memory of Elizabeth or John d'Hautain, but of the young Elizabeth Hatton, dead at the age of eighteen in 1887.

Where is his heart?
The question forced upon a young girl just entering into woman-
  hood,
To rob her of her life and loves.
As if those lovers of past times
Could, with vicarious passion
Replace her own experience
As a stone might stand for a heart.
"Where is his heart?"
Better to ask, "Where is _hers_?"

The last word was underlined. Lizzie wondered who it meant. The young woman who killed herself? Or Elizabeth d'Hautain, viewed not as a martyr for love, but as a curse of sorts, carried down through the generations.

Lizzie sighed and felt her concerns about her own safety evaporate. None of this was about Lizzie Manning. She had a life and a love and she would not risk them further in this business. She had a moment of sudden clarity; there was no danger now that this information would harm her, or that she would harm herself.

She realized that she, like Rossetti's lover, had regained herself before it was too late. If she had lived in this house and experienced the feelings of two nights ago when she was twenty years younger she wasn't so sure that she would have gotten to this point. But she had, fortunately, blundered her way into the story when she was closer in age to the woman who had written this poem than to the girls who had written all the others.

There was a sound behind her and she turned to see Edmund come into the room. With everything that she had learned this morning, she hadn't had time to think about how she should greet him, or prepare herself to do so. She stood up as he came toward her and kissed him on the cheek. When she turned back to the table to sit down again, he touched her softly on the waist, as if to escort her back to the chair.

They had barely said hello when George came in, followed by Helen, who stood just inside the door, seemingly waiting for instructions from her employer. Lizzie was glad to have her nearby.

"Are you all right?" George asked with real concern.

"I am completely recovered," she said. "Thank you."

He pulled up the chair beside her at the table and looked at her intently. "Are you sure?"

"I am sure."

Edmund pulled up a chair at the opposite side of the table.

"And what about all this?" George asked, gesturing at the documentation that Lizzie had gathered. "What do you plan to do about this?"

"At this point, nothing," Lizzie answered emphatically, separating the manuscripts from her printouts, and putting the latter into her bag. "I'm going to hand these over to you," she said, piling the scraps of poetry into a pile, "along with the triptych, and I am going to let you decide how to handle them."

"There's Lily to think of," Edmund murmured.

Lizzie nodded. She had already decided not to tell them that she had learned that she was related to them. It would only make the link to Lily more tangible. "It would be better that she not see these things," she said. "Though I don't think that just seeing them necessarily leads to the obsessive paranoia, or whatever it is." She pointed out the case of the Elizabeth Hatton who had been Rossetti's model and said that it was possible to know the details, feel the pain, and still move on and live a long life. "I honestly believe I have moved past this," she said.

"But Bette never got over it," George said. "She still lives in a medieval fantasy world, even thirty years later."

Edmund gave Lizzie a look. She knew that a significant part of Bette's mental state was due to mental illness and drug use, but she didn't know if George acknowledged it.

"I wish I had a better sense of what, exactly, triggered this obsession over the years," Lizzie said thoughtfully. "Clearly there were plenty of Hatton women who were completely unaffected."

George paused in looking through the papers Lizzie had handed him. "There is a document that you haven't seen that might help explain this," he said.

Lizzie looked at him, clearly puzzled. George looked back at her steadily, and then pushed several pieces of paper toward her.

"I got these out yesterday," he explained, "thinking that you might like to see them."

Edmund sat silently watching the exchange.

"This letter was written to my father by his great-aunt when he was still at Oxford."

Lizzie pulled it forward and began to read. It was the letter Bette had described in her diary.

```
Dear John,
    I cannot help but feel that you did not
take our conversation of last week very
seriously. I know you think me an eccen-
tric and somewhat amusing relation, and
I do not doubt but that stories of me and
my unorthodox choices in life have been
the subject of many conversations around
your family table. I must, however, be
very firm in stressing that should you
```

ever have a daughter, the information I am giving you <u>must</u> be made known to her.

While this notion of a "family curse," especially one surviving from Mediaeval times, must seem very silly to a well-educated man of the modern era, you can see the proof of it in the history of our family. This is not a legend but a legacy. That so many Hatton girls would die at their own hands is the sad testimony of the power of this horrendous obsession.

I am currently the last link in a long chain of events that culminated most recently some thirty years ago in the death of your aunt. Your father knows, of course, the sad story of his sister, but his more recent tragedies have clouded the memory. With the loss of your older brothers in the war, the responsibility will fall to you.

Even though you probably do not wish to take this seriously, please save the statement that I will attach to this letter describing what I know of this story, and pass it on to the next generations. In time, your father will give you important family papers and my request is that you include this among them. If you do not believe me, John, at least humor an old lady who has seen too much tragedy in her life, and trust me that this knowledge will become important again one day.

It was signed "Fondly, Elizabeth Hatton." Two typed pages were attached, the top one entitled: "Statement of Elizabeth Hatton, Given at Birchington-on-Sea, September 13, 1921." It was notarized by a London solicitor a few days after it was dated. It basically told the history as Lizzie now knew it, but added information from the personal experience of the author that was new to Lizzie. "I first felt the power of this legacy when I was eighteen years old," she read. "Disappointed in love, I found myself captivated by this story of a love seemingly so grand that it made death seem like an eloquent gesture."

> For each of these young women there were lovers lost to war, abandonment, misunderstanding, or family interference. Other families faced these same tragedies, but moved beyond them—such suffering was incorporated into the process of maturation. But in my family, the glorification of dying for love became legendary, even desirable.
>
> Though I do not know the specific details of each of the tragedies, I can relate the stories of two of the women affected, myself and my niece.

She described her own engagement to a young man who was subsequently killed in a riding accident, and the deep depression that followed. Her parents sent her to London where she drifted into the artistic circle of the Pre-Raphaelite Brotherhood. She admitted that part of her long affair with the artist Dante Gabriel Rossetti was based on a mutual interest in the relationship between love and death. That they never married led to an estrangement from her family and consequently a deep regret on her part that she had not been at Hengemont to guide her niece through her own period of depression.

> For a family so often touched by similar tragedies, the Hattons have been remarkably obtuse in recognizing the symptoms. I can only attribute this to the fact that the time between episodes was long enough to prevent rational people from expecting that such a history could apply to them. My understanding of my niece's story is this: Her father arranged for her to meet and be courted by a young man from the north of England. His fam-

ily had enormous wealth from the factories, but no position; the Hattons have
position, but rapidly declining wealth.
He was a dissolute and wretched crea-
ture whom she, nonetheless, was convinced
to love, and once having been convinced,
loved ardently. When her eyes were opened
to his true character, and to his vile
treatment of numerous women, she chose
to end her life. There can be no doubt
but that Elizabeth's tragic death led her
brother to the same horrible conclusion
just a few years later.

The statement concluded by saying that Elizabeth Hatton had compiled a list of the women affected, which was attached, and that she'd had the memorial stones placed in the church. Lizzie quickly read down the list; it was identical to the one she had prepared. She pushed the pile of papers back to George.

"Thank you for letting me see that," she said. "It helps explain things."

The three sat silently for a few minutes.

"I think I'll go to London tomorrow and do some of the research that still needs to be done there," Lizzie said finally.

George offered her a place to stay at his house in London but Lizzie refused. She did not want to encounter Richard, but used the excuse that she was expecting her husband to join her shortly and would prefer to stay in a hotel. George then offered Mrs. Jeffries' assistance in making a reservation. Lizzie turned to see if Helen was still in the room, but the housekeeper had slipped silently out at some point in the conversation. Lizzie excused herself from George and Edmund and went to find her in the kitchen.

Helen was sitting at the table, waiting for her. Lizzie refused the inevitable offer of something hot to drink and sat next to her.

"I'm sorry, Helen," Lizzie started, "that when I arrived here I was too thick to be able to appreciate the story that you had to tell me. I'd like to hear it now."

Helen looked somewhat surprised. "Did Sir George acknowledge his relationship to you?"

Now Lizzie was surprised. "No. Do you think he knows? I found out about it in a letter that the priest has over at the Catholic church in the village."

Helen shrugged. "When I heard your name, I just assumed he must have brought you here to make things right."

"He hasn't mentioned it, or even given a hint that he knows. I honestly think he invited me here because I have certain expertise that he needs."

"Well then it is certainly the biggest coincidence I've ever heard of," Helen snorted.

Lizzie smiled. She wasn't certain what to think about George at this point. "Tell me what you know about that other Lizzie Manning," she said. "Was your grandmother in contact with her after she went to the U.S.?"

Helen shook her head. "From the day she left they never heard another word from her. It broke my gran's heart with worry." For several minutes they talked about the first arrival of the Manning girls at Hengemont.

"How did Lizzie begin her relationship with Edmund?" Lizzie asked finally, feeling awkward again at the historical echo in the names and hoping that Helen wouldn't notice her discomfort.

"It started on the day his sister committed suicide."

Lizzie was glad that she was sitting down; she could not form any words in response.

"Jumped off the roof," Helen continued, "like so many of the Hatton girls."

She described how "that other Lizzie," a parlor maid, had been in the library at the time. "According to my gran, she was always volunteering to dust the library, and then spent hours in there. The housekeeper knew she was reading the books but indulged her if there was no other pressing work."

"Oh my God," Lizzie said softly, closing her eyes and picturing the event. "She landed right there on the terrace, didn't she?"

"She was still alive when Lizzie got to her, but died before anyone else had a chance to see her. The brother could not be consoled, and sought Lizzie out, always hoping there had been some message for him, but of course his poor sister had been all broken up and couldn't speak."

A tear rolled down Lizzie's cheek and she reached up to wipe it away.

"When she found out she was pregnant the brother offered to marry her, and my gran thought that they *had* married, but then Lizzie was gone and he was still here."

"And did your grandmother know that her sister had emigrated?"

"Yes, and that is all she knew." Helen took out a handkerchief and dabbed at her eyes, then returned it to her pocket. "When I heard you were coming and learned your name, I was expecting that something would happen, but you didn't seem to know anything about this, and none of the Hattons made any acknowledgement of their relationship to you."

Lizzie felt quite sure that Edmund knew nothing about it. Of George she wasn't so sure, but she couldn't see why he would have brought her all this way and interacted with her on a daily basis if he knew they were related and didn't mean to tell her. Could he have been looking to see if she knew it herself?

It was obviously a topic designed for secrecy, and a house where deception rested very comfortably. Even Helen had not always been straight with her, Lizzie thought.

"Why did you tell me that Bette was dead?" she asked.

"Partly to protect her, I think." Helen paused. "I just blurted it out without thinking. No one has asked me about her in such a long time." She paused again. "Maybe to protect you, too," she added softly. "I didn't want you worrying about her being insane."

"Because you thought I might be going insane as well?"

Helen tried to smile. "It doesn't seem to make much sense now, looking at you. You seem to be taking all this pretty well."

The two women rose and moved toward the door to the kitchen.

"On a more mundane topic," Helen said, "Sir George called just before you came in and asked me to make some arrangements for your stay in London. Where do you like to stay in town?"

The first hotel Lizzie had ever stayed at in London was the Grosvenor, into which she and Martin had stumbled late one night from nearby Victoria Station. She began to mumble a sort of explanation of that trip years before, from which the housekeeper caught only the name of the hotel. That was enough for her to take care of the reservation and the next morning Lizzie was back on the train from Minehead heading east.

She and Edmund had said the briefest of good-byes; warm on both sides, but more restrained than previously. There was much to think about. On the train she pulled out her laptop and began to go through her notes and files. She would have so much to tell Martin, she thought, and just as much to keep to herself.

Chapter 19

The suite at the Grosvenor Hotel was really elegant. Lizzie would never have splurged on anything so extravagant for herself, but she appreciated the gesture that Helen had made for her with George's money. There were two rooms, a sitting room and the bedroom. The former had an expansive view toward Buckingham Palace and even a small gas-powered fireplace that Lizzie could turn on with a remote control.

It had now been more than three weeks since she had talked to her parents and after she unpacked, Lizzie sat down at the desk and called them.

"Hello dear," her mother said as soon as she heard Lizzie's voice. She wanted to know all about Hengemont, being enthusiastically interested in the house and its occupants.

"Why are you such an Anglophile?" Lizzie teased.

"Jane Austen," her mother answered without hesitation. "The Anglophobe is here too," she continued wryly. "Shall I put him on?"

Lizzie had been wondering all this day and the previous one what she should say to her father about her new knowledge of their relationship to the Hattons. Was he entirely ignorant of it? Did he want to be? The sound of his voice brought back a flood of emotions.

"Hi Pop!" she said, answering his greeting.

He asked all the expected questions about her research, her travels, even getting to the weather. She answered all of them with an enthusiasm she didn't feel.

He did not mention the Hattons, so she did, reminding him of the name of her employer.

"Oh that's right," he said, sounding surprised. "I had forgotten."

"It's a pretty swell place they have," she said, trying to make her voice sound cheery. "I don't suppose there is any chance that we're related?"

He laughed. "Not a chance, sweetheart, sorry about that."

He didn't know. It was clear from his voice.

As she hung up the phone she knew that it would not make him happier to know and she decided then that she would not tell him.

She took a long bath, stretching out in the big tub and pondering all the things that had happened at Hengemont. She felt entirely relaxed for the first time in three weeks, and though it was only about seven o'clock crawled into the bed and fell quickly to sleep. She woke around midnight to feel the weight of someone joining her. It was Martin.

"Hello, love," he whispered, wrapping his arms around her as she woke.

"Oh Martin," she said, turning toward him and rubbing her body against his. "I'm so glad to see you."

Martin looked at her for a long moment and then kissed her softly. "I've really missed you," he said. "And I was worried."

She held him tightly, then kissed him passionately. Their caresses led to tender lovemaking. When it was over she fell into a deep and dreamless sleep, the best she had had since she'd arrived in England.

It was still early when she woke. Martin was snoring softly as she slipped out of bed and padded across the carpet to the bathroom, and he was still sleeping soundly as she dressed and went down to get some coffee and baked goods for their breakfast. Martin wouldn't be very hungry given the time change, but he would need the coffee and might appreciate something light to eat when he woke.

The city was bustling as she stepped out the front door of the hotel onto Buckingham Palace Road. It was only a few blocks to the shops at Victoria Station where she had noticed a promising coffee shop the day before. She returned to the hotel room with coffee, cinnamon rolls, and *The London Times*.

At ten o'clock she kissed Martin on the lips and whispered "Good Morning, love, welcome to England."

He managed a weak smile, rolled over and slept for another hour as she scanned the *Times*. At eleven she tried again.

"Martin, sweetheart," she said softly, "you don't want to sleep too long or you won't get over the jet lag."

He stretched out his arms, caught her in one and pulled her to him for a long kiss.

"Miss me?" he asked.

"Like crazy," she answered, kissing him again.

Martin went into the bathroom for several minutes and when he returned to the bed he had a cup of coffee in one hand.

"Yuck," he said, taking a sip, "this is cold."

"I thought you'd be up an hour ago," Lizzie shrugged.

"Come on, dear wife," he said, "I'll take you out for a real English breakfast."

Lizzie told him that he was too late, but could take her to lunch. She knew that he was anxious to hear about her adventures at Hengemont, and she was just about ready to tell him. He dressed quickly and before long they were walking arm and arm through the chilly London day.

The both saw "The Ship" at the same moment and agreed that a pub lunch in an ancient-looking establishment was perfect for Martin's first foray into English food. The pub had a low ceiling, lots of wood, dark recesses, and slightly tilting beams. It was still early enough that they could occupy one corner entirely by themselves. Lizzie slipped in along the cushioned bench and Martin followed, sitting close enough to slip his hand onto her thigh. A waitress took their order for fish and chips and salad, and Martin ordered a pint of beer for each of them.

As he spoke with the waitress, Lizzie looked around at the advertising art, the dusty ship models, and the hundreds of coasters tacked to the walls, trying to decide where she should start. Martin anticipated her, asking what had led her to the Hengemont roof.

She started slowly, telling him about the dreams and the poems, how she had matched them up with actual women.

How she had seen the ruby worn repeatedly in the portraits, and how she had seen the memorial stones in the Hatton's church. She told him about John and Elizabeth, about Rossetti's lover, Bette's diary, and the missing heart. When she finished they both sat silently for several minutes.

Martin took a sip from his pint-sized glass of beer and looked at her over the rim. "What is bothering you the most about all this?" he asked.

She was thoughtful for a moment. "I had these dreams," she said finally. "They were so vivid, so filled with detail. I felt like I was *in* the past, not just viewing it from a distance, but then I can't remember if I read those details, or saw them somewhere in some document or painting." She took a long swig from the beer and put the glass down on the paper coaster. She wasn't prepared to tell Martin of the erotic nature of the first dream and of Edmund's role in it, or of the intense desire for her lover in the other two dreams. "It's a bit frightening," she said finally, "because I feel like I learned much of what I know about this story directly from the dreams."

"And the Hattons knew this story and what it could do?"

"George knew it primarily through the experience of his sister, and Edmund as a sort of interesting medical problem. I think the women in the family have always been more knowledgeable about this story than the men, and the only woman who qualifies right now is locked in a convent in France."

"How many did you say there have been?"

"If you count me, twelve," she said, "over a period of some seven hundred years." She looked around the pub, hoping to find comfort in the "Olde England" decor. Carved faces emerged from the ends of the dark wood beams. Once she would have found them amusing, but now they just seemed sinister.

"There's something else," she whispered. "I just found it out two days ago."

Martin took another sip of beer and waited for her to continue.

"This is the strangest thing," she said slowly, "and I'm still trying to come to grips with it myself." She paused and took another sip from her glass.

Martin looked at her with real concern. "What is it?" he asked.

"I found a document in the local church down at Hengemont that seems to indicate that I am related to the Hattons." Since she had visited with Father Folan, Lizzie had acknowledged this fact only to Helen, who had already known more about it than she had.

Her husband waited for her to continue.

"It appears that George Hatton's great-uncle was my great-grandfather," she said quickly. "He fathered the child of a young parlor maid—she was my dad's grandmother."

Martin looked stunned. "Does George Hatton know this?"

"I don't know," she answered. "I don't think so."

They sat in silence for several minutes as Lizzie gave Martin time to digest what she had said.

"So what do you think is happening to me then?" she asked finally. She had tried to keep the mood light, but she could not disguise her disquiet from her husband.

"What do *you* think is happening?" he asked back.

"I like Edmund's explanation that I was in a fugue state brought on by an idiosyncratic reaction to valium," she said, half joking. She fingered the glass on the table in front of her as Martin waited patiently for her to continue. "But I can't help worrying about this other thing that he said."

Martin reached over and took her hand and held it. "What was that?" he asked gently.

"When he told me this, neither he nor I knew that we were related. In fact, I'm pretty certain he still doesn't know. . . ." Her voice trailed off again.

"And?"

"And he thinks that there is a genetic predisposition to mental illness among the women in his family," she said quickly. "Edmund is a doctor and he wants to explain all this by science and genetics," she went on, "but I can't help feeling there is something weirder at work here. All of the women who experienced this phenomenon were named Elizabeth Hatton."

"But that's not your name."

"No, but if my grandfather had had his father's surname,

rather than his mother's, then my name *would* be Elizabeth Hatton."

She took her hand from Martin's and took another sip of the beer. As soon as she set the glass down he grabbed her hand again. He squeezed it until she looked up at him.

"Is that all that's worrying you?" he asked. "That you've inherited some madness?" He was actually smiling, and Lizzie pulled her hand away again angrily.

"Thanks for your concern."

"Oh now Lizzie," he said, putting his arm around her and giving her a hard hug. "Lizzie, Lizzie, Lizzie, this situation is *much* weirder than that!"

She looked at him with astonishment.

"Do you really think," he continued, "that some sort of madness would transmit itself down through what, twenty-five or more generations, and that each of the sufferers would have precisely the same delusion? If I understand what you told me, the details were the same every time. It was always about the same two people and nothing got altered over seven hundred years, even down to you. Does this really sound like some bad drug reaction?"

Lizzie pondered his words for a moment. "Are you saying I'm being haunted or something?" she asked. "Because you know I can't buy that." She turned her whole body toward him to continue. "And frankly I can't believe that you would either. You don't even read your horoscope."

"Well I'm not going to start living my life by signs read in stars or cards or chicken bones," he said, "but I'm also not willing to discount that there might be things out there that we don't understand."

"Supernatural things?"

"I'm not sure how I'd define the thing I'm thinking about. But I think that between people who have a deep love there is a connection that can be felt somehow." He took his arm from behind her back and took her hand again. "I knew that I would marry you the first time I saw you. How do we explain that?"

She shrugged.

"There is something here," he tapped his chest and then

moved his finger up to tap his temple, "and here, that is more powerful than science can explain."

Lizzie sat quietly, thinking about several other occasions in her life when she had felt that loved ones were in danger, or that something extraordinary had happened to one of her siblings, only to have the phone ring soon after.

"So this Elizabeth d'Hautain, then," she mumbled, struggling to find words, "she transmitted her pain through her DNA or something?"

"Maybe. Maybe she felt the love and the loss so strongly that sensitive women among her descendents could feel it somehow."

"But most of them killed themselves! It's hard to believe that she would curse her unborn granddaughters for generations to come." Lizzie thought about this for a few moments before continuing. "You know, she was still only a teenager when she killed herself. I don't think she gave much thought to any future." She took another sip of the beer. "And maybe that's why all those women who committed suicide were so young. They hadn't begun to think in terms of the future either."

They sat for several minutes in silence.

"George showed me a very interesting statement, written to his father by his great-aunt," Lizzie continued, breaking the silence. "She explained all this by saying that the Hatton family romanticized death to such an extent that girls who knew the story would turn to suicide when they were disappointed in their own love lives."

"A *Romeo and Juliet* phenomenon?"

Lizzie nodded.

"But you didn't know the story."

Lizzie took a swig of beer. "This is where I am most confused, though," she said thoughtfully. "I *did* know the story. Edmund told it to me and the clues to it were all around me, in the paintings and the poems. How much did I learn and incorporate into the dreams? My memory has become very fuzzy about the order in which the information came to me."

"You're looking for a rational explanation."

"Yes."

"And are you satisfied that you have now described one?"

"Almost." She smiled.

Martin looked at the far end of the bar and Lizzie could see that he was processing all the information she had given him. Finally he spoke again.

"He knows," Martin said bluntly. "George Hatton knows."

"How could you possibly know that?"

Martin turned to look straight at her. "Because I know what you have to do," he said. "And so does he."

Lizzie felt the hair along the back of her neck tingle. Martin's expression was new to her and she had never seen him look so pale. He waited until she nodded nervously, then he continued.

"I think there's a task in all this for you," he said seriously.

"A task?"

"A job, Liz. A quest. A familial responsibility."

She looked at him quizzically.

"You have to find the heart," he said finally.

Lizzie drew her hand out of his and ran it through her hair. She massaged herself lightly on the neck to stop the tingling sensation, which persisted. Her hand felt cold and clammy against the warm skin under her hair.

Martin was looking at her very seriously. He was clearly concerned.

"Frankly, Mart," she said hoarsely, "You're scaring me. I expected you to help me rationalize all this, to support the logical explanation." She gulped down everything left in the pint glass and held it up in the direction of the bar man to order another. "You are implying that I'm getting a message from seven hundred years ago to go out and find a disembodied human heart?"

"It sounds strange, I know," he said gently. "But sometimes there is no rational explanation. This is clearly not just some kind of congenital mental illness. These are very strange circumstances—how else can you explain them?"

"But why would it have to be *me* who finds it?"

"Because you can."

She stared at the empty glass as she twirled it around and

around in her hands. Martin took the glass from her, put it firmly on the table and took both her hands in his. She looked up to meet his warm brown eyes.

"You can," he said again. "None of those previous women was in a position to do it. George Hatton knows it too."

Lizzie pondered that. "I don't really think he knows," she said. "He was really upset when I had that fit or whatever it was. He made me move out of the house that very day."

"I'm not sure he necessarily acknowledged it consciously," Martin said, "but he knew that you had the skills to dig into the past and end this thing once and for all."

"What if there is no heart?" she asked.

Martin withdrew his hands and adjusted himself on the bench as the bar man approached with two new pints and their lunches on a tray.

"I don't think this curse would have survived if the heart hadn't," he said when they were alone again. He chose his words carefully. "This is a request," he continued, "an assignment. This ancestor of yours is looking for someone to take away a pain so great that it has outlived her by centuries." He held up the new glass of beer as if to make a toast and then brought it straight to his mouth. Lizzie waited for him to speak again.

"I can't believe the pain would last without the possibility of a solution." He saw her worried face and smiled. "Of course I'm just speculating," he said with a laugh.

Lizzie smiled uncomfortably. "How much of my life should I dedicate to this search?" she asked.

"Don't let it become any more of a life-altering obsession," he answered seriously. "And don't ever let yourself get so caught up in *her* life that you lose your own." He reached across and gripped her hand again tightly. "You planned to stay another week in England anyway. Why don't you put all your skills to work on this and see what you can find. Just think of it as a research problem, and then if there's nothing to it you can go home and leave it behind you."

She thought for a moment and then nodded. "Okay," she said. "I'll give it a shot. But now that you're here, you'll have to protect me from the forces of evil."

"Can do," he said, raising his glass again. "Here's to luck in your quest to uncover the secrets of the human heart."

Chapter 20

Martin raised certain fears in the deep, superstitious part of Lizzie that, until that point, she had not consciously confronted. Despite the voicing of things she might have preferred to leave unsaid, however, she still could not countenance a supernatural source for the misfortunes that had befallen the Hattons over the years. As to her own experiences, however unusual and startling they might have been, she could not and would not attribute them to the ghosts of a couple of aristocratic teenagers whose romantic notions got the better of whatever good sense they might have possessed.

It was necessary, therefore, for her to approach the problem logically. There were three subject areas for which she required quick history lessons: medieval heart burials, the Crusade of 1250, and the Knights Templar. Martin agreed to look into the first and headed off to Westminster Abbey, the great mausoleum of English History, to see what he could find. Lizzie headed to the British Library, expecting that some previous scholars had already done the work on the other two topics. Both the Crusades and the Templars were represented by hundreds of titles. Several books actually discussed both topics and Lizzie ordered a stack and then went to wait at the numbered seat assigned to her in the reading room.

As she looked around the room at the bowed heads of other researchers Lizzie thought about Martin and what a rare man he was. He provided her with perspective while always taking her seriously. The thought of Edmund Hatton made her blush. Now that she had held Martin in her arms again, had Edmund's attractions vanished? She could not deny that he was wonderful, and not just physically. He was gentle and kind, really thoughtful, and he had saved her life, which made him particularly compelling. But Lizzie wondered if part of the attraction to Edmund might not actually be an attraction to Hengemont and the life there. Distant from him now by a few days and a hundred miles she couldn't even remember if he felt anything for her. Could she have projected onto him her own fantasies? She made a determination that she would not threaten her relationship with Martin by any further thoughts of Edmund Hatton. But she wondered where he was at that moment. Had he returned to Bristol? Was he with George? With Lily? With a patient?

Her multi-volume *History of the Crusades* arrived and Lizzie began to scan the table of contents. She quickly passed over the First Crusade of 1090. There was a lot on Richard the Lionhearted and the Third Crusade a hundred years later. Richard was apparently the favorite Crusader of Englishmen, while King Louis IX of France, who became St. Louis, was the clear leader among French authors.

Lizzie skimmed rapidly over the early material, remembering the other knight-effigy crypts in the Hatton church and the history of the family she had read at the White Horse. She vaguely remembered that someone, probably an uncle of Alun d'Hautain, had gone crusading with Richard and never come back. "That was 1190 though and sixty years too early to have anything to do with the heart," Lizzie mumbled to herself. Richard himself, she was reminded, was captured on his return journey and held prisoner until 1194 by the German emperor. Names jumped out from the page as she flipped through the thick book: Messina, Acre, Saladin.

Richard was succeeded by his brother John, who Lizzie remembered principally as the villain of Robin Hood movies, and then by John's son, Henry III. The next king, Edward I, called "Longshanks," had also gone on a crusade, but that was 1271 and twenty years too late. Lizzie thumbed back to the reign of Henry III, looking for a description of the English participation in a mid-thirteenth-century crusade. John d'Hautain had died at a place called Mansoura, according to the Hatton family history.

She finally found the episode she was seeking. Crusading had lost much of its appeal by the time Alun and John d'Hautain set out from Hengemont in 1248. Even with a tremendous sacrifice of lives, European Crusaders had been losing rather than gaining ground in the Holy Land. It was the king of France, Louis IX, who really inspired the European return to the wars, after a charismatic religious experience some five years earlier. He led the force that set sail from Marseilles toward the Holy Land in August 1248. The book reprinted a description of the departure from the account of one Jean de Joinville.

> When the horses were embarked, our master mariner called to his sailors, who were in the prow of the ship, "Is all fast?" "Aye aye, sir," they answered; "the clerks and priests may come forward." As soon as they had done so, he called out to them, "In the name of God, strike up a song!" They all sang in unison VENI, CREATOR SPIRITUS; the master called to the sailors, "In the name of God, make sail"; and so they set the sails.

Lizzie could picture the armored John d'Hautain among them. The force wintered in Cyprus and set out the following May with a large fleet, many more soldiers having joined them in the interim. Their objective was to take Cairo and proceed from there toward Jerusalem. On Christmas Day they were within sight of the Egyptian walled city of Mansoura, but it was more than a month before they were able to enter it. When they did so, it was in an ill-judged and poorly executed maneuver that led the Europeans by the hundreds into the narrow streets of the town, where they were massacred by archers stationed on the rooftops. As many as two thousand armored knights may have died on the first day.

Louis, camped beyond the walls of the city, held out for two more months, while the rest of the European force dwindled from disease and starvation. Finally beaten, the last survivors of the fleet walked away. Louis was captured. Later he would pay a ransom for his release and become a saint.

Lizzie didn't know if John d'Hautain and his father had

died in the bloody rout in the streets of Mansoura, or from hunger or disease in the weeks that followed. Was there any way that his body could have been recovered and identified in all that mess, she wondered? The Templars were certainly there in numbers in the battle, but they had sustained devastating losses as well.

The shadows in the reading room were lengthening as Lizzie turned to the book on the Knights Templar. On the title page was the seal with the two knights sharing a horse. She looked at her watch. She had an appointment at four o'clock with Tom Clark, the curator of the British Museum, who was squeezing her into his schedule as a personal favor. She had about fifteen minutes to copy down the basic timeline of Templar history. Like most libraries, the British Library allowed only pencils, so Lizzie stacked a pile of sharp ones near the top of the desk and wrote quickly in her notebook under the title "Templar Chronology."

1118: Order of Knights Templar founded for the protection of Pilgrims to the Holy Land. (Named after a wing of the king of Jerusalem's palace which was built on the foundation of the old Temple of Solomon.)

1128: Recognized as a religious military order, answerable only to the Pope.

1147: Embarked on the second crusade. Established trade networks, money transfers, etc.

1305: Beginning of the suppression of Templars by the king of France. Under torture they confessed (supposedly) to Devil Worship and Denying Christ.

1312: Order is dissolved by a Papal Bull.

According to one historian, the Templars left a great treasure that had never been discovered; according to another, a nineteenth-century French priest discovered cryptic parchments, which supposedly held the key to where the Templars hid their fabled wealth. Lizzie flipped to the index and looked under "England." The Templars had property and religious houses all over the country. In London, their home church now stood in the middle of the British Law Courts, commonly called "Temple Bar." Lizzie closed the books, slipped the pencils and her notebook into her bag, returned the books to the desk, and walked quickly out the front door of the library. She was lucky to find a cab, and pulled up to the British Museum at five minutes to four.

Tom Clark was his usual amiable self. Literate and funny, he had always been Lizzie's model of the cultured Englishman. After exchanging information on mutual friends and institutions, Lizzie told him that all was not going well with the Hatton project.

"Not finding what you hoped?" Tom asked.

"Just the opposite," she laughed, "there is too much to process, and it's not all about Francis Hatton and his collection."

Tom looked curious. "How can I help?"

"For now," Lizzie said, "I just want to see if you can help me locate a Tlingit bentwood burial box and a Chilkat blanket."

"Part of Lieutenant Hatton's collection?" he asked. "I don't remember ever seeing those in any inventory."

"That's just it," Lizzie continued, "Francis Hatton himself hid all references to them because he was mortified to find himself a grave robber. It was clearly his intention to return them, but I can't find any record that he ever went back to the Northwest Coast."

"You don't think those things are here do you?"

"I don't know. I just thought it would be worth checking among the other Cook collections here and elsewhere, and I figured you were the man who'd know."

He turned to his computer screen and brought up the information on the Museum's collection. "Any details on the iconography?" he asked.

"Both pieces have a bear crest, and if Hatton's eye is any good they are rendered very similarly."

"Anything else?" he asked.

"The burial box still contained a human corpse, not fully cremated, when Hatton had it in the eighteenth century," Lizzie said grimly.

Tom Clark didn't even flinch. In his years as an anthropologist at the British Museum he had handled many old body parts. After several minutes he turned back to Lizzie.

"This is a pretty complete catalogue of the Cook material," he said, "and I don't see anything like what you describe, but let me keep an eye out for it."

"There's another interesting thing down at Hengemont that you should know about," she added. "Or did you already know that Joseph Banks gave Francis Hatton a boomerang from Cook's first voyage?"

"No," Tom said slowly, scanning his computer terminal again, "and I don't see any reference to it here. Thanks, that's great to know."

"It gets better," Lizzie said. "There is a Dance portrait of Francis Hatton all suited up and ready to go on the voyage, and he's standing next to a table that has the boomerang on it!"

"Brilliant!" Tom said in a very British declaration of excitement. "You know, Lizzie," he continued, "I am planning a major exhibition of Cook material a year or so down the road. Should we try to incorporate the Hatton material into it? Or do you feel that collection warrants a separate exhibition."

"Frankly, it all fits into a cabinet no bigger than your wall there," Lizzie said. "It's terrific stuff, but even with the painting it makes a better part of an exhibit than a stand-alone, and your Cook exhibition would be the stronger for including it."

"There's some politics in all this, as I'm sure you will not be surprised to hear."

"Having come to know George Hatton a bit, I would put my money on his son Richard being the political one."

"Exactly," Tom confided. "He is keen to become a trustee of the museum."

"I'm sorry to have to tell you that he and I did *not* hit it off."

"Well the scuttlebutt here in the city is that he is burning bridges pretty fast, so you aren't the only one." He paused, as if wondering if he should tell her more. "Just for your information, Lizzie, I'll tell you that I have heard that Richard Hatton has lost a fortune in some bad investments, and may be facing some social embarrassment from it all as well. He convinced a number of his friends to join him on big deals that never materialized as promised. I think he sees the Museum relationship as one that can solidify an increasingly shaky reputation here in London, especially among the new wealth that love aristocratic connections and old families."

"When you say 'lost a fortune,' how much do you mean?"

"Several million pounds."

Lizzie sat slowly back in her seat. "My God," she gasped. "I wonder if his father knows?"

Tom leaned forward. "I hope you won't mention any of this to him."

"Of course not," she assured him. "I like him, though, and I hate the thought of seeing him embarrassed."

"Did you know him before this project came up?"

She shook her head. "And I have been wondering how you came to recommend me for it."

He seemed more comfortable with the subject changed. She knew that he feared he had told her too much, but she was very glad to have the information about Richard. It explained, but did not excuse, his outrageous behavior.

Tom told her that Richard Hatton brought his father by the museum one day, encouraging him to support the idea of a publication and exhibition on Francis Hatton.

"I was showing them different publications, as models of ways these early collections could be presented," Tom said, "and Sir George was positively bowled over by your book. Said instantly 'She's the one! How do I contact her?'"

"Had he actually read it?"

"No. And not that you wouldn't have risen to the top of the list anyway, Lizzie, but Sir George almost seemed to make the decision based simply on your name."

Lizzie started. George *did* know of her connection to the Hattons. There was no other explanation. She wanted a chance to think about this, and she didn't want to do it sitting in Tom Clark's office. She made a show of looking at her watch and stood up.

"This has been a most interesting conversation, Tom. How should we proceed from here?"

"Well, if you are inclined to think that I should approach Richard Hatton with the Cook exhibition project, then I will do that. He's eager to find some way to get his name up on the wall."

"I'll mention it to George," Lizzie said. "I think he would be inclined to take my advice on this."

"Great," Tom said. "I'm glad you stopped by today. This has been very productive for me."

"And for me," Lizzie responded. "It takes the pressure off me to package this material in some specific way."

"And what about a publication?"

"Hatton's journal is really a treasure, very open minded, sensitive to cultural issues, and filled with great descriptions. It's not long, and I think a publication of it would make an important contribution, especially if it included photographs of the artifacts he collected on the voyage."

"Would you like me to look into having it published by the museum?"

"That would be great!" Lizzie said, delighted. Something would come out of this whole experience that would be to her benefit after all.

"Maybe we could get it to coincide with the larger exhibition project, or maybe it could even be a long chapter in the catalogue," Tom Clark continued.

"Let me talk to George about it and see how he wants to proceed."

"All right then. If I find anything on that box or blanket, should I contact you at Hengemont?" he asked.

"No, I'm doing some work in London," she said. "I'm at the Grosvenor."

He walked her to the door of the Museum, clearing her access through the security systems as the guards locked the building for the night.

The two exchanged what Lizzie liked to think of as "professional kisses," where their lips almost, but not quite, touched the other's cheek, then Lizzie hailed a cab to take her back to the hotel.

Martin was fast asleep when she got back to the room. Lizzie wondered if she should wake him, since she knew that he would never get over his jet lag this way. But he looked so peaceful and comfortable that all she could do was slip in beside him and before long she was asleep herself. When she awoke, the room was dark.

"Martin," she called softly, "Martin, wake up. We've slept too long."

She rolled over and slipped her arm over his shoulder, kissing him on the back of the neck and breathing in the warm smell of him.

"What time is it?" he moaned.

"Eight o'clock," she said, looking at the clock on the bedside table.

"Don't tell me," he said, "you've been asleep too, haven't you?"

He rolled over and slipped his arms through hers. She nodded.

"Any dreams?" he asked.

"Not a one," she smiled.

"Let's go have dinner and I'll show you what I found," he said.

• • • • •

"I wonder what else George Hatton knows that he hasn't told you?" Martin said bluntly after they had ordered their dinners in the hotel restaurant.

Lizzie swirled the plastic stirrer around in her drink. "I'm mostly wondering if he has other documents that I haven't seen yet."

"You don't think you saw them all?" Martin asked.

"I think I saw all of the papers related to Francis Hatton and his voyage," she answered. "In fact, I found more than even George Hatton knew existed." She paused a moment and continued, thinking aloud. "I know that he didn't know anything about the grave robbing that Frank did on the Northwest Coast, and I don't think he knew that Bette had left the poems and her diary in the cabinet." She looked up to meet her husband's dark eyes. "Oh Martin," she laughed, "You are way too suspicious. He is not as cunning as you are thinking."

Even with what she had learned from Tom Clark, Lizzie was not inclined to doubt George's fundamental nature. She had become rather fond of him. She did, however, tell Martin that she now suspected that George had known about their relationship when he offered her the job.

"A ha!" he said. "And what are the other papers that you think he may be holding back?"

"I'm just wondering if there are any more thirteenth-century documents, like the one Father Folan got from Rome. They would have nothing to do with Francis Hatton's voyage, and George would have no reason to think that they would be important to me."

The two of them determined that Lizzie should call George Hatton to ask, and she decided to do it quickly, before their dinners came. She rose from the table, gave Martin a quick kiss, and went into the lobby to phone Hengemont.

George Hatton answered the phone himself.

"Lizzie," he replied, clearly surprised to hear from her. "How are things going in London? Mrs. Jeffries says you're at the Grosvenor. I hope you're comfortable there."

"It's just fine," she said.

"Have you arranged for your return to Boston?"

"I'm still leaving next week, as planned," Lizzie said. "Before then, George, I'm thinking I might make one more trip down to see you and go through the family papers again."

"I thought you had already entered everything you need into that computer of yours," came the answer. Lizzie could tell that George was trying to sound lighthearted, but wasn't particularly eager to see her again at Hengemont.

"I've seen all of Francis Hatton's papers," she said. "Now I want to see all of the letters and contracts that were in the possession of Elizabeth d'Hautain."

"How do you know there are any?" George said.

"I don't," she replied, honestly, "but if there are, I need to see them so that I can find the heart."

There was silence at the other end for a long time.

"I'll bring them to you," he answered finally. "I'm coming into town the day after tomorrow. Can I meet you at your hotel around seven in the evening?"

Lizzie agreed and hung up the phone. The waiter arrived with their dinner just after she returned to her seat at the table.

"Perfect timing as usual," Martin said. "How'd it go?"

"He's coming here the day after tomorrow at seven."

"Good," Martin nodded. "I want to meet this guy."

Lizzie was hungry, and this looked like a very good meal—salmon with small roasted potatoes and several sprigs of greenery that she thought must be watercress. "So," she said, digging in, "what did you find at Westminster Abbey?"

Martin had ordered roast beef and now as he cut off a piece he said, "It's only because I know that you aren't squeamish that I can tell you this while eating, but that whole place is filled with the heartless nobility, and I'm not joking." He put his fork to his mouth and chewed.

Lizzie smiled, "Success, I take it?"

Martin nodded, picking up his wine glass. "There is hardly a Medieval monarch there that didn't have his or her heart sent off to France or Jerusalem or somewhere. And it wasn't only hearts." He took another bite. "Some of this could actually spoil your dinner," he said, "so let me just insert at this point that you could not have had a better ambassador on your mission today."

"No?"

"No," he said with a grin. "Believe it or not, I got to talking to one of the clergymen there, and he actually knew some of my work."

Lizzie gave him a nod of encouragement. "I knew that having a famous artist for a husband would come in handy some day."

"This guy is retired now," Martin said, finishing off his meal, "but he used to be a pastor in a neighborhood of what they call 'Council Housing'—what we would call 'projects.'" He leaned back, picked up his wine glass and pushed his plate away. "Hence his knowledge of public art works done in similar neighborhoods in the U.S. A nice guy, liberal and open minded. I guess he's not exactly what I expected to find at Westminster Abbey."

The waiter arrived as Lizzie finished her dinner, and took their plates away and brought coffee. Martin pulled several sheets of folded paper out of his jacket pocket.

"Anyway," he continued, "he was very helpful. Showed me around and even took me up to their library."

Lizzie leaned forward with interest as Martin began a litany of heart burials.

"Well, to start with the Crusaders," Martin said, "Richard the Lion Hearted's remains are scattered across France. Most of him was buried at Fontrevault Abbey, but his heart went to Rouen, and his bowels were buried at Chaluz, apparently as an insult, because he was killed there." He looked up from his notes. "And you'll love this," he added. "His heart was buried under a little king effigy, and in 1838 they dug it up and put it in the local museum."

Lizzie felt that Martin wanted her to make a witty remark, but she couldn't help wondering if something similar could have happened to John d'Hautain's heart. He continued, describing the hearts of Kings John and Henry III, both sent to Fontrevault, while their bodies remained in England. "Then there was a Prince Henry," Martin read from his notes, "who was murdered in some place called Viterbo in 1271, and whose heart was brought home in a golden cup and placed in Westminster Abbey."

He turned to the next page. "You know the Charing Cross Railroad Station?" he asked.

Lizzie nodded.

"Well that's named after a cross that was placed there to mark a spot where the body of Queen Eleanor lay on its way from Lincoln to London in 1291," Martin said. "They left her entrails back in Lincoln, and then deposited her heart at the Blackfriar's monastery in London before burying her in Westminster. She had several children who died young, and they are buried in the Abbey too, but the heart of one of them, her son Alfonso, is with her heart at Blackfriars."

"Charming," Lizzie said.

Martin looked up and smiled. "It's really weird, isn't it?"

Lizzie nodded.

"There's more," he said. "Now we're getting to the really sick guy, Edward I. He instructed his son to boil the flesh off his skeleton so that his bones could be carried around with the army until the Scots were crushed, and, as he had been on an unsuccessful crusade in his youth, he wanted his heart sent to the Holy Land."

"Even more charming," Lizzie snorted.

"And his son, Edward II, was such a rotten king that his queen, Isabella, and her lover had him imprisoned and eventually murdered." He gestured to keep Lizzie from interrupting with a comment. "But that's not the good part for our purposes," he continued. "Isabella repented somewhat after her son, Edward III, had *her* lover executed, and when she was dying she asked that the heart be removed from the long-dead corpse of her husband-victim, to be delicately placed in a silver casket and laid on the breast of her own corpse when she was buried."

Martin looked up in triumph. "What a country!" he said smugly, laying down his pile of papers and lifting his glass to his wife.

"So, it wasn't so strange after all that Elizabeth d'Hautain wanted her husband's heart sent back."

Martin shook his head. "And, I've saved my favorite for last." He handed Lizzie a Xerox of a grainy black and white photograph taken from a book in the Westminster Library collection. "There's a place in Scotland called Sweetheart Abbey, which is named for the founder, Lady Devorguilla, who carried her husband's heart around with her at all times." He tapped his finger on the photograph. "Here's a picture of a carving of her at the abbey."

Lizzie looked at the picture of the headless statue in disbelief as Martin went on.

"That thing in her hands is the silver and ivory casket she had made to hold his embalmed heart, and she wore it around her neck for at least sixteen years."

"Ick."

"Oh, come on. I think it's romantic."

"Don't get any ideas Mart." Lizzie took a sip of her coffee. "When was this, anyway?"

"Middle of the thirteenth century, just like your missing heart. And there are more. There's a well-known heart burial in Somerset at a place called Sampford Arundel, and another at Salisbury Cathedral."

As they left the table Lizzie took the papers that Martin held out to her. They walked toward the elevator in the lobby and he slipped his arm around her. "You really didn't think that Scottish thing was sexy? That Sweetheart Abbey story?" he teased.

"Ha, ha, ha."

"Want me to lay my heart on your breast?"

"Only if it is still beating and remains within your hairy chest."

"You've got it," he answered.

Chapter 21

The next day Martin took the train early to Newcastle to scout out his mural project. He was scheduled to visit the proposed site and meet with town officials, potential financial backers, and some of the people in the community who would help him with production if he accepted the offer. Seeing Lizzie had lessened his fears for her, and he planned to stay the night in Newcastle to finish up the business. He promised he would be back in time to meet George the following evening.

Lizzie walked with him to Victoria Station, then headed for the Public Record Office, where she had spent many hours when she was researching her dissertation, and where she hoped to find some information about the Knights Templers, and possibly about their role in the transportation of the John d'Hautain's heart from Egypt back to England after the battle of Mansoura. She walked briskly, feeling smart and professional. She was confident that she was a good researcher, and that this was a problem she could solve.

A few minutes with the catalog was enough to shake her confidence. Most of the surviving materials consisted of detailed inventories of Templar property confiscated by the British Crown at the time of the dissolution of the Templar order. There were lists of household goods, religious regalia, and documents. They were in a combination of Latin, French, and Middle English, and Lizzie quickly became frustrated. She wasn't comfortable enough in any of the languages to be sure that she wasn't missing the object of her search. After three hours of exasperating work, she had made no progress. If she went out and learned the languages, or found someone competent to translate them for her, she would have to begin again at the beginning.

The librarian arrived with another file box of documents and asked Lizzie if she was ready to trade the one she was working on for this new one. She shrugged. What the hell, she thought. She pulled out a file, opened it and started looking quickly at endless old pieces of paper covered with lists, numbers, and incomprehensible foreign words. The pages shifted, one after another from the right side of the folder to the left as she moved them face up to face down. She closed the folder. She had no memory of even a single word.

It was past noon. Maybe she should take a lunch break, she thought. At any rate, she could stop at a book store and get herself a couple of pocket dictionaries. She returned the document box to the desk and left the building. It was bitter cold as she walked up Chancery Lane. She saw W.H. Smith, the bookstore chain, and bought two dictionaries, Latin and French.

There was a small pub tucked into the alley behind the bookstore and Lizzie decided to stop in there for lunch. It was crowded, but she found an empty booth and slipped in, removing her bulky coat, muffler, hat, and knitted gloves before she sat down. There was no menu on the table and when she looked up at the bar, she didn't see the usual blackboard with specials. She left her coat in the booth and went to the bar. No hot food served, she was told.

"We have crisps," the man behind the bar told her.

Lizzie thought of the trouble it would take to get her cold weather gear on again and find a restaurant. She had seen nothing in the neighborhood but law offices.

"I'll have two packs of crisps and a pint of bitter," she said. She looked around the place. There had been a time when a single woman wouldn't have been served beer in a pub, but this seemed a pretty hard-drinking crowd, and she was not the only woman drinking alone.

She went back to her booth and opened one of the small bags of salty potato chips. What to do now, she wondered? She took a long drink of the bitter. It was misnamed, she thought. It wasn't bitter at all and she had become fond of drinking it on her earlier trips to England.

She took a notebook and the two dictionaries from her bag and laid them on the table in front of her. "Okay," she said to herself, "where am I on this ridiculous project anyway?" She finished the pint and the crisps and went to the bar for the same thing again. She was feeling warmer and calmer and thought she might actually be able to get a little work done as she sat there. Around her was the low rumble of conversation, the clink of glasses as the barman wiped them and set them on the shelf above him, and the different clunk of glasses as they touched the wood of nearby tables.

A list of pertinent words would make her afternoon more productive. Lizzie took up a pen and began to write down all the words for heart from the Latin dictionary, and then did the same for French. She also wrote down the words for corpse, preserved, travel, widow, soldier, knight, Crusades, and all the versions of dead, death, and dying. For the first time that day, she felt like she was making some progress. Would it be too much to have a third pint? She had seen some of her English friends down five pints at lunch and had always been astonished, especially since they then went back to work. She felt a comfortable buzz and thought the beer was helping. At the bar she ordered another pint, but shook her head when the publican held up yet another bag of crisps.

Back at the table she looked at her growing column of words, then turned to the notes she had taken that morning at the Public Record Office. She started a list of questions:

1. Were all the Templar properties in England confiscated by the Crown?
2. Was there any attempt to return to private individuals personal property held by the Templars at the time the order was dissolved?
3. What happened to the remains of Templars killed at the battle of Mansoura?
4. Where is his heart?

As she dotted the last question mark, Lizzie dropped the pen with a start. She had actually written, unthinkingly, the very line that had started her on this strange chase. She stared at it while reaching to retrieve her pen and sent the beer glass clattering across the table. The barman approached with a towel to wipe up the spilled beer and Lizzie reached for her napkin to stop the flood headed her way. Most of the pint glass had spilled onto her coat and scarf, lying on the bench opposite her in the booth. Lizzie could do no more than murmur an apology for her clumsiness as she slid out of the booth. The man gave her a look of grumpy exasperation; he clearly did not appreciate her kind of damsel in distress.

Lizzie picked up her coat and brushed it off as well as she could. Her knitted muffler was soaked with beer, as were her hat and gloves. She went into the bathroom and wrung them out in the sink, then held her coat up to the hot blower provided to dry hands.

"Where is his heart?" It was written on a scrap of paper sitting on the table in the pub, and she had written it. Should she add it to her assemblage of poems? She wasn't sure if this was humorous or terrifying. Was she now one of the Hatton girls? Or, could it be, she wondered for the first time, that someone else had written that question as she had, simply because they actually wanted to know the answer to it and not because they felt some centuries-weight of tragedy about it.

Her muffler and hat were still soaking wet. To go out into the cold with them was out of the question. She laid them across the sink and left them. Maybe when they dried somebody else could use them.

Her soggy papers were at the bar. A couple had already replaced her in the booth and the barman didn't seem sorry to see her go. She wiped off her notebook as well as she could, shoved it into her bag, paid the bill, and left the pub. The cold air hit her with a blast in the face. She pushed her fists into her pockets, missing her warm scarf and gloves. Her coat was damp, but she still felt dry enough inside it, so with her head down she started walking.

There was a warren of small alleys in the neighborhood and Lizzie wasn't sure exactly where she was. She knew that eventually she would come back out onto Chancery Lane or Fleet Street, but in the meantime she would walk until her head cleared. Where should she go now? She had no idea how to proceed. This wasn't anything like her usual research problem. For one thing, the language barrier seemed insurmountable. And the resources available were totally unfamiliar to her. In her own field of late-eighteenth-century voyages she felt confident that she had a good handle on the sources that survived and what they represented of the mercantile and scientific efforts of the period, but here she was really out of her depth.

The cold nipped at her exposed face as she progressed in a blur, moving swiftly through crowds of people, crossing streets, passing building after building. At one point she caught a glimpse of her reflection in the display window of a store. She looked awful. Her hair had frozen into a tousled mess, her coat was stained from the beer.

Occasionally she saw on a building or sign the name of a street she passed: Cursitor Street, Furnival Street, Fetter Lane. Eventually she emerged onto busy Fleet Street. Lizzie looked down the length of it. Here and there Christmas decorations were still visible, clinging sadly to lamp posts. She didn't think she could face the crowds that jammed the sidewalk, so she crossed the street and continued on in the same direction, toward the River Thames.

On her right was a large complex of buildings, set into a walled park. It was the great legal heart of England, the Inns of Court and Chancery. Lizzie had not meant her steps to lead her here, but as she looked through the gate she realized that she was near the Temple Church. These grounds, now swarming with lawyers, had once held the headquarters of the Knights Templar in England. It had occurred to her during the course of the morning that she might want to go to the Temple Church, but she hadn't realized she was so close to it at the Public Record Office.

A map of the grounds was mounted on the gate; it showed the buildings directly in front of her, still called the "Inner Temple" after a thousand years. She traced her finger along the path that would take her to the Temple Church, the only part of the complex that survived from the time of the Templars. Her heart was beating fast and she tried to take a deep breath but found that the cold prevented her.

The church was smaller than she expected. It was famous for its round shape, modeled on the Temple of Solomon in Jerusalem, after which the Templars had taken their name. Lizzie went to the door and found it locked. She looked at her watch, it was three-thirty. She walked around the circular wall to another door, this one set inside an old Norman porch. No luck. There were a number of graves scattered here and there around the church, and as Lizzie looked at them she wondered what she should do. She was feeling slightly queasy.

She sank down onto the small bench on the porch. Of all the nights that Martin should be away, this was going to prove the worst. She just knew it. The whole situation was frustratingly out of control. Suddenly, *she* seemed out of control. How could she possibly have thought that she would be able to find the damned heart! Lizzie couldn't keep back the tears any longer, and as she sat on the porch of the Temple Church they began to flow freely until eventually she was sobbing loudly, her body convulsing with uncontrollable hiccup-like jerks.

Eventually her sobs drew the attention of a young woman, who came around the church to investigate. "Are you all right?" she asked sympathetically, leaning toward Lizzie but not touching her.

Lizzie nodded and reached in her bag for a tissue. "I'm disappointed the church isn't open," she said, wiping her eyes.

"Are you cold?" the woman asked. "Do you need a warm place to sit?"

Lizzie couldn't help smiling. This girl thought she was a bag lady. She looked down at her stained coat; her hair was matted and she still had a pretty hearty beery smell.

"You could come inside for a minute to get warm," her companion said, "but you won't be able to stay."

Lizzie blew her nose and stood up. "Do you have a key?"

"I'm with the florist. We're setting up for a wedding this evening."

They walked together around the church and Lizzie saw the white van of the florist, and a young man carrying a gigantic bouquet into the church. This was at least an opportunity to see the interior.

"Thank you," she said to the woman. "I'd like to see inside just for a few minutes if I could."

"I don't see any reason why you couldn't come in while we set up."

A young man at the door of the church obviously disagreed. He held up a hand to stop Lizzie as she mounted the few steps.

"I'm sorry," he said curtly, "the church is closed to the public."

"Can I just have quick look around?" she asked. "I've come a long way to see it."

He shook his head. "Sorry," he said dismissively. He turned away.

"Wait," Lizzie said, her frustration growing. "It's not even five yet."

The man turned back with a look of haughty disgust. "This is a private church," he said. "We have limited hours for the public. You'll have to check in advance before your next visit."

"Do you have a library here?" she asked.

He practically pushed her away. "No."

Lizzie hoped he wasn't a clergyman. She turned and said goodbye to the young woman who had been kind to her. "What time is the wedding?" she asked.

"Seven o'clock."

Lizzie thanked her and turned to go. The confusion and disappointment of the day's events were overtaking her, and all the feelings she had been resisting or denying about the strange situation in which she had found herself for the last several days rose to the surface. This was *not* just a research problem, as much as she tried to justify to herself that it was. She had learned things about her family and herself that were unexpected and difficult to digest. The chain of evidence she had uncovered about the Hatton women, a group to which she now belonged, was both extraordinarily exciting and frustratingly confusing. At this moment all those feelings were being manifested in an irrational, almost obsessive need to see what was inside this church. She couldn't explain it. She didn't know if there was anything important or useful there, but she didn't think she could go any further if she wasn't able to examine the interior.

There was nothing to be done but crash the wedding.

Fleet Street was busy with end-of-the-work-day traffic and it took almost twenty minutes to get a taxi to take her back to the hotel. There was a message from Martin and she called him at the number in Newcastle.

"How does the project look?" she asked after they had exchanged hellos.

"This is a great one, Liz," Martin answered. He was obviously excited. "I'm going to dinner with the mayor tonight, and then meeting with people from the community again for most of the day tomorrow." He described the site where the mural would be. Lizzie found it hard to give him all her attention. She was wondering if any of her dresses were nice enough to wear to an evening wedding.

"What time will you be back tomorrow?" she asked.

"About seven, I expect."

"Good," she replied. "Don't forget, George is meeting us."

"Are you okay?" he asked.

"Of course, why do you ask?"

"You sound a little funny."

"Sorry," she said apologetically. "I don't want to put a damper on your enthusiasm." She paused for a moment. "Not a good day of research."

Martin asked for details but Lizzie was unwilling to furnish them at this point.

"You sure you're okay?"

Lizzie finally convinced him she was. "I'm going to miss you tonight, though," she said.

"Well you should just have a quiet night in," Martin suggested.

Lizzie smiled. "You're a sweetheart," she said as she hung up. It just wouldn't pay to tell him her plans at this point.

• • • • •

Getting a hairbrush through her hair took a good part of Lizzie's preparation time. She showered, brushed her teeth, put on her best dress and looked at herself in the mirror. It simply wouldn't do. Not for a formal wedding. Not if she didn't want to stand out like a sore thumb. Besides, what would she wear for a coat? And she certainly couldn't go into the church toting the big bag that she always carried. She liked it because it was big enough to carry her computer in, but it would make her stand out this evening and she didn't have a smaller purse.

The plot would only work if she was willing to invest some serious cash, she decided. There was a women's dress shop in the lobby of the hotel. Lizzie left her coat in her room, and taking only her wallet and room key, went to buy a nice coat and bag.

The store was expensive, but they had a beautiful forest green wool coat that fit Lizzie perfectly. It was more tailored than she usually wore, but very flattering. She told the shopkeeper that she was going to a wedding.

"You know you'll need a hat too."

Lizzie thought of her knit hat, soaked in beer and sitting in the sink of the pub behind W.H. Smith.

The woman held out a hat for her to try. Dark grey with a band of forest green, it would match the coat perfectly. Lizzie tried it on. The effect was not quite right. The brim was too big.

"You should put your hair up."

Lizzie turned and smiled at her new fashion advisor. "I didn't bring a hairbrush," she said. A hairbrush and clips were soon produced and Lizzie pinned her hair firmly on top of her head. Now when she added the hat the effect was perfect. It was necessary to buy a small grey clutch bag and a new pair of shoes to complete the ensemble, and the whole thing set Lizzie back almost four hundred pounds, but she felt ready to march confidently into a wedding to which she had not been invited.

She got a cab and arrived back at the church. In the darkness, the stained glass windows stood out as pale patches of color. The light inside was not bright enough to make the patterns distinct, but the effect was beautiful. A small crowd of elegantly dressed guests stood smoking just outside the door. Lizzie mingled for a moment, eavesdropping on conversation.

They all seemed to be lawyers. The rude young man from earlier was still at his post and Lizzie flashed him a broad smile as she went into the church. He nodded politely, showing no sign of recognizing her.

She slipped into the interior and took a moment to get her bearings. Her attention was immediately drawn to the effigies of several knights, carved in stone and set directly into the floor in the center of the round part of the church. There was a small stack of printed guides on a table near the door and Lizzie picked one up. A wedding program was handed to her immediately after and she slipped the guide inside it. There was no time to do more than glance around the church before the smokers were herded in from outside for the start of the service.

The church was almost full and as one of the last to be seated, Lizzie found herself on the aisle at the back. As the organ started, she opened the wedding program, positioning the guide to the church inside it so that she could study it without attracting the attention of the people around her. She felt a bit like a teenager smuggling a comic book or a *Playboy* magazine inside his school textbook. She stood and sat as the movement of the crowd dictated, but paid no attention to the ceremony, other than to note that it was filled with beautiful young people, lovely and expensive clothes, and a smattering of adorable children. There were no visible tears. The organ, which the guide informed her was one of the primary attractions of the church, filled the space with sound at the appropriate moments and the flowers with which her Good Samaritan had filled the church a few hours earlier added a delicate but definite perfume to the air.

Lizzie's attention went from the guide in her hands to those parts of the church described in it. The floor plan was simple. In 1185 the Templars had constructed a round church, just under sixty feet in diameter, and in 1240 they added a rectangular addition to its eastern edge. The addition, called the "chancel," was about one and a half times the length of the round nave. The resulting outline had the shape of a thick, blocky, lower-case letter "i." It looked to Lizzie like the icon that indicated tourist information, or the silhouette of one of the little people that populated her nephew's favorite toys, with their big round heads and short, armless, columnar bodies.

Two small porches had been added later, one at the neck where the round head of the church met the rectangular body, and one that sat like a little hat on the top of the head at the western edge.

The altar, where the happy couple stood amidst the flowers, was at the end of the chancel farthest from the original round structure of the church. The pews in the chancel were set up for a choir, facing the center aisle and with a slight rise. Folding chairs had been placed along the center aisle to accommodate wedding guests. Lizzie was seated in the highest row of the choir and at the end farthest from the altar, and it was a perfect position from which to observe the church.

In addition to being able to see the whole of the chancel, she could look in the opposite direction from the action of the wedding and examine the round nave without attracting attention.

The circle of the nave was dominated by six columns and ten tombs. Unlike the knight effigies in the Hengemont church, these were lying right on the floor. One of them was a simple coffin shape, but the others were portrait sculptures of knights, presumably Templars. They were all at least a few decades too early to have been associated with John d'Hautain, but Lizzie couldn't help wondering if his heart had come to this church. It would be a logical place for it to have lain upon arriving back in England, though she could not imagine why it would not then have been sent on to Hengemont.

The church had sustained heavy damage in the bombing blitz of London during World War II, and had been "extensively restored" both before and after that event, according to the guide. Lizzie looked around her. How much of what she could see from where she sat was original to the thirteenth century? The chancel's surface features all looked newer that that. If there was anything to be found in the Temple Church, she decided, it would be in the round nave. The graves were all identified by name in the guide, and none was familiar. The rest of the stones in the floor were worth looking at for old markings, though she couldn't see any from where she sat.

Around the circular wall, the surface was decorated with a repeating pattern of relief-carved columns and gothic arches, reaching up to a height of about ten feet. The shallow niches that were created in the process looked like they could once have contained memorials of some kind.

The ceremony merging the attractive young attorneys into one firm wrapped up with a round of applause, and Lizzie followed the bridal party into the round nave of the church. As the bride and groom received their congratulations from a line of well-wishers, Lizzie circled the church, examining the stones of the floor and wall as quickly as she could in the dim light. It became apparent that there was not going to be time to do it carefully before the party moved to the reception in a nearby building on the Temple grounds. Around her, people were bundling themselves up in preparation for going out into the cold.

The minister who performed the service was standing near the door talking to people as they passed, and Lizzie moved herself into position to chat with him a bit before she left the church.

"This is such a lovely building," she said casually.

The minister replied that it was. He asked if she was a friend of the bride. She lied and said that her husband had gone to school with the groom. He recognized her American accent. It seemed a good opening.

"Do you get many American visitors?"

"Yes, many thousands every year."

"Does the tourist traffic ever conflict with the weddings and other services you perform?"

He explained that the Temple Church held a rather unique position among English Churches. It had no regular parish population and was not supported under the usual management of the Church of England. "We operate for the benefit of the attorneys and solicitors who occupy the Temple grounds," he concluded, "and with their support."

Lizzie understood this to mean that the church didn't have the usual obligation for regular public access. Weddings, funerals, and other services for the legal community always took precedence. The minister turned his attention to other guests, waving and shaking hands simultaneously. Lizzie thanked him and turned back into the church, pretending to look for someone.

"Is the church open tomorrow?" she asked the rude young man.

"Not to the public," he answered.

"What about for research?" she asked.

"What kind of research?"

"Templar research."

"We don't have any of those records here," he explained. "You can do legal research at the Law Library, but the surviving Templar records are mostly at the Public Record Office."

The crowd was thinning and Lizzie had to make a decision. There wouldn't be another opportunity to visit this church while she was in London. The old Norman door on the far side of the nave had a red exit light above it and Lizzie meandered over to take a closer look. A small sign on the door above a modern-looking push bar said "Emergency Exit Only, Alarm Will Sound." She breathed slowly. If she could find a place to hide, she would not need to see everything quickly. She made a motion of looking for something, opening and closing her purse and glancing around her on the floor, then returned to the pew where she had been sitting during the wedding. When she was certain that no one was looking in her direction, she slid down to the floor. If, by some cruel act of fate, she was discovered, she would say that she was looking for a lost glove.

It was not long before she heard the minister and the rude man exchanging good-byes. "Is everyone out then?" one asked the other. Lizzie didn't hear the rest of the conversation as they disappeared into the vestibule that led to the porch. The lights began to go out one row at a time until the church was in total darkness. Lizzie sat up in the pew and waited for her eyes to adjust.

The only lights were the ones that marked the emergency exits and one on the altar. Lizzie felt her way carefully down the steps that led to the main floor of the church and proceeded back to the nave. Her new shoes were not comfortable and the heels were higher than she was used to. She felt her way around a column and stumbled on the carved foot of one of the effigies.

She fell hard and landed in the narrow space between two of the stone knights.

She lay perfectly still for a moment until she caught her breath again. Her hip and elbow had taken the force of the fall. There would be an impressive bruise on her hip the next day, Lizzie could tell already, but she was not seriously hurt. She reached out her hand, found the arm of one of the knights and pulled herself up into a sitting position. She took off her shoes and rubbed her stockinged feet, then reached around and found her small purse. If only she had her regular bag, she thought, she'd have a flashlight.

The switches for the lights were undoubtedly in the vestibule; that was where the minister and his assistant were when the lights went out. But turning them on might draw attention from the outside. Lizzie sat thoughtfully. On either side of her lay the knights, just barely visible in the red glow of the emergency exit sign. She wondered if anyone was buried under the stone on which she sat. Strangely enough, though she was locked in a mausoleum in the dark, she wasn't scared. She hadn't consumed anything but potato chips and beer since breakfast, and after her fall she felt a little bit disoriented, but she gradually began to feel her decision-making power returning.

Laying her shoes and purse gently at the base of the knight who'd tripped her, Lizzie took off her coat and hat and laid them carefully across the effigy. There had been a large candle used as part of the marriage rite and if she could find it she would use it to look around the rest of the church. In her stocking feet she padded up the aisle of the chancel, moving carefully and feeling with her toe for obstacles, especially as she neared the steps to the altar. The candle was where she remembered and Lizzie groped around the altar near it, hoping to find something to light it with. Three long sticks under her hand felt like matches as she moved her fingertips up to the heads. She struck one against the altar and it made a satisfying sound as it first scratched along the stone and then popped into flame.

The church was cold, especially for someone without shoes, but Lizzie felt no apprehension as she made her way back to the circular wall of the nave, holding the candle in her right hand and shielding the flame with her left. She took up her position at the place where she had been forced to abandon her examination earlier and began to walk, counter clockwise, around the whole of the church. She moved the candle up or down as needed and explored the surface of the floor and walls.

How many Templars had walked this path with a candle in their hands? She hummed as she proceeded. She didn't really expect to find anything here. What could she find anyway? If John d'Hautain's name were engraved on some stone, surely some member of the Hatton family would have discovered it by now. Nonetheless, she felt like she was going through an important process, if for no other reason than that it gave her a sense of connection with the days of John and Elizabeth d'Hautain.

When she had gone around the whole wall of the church she returned to the effigies at the center and, one by one, examined them by candlelight. They wore much the same costume as John d'Hautain did on his tomb and in his portrait in the triptych. Chain mail under a loosely belted cloth tunic. Each of these knights had a sword and shield. A few had their hands folded in prayer, several had crossed legs, two of them rested their chain-mailed feet on the backs of small lions or dogs. Lizzie laid her coat on the stone floor and sat on it, leaning back against the stone shield of one of the knights. The burning candle was lodged safely between his legs.

Three times today she had completely lost perspective. The first time was in the Public Record Office when she had abandoned the quest. The second time was in the pub when she found herself writing the question without thinking. The third was her emotional outburst on the church porch when she thought she would never be able to get inside the building in which she now sat, cold but comfortable. Even feeling such an irrational compulsion to see the church was evidence of the out-of-control state of her emotions at the time.

If she worked backwards through the episodes, she could

now tick them off on her fingers as being soluble or understandable. The third, of course, was solved. Here she was. Admittedly here she was sitting in the dark and breaking some trespassing law, but here she was.

Was it all that strange for her to have written that question in a list of questions, she wondered? As she thought about it with rational calmness, Lizzie acknowledged that it was not.

"Where is his heart?" She said it aloud. It was not so scary. She was looking for it after all.

The question of the research was the one that required the greatest concentration. She actually laughed when she realized what a state she must have been in to think that she could, with two pocket dictionaries and a list of words, approach hundreds of boxes of documents in languages that she could not read.

She turned to one of the knights lying near her. "You know," she said, "there is a process to doing historical research." She laughed again. If an amateur had approached her own field by going directly to miscellaneous manuscripts, without knowing anything of the finding aids, indexes, reference works, or secondary sources, she would think her an idiot—or a lunatic. Today, she had been both.

The eyes of her friendly knight seemed to move slightly in the flickering candlelight. Lizzie patted him on the cheek. "Thank you for listening," she said. "You are absolutely right. This is a research problem."

She was clearly at a point beyond which she could only proceed with extraordinary good luck. Or if not luck, then expert assistance. She stood up. She would start the next morning at the Public Record Office as soon as it opened, and she would begin by asking for help with her quest for information.

She put on her shoes, her coat, and her hat, tucked her ridiculously small new purse under her arm, and charged the door. A bright light came on, an alarm bell sounded, and the cold air rushed at her. She let the door slam behind her and proceeded, calmly but quickly, around the church to the footpath that led to Fleet Street. A bell chimed midnight as she got a cab for the Grosvenor.

Chapter 22

The next day was sunny and clear. Lizzie woke refreshed and famished, went for the full English breakfast in the hotel dining room, and still had time to walk the few miles to the Public Record Office. The air had a crisp snap to it, and she felt ready to work when she arrived at the library just as the doors were opening to the public.

"Is there anyone on the staff who is particularly knowledgeable about the Knights Templar?" she asked the woman at the information desk.

"I think Mr. Parker has done some work on that topic."

"Would it be possible to speak to him for a few minutes?"

Lizzie waited as the woman spoke on the phone, and was then directed to an office at the far end of the reading room.

Anthony Parker sat behind a big desk piled high with papers. A kindred soul, Lizzie thought. She dug in her purse for a business card and handed it to him as she introduced herself. He looked at the card and then back to her.

"I remember you," he said, "from when you were here several years ago working on the Pacific trade material."

Lizzie smiled with surprise. "You have a good memory." She was embarrassed that she did not remember him.

"Congratulations on finishing the Ph.D.," he said, filing her card in a box on his desk. "What are you working on now?" He gestured to the chair opposite him.

Lizzie sat down and explained very briefly about the Francis Hatton project.

"I've gone off on a bit of a tangent, though," she continued. "Back into the family history at the time of the Crusades." She pulled a file folder from her bag and took out a photocopy of the Henry III document at the Hengemont church. Father Folan had had no qualms about sticking the ancient document on his office copy machine. She handed it across the desk to Anthony Parker.

"Ah, now you're getting into my period," he said, taking it with interest.

"I am at a loss with this," Lizzie said, "though I find it very interesting." She gave him a moment to read it before continuing. "I need expert advice and I hope that you are the person who can give it to me."

"It's a contract between Henry III and the Knights Templar. In case of the death of a certain young Crusader knight, the Templars agree to preserve his heart and ship it back to England." He looked up from the document to Lizzie. "I've seen other manuscripts like this. What do you want to know about it?"

"Where is his heart?" she asked. She could not help smiling as she said it.

He smiled back, but his look was puzzled.

She continued. "The knight in question was John d'Hautain, an ancestor of Sir George Hatton. They never got the heart."

"And they are still looking for it?"

She nodded. "I know this is a very strange sort of search, but do you think I might be able to find any other information about this in the records of Henry III or the Templars?"

"Well, the official documents from the reign of Henry III have all been published," he said. He stood up and walked to one of the crammed shelves in his office, pulling down a big volume. "Let's see what we can find," he said, returning to his desk and turning to the index of the book.

Lizzie leaned back in her chair with a sense of relief. She should have started here yesterday. It was stupid to have wasted a morning of research without asking for assistance. She looked at Anthony Parker. He was the sort of man who would, in America, be called a geek, but here represented a certain class of well-educated, rumpled Englishmen of middle age. She liked him. She admired knowledge and expertise and Anthony Parker clearly had both.

"The fact that you have one document identified already gives you a good starting point," he mumbled, turning back and forth from the index to the body of the book. He looked up at her and smiled. "This is my own field of interest," he said, "the Templars and the Plantagenet kings."

Lizzie could not believe her luck.

"Here's your document," Anthony said, turning the book toward Lizzie and pointing to the index. "And here's something that seems to be related." He flipped through the book to the page indicated. She looked at the page of Latin text in front of her and apologized for her ignorance. The librarian gallantly agreed to translate.

"It seems that William Longespèe, the Earl of Salisbury, was on the same Crusade as your man, John d'Hautain," Anthony said slowly, running his finger back and forth across the page. "He was eager to have his remains lie in England and so, on his behalf his wife, the Countess of Salisbury, asked Henry to make the arrangement with the Templars." He looked up. "Henry III was a special friend to the Templars."

Lizzie gave a nod of interest.

"He wanted for a long time to be buried in the Temple Church in London, but then he spent so much time rebuilding Westminster Abbey and the shrine of Edward the Confessor that he ultimately decided to be buried there instead."

Without giving the details, Lizzie told him that she had been to the Temple Church the previous day.

Anthony pulled the book back to his side of the desk and continued to thumb through the index, all the while giving Lizzie a running commentary on the burial practices of the Plantagenet kings.

"And of course the Templars were masters of organ preservation," he said at one point.

"Really?" Lizzie asked, her interest especially piqued by this bit of information.

"Oh yes," he continued. For a moment he looked up at her. "One of the Provincial Grand Masters, the head of the order in England, died on a trip to France about 1275." He looked back down at the index as he continued to talk. "His chaplain was traveling with him and actually boiled his corpse, stripped off his flesh, buried that in Spain, then preserved the heart and brought it and the skeleton back to England."

"He actually boiled up his boss?" Lizzie said, recoiling slightly.

The librarian nodded. "And he wasn't just his boss in the Templars, he was also the Bishop of Hereford."

"But he knew him," Lizzie said with horror. "I mean this wasn't just like dropping a chicken into the pot."

He smiled knowingly at her. "Ghastly, isn't it?"

She nodded.

"Anyway," Anthony continued in his droning accent, "Henry received letters on behalf of these two men, the Earl of Salisbury and your man, and he wrote to the Templars on their behalf, enclosing some money to cover the expenses." He turned back to the master list and flipped forward in the volume several pages. "Here is the response from the Templars; Henry added a note and then sent it on with his own seal. That's the one you already have," he said, nodding at Lizzie's photocopied document. "There is another here sent to the Countess of Salisbury. And here's something interesting," he said, flipping to another page in the volume. "This is a letter from the Templars to Henry, telling him that both men are dead, and describing the bloodbath at Mansoura." He looked up at Lizzie, "That was a horrific battle," he said.

"Yes, that much I *do* know." Lizzie said.

"The Templars say that they have preserved the heart of Jean d'Hautain in a golden box with his mark on it." Anthony looked up. "That must be arms of some kind, but it's rather early for regular heraldic markings."

Lizzie was sitting up straighter and leaning across the desk. She felt a surge of excitement. She knew what the crest was. Her heart was pumping faster.

Anthony Parker had gone back to the book and was reading with interest. "Oh I say," he said, suddenly, "this *is* interesting. Apparently, as they are in Egypt, they are going to try a sort of modified mummification process and send the whole corpse of Longespèe back."

Lizzie mumbled something about it sounding very unusual, but wanted him to get back to John d'Hautain's heart.

"I've never seen anything like it," Anthony said. "In fact, I'm surprised I've never noticed it before." He inserted a strip of paper from a pile on his desk as a bookmark and then went back to the index. "There's one more thing that deals with Longespèe here, and it is several years later." He turned again to the volume of documents and took a few minutes to read through the Latin before attempting a translation.

"All right," he said, "I think I've got it and this could be very interesting to you." He turned the volume around again so that Lizzie could see it. "The head man of the Templars, the Grand Master, was almost always a Frenchman." He gestured at the Templar list that Lizzie had been looking at earlier. "It was really the French king, Philip the Fair, who brought them down, though Edward II didn't do anything to support them here."

He pointed to the book again. "But there was one English Grand Master, Thomas Berard, and that was during the reign of Henry III, when the Templars had a lot of support here. According to this letter to Henry, written in September 1256, Berard was going to be returning from the Holy Land to England, and he would bring with him the remains of William Longespèe and a heart casket, but there is no name mentioned in association with it."

Lizzie felt such a pronounced tingling in her scalp that she worried for a moment that her hair might be standing straight up from her head. Her voice was a hoarse croak when she asked again, "So where is it? Where is his heart?"

"Well, not to be too disrespectful, but Longespèe is clearly the more influential guy here," Anthony said. "You know he was the cousin of Henry III?"

Lizzie shrugged her ignorance, wishing he would get on with it.

"Oh yes, his father, William Longespèe the elder, was one of the famous illegitimate sons of Henry II," Anthony continued. "So the corpse in question here was the king's cousin."

"And where did *he* end up, this younger Longespèe?" she whispered.

"Haven't you been there?" Anthony asked. "He's in Salisbury Cathedral and it's well worth seeing if you haven't been there before."

Lizzie collapsed back in the chair. "He's buried in Salisbury Cathedral?" Her mind was racing.

Anthony Parker continued to jabber on, as if this were the kind of knowledge one stumbled onto every day. "Oh yes, the knight effigies of the Longespèes, father and son, are some of the best Medieval tomb carvings left in England," he said. "And some of the oldest carvings in the cathedral."

Hadn't Martin said that there was a heart burial in Salisbury Cathedral? Lizzie warned herself not to get too excited. There were plenty of heart burials around and it could be anybody. She asked Anthony Parker if he knew, but he couldn't remember anything that might be the heart burial of John d'Hautain. She began to pile up her papers.

"I might have something else of interest to you however," he said, turning his chair around and pulling a catalogue drawer out of the cabinet behind him. He looked up at Lizzie. "I still like the old cards, even though we're now trying to get it all on computer."

Lizzie smiled sympathetically. She liked the old card catalogue too.

"If I remember correctly," he mumbled, flipping through the cards, "we may have some correspondence of Lieutenant Francis Hatton in the Admiralty papers."

She had almost forgotten about Francis Hatton, now her ancestor. She asked what the correspondence referred to.

"Lieutenant Hatton was an interesting character," Anthony started. "There are several letters here to Captains heading to the North Pacific, always asking if they are going to touch on the coast of the North American continent." He shoved the box across the desk to Lizzie. There were inquiries to George Vancouver, George Dixon, and James Colnett; all of them had been his shipmates on the Cook voyage, and all led subsequent expeditions to the Northwest Coast. There was even a letter to William Bligh about the *Bounty* expedition.

The librarian pointed to the next batch of cards. "These are responses from the Admiralty and the captains, almost always inviting him to accompany them if he wants to." Lizzie quickly flipped through them. The next group of letters was again from Hatton.

"These are the strange ones," Parker said, "having expressed such interest and received the invitation, he always regretfully declines."

"His father, brother, and sister, all died around this time," Lizzie said, by way of explanation.

"It's still strange though," Parker continued, "it's as if he *needs* to go, but doesn't really want to go."

He was so close to the truth that Lizzie decided to tell him about Francis Hatton's inadvertent grave robbing and subsequent feelings of guilt.

He nodded. "That explains it then," he said. "It seems logical that it had to do with his collection. I thought that maybe what he was really fishing for was someone to collect items for his famous specimen cabinet."

"Not far off, I think," Lizzie said. "I don't think that any of those other guys, Vancouver and the lot, would have understood his wanting to return a Native American corpse to its original burial site." She watched him return the catalogue drawer to its cubbyhole. "In the end, I don't think he could bring himself to ask it, and the demands of his own estate prevented his leaving again."

"So what became of those things?"

"I have no idea," she answered. "They've gone the way of the heart, I guess."

He gestured at the box. "Do you want to see any of these documents?" he asked.

Lizzie shook her head. "Not today, thanks." She asked for photocopies of the transcriptions of the Templar and Henry III documents though, which Anthony quickly provided from the book.

"You have been so helpful," she said, standing and extending her hand, "thank you."

It wasn't even noon yet as she walked out into the grey January day. George wasn't due until seven o'clock and Martin probably wouldn't be back until at least then. Lizzie hailed a cab and asked the driver which station she should go to for a train to Salisbury.

"That would be Waterloo," he answered. "Is that where you're headed?"

"Yes please," she said, tossing her bag onto the seat and following it in.

There was a train leaving for Salisbury some twenty minutes after her arrival at the station, so she just had time to buy a ticket, a prawn sandwich, and a cup of coffee. The train was one of the old ones that still had private compartments and, as few people seemed to be heading to Salisbury in the middle of the day in the middle of the week in the middle of the winter, she had a compartment to herself. She spread her notes out around her and looked for the paper that Martin had given her with the information he had found about heart burials. It said there *might* be a heart burial in Salisbury cathedral, but it might also be the tomb of a boy bishop.

Lizzie cracked open the plastic lid of her coffee cup, wondering what strange politics would have led to the ordination of a kid. Then she sat back and gazed at the countryside as the train rumbled along. Here and there was snow, but mostly it just looked bleak. Frozen fields and cold-looking cows and sheep. Occasionally the train passed near a village, but with such speed that it could only be seen clearly in the distant views. Up close the churches and cottages and country pubs all became a blur. Lizzie finished her lunch, repacked her papers and began to look anxiously for the spire of Salisbury Cathedral, which finally came into view as a tiny white needle in the distance.

With every minute and every mile it became larger, nothing ever obscuring the view of it. No hill, no building, not even trees came between Lizzie and the steeple of Salisbury Cathedral from the moment she first saw it through the train window until she rolled into the city, and her eyes never left it. It was hypnotic to her as it grew larger and larger.

It wasn't a long walk from the station to the cathedral, but she was so anxious to get there quickly that she hopped into one of the cabs waiting out front. The route through the town began on broad streets but finally ended in the narrow tangle around the wall of the cathedral grounds, called the "close." Though she had seen the tower of the cathedral from a distance of several miles on the train, now she couldn't see it at all until the cab drove through the gates of the close and the vast open area around the cathedral gave her a magnificent view. The front face was entirely covered with the carvings of saints, standing in remote stillness. Lizzie felt her heart beat rapidly as she paid the driver and, with her bag over her shoulder, saluted the saints on the massive front wall. Whatever expression might have been on their faces once was worn away by time and the elements, and they gave Lizzie no clue of what she would find inside.

She paid the entrance fee, picked up a guidebook and stood for a long moment staring down the length of the cathedral when she first entered. Unlike at Westminster Abbey, she could see from one end of Salisbury Cathedral to the other, and it had nothing like Westminster's profusion of tombs. The inside cover of the visitor's guide showed an outline map of the church with highlights for tourists.

She skipped over the description of the ancient clock, which she could see against the wall opposite her, and read quickly down the list: "Hungerford Monument, St. Osmund's Shrine, Beauchamp tomb, Longespèe effigy." Lizzie stood still for a moment and read the words again: "Longespèe effigy." Her skin felt clammy and she could feel her heart beating in her neck as she walked down the long aisle to the place marked with the small circled number three on the map.

Past a cluster of delicate columns and under a gothic arch of stone lay the tomb of a knight. The stone effigy was wearing armor and was almost half-covered by a large shield decorated with animals standing or running. Lizzie caught her breath. There was a lengthy written description posted on the column nearby, and a full-color illustration of what the tomb had looked like when it was covered with its medieval paint. "William Longespèe, Earl of Salisbury, was half-brother to King John," read the label. "On his death in 1226 he was the first person to be buried in the cathedral."

Lizzie sighed audibly. This was the father, not the son. She looked at the map again, but there was no mention of another Longespèe tomb. The afternoon sun was inching its way across the stone floor of the cathedral from the high arched window behind her. Lizzie followed the track of a beam of light back to the west end of the cathedral where she had come in. On the far aisle was another knight effigy, with a smaller tomb at its head. She bundled her jacket a little closer against her and walked tentatively across the church and down the other aisle to the end of the cathedral.

Even before she read the accompanying panel of text she knew it was the place. "William Longespée the Younger, Son of William, Earl of Salisbury, was General of the English Crusaders and died heroically, fighting the Saracens in the assault on Mansoura, Egypt, in 1250." She hurried to the next label, over a miniature effigy in religious vestments. "This figure has been believed to commemorate a Boy Bishop of the thirteenth century, but it is possible that it covered the heart of Bishop Richard Poore (1217-1229), founder of this Cathedral, whose body was buried at Tarrant Crawford in Dorset."

"Oh God, it's here," she said, surprised that she had spoken aloud, but knowing without a doubt that John d'Hautain's heart was under the stone in front of her. For several minutes she stared at it, not knowing what to do. Then she went around the raised platform on which the tombs were mounted to the other side. She sat in one of the folding chairs set up in rows along the nave of the cathedral and stared again at the effigy of the "boy bishop" from the other side. It was certainly not meant to represent John d'Hautain, but she still felt absolute confidence that his heart was here. If she could pass her hand through the stone she would touch it. As if to confirm her belief, the wandering beam of sunshine now reached into the dark corner and played on the worn features of knight and boy. Lizzie looked at the younger Longespèe; he had been John's comrade-in-arms.

It was almost ten minutes before Lizzie moved again. She massaged her temples and considered how to proceed. George Hatton probably had enough influence to get the tomb opened if she could marshal the evidence to warrant it. But where to begin? The Templar documents made the link between William Longespèe the Younger and John d'Hautain, but the effigy that now lay over the heart muddied the waters considerably. Where had *that* come from? She knew nothing of boy bishops and would just as soon not tread down that path. She did know enough about medieval heart burials to believe that one could have been confused for another, and the label here was ambiguous. Whoever wrote it was clearly in doubt as to the identity of these remains.

Lizzie stood up and walked back to the desk where she had purchased her ticket. "Who wrote the labels in the cathedral?" she asked the young man behind the counter.

"I'm not sure," he said, shaking his head. "It might have been the librarian."

"Is the library open now?" she asked hopefully.

"Yes it is," he answered, looking at his watch, "for another hour." He looked up at Lizzie again and added, "but it's not open to the public. It's just for scholars."

Lizzie dragged her wallet out of her bag and gave him one of her business cards. "I'm a historian," she said, "working on a project for Sir George Hatton."

The young man pointed the way. Up a flight of ancient stone steps Lizzie found a carved oak door that had an index card tacked to it reading "Library. Researchers Only." Inside she found herself in an organized but overstuffed room of bookshelves, tables, document boxes, and bundles of papers. Behind the desk a woman of about her own age looked up and smiled.

"Can I help you?" she asked.

Lizzie got out another business card and passed it across the desk, explaining that she was in England to do some research for George Hatton. The woman gestured to the chair opposite her and Lizzie sat down.

"Our collection is pretty specific to Salisbury cathedral," the librarian said. "I'm not sure what you'll be able to find here." The nameplate on her desk read Nora Stanley, though she didn't introduce herself.

Lizzie was thoughtful for a moment, wondering how to explain her weird task to this straightforward Englishwoman. Best not to tell her that she had been influenced by dreams or stolen glimpses into Bette's diary, she thought. She pulled her notebook out of her bag and found the copies of the Templar documents that had been made for her by Father Folan and Anthony Parker.

"Sir George Hatton had an ancestor who fought in the Crusades," she started, pushing the first of the documents across the desk, "and he died at Mansoura with William Longespèe the younger."

"Ah, I see the Salisbury connection," the librarian said, "but we don't have much here of the Longespèes—beyond their physical remains, that is. There aren't a lot of documents describing the Crusade, for instance."

"Strangely enough," Lizzie said hesitantly, "what the Hattons are seeking are missing remains from their own ancestor."

Nora Stanley looked up quizzically. Lizzie looked back at the other woman. She looked intelligent, compassionate, she didn't seem stuffy, and she dealt every day with the medieval world. What the hell, Lizzie thought, passing the rest of the Xeroxes across the desk.

"The Hatton family, then called d'Hautain, arranged for the heart of John d'Hautain to be sent back from Egypt in 1250, and all the evidence points to it having been transported with the body of Longespèe." She sat back and allowed Nora to look over the documents before adding, "but the heart never got to them."

"How can you be sure?" the other woman asked without looking up, and reaching for a Latin dictionary on her desk.

"Very, very strong family tradition," Lizzie said.

Now Nora did look up. "Very, *very* strong tradition?" she asked, smiling.

Lizzie smiled back. "Almost a curse, you could say."

Nora put her hand on the papers. "These really are interesting, but what are you hoping to find here?"

"Is there a chance that John d'Hautain's heart came here and is buried in the cathedral?" Lizzie asked bluntly.

Nora nodded. "There are a number of miscellaneous bones and other body parts that have turned up in various building projects around the cathedral." She leaned her elbows on the desk and touched her fingertips lightly together, creating, Lizzie thought, a miniature cathedral shape.

"As you might imagine with a building more than seven hundred years old, a lot of things have shifted around over the years," Nora continued, "not to mention that all the graves were moved in a big restoration project in the late eighteenth century."

"Did they keep a record of what or who they were moving?" Lizzie asked.

"Not to the detailed standards that we expect today," came the reply.

The two women sat thoughtfully for a moment.

"Do you have any idea what's actually buried under that little bishop effigy adjacent to the younger Longespèe?" Lizzie asked, finally.

"Not off the top of my head," Nora answered, "but we might find that in the reports of the Keeper of the Fabric." She rose from her desk and crossed to a shelf of document boxes. As she pulled down an index ledger, Lizzie couldn't help asking what or who was the Keeper of the Fabric.

"The manager of the building, also called the clerk of the works," Nora explained. She ran her finger down the page. "Here we go," she said, "tombs, heart casket." Two boxes were indicated and Nora took them both off the shelf and back to her desk.

Lizzie wished her own heart would stop beating so hard. She was actually beginning to feel slightly light-headed, and Nora was not going fast enough to satisfy her.

"For one reason or another," Nora began to explain, "the tombs have to be opened on occasion, and the Keeper of the Fabric indicates it in his report." She pulled out the first group of papers. "That grave was moved about two hundred years ago, along with the Longespèes, father and son, from the Trinity Chapel up at the top of the cathedral to the plinth in the nave where they are now."

She went methodically from page to page. "I'm hoping to find some note from the architect, James Wyatt," she explained, "about what exactly got moved. Ah, here it is."

Lizzie leaned forward to look from across the desk.

"It was some sort of small gold casket," Nora said, "with a heraldic device on it."

"That's exactly how the Templars described John d'Hautain's heart," Lizzie said excitedly. "Did he describe the heraldic device?"

"No," Nora said disappointedly, "though it says they had someone search through the coats of arms of English families without being able to identify it." She put the papers back in their box and proceeded to the next group. "Of course most arms changed a lot between the thirteenth century and the eighteenth." As she shuffled through the papers of the second box she explained to Lizzie that the tomb had been opened again after a flood in 1915, and that the index indicated another reference to the contents.

"Here it is," she said, "and this time the Keeper made a sketch."

She turned the paper around so that Lizzie could see a crudely drawn shield on the page. On it were three elements—two hearts above, a series of blocks in the middle, and a wavy line below.

"Oh my God," Lizzie blurted out, "that's it!" She looked up at Nora Stanley. "That's it," she repeated, tapping her finger on the paper, "that's the heart of John d'Hautain."

"Are you sure?"

"Absolutely. There is no question."

"The Hatton family crest is pretty famous for its pierced heart," Nora said, turning the page back around to look at it herself, "and none of these other things is on it."

Lizzie described in detail the evolution of the Hatton family crest, the crenellated battlement of the castle tower, which had been interpreted in this sketch as a line of blocks, and the wave of the sea beneath it. She even described the scene at the tournament where it had been worn.

"I am impressed with the amount of material you've unearthed there at Hengeport, Dr. Manning."

"I told you there was a *very* strong family lore," she said with a forced laugh, "but you can also see this same crest on the effigy of John d'Hautain in the family church."

"I assume you'll tell Sir George about this?"

"Indeed I will," Lizzie said, looking at her watch, "which reminds me I must catch a train—I'm meeting him in London."

She collected her papers, shook hands heartily with Nora Stanley, and thanked her for her help. Then she ran all the way to the train station.

Chapter 23

George Hatton was right on time. Lizzie met him in the lobby and escorted him back to her suite. As they went up in the elevator, she couldn't help but notice the leather-bound box under his arm. She wondered if what he had to show her could possibly be as exciting as what she had to tell him.

"I hope you've had an enjoyable stay in London," he said nervously. His eyes were on the numbers of the floors as each lit up in succession. Lizzie could see that he was still uncomfortable about her experience at Hengemont.

"Yes I have," Lizzie said. "It's been very productive."

"Seen any shows?"

Lizzie turned to give him a withering look but he was still avoiding her eye, as if they were strangers in the lift together. She was surprised at how awkward it seemed.

"I've been working," she said, somewhat curtly.

Now he turned to look at her.

"I'm sorry," he said.

The elevator doors opened and Lizzie took out her key to lead him into her suite. She had arrived back from Salisbury just in time to order some wine, cheese, crackers, fruit, and patè from Room Service, and they had been delivered while she was down meeting George.

"Would you like a glass of wine?" she offered, gesturing to a seat for him. There was a good-sized table near the window where she thought he could show her whatever was in the box he carried. Beyond it, London twinkled in the dark winter sky.

"Thank you," he said, placing the box on the table and sitting. "A glass of wine would be very nice."

Lizzie made up a small plate for each of them from the

food on the sideboard, poured two glasses of wine, and sat down opposite him. She was wondering how to tell him that she had found the heart. In fact, she was hoping that Martin would get back soon, because she wanted him to be here when she related the story for the first time.

George took a sip of the wine and pushed the box toward Lizzie.

"You'll probably be able to figure out what's in here as well as I did," he said. "This box was given to me when my father died and I inherited the title and property." He turned his chair to look at the lights beyond the window and took another sip of the wine. "I've never shown it to anyone else," he said softly, "not my sister, not my solicitor, not even my sons, though Richard will see it soon enough when I'm gone."

The box was old but very solid and obviously well cared for. The leatherwork reminded Lizzie of a seventeenth-century book, and she guessed that it had been made at that time. It had a sort of belt around it with a locking clasp that clicked open easily. The papers inside represented the history of the Hatton family, organized carefully from the oldest on the bottom to the most recent on the top. Lizzie turned the pile over so that she could begin with the oldest, but she couldn't help noticing that the most recent document, dated 1966, was a court-ordered committal of Elizabeth Hatton to a mental institution. She thought with a guilty conscience of Bette's diary, which was still in her possession.

The oldest documents in the pile were written on vellum and marked with ribbons and wax seals. Though they had all been rolled when new, the passage of seven hundred years, with most of them in a box like this one, had straightened them out flat. For a moment Lizzie regretted that she would not be able to read the ones in Latin or French, but she soon found that interleaved between each of the old documents was a newer one with a translation written in a neat nineteenth-century hand on a stiff piece of Hatton stationery. One after another, she turned over a dozen or so papers related to early titles and landholding, all bearing the seals of Kings Henry II, Richard I, John, and Henry III. A special writ called Richard, Margaret's husband, to Parliament in the reign of Henry

III. It had a big wax disk, impressed with the Great Seal of England.

There were the Templar documents she had seen transcribed at the Public Record Office, and she thought of the copies that lay now in her book bag. The translations were very consistent with the information she had gotten from Anthony Parker and Father Folan.

The next paper she turned over was a letter from Elizabeth Pintard d'Hautain to her son. Lizzie touched her fingertips very gently to the signature mark. It was her first physical encounter with the woman who had started the Hatton obsession with dying for love. She sat silently for a moment until she heard George turn from the window to look at her.

"I see you've found it," he said.

Lizzie nodded. She took the translation and laid it beside the letter, moving her eyes back and forth between the two, one in old French, the other in a stylized English.

"My God," she said after a moment, looking up at George, "it's her suicide note."

Now it was George's turn to nod silently. He turned back to the window, his empty wineglass on the table beside him.

The letter described the sequence of events that Lizzie had learned from her other disparate sources, though in terribly sad and poignant detail. Elizabeth d'Hautain knew that by pledging her son to marry the daughter of her sister she was insuring that he would inherit the d'Hautain family titles and property. She asked his forgiveness for abandoning him, but said that she could not live without her husband. There were instructions to place his father's heart in the tomb in the family church if it should ever come into his possession.

"Though you will not remember your parents," the translation read, "think on them with kindness. Always remember their story." The letter concluded with a message that it would be left with Elizabeth's priest and was to be delivered to her son only on the death of his uncle and his inheritance of Hengemont. Her signature was scrawled on the bottom. Lizzie touched it again.

The next page included two shield-shaped drawings. The first showed the crest of John d'Hautain, which Lizzie had seen so recently at Salisbury Cathedral; the other drawing showed the sword-pierced heart, with instructions from Jean-Alun d'Hautain that he was adopting the new crest in honor of his parents. The motto was from his mother's letter: "Semper Memoriam."

"This is powerful stuff," Lizzie said, looking up at George's impassive back. He had not stirred in several minutes, but now he turned and nodded again.

"Can I pour you another glass of wine?" she asked.

"Yes, thank you," he said, turning his chair back to the table again.

Lizzie rose to pour the wine and George began to nibble a cracker. The time had come to tell George about the heart; it couldn't be delayed any longer. Lizzie looked at the door, wishing that Martin would return and, as if on cue, it opened and her husband entered the room.

"Hello," he said, looking from Lizzie to George and back to Lizzie. "Sorry I'm later than I expected." He crossed the room and held out his hand. "You must be George Hatton," he said. "I'm glad to meet you." He turned and kissed Lizzie and then excused himself into the bedroom to get rid of his coat.

The silent spell that the room had been under for the last half hour was broken. Lizzie breathed a sigh of relief and prepared to break her big news to both men. It didn't take long for Martin to return to the sitting room, fill a plate of snacks and join them at the table. Lizzie passed a wine glass to each man and held her own up.

"Cheers," she said, taking a gulp. She sat down again, opposite George, but she caught Martin's eye before she began speaking.

"I have news," she said. "I found the heart."

The reaction of the two men could not have been more different. George Hatton sat perfectly still, his face growing ever more pale as the blood drained from it. Martin rose from his chair with a cheer and gave her a kiss of congratulations. "I knew you could do it," he said.

"How? Where?" George was almost inaudible beneath Martin's excitement.

"It's in Salisbury Cathedral," Lizzie said gently, looking directly at George.

"And you're sure?" George stammered. "You've only been looking for it for two days! My family's been looking for it for seven centuries!"

"I know this is a very peculiar situation George, but in a way it was hiding in plain sight. A number of people had seen the casket over the years. They just didn't recognize the crest."

"You're really sure?"

"There can be no question," Lizzie answered, pulling out the various documents she had collected and showing him the references.

"The real proof is right here, though," she said, tapping her finger on the picture of John d'Hautain's shield. "The heart casket bears this coat-of-arms."

George rose from his chair and paced the room. Martin reached under the table and squeezed Lizzie's knee. She smiled at him, then rose and stood with George.

"What should I do now?" he asked.

"My recommendation is to contact the people in charge at Salisbury and claim it," Lizzie answered.

"It will seem a bit strange after seven hundred years," he mused

"These things sometimes take a long time," Lizzie said with a smile.

George nodded. He was not in a state to appreciate Lizzie's humor.

Martin called softly to Lizzie from the table. She stepped over to him and found that he had turned the stack of papers over and searched through them from the more recent end.

"Ask him about this," he whispered, showing her a receipt for the £300 paid to her great grandmother, with a notation about her pregnancy and departure.

Lizzie shook her head at him. He gave her a meaningful glare and held up the receipt again, mouthing the words, "Ask him!"

"Let me do this in my own way," she whispered sharply, turning back to face George.

Martin folded the paper and slipped it into his pocket.

George seemed to be recovering somewhat from his shock. "I have a friend in Salisbury who should be able to help me present the case to the Dean and Chapter at the cathedral there," he said. "Let's just get this over with. Could you clear your schedule and go there with me tomorrow?"

Lizzie nodded.

"My schedule is clear too," Martin added dryly. Lizzie gave him an arch look. She could tell he was itching to confront George about his knowledge of her relationship to the Hatton family.

George began to put the papers back in the box.

"Bring this one to Salisbury," Lizzie said, reaching for the page with the sketch of the crest and setting it aside.

"I can't tell you how much I appreciate all the work you've done on this," George stammered. He seemed to sense Martin's hostility and added with a nod to him, "and your support, too." The box closed and the sound of the old lock snapping into place was the only sound in the room.

George's departure was as uncomfortable as his arrival. He shook hands with Martin and gave Lizzie an awkward kiss on the cheek as she walked him to the door of the suite. When it had closed and latched behind him, Martin put his hands on Lizzie's shoulders and looked at her.

"He knows," he said. "He feels guilty that his family shafted your great-grandma, and he knows that you are actually his niece or cousin or something."

"I know," she admitted, "and I concede that he knew it all along."

"Aren't you angry that he put your life in danger?"

"Oh come on, Mart," she said, pulling away. "How was my life in danger?"

"Are you forgetting that you managed to climb up onto the roof of his house?"

She could see that he was very serious.

"I don't understand why you didn't confront him when we had the evidence right in front of us," he said, following her toward the bedroom.

As she turned the spread back, Lizzie explained again that

she didn't think George Hatton had ever even considered that she might be susceptible to the madness that led to suicide.

"Then why did he ask you here?"

"Because I'm a good historian," she said bluntly. "Maybe he did want to repay some debt, or maybe he secretly thought I might do exactly what I did—find the heart—but to suspect him of more than that is to make him more sinister than he is." She was angry with Martin for pushing the subject. "You shouldn't have gone through those papers," she said. "This is my problem and I'll handle it."

Martin came around the bed and touched her softly on the hair. "You're right," he said, "I shouldn't have gone through those papers."

Lizzie resisted for a moment his attempts to pull her into his arms.

"But you have no problems that I don't share," he continued, "and I still don't think you are taking the dangers here seriously enough. Don't think because I worry about you, or am suspicious of him, that I am not still your greatest admirer." He kissed her on the forehead.

"I know," Lizzie said softly. "But you shouldn't worry so much about George. He's not so wily that he could manipulate me."

Martin laughed. "You know you shouldn't be so flip about the English aristocracy now that you *are* one."

She sat on the bed and leaned against the headboard, reaching out for his hand. "You know, Martin," she said, locking her fingers through his, "I have to admit that there was a moment there when I found that whole way of life at Hengemont quite seductive."

"Planning to claim your rightful place in the Hatton family?" he asked gently.

She placed her free hand against his face. His eyes, deep and warm, made a small movement as they met hers. Lizzie laughed.

"Hardly!" she said. "Can't you just picture it? My whole family traipsing over here to move in with the Hattons?"

Martin was smiling, but trying to be serious.

"You admit it's seductive, though," he said.

Lizzie still smiled. "Of course it's seductive. The idea that you don't have to work, that there are no worries about money, no credit card bills, no anxiety over tenure. God, who wouldn't love to have someone clean their house, do their laundry, keep the yard beautiful, drive them around."

"Not to mention the feeling of importance," Martin added.

"You know, Martin," Lizzie said emphatically, "I'd rather be known for something I *did,* some accomplishment."

"I'm sorry that I am not able to keep you in the style to which you have become accustomed," he said, half seriously.

"Don't worry sweetheart," she said, "I did not become accustomed to it. In truth there is a point at which you realize that even though you're not doing it the laundry is still getting done, the house is still getting cleaned, the garden is blooming beautifully, and that if it's not the Lord of the Manor doing it, then it is some serf." Lizzie grabbed a tissue and blew her nose. "I may be descended from the Hattons, but I'm also descended from their servant. I'm prouder of her and what she did than I am of them and what they did."

"Then you're still my Lizzie Manning, and not her high and mighty Lady Elizabeth Hatton?"

"Heck, Mart," she continued, "if I wouldn't change my name to Sanchez when I married you, why would I change it now for a much stupider reason?"

"Are you going to tell old George that you know?"

"Yes," she answered, "when the time is right."

Chapter 24

When Lizzie climbed into the back seat of George's Bentley the next day, she found that he had recovered his aristocratic calm. He was friendly without being warm, authoritative without being overbearing, the perfect gentleman. The two of them talked strategy during the ride to Salisbury, as if the item they were claiming was some ordinary piece of property and not a human heart. In the front seat, where he had insisted on sitting, Martin chatted amiably with Peter Jeffries.

George had used his connections to make an appointment with the Dean of Salisbury Cathedral at 11:00. At Lizzie's recommendation, he had asked that Nora Stanley, the librarian, attend the meeting and bring the report of the Keeper of the Fabric, which showed the drawing of the crest on the heart casket. George had his own copy of the same from the hand of Jean-Alun d'Hautain, and Lizzie had copies of the correspondence among Henry III, the Templars, and the Longespèe family. There was no doubt that they had very good evidence to claim the heart. The question was, after more than seven centuries, was it just too late? Did it belong to the Cathedral?

It wasn't until the car was driving through the gate into the cathedral close that George mentioned casually that Edmund would be joining them. Lizzie found herself suddenly flustered, not so much at seeing him again as at introducing him to Martin. She had not yet sorted out her feelings and had no time to prepare for the scene before it was upon her.

Martin opened the car door and took her hand. He looked at her closely.

"You're nervous about this, aren't you?" he said softly into her ear.

She was surprised by the question and laughed nervously. "I am," she said, avoiding his eye and knowing that his "this" was different from hers.

Edmund stood at the door of the church, watching the exchange. Lizzie introduced him to her husband and as the two men shook hands she looked from one to the other. One was fair, one was dark, but that was only the superficial difference between them. She knew everything about Martin from having lived with him for more than fifteen years. She absolutely believed him to be a genius. He was passionate, animated, and loved her absolutely. Edmund was less well known. In the last three weeks she couldn't say if she had spent fifteen hours alone with him and was uncertain about his feelings for her. Once again she asked herself how much she was attracted to Edmund himself, and how much the attraction might be to Hengemont and the Hatton history that he represented. She dismissed the thought almost as soon as it came into her head. It wasn't fair to him. He was much more than that. He had been the calming influence that supported her, and his father, through all the ordeal of the last few weeks. In a hundred ways he had proven his thoughtfulness.

The two men were not at all alike, but she was in love with them both.

How far would she have gone toward having an intimate relationship with Edmund that morning at the White Horse? Her thoughts were making her uncomfortable as she watched them talking to each other. Did Martin have any suspicion of her feelings for Edmund? She didn't think so. He knew that Edmund had rescued her that night and that she liked him very much, but no more.

George came to stand beside her and for the first time that morning, his reserve cracked. He set his hand on Lizzie's arm and asked her one last time if she was sure this was the right heart.

She put her hand over his as she replied, "I am absolutely certain."

"Are you saying that as an historian?" he asked.

"Yes," she answered, "all the evidence is there. But I also feel it intuitively."

"In your heart?" Edmund asked. It was the first thing he said directly to her that day. They had mostly avoided looking at each other or speaking directly during the exchange of introductions, but now Lizzie turned to him and smiled.

"Yes," she said. "I feel it in my heart."

They went into the cathedral, where Martin went off on his own to look around while Lizzie and the Hattons met with the staff. The dean was impressed with the evidence they had assembled, as was Nora Stanley. They seemed perfectly willing to agree that the heart buried near William Longespèe the younger was, in fact, that of John d'Hautain.

"What would you like us to do about this now, Sir George?" the dean asked him. "We can certainly change the sign and acknowledge your ancestor." He turned to Nora. "That's not a problem is it Mrs. Stanley?"

"Not at all," she answered quickly. "I'll write it up this afternoon and get it to the calligrapher." She rose as if to tackle the task immediately.

"No wait," George said, "that might not be necessary."

"You wish to keep this anonymous then?" the dean asked.

"Well, yes and no," George said, fumbling for words. "Yes, I do want to keep the whole business quiet, and no, you don't need to make a new sign because I want to take the heart back to my family crypt in Somerset."

The clergyman and the librarian could not have been more surprised.

George seemed to gain eloquence and assurance in equal measure as he explained that the legacy of the heart had weighed so heavily on his family over the centuries that they could not be at peace until it was buried in their own church. Almost as an afterthought he acknowledged the honor of having it for so many years in Salisbury Cathedral, but Jean d'Hautain was, he insisted, "intended to be buried in *our* church, and there he must go."

The silence that followed was so thick that Lizzie felt she could taste it in the cold air. The dean put his elbows on the desk and tapped the tips of his fingers together in the same motion that Lizzie had seen Nora Stanley use the day before. With his long thin fingers, the cathedral effect was even more pronounced.

"Well," he said finally, "I can't very well refuse to return remains of which the identity seems so certain, and where you have proof that Salisbury Cathedral was not the intended place of interment."

He put his hand on the phone. "It will, of course, take a few days to make the arrangements. Were you serious about wanting to keep this all quiet?"

George said that he was.

The dean picked up the phone. "Let me just ask the Keeper of the Fabric when he can work it into the schedule," he said to George as he dialed. "It should be easy enough to do it one evening this week under the guise of usual maintenance and repair."

Lizzie, George, and Edmund exchanged looks of excitement, anticipation, and anxiety while the man at the desk talked on the phone. He explained the situation to someone on the other end, heard the response, and turned to George. "It turns out that this evening is the most convenient time for him, as he will have the necessary equipment in the cathedral to make some repairs to the plinth," he said. "Will you stay for the exhumation?"

George nodded with remarkable composure.

"Right," the dean said into the phone. "Then we'll meet you after Choral Evensong."

• • • • •

George treated the foursome to dinner at an ancient inn called the "Haunch of Venison," not far from the gate to the cathedral close. Much of the discussion revolved around Martin's upcoming mural project in Newcastle. No one brought up the subject of their bizarre and macabre plans for the evening, though those thoughts were in the minds of all.

They walked back along the narrow streets of the oldest part of Salisbury. The night was cold but exceptionally clear and the white face of the cathedral was lit against the dark sky. The dean's reference to the night's business as an "exhumation" made the hairs on Lizzie's arms stand at attention as they walked across the dark lawn of the close. Martin reached out and found her hand and held it tightly.

From the church they could hear the sounds of Evensong, the last service of the day. The ancient hymn, simply sung in a building of such immense age, size, and grandeur, had a powerful effect on each member of their party as they slipped through the side door of the church and into the last row of folding chairs. Unlike earlier in the day, when the winter light had streaked in through the windows, now the cathedral was lit only in small pools around the lamps and candles. Lizzie couldn't help but look at the small effigy of the boy bishop lying nearby, his blank eyes wide open and staring straight up. He had no idea that he was about to donate the heart that had lain beneath him for centuries, for transplantation into a new effigy.

As the service ended and people began to exit through the side door, Lizzie saw three men with tools and what looked like a large easel waiting at the back of the church. When everyone had gone except themselves and the clergyman, the three men came forward. One was introduced as Bill Bracken, the Keeper of the Fabric; the other two were his assistants. Lizzie nodded to them. This Bill was not at all what she expected. A burly man with white hair and a red face, he seemed an unlikely exhumer. While the two younger men chipped the cement away from underneath the effigy, he set up work lights and a framework with a pulley over the tomb. It was only half an hour before they were ready to attach felt-padded metal clips to the corners of the effigy, and with the three of them, the job of lifting it off its bed with a rope through the pulley was easily done. As his assistants held the stone suspended, Bill Bracken reached into the narrow cavity beneath it and pulled out a box. In the darkness, Lizzie could hear the voice of the dean of the cathedral, praying for the soul of John d'Hautain.

Everyone in the church waited silently as Bill handed the box to the dean and turned to help his comrades ease the stone back into place on the tomb. The only sound was the loud ticking of the old clock works displayed in the aisle where they were standing, and the scraping of a steel trowel as new cement was laid in between the effigy and the stone beneath it. Though she knew she was awake, Lizzie felt as if she were in a dream. The cathedral was now dark except for the single pool of light around them. It seemed almost slow motion as George Hatton was handed the box and turned it to look at the design on its surface. He sat in one of the chairs with the box cradled in his lap and looked up at Lizzie, as if for confirmation that this was indeed the right thing to be doing.

Lizzie went and sat next to him. George tilted the box toward her and into the light. Even with the grime of centuries on it, there was no mistaking the dull gleam of gold, or the device enameled on its top. The hearts, the castle tower, the sea, were all perfectly visible.

"That's it," she whispered.

"Yes," George nodded, "I know." He handed it to his son and turned back to Lizzie. "Even I can feel it," he said.

Edmund was the only one who had thought to bring a towel to wrap it in and a travel bag in which to put it, and he now carefully packed it up. His father stood up and turned to the dean.

"Thank you," he said, reaching out to shake his hand. "And thank you for keeping this quiet."

Behind them, the two young workmen were almost finished cementing the stone back into place.

"I would like you to sign a document for me," the dean said, gesturing the way back to his office, "just to make the transfer of the remains legal."

George nodded and went with him.

Edmund indicated that he would prefer to wait outside and Lizzie and Martin quickly echoed his sentiments. They went out to the side porch of the cathedral and from there walked out to the expansive lawn. The stars were bright above them.

"Hengemont or London?" Lizzie asked Edmund.

"Well, if you two don't mind," he answered, turning the collar of his coat up and securing the bag with Jean d'Hautain's heart under his arm, "I think we'd like to get this back to Hengemont as soon as possible."

"Yes, of course," Lizzie said, hurriedly. "How about a night at the White Horse?" she said to Martin.

"By all means," he answered. "I'm dying to see the place."

Chapter 25

"Now that we have this thing, I assume we're supposed to bury it in the tomb intended for it," George Hatton said as he sat with Lizzie, Martin, and Edmund at the White Horse pub. The gold casket with John d'Hautain's heart was in the middle of the table. Lizzie, Martin and Edmund had each examined the box to see if it could be opened, but it would have required breaking through the solder; it remained tantalizingly mysterious.

Lizzie had been thinking about where the heart should be buried, and now she answered George's question carefully. "I'm not sure it's as simple as putting it in the Crusader's tomb."

"What do you mean?" George asked with surprise. "Now that we've got the heart back after all these years, don't you think that she intended it should be buried?"

Lizzie looked to Martin for moral support. He looked back steadily. She turned to George and then to his son. "I've been thinking about this a lot, and the truth is, I don't think that there is any consciousness in any of this."

"What?" George sputtered. "You can't mean that my sister spent her whole life in an institution for nothing."

"That's not what I mean," Lizzie said calmly. Under the table Martin slipped her hand into his. "What I mean is that I think it is her *feelings* that have lasted all these years, not her *intentions*." She did not speak the name of Elizabeth d'Hautain.

"I'm not sure I understand you," Edmund interjected.

"This is not really clear to me," Lizzie answered, struggling to put her barely developed concepts into words. "It's

326 • Mary Malloy

just that I'm not sure that simply burying the heart in the tomb will break the cycle."

George sighed. "What the hell are we supposed to do with it then?"

"I think we need to bury it *with her.*"

"Not in the Crusader's tomb?"

"We can bury it there, but then I think we need to find her and put her there too."

He seemed a bit perplexed. "Isn't she there already?"

"No," Lizzie said emphatically. "She's in that little plot set aside for suicides."

George looked at her with amazement. "All right then, Lizzie," he said finally, a hint of exasperation in his voice, "you're the doctor. I'll just let you take care of the details."

"This all sounds fine to me," Edmund said softly. "But I think that we need to be careful about what stock we place in all this." His turned to his father and continued gently. "I'm sorry Dad, but as far as Bette is concerned, I think you have to consider the possibility that this story with which she has been obsessed for so long is a *manifestation* of her mental problems and not the cause of them."

Lizzie found herself caught up in the moment between father and son and consequently did not fully comprehend Edmund's meaning. She looked at her husband. Martin had understood Edmund perfectly, and his face was such an open book that in his expression Lizzie first realized what she had missed from Edmund's words.

"What do you mean?" George asked.

"I mean that Bette's not haunted or possessed by this woman, Elizabeth d'Hautain," Edmund answered. "She is mentally ill."

George reached up to take off his glasses and rubbed his eyes. Edmund continued. "Because this disease has manifested itself the same way so many times, we have allowed ourselves to accept, too easily I think, what is essentially the medieval explanation. In Bette's case it is certainly schizophrenia, accelerated by her drug use. It probably was that or some other diagnosable mental illness in the other cases as well." Edmund looked at Lizzie. "I don't think it's healthy to indulge in these fantastic suppositions. Bette's recovery at this point is very unlikely."

Lizzie suddenly felt embarrassed for having entered so fully into what Edmund had called the manifestation of the obsession. She wondered if he would feel any differently if he knew that she was also a descendent of Elizabeth d'Hautain, but felt pretty confident that he would not. Martin, she could see, was not convinced.

• • • • •

Because Elizabeth d'Hautain's grave was seven hundred years old, it seemed logical to Lizzie to hire an archaeologist to exhume her corpse. It consequently took two days for the young man recommended by Tom Clark to obtain the necessary licenses and permissions, and to map and sample the area around the graves of the ten suicides to determine which was the oldest grave there. An acorn had fallen at some point near Elizabeth d'Hautain's grave, and had subsequently grown into a very large oak tree.

"This could be something of a problem," the archaeologist said to Lizzie. His name was Dennis Aiken and as he spoke to her he tied a string around one of the sticks now set at regular intervals throughout the area beyond the cemetery wall. Because the frost-bound ground was so hard, he and his team were using small power tools to break up the soil for removal.

"How so?" Lizzie called, raising her voice to be heard over the sound of the noisy tools.

"Well, she could actually be under this tree," he called back.

"Yikes," Lizzie muttered.

"Yikes indeed," Dennis echoed, stringing his thin cord from one stake to the next. "On the other hand, however," he continued, "oak tannin is a very good preservative and it may have contributed to a better state of preservation than you might otherwise find in a grave this old."

She pulled her coat around her. "If you find something, would you give me a holler?" she asked. "I'll be in the church." Out of the corner of her eye she could see Bob Moran standing at the edge of the graveyard, keeping an eye on things, but not participating. She waved to him and he waved back. Since the evening she had dinner with him and the Jeffries she had seen him only occasionally, and always from a distance as he went about his chores around the grounds.

Dennis assured her he would keep her informed of their progress, and Lizzie walked through the gate and up the path to the church. Inside she could hear voices; it was Father Folan and the local vicar, Reverend Moore, talking about the reinterment of John and Elizabeth d'Hautain.

She paused just inside the door and eavesdropped on their conversation. They were discussing the removal of Elizabeth d'Hautain's corpse from unhallowed to hallowed ground, and church policy on the burial of suicides. They talked of depression and mental illness and cases they knew from their personal experience as pastors. It was clear that both men believed that their benevolent God looked upon those poor desperate souls with more mercy than did their respective churches.

"One way to solve this," Reverend Moore said quietly, "is just to go out now and consecrate that part of the cemetery. I've thought of doing it for some time anyway."

Father Folan touched his colleague on the arm. "In truth," he admitted, "I already have."

Lizzie walked quietly down the aisle and slipped into the pew behind the two priests. Both men nodded to her and Father Folan actually turned around to smile and reach a hand out in her direction. She had described to him the burial service she thought most appropriate for John and Elizabeth, and Edmund had explained it to the vicar; their talk now turned to the service.

The Irish part of Lizzie told her that Father Folan was likely to be superstitious as well as religious, and she had played up to that somewhat in explaining the situation of the lost heart. She doubted that Edmund had used the same tactic with Reverend Moore, expecting rather that, as the son of the Lord of the Manor, his request for action, no matter how sympathetically or politely delivered, would simply be accepted and carried out without question. In any case, Reverend Moore seemed prepared to allow the Catholic Litany of the Dead to be chanted in Latin as she had requested. She thought it was what John and Elizabeth would want.

"The Hattons want an ecumenical service, Michael," the vicar was saying, "and that is what they shall have."

Father Folan smiled at him. "Now Ian," he said, "I don't want you to think that I'm a showoff, but I think I'll sing my part."

The vicar returned a more shallow smile. "If you think that is necessary," he said.

Father Folan clapped him heartily on the back. "Come now," he said, "I expect you to sing the responses for me."

"In Latin?"

"Of course, lad." He smiled now at Lizzie, adding, "And you too, my dear."

The three talked comfortably in the cold church for several more minutes before they were interrupted by a shout from outside.

"Dr. Manning," one of Dennis Aiken's assistants called, running up to the door. "We think we've found her."

Lizzie felt a cold wind on her face as she, the vicar, and Father Folan stepped onto the stone porch of the church. She pulled her new muffler up to her nose and moved tentatively across a rough patch of ground to the stone wall that divided the old unconsecrated ground from that directly adjacent to the church. She could just see over it to the site where Dennis Aiken was excavating. He motioned to her to come through the gate and around.

"It hasn't been easy with this frozen ground," he said as she approached with the two priests. He tapped on a thick piece of wood with a long pole. "But as you can see, we've found a coffin that could very well be from the thirteenth century."

Father Folan made the sign of the cross, and Lizzie was tempted to do the same.

Dennis Aiken was standing on the edge of a growing hole, which his assistants were working to enlarge further. As the whole crew of six began to concentrate all their energy on it, the hole rapidly took on the appearance of a grave rather than an archaeological site. Dennis took continuous photographs of the process, pausing occasionally to log information onto a form on a clipboard, and it was not long before everything that remained in the ancient grave was clearly visible. At a signal to the working crew, all of the power tools suddenly ceased and in the silence that followed Lizzie thought she could hear her heart beating.

It was not a large coffin, though the oak boards from which it was made were several inches thick. As they cleared away the top board, Lizzie turned to look at the tree that towered above the grave. She had thought so much about Elizabeth d'Hautain as a living, breathing woman, feeling her emotions, almost thinking her thoughts through her strange dreams, that she suddenly questioned if she wanted to see her corpse. Would she be a skeleton? Would there be even that much left after all this time? Images of bodies in various states of decomposition raced through her mind. She shuddered, and pulled her coat closer around her. Father Folan came over to stand near her and she gave him a weak smile.

Dennis jumped into the hole to help with the last tug as the coffin came from its grave. As the lid was loosened, he instructed his men to lift it and set it aside. Lizzie heard him say, "My God, she's beautiful."

Father Folan left her side to look into the grave, and then came back and took Lizzie by the arm. "There's nothing to fear here, my dear," he said with his soft brogue. "She's remarkably well preserved."

Dennis was explaining to his crew about the miraculous properties of oak tannin and the bog that had preserved the corpse for more than half a millennium as Lizzie approached the hole with trepidation and looked in. There, lying against one side of her coffin, her hands folded in prayer and her eyes closed as if in sleep, was Elizabeth d'Hautain. Her skin and clothes were all the golden brown color of leather, her face was serene and beautiful. Under her wimple, Dennis pointed out a few strands of auburn hair.

"She's so tiny," Lizzie said. Looking into the open grave at the beautiful corpse of Elizabeth she felt only peace.

The two clergymen stood on either side of her. Each of them was saying a low prayer. When he had finished, Lizzie asked the Reverend Moore if it would be appropriate to ring the bell of the church to let the family know of the find, or if one of them should go up to the house.

"The bell's a good idea," he said, turning to go back into the church.

Dennis looked up from his position kneeling beside the coffin. "There's extensive damage to the back of her skull," he said, gently rolling the corpse.

"She fell or jumped off a tower," Lizzie said.

"Ah, that explains it then. She would also have lost a lot of blood, making this tanning process more possible." He came around the grave as his assistants pulled themselves up out of it. "You must be pleased," he said to Lizzie, as he wiped his hands on a towel and took the clipboard from his awestruck employee.

"I don't know what I expected," Lizzie said. "I guess I thought you might find a few bones or something, but this. . . ." She gestured at the corpse, not knowing what to say.

· "It is remarkable, isn't it," Dennis continued. "I've seen so-called 'bog people' before, prehistoric bodies perfectly preserved in the oxygen-free and pest-free environment of a peat bog. I can only assume this was a bog at some time. Of course I'll have to take the remains back to my lab for some tests, and then I think there are some archaeologists at the British Museum who would be very interested in seeing it."

Lizzie shook her head. "I don't think that's going to be possible," she said. "The family is committed to burying her inside the church immediately. In fact," she said, hearing the church bell begin a rhythmic clanging, "I expect we'll see Sir George soon enough."

Dennis tried hard to convince Lizzie that she should support his scientific curiosity and use her influence with George Hatton. At first she was sympathetic. This was, after all, an extraordinary find and Dennis Aiken had done a good job locating it.

"I'm sorry," she said, as supportively as she could. "I think I know just how you feel, but there are other, private, issues here."

Dennis pushed harder and Lizzie responded with greater

332 • Mary Malloy

firmness. They spent several minutes going back and forth. She could tell that he was reaching the limit of his patience, and she knew that she was certainly reaching the end of hers.

"Now wait," Dennis said finally, a certain anger appearing in his voice for the first time, "this is a major archaeological find. We must share it with the public."

In the distance, Lizzie could see George and Edmund Hatton approaching the gate from the house. She waved to them, then said to Dennis, "We might as well wait until Sir George gets here. It's his decision in the end."

"By God, it's *not* his decision," Dennis returned angrily. "This is a matter of national significance."

"There is no mystery here," Lizzie answered. "We hired you to excavate a specific grave, whose occupant was well known to us. We already knew how she died, and our purpose in exhuming her was to move her into the family church. You said yourself that this kind of preservation, while not common, is certainly not unknown. The scientific value here is secondary to the human needs."

"It's still an important find, and of national interest."

"I know that you could enhance your professional reputation with this," Lizzie said, losing her patience, "but it is a personal matter of family to these men." She gestured toward the approaching George and Edmund as she finished. "You're on private property, you're being paid a good wage, this is *their* ancestor, don't push it if Sir George doesn't want it pushed." She began to walk toward the Hattons.

Dennis Aiken followed. "Now wait," he said, reaching for her arm, "why wouldn't they want to follow up on this?"

Lizzie shrugged him off.

"You know," he said, "I can always bring in the police, what with the suspicious nature of her death and all. I can make it uncomfortable for them."

Lizzie stopped and turned to face him. "You're going to bring in Scotland Yard to investigate a seven-hundred-year-old corpse found in a graveyard?" she said angrily. "That should certainly make a name for you." She turned her back on him and continued on to meet the Hattons. "Don't follow me," she hissed. "I hired you and now I'm firing you. Get out."

"I'll speak to Sir George if I want," he insisted.

"Then wait back at the church, you can speak to him there." Lizzie now turned and gave him the look that she saved for her worst students; it had silenced coughers in theaters, it had brought auditoriums to complete stillness. Dennis Aiken backed away and went to the church.

"Oh brother," Lizzie said under her breath. George and Edmund reached her and she explained the find as they walked to the graveside.

"Remarkable," Edmund sighed, looking into the open coffin.

"The archaeologist says she was preserved by the boggy ground associated with this oak tree."

They stood silently for several minutes and were eventually joined by Martin, who had heard the church bell ring from the White Horse.

As they turned from the grave and started toward the church the impatient Dennis Aiken cornered George. He avoided Lizzie's dangerous look as he rapidly explained the importance of this archaeological find to the nation. George tried to wave him off, but he would not take the hint. Edmund gently took him aside and told him this was not the time, but he still would not be stopped. Walking backwards in front of George he pressed him to let him bring in some other archaeologists and to prepare the body to be transported to London for further study.

Finally George stopped in his tracks. "Go away," he said softly.

"What?"

"Go away," he repeated with greater firmness, resuming his walk toward the church.

"I'm sorry Sir George, but I don't think you understand," Dennis replied. He began to say that he thought Lizzie had not advised him well.

George stopped again. "Are you deaf?" he asked.

"Of course not."

"Then get off my property."

"I can't in good conscience just abandon such an important find."

George turned to his son, "Call the police," he said. "Get this man, and all the rest of these people, off my property."

"I'll be back," Dennis Aiken said, motioning to his crew to pack up their things.

"And I'll have you arrested," George said dismissively.

Lizzie was impressed. George had appeared to lose his natural confidence since her episode on the roof, but now he was clearly getting back to his old self.

The two clergymen came out of the church to meet them and George asked Reverend Moore to "get Bob Moran and some lads from the village to move the coffin to the church and fill up the hole again."

The vicar nodded and went to recruit the help. Bob Moran had been hovering at the fringes of the crowd and hearing his name stepped forward.

"Let's get this over with," George continued, turning to Edmund. "There's Bob. Tell him to get a crew together. Let's open up the tomb and bury these people."

It took several hours to assemble the necessary labor and equipment, and it was not an easy matter to raise the stone lid from the tomb chest. It was much more difficult than the exhumation of the heart a few days earlier at Salisbury Cathedral, where the stone had been relatively small and the crew experienced at the job. Bob Moran called in the local stone mason and he, in turn, called a rigger up from the port with heavier tackle and gear.

Edmund supervised the move of Elizabeth's coffin into the church where it was laid in front of the altar. He put the heart casket on top of it.

Lizzie sat in one of the side pews and stared at them, feeling a mixture of emotions. There was awe mixed with pride that she was the one who had reunited John and Elizabeth after so many centuries. There was also confusion about how, exactly, it had all happened. The last several weeks were something of a jumble.

Martin went back to the White Horse to bring some blankets and pillows and when he returned, Lizzie lay down in the pew with her head in his lap and slept. She woke two hours later to his kiss.

"Wake up, darling," he whispered, "they have found something wonderful."

Lizzie wrapped a blanket around her shoulders and walked with Martin over to the tomb. The stone lid was now propped open with boards at the two corners furthest from the wall, and a heavy chain was suspended over each end. Lizzie blinked to adjust her eyes to the strange light. The work lights were very bright but the interior of the sarcophagus was deep in shadow and it took a moment for her eyes to adjust. When she could finally make out the contents she gasped. Folded on top of a carved and painted Tlingit bentwood box was the Chilkat bear-crest robe.

"My God," she whispered, "Frank Hatton must have put them in here when he had the tomb opened for Eliza."

"Would you like to take them out?" George asked.

"Of course," Lizzie replied. She gently touched the woven robe, astonished to see how bright the colors were after two centuries. The fibers were still strong and she lifted it carefully and laid it on a nearby pew. She then reached back into the burial chest to test the weight of the box. It was light enough for her to lift out by herself and she removed it from the tomb and set it down next to the blanket.

"My God," she said again, sitting in the pew next to them and lightly touching the box. "What a day."

"What a week!" Martin laughed.

"You haven't even been here a month, and think of everything that's happened," George said, sitting down beside her. "You know, Lizzie," he added thoughtfully, "it was really rather a nice gesture of Francis to put Eltatsy in the tomb."

"It was indeed."

They took a short break before continuing with the grim task that lay before them, and shared coffee and food with the work crew. Father Folan went across the street to fetch his colleague and the two clergymen made preparations for the burial service. When they were ready, Reverend Moore spoke briefly to George and he motioned to Edmund, Lizzie, and Martin to join him in the front pew. Helen and Henry

Jeffries, Bob Moran, and the workmen from the village filed into the pews behind them.

As promised, Father Folan chanted the Litany of the Dead in Latin, and Reverend Moore chanted the responses back. Lizzie couldn't help thinking of the two passionate teenagers who now, centuries later, lay in the small boxes in front of the altar. She imagined that the chants sung at their wedding, in this same chapel, had sounded very much like those she was hearing now.

When it was concluded, George and Edmund went forward and helped the priests move Elizabeth's coffin to the tomb that had been built to hold it seven centuries earlier. The small crowd in the church gathered around them to help if needed. When the coffin was settled, George turned to Lizzie. "Where should we place the heart?"

She stepped up to stand beside him and looked at the oak coffin, now resting securely in its stone chest. "I think you should push the lid back and lay it inside next to her," she said.

George nodded and began to return to the altar for the heart casket as Edmund and the priests pushed back the top of Elizabeth's coffin.

"Why don't you let Lizzie do it?" Martin interrupted. "She's part of the family too."

Edmund looked surprised. His father, embarrassed, stepped back a step and gestured toward the small golden box.

"Of course," he said turning to Lizzie. "Elizabeth, would you place it where you think she would want it."

Lizzie was furious with Martin for having announced to everyone in the church her relationship to the Hattons. She still hadn't decided how far she wanted the knowledge to go and now her husband had robbed her of whatever control she had over it. Whatever calm had existed in the moment vanished and she felt herself shaking as she took the few steps to the altar. She looked around the church and felt all the weirdness of the situation, now made even more awkward by Martin's declaration.

Wordlessly she gathered up the small casket. As she walked

with it to the tomb, she could feel the small hard lump that was the heart of John d'Hautain roll around inside the box. Had this thing held his passionate love? Would *she* have been satisfied with it had she gotten it all those years ago? Would any of those women who had asked for it for so long? She stumbled up the stairs to the tomb, blinking back tears.

The bright work lights had been adjusted so that they shone directly into the interior and the sight was ghastly. Elizabeth's corpse had a shriveled dead look that Lizzie hadn't noticed in the earlier softer light of the winter afternoon. The face was tight, the lips drawn back to reveal small crooked teeth. The eyelids were open slightly but there were no eyes inside. Her hands, which had appeared clasped in prayer, did not in fact touch and now looked more like claws, grasping at the air between them, as if seeking, seeking still, the thing Lizzie held in her hand.

She put the box into the tomb, resting it against the elbow of one rigid arm of the corpse. The gold glinted against the harsh light. Lizzie could not tear her eyes away. Was this moment worth all the suffering it had caused, she wondered? She had expected some feeling of serenity, of closure, some glow of recognition between these long-dead wretches, but they just lay there shriveled, and she felt nothing. Had Martin ruined the moment by making her so angry, she wondered?

Lizzie stared into the coffin until Edmund and George came up and pulled the oaken lid back into place. George motioned to the workmen to lower the heavy stone lid of the tomb, which was quickly done. When the work lights were turned off, the church was plunged into darkness. They had begun the grim business in daylight and now it was almost midnight. Reverend Moore found the switches to turn on the lights in the church, and the assembled company began to leave silently.

George turned to Lizzie and indicated that he wanted to speak to her. She went to stand beside him and he leaned toward her.

"From your husband's comment, I guess you know about our relationship," he said. His spoke softly; Lizzie couldn't read any emotion in his tone.

She nodded. When she raised her eyes to look at him, he was studying the memorials to his departed family members packed into the dark church. *Their* departed family members, Lizzie thought.

He turned to meet her gaze. "I'm sorry," he said simply. He seemed at a loss to find any other words and so repeated his apology again. "I'm sorry."

They moved out of the church to find Martin and Edmund. Lizzie's husband gave her an impatient and searching look. Edmund was disguising his curiosity better as he looked from Lizzie to his father and back.

George looked at his son. "Lizzie is the great grand-daughter of my great-uncle," he said, so softly that his listeners had to lean forward to catch the words.

Edmund looked at Lizzie with some confusion, then looked down, and then back at the church.

"Which great-uncle?" he whispered to his father.

"The one after whom you are named."

Edmund accepted the information silently. It had begun to snow, and he took his father by the arm and started to lead him back toward the house. George moved slowly, solemnly. For the first time since she met him, Lizzie thought he looked every bit his age.

In contrast to the peace that had permeated the party that evening in Salisbury cathedral, now they all seemed exhausted, tired of the business, as if they were only now feeling the delayed grisly horror of the spectacle.

Martin tried to take Lizzie's hand but she pulled away. She was not happy with her husband's behavior in the church.

"Why did you have to blurt out my relationship to the Hattons that way?" she whispered furiously. "I told you that I would handle it. I wanted to talk to George about it privately, and you made it into a public declaration."

She didn't wait for an answer but turned and went back into the church. She was angry with Martin and she was angry with Edmund, who had made no comment to her, no gesture of understanding when he learned that they were related. He could barely meet her eye. And George. His mumbled apology was hardly worth the effort. Her thoughts went back to

Edmund. After all the closeness they had shared, how could he just stand there, avoiding looking at her? Was he embarrassed about the relationship that had formed between them over the last few weeks? Or over the relationship that had existed between them all their lives, but which neither had known about until now? Or did he think she *had* known?

Her first intention had been to go back one last time to the tomb of Elizabeth and John, but her footsteps veered right instead of left as she reached the altar. Moving to the last row of the wooden pews, she sank down into it. The church was completely silent. Lizzie could feel her heart beating. She leaned forward until her head touched the back of the pew in front of her, and then she cried hard.

Men, she thought, were disappointing creatures. Not disappointing enough to die for, but disappointing nonetheless. She stopped her sobbing, sat up, blew her nose and looked around her. She was sitting right on top of the memorial stones. She pushed the bench she was on back with her feet so that she could look at them again. All those poor Elizabeths, she thought, nine of them, and one Edmund.

One Edmund.

She stood up and pushed the two pews further apart so that she could see that stone again and read it: "Edmund Hatton, 1864-1889." It was her great-grandfather. He had committed suicide, just like all those miserable girls. Another sob caught in her throat. Had he killed himself for the loss of Elizabeth Manning, she wondered? Or grieving for his sister? Either way, he was a pathetic wimp. Twenty-five years old. He could have found his lover and child if he wanted to.

Lizzie backed away from the pew and moved down one of the side aisles of the church. What had seemed so comforting to her just a few days earlier now seemed false, all these monuments to devoted sons, loving spouses, caring parents and valiant heroes. As far as she was concerned, it was all just for show. Where was all that caring and devotion when they lived?

Martin hadn't spoiled the moment. There was no moment. All this agonizing over hearts and corpses was meaningless.

Her husband stood silently at the back of the church. Lizzie saw him as she neared the door and did not resist as he pulled her into his arms. She looked up and met his eyes. He was sorry for having disappointed her; it was all over his face.

"Could you live without me?" she demanded.

He turned and led her out of the church, pulling the door closed behind them. On the porch he slid his arm through hers. "That's a strange question," he said. "Are you worried about something?"

Lizzie pulled on her gloves and wrapped her new scarf around her neck.

"My great-grandfather, Edmund Hatton, killed himself for love," she said.

They worked their way through the tangle of graves, past the wall and the plot that lay just outside it, now with a fresh mound of earth where Elizabeth had lain. The snow was just beginning to cover it. Edmund, the lover of her great grand-mother, he must be there too, Lizzie thought.

"Too many thoughts of death, sweetheart," Martin said finally. And then, after another long silence he added, "Would you want me to follow you if you died?"

"Not at all," she said, without hesitation. "But I'd want you to feel really really bad for a long, long time."

"I promise you, I would," he said.

They paused as she pointed out the plots beneath the oak tree.

"I wonder if his family preferred him dead to married to her."

"A century ago would you have loved me?" Martin asked softly.

"Of course!" she proclaimed instantly. "How can you even ask that?"

"Because Mexican men didn't marry the daughters of Irish immigrants and find themselves welcomed with open arms into the family," he said bluntly.

Lizzie felt tears welling up in her eyes again. It was a thought she had never, ever, considered. Life with Martin was not always easy. He was so impulsive and unguarded in his responses that he often provoked her, and yet the fact that he was so candid meant that she almost always knew what he was thinking and feeling. Right now he was filled with concern and regret; concern about her response to his stupid and unthinking exclamation in the church, and regret that he had hurt her by his actions. In many ways he was unpredictable, and yet he would never, she knew, ever have abandoned her as that earlier Edmund Hatton had abandoned her great grandmother. She dabbed at her eyes with her gloved hand. Her husband wasn't always easy to live with, but he was easy to love.

"I think we would have been together in any age," she said softly.

Martin was thoughtful. "Of course we would have loved each other," he said. "But if your family—or mine—had made it impossible to be together, would I have considered killing myself?" He paused for a moment before continuing. "I understand the impulse, as horrible as it is."

She slipped her arms inside his coat and hugged him. Tears rolled down her cheeks and she rubbed her face against his shirt to dry them.

He held her tightly. "There are many worse things that men have died for, Lizzie."

They stood there for several minutes, snow falling softly around them. Lizzie was the first to move, and they turned and started their walk toward the White Horse.

"What is worth dying for?" she asked him.

"I thought about that a lot during the Vietnam days," he answered. "Fortunately for me the draft ended just as my year was coming up, because I knew that I did not think that war was worth dying for," he continued.

She asked if any war was worth such a sacrifice.

His answer was delivered softly, thoughtfully. "I think I would have gone with the American troops in World War II; I think I would have joined the Union against the Confederacy; I think I might have followed Pancho Villa or Zapata for Mexican Independence." He stroked her hair. "The decision would have depended a lot on whether or not I had my Lizzie in my life."

She leaned against him.

"I think young men are easier to sacrifice in wars because

they don't often yet have the ties of real love to hold them back," Martin continued.

"Jean d'Hautain left Elizabeth to fight in the Crusades."

"Well that's one I definitely would have passed on," Martin said with a quiet laugh. "He was on the wrong side in that conflict if you want my opinion."

Lizzie nodded. "He felt it was his duty."

"Duty is something of a strange concept to me," he said. "I feel a strong sense of duty to you, to my parents, to my work, but I can't imagine the circumstances that would convince me to feel a duty to follow some king for a cause like the Crusades."

"It was pretty much a massacre of people for no reason other than their religion," Lizzie said softly.

"The Unholy Wars."

"Like most wars, I guess." She kicked at a clod of snow in the road. "There is something intensely romantic about war though," she said. "The danger, the separation, I don't know, there is something there that heightens the sensations and makes them all more intense. Fear is there, but passionate love, too." She looked at her husband. "I guess the feeling that *this* encounter might be your last makes you invest everything you have in it."

"Is it worth risking death to feel that passion?"

"No," she said shaking her head.

"And that level of intensity is not how you want to live every moment," Martin said, stopping and taking one of Lizzie's gloved hands in both of his.

"Are we too comfortable in our relationship?" she asked.

"Not at all," he said, squeezing her hand. "We are comfortable in our relationship because we trust and know one another. That is what creates intimacy."

"Is that better than passion?"

"You can't catch me, you know," he said laughing. "I love you passionately, you know it."

"And we're not boring or complacent after fifteen years?"

"I don't find you boring," he answered. "Do you find me too comfortable?"

Lizzie thought with a twinge of guilt about her attraction

to Edmund Hatton, then turned and looked into Martin's beautiful face. She knew every line, every hair, she loved his deep brown eyes, his intelligent good-humored expression, the look of love that she saw reflected back.

"No, my darling," she said, "In fact, I don't know how I got so lucky."

He smiled. "Thank God," he said, starting to walk again, "I was afraid I was going to have to go off and find a war somewhere to win you back!"

"There is something very sexy about the thought of you strapping on a sword or a gun to go off and protect me."

"You don't really believe that," he said. "You have never needed me to protect you from anything."

Lizzie smiled. "You're right. It's not sexy in terms of *our* lives. I was thinking about that Medieval situation again." She stopped. "That brings me back to my question, 'Could you live without me?'"

"No."

"Just like that? No?" she pressed.

"Just like that."

"But you wouldn't kill yourself?"

"I don't think so. There are some other reasons for going on, but my life would be forever diminished; something in me would die."

"Would you die for me?"

"You are really pushing this, you know."

She laughed. "I know. It's just been such a weird day."

He was thoughtful. "I wouldn't just lie down and die because you did, but if you were about to be hit by a truck and I could rush in and push you out of the way and be killed in the process, would I do that?"

She waited for him to answer his own question.

"I can't say for sure what I would do if I thought about it," he said, "but I think my instinct would be to do it."

"Thanks," she said. "I feel better now."

They both laughed. The snow had stopped and the sky was clearing as they continued on hand in hand.

After several minutes of silence Martin asked Lizzie if she was attracted to Edmund.

"Why do you ask?" she said, trying to make her voice sound calm and normal.

"He saved your life," Martin said, squeezing her hand. "I wish that had been me."

Lizzie didn't say anything.

"He's in love with you, you know," Martin said after another momentary pause.

Lizzie stopped and turned to him. "And I'm in love with you." She said it without any doubt in her mind or heart. "I love you."

Martin leaned his head down and kissed her.

• • • • •

That night, lying in their too-narrow bed at the White Horse, Lizzie asked Martin what he thought of Edmund's explanation of the Hatton family phenomenon. "Can all of my experiences of the past few weeks be rationally and scientifically explained?"

"What do *you* think?" he asked back. "Do you feel more comfortable thinking that George's sister suffers from schizophrenia than that she inherited or intuited thoughts and feelings from her ancestors?"

Lizzie turned slightly in his arms. "It's a bit frightening either way, I guess. Whatever Bette inherited, I may have inherited too."

"And is that necessarily bad?"

Lizzie pushed herself up on her elbow and looked at Martin. "How can you ask that? This is something that caused young women to kill themselves. It's kept George's sister in an institution for over thirty years."

Martin sat up in the bed and pulled Lizzie back into his arms. "But despite the death, there has also been remarkable passion."

"Are you fearful for my sanity?"

"No more than I was before you left for England," Martin joked.

Lizzie gave him a meaningful look and he kissed her. "Not at all," he said emphatically. "I feel confident that you have now played your role in this drama and can leave it behind when you go home."

She settled back down into the crook of his arm and after another silence asked him where he would like to be buried.

"Boy, you are just not going to let this morbid stuff go, are you?" he said.

"Well, it's something I think we need to talk about sometime."

"Right now?"

"No, but sometime."

Martin squeezed her in his arms. "You know," he said, "I can very truthfully say that I don't care."

"Not at all?"

"Not at all. You decide where you want me to be."

"You don't want to make some artistic statement in death?"

"Like what? A big funerary mural?" he laughed. "No wait," he continued, "you could have me cremated, mix my ashes into paint, and do a repro of one of my murals."

"Okay," Lizzie said. "We don't need to talk about it."

"But I'm on a roll," he said. "Forest Lawn in Glendale might even allow such a thing on one of their walls."

"I was serious," Lizzie said.

"I know," Martin said. "But this is a subject that is not worth the attention that you have been giving it recently. It's not healthy." He hugged her tightly. "I know where I want to *live,* and that's with you in our own house in Boston, Massachusetts."

"Me too.

"Then let's go there."

Lizzie nodded and hugged him back.

Chapter 26

The next day was warm for January and the snow from the night before was melting rapidly. Lizzie wore a heavy pullover sweater but no coat as she walked in the early morning mist to the church. Martin was still fast asleep at the White Horse, and she wanted to visit the tomb again by herself after the tumultuous activity of the day before. She picked her away along the side of the road, listening for the sound of oncoming vehicles hidden by the high hedge on either side.

When the hedge broke to reveal a barren field of earth, there was a "Public Footpath" sign, indicating the most direct walking route to the edge of the Hengemont estate. At the far end of the field Lizzie could see the square Norman tower of the Hatton's church. She pushed open the gate and made her way over the clods of earth, plowed into furrows and filled with small flinty stones. At the far end she climbed over the fence by way of the two-step wooden stile; the rest of the path was through the small woods that surrounded the church, still choked with the fallen leaves of oak and maple and all frosted with snow. The brown and white patterns of color were broken only occasionally by an evergreen yew tree.

The gravestones in the churchyard looked cold. It suddenly felt like winter again, to see the slatey stones in their frozen ground. Lizzie pushed open the door of the church and walked up the side aisle toward the altar. Her sneakers made no noise on the stone floor and her attention was on the ground in front of her, reading again the names and dates of Hattons and their neighbors buried beneath.

She went to stand again by the tomb of Elizabeth and John. Were they happy now? she wondered. Did any of this matter? Lizzie decided that it did. It mattered to her. She felt better today, as if something good had been accomplished. It didn't even matter if out there in the ether somewhere whatever ancient molecules that might survive of the woman they buried yesterday had any notion of what had been done in her name.

Turning around, she slid down to sit on the top of the two steps that raised the tomb above the floor, and rested her back against the cold stone. It was, she thought, only a thin wall that divided her from the last mortal bits of John and Elizabeth d'Hautain. That shriveled thing that was John's heart had once pumped blood through his young and virile body, and some part of that blood still circulated through her own system.

She looked around her at the other Norman graves in the chapel. In those tombs were the desiccated fragments of people who had known these two behind her as vibrant teenagers, full of hope, passion, fear, envy, and all the other noncorporeal parts of a human being. And now all of them were a part of her. Did she feel a part of them?

On the day that she first confronted the fact that the Hattons were her ancestors, she had felt such conflicting emotions. On the one hand it connected her to something important that she had always thought was lacking in her life: a sense of belonging to a place and to a known history. On the other hand, not having had those things for her whole existence up to that point had formed her identity in a different way, and the sudden acquisition of such an unexpected legacy threatened to overwhelm her very sense of herself.

For a moment she indulged the fantasy and imagined herself living the life of the Hattons in medieval times. She loved the idea of that life, the clothes they wore, the landscape through which they walked. But she would not really ever want to be there rather than where she was. She would never have been able to do the things she had done, to go to the places she had gone, to have loved Martin.

It was more than a slab of stone that separated her from Elizabeth and John, she thought, as she leaned against their tomb and stood up. It was seven centuries and a world of ideas, expectations, and possibilities. She did not need them to give her a sense of herself. She did not need that other Lizzie Manning, either. Her identity was neither from the master nor the maid. In all the essentials of her life she had created her own identity and at that moment she felt quite satisfied with it.

The sound of footsteps coming up the main aisle of the church broke her reverie and brought her out of the niche in which she was standing. It was Edmund, and he seemed startled to see her.

"Lizzie, I didn't expect to see you here so early."

"I'm saying good-bye," she said.

"Good. I would hate to see you invest any more in this business."

She sat down in a nearby pew and he sat down next to her.

"What are you doing here at this hour?" she asked.

"I came to get the Indian things."

The bentwood box and Chilkat blanket were still where she had left them the day before.

"I'm glad to get a chance to talk with you alone, Lizzie, because I don't know when the opportunity will come again and there are some things I need to tell you," Edmund continued.

She was almost afraid that he was going to admit feelings for her that she didn't want to know, but he began to talk about Richard.

"I called my brother last night," he said, choosing his words carefully, "to tell him about all of this business with the heart. And I've found out some things that are important." He fumbled with his words. "I hardly know how to tell you this."

"Is this about his financial problems?" she asked candidly.

He looked surprised that she knew about them.

"Yes, and no," he said. "That night that you had the episode up on the roof, I took a blood sample."

This was not the direction she had expected the conversation to go.

"Did you find anything?" she asked.

"Yes," he said uncomfortably. "There were traces of belladonna in your blood."

"What?"

"I specifically asked the lab to look for it."

"What?" she said again, louder this time. "That's impossible! I never even knew what it was until you told me about it a few days ago."

"It was that conversation that got me thinking about it," he continued. "The chocolates Richard sent you were laced with it. I sent them, and a sample of your blood, to a lab to be tested."

Lizzie felt as if she had been struck by lightning. For several minutes she couldn't say a word, and Edmund remained silent through it all, waiting for her to process the information.

"He tried to kill me?" she asked incredulously.

Edmund was emphatic in denying that was his brother's intention. "He swore to me that he didn't mean you any real harm. He hoped that you would just get sick, and maybe frightened, and leave."

Lizzie started to rise, but Edmund put his hand on her arm to detain her. "I told you that he had taken it himself on several occasions, but your experience was worse than anything he experienced or expected."

She slumped back into the pew.

"Your symptoms," he said, clearing his throat. "Your symptoms were so extreme. When you told me that it had happened two other times, and that each time you had ingested something conveyed to you by Richard, well. . . ." He didn't know how to end the sentence.

It was clear to Lizzie that Edmund was working very hard to maintain an air of calm professionalism as he told her all this, but his hand was shaking as he touched her, and she was getting more and more angry as the implications of what had happened to her sank in.

"He can't possibly have done this to me just so that he could get someone else to work on the Cook material?" she said angrily. "I can't believe. . . ."

Edmund interrupted her. "It's much more serious than that."

She pulled her elbow away from his hand and folded her arms tightly across her chest.

"All right," she said, "explain it if you can."

"Richard has lost a great deal of money in the last few years."

"And he wants to curry favor with the British Museum," Lizzie fumed. "I know."

"It's not that, Lizzie." Edmund leaned forward so she would have to look at him. "He's lost more than two hundred million pounds."

Lizzie stared at him in disbelief.

"He's sold or leveraged all of my family's property except this estate," Edmund continued. "The house in London, the agricultural lands and probably much of the art will have to be sold."

It took a minute for all of this to sink in. "But how could he?" she asked. "Don't those things belong to your father?"

"Richard will inherit it all and he used that fact to leverage huge sums; he also convinced others, many of them old family friends, to invest *their* money, using my father's property as collateral."

"But that still doesn't explain why I was a problem for him," she said slowly, pondering the enormity of what it all meant. "If it wasn't the British Museum business, then why would he care about me at a time when his other problems were so enormous?"

"You and your family presented a potential claim on the estate, and that was a prospect so frightening to Richard. . . ."

Lizzie cut him off. "What?" she asked incredulously. "Are you saying that *your* family has known about *my* family all along?"

"No," Edmund said convincingly. "When Richard asked my father why he hired you for this job, Dad told him about that other Elizabeth Manning. That was the first he knew of her. Then when Richard saw that you had access to many of the papers around the house, he became terrified that you would discover the relationship."

Her mind was working furiously, trying to comprehend the timeline of who knew what and when.

"When did your brother find out that it was more than a coincidence that my name was the same as your ancestor's lover?"

"Richard knew sooner than my father, I think. He is rather sophisticated about using technology to answer questions of this sort. For him, it was easy enough to follow your family tree back four generations on the Internet."

Lizzie was not convinced. "I've looked for information on my great grandparents for the last two decades," she said, "and never found anything—and I'm no slouch on the Internet." She thought about this for a few minutes. Richard had known what she hadn't: that Manning was the woman's maiden name. She had always been searching for the wrong great-grandfather.

"Damn him!" she exploded, beating her fists on the back of the pew in front of her. "Damn your brother!" She turned to look at Edmund. "I'm sorry to say this, but I hope he goes straight to hell. I hate him for what he did to me!"

"I'm not so fond of him myself at the moment."

Lizzie slumped back for a moment and then came forward again and hit her fist once more on the back of the pew. "Damn him!" she said again. She pulled at her hair and groaned with anger. "And it's not just because he tried to kill me. He made me doubt my sanity! He made me lose all perspective! Oh damn, I have been such a dope!"

She looked at Edmund and laughed at the ridiculousness of her behavior. "God, you must have thought I was a fool."

"No, Lizzie. No, how could you say that? You were a victim."

She leaned back again and crossed her legs. "You know all this supernatural stuff?" she said. "The only, I repeat the *only* reason I fell into that damned trap was because of those dreams. They were so vivid, they were like hyper-reality, with the colors and the smells and the emotions all heightened beyond anything I had ever experienced." She uncrossed her leg and stomped it on the floor.

"Damn him to hell!" she said again. "All the time they were drug-induced hallucinations."

So many questions were swirling around in her brain. The first was whether or not there were likely to be any long-term repercussions of the drug. Would she have flashbacks? Edmund assured her that it was extremely unlikely. Belladonna was not as potent as LSD, and the fact that she had vomited after every episode was a good sign.

"Why did you tell me this?" she asked.

"Because you had to know." He looked up at her again. "You aren't crazy and you aren't haunted."

She tried to smile.

He continued. "It is rather ironic, though, that Richard's stupidity led you into an experience that paralleled those of the other women even more closely than you imagined."

She thought about that for a moment, then asked Edmund what he wanted to do about the situation with his brother.

He seemed surprised by the question. "Whatever you think is right," he answered finally. "Whatever you decide, you will have my full support."

"Did you notify the police?"

"Not yet, but I certainly will if you want to press charges against him for assault."

"What would that do to your father?"

"I think that the knowledge that you might have died because of Richard's actions against you would be a blow from which he would not recover. Far, far worse than the financial losses, even the loss of this estate. And," he added, "one way or another, Richard is probably going to jail anyway."

There was a certain satisfaction in that, and Lizzie did not look forward to returning to England in order to testify against one of the Hattons. It would be devastating to George, embarrassing to Edmund and Lily, and would bring out a story that would do her no credit, despite the fact that she was the victim.

"There's one more thing," Edmund said haltingly, "and then I think you will know everything that I know."

It was difficult to believe that there could be anything worse than what she already knew, but Edmund's tone was so serious.

"They were married."

He blurted it out as if it was the most important piece of information of the day, and then looked surprised that Lizzie didn't seem to accept it in the same way. She shrugged.

Edmund went on tentatively. "Richard found a record of a marriage. That other Edmund married that other Lizzie Manning, but when his father found out, he had the marriage annulled. I think the father must have tried to convince the poor girl that the whole thing was a sham."

Lizzie blinked hard several times. That would explain why she had gone back to using the name Manning and had never tried to contact him. "What a cruel bit of business," she mumbled. "To both of them."

He seemed to be waiting for her to say something more, and finally asked, "You know what this means, don't you?"

She shook her head.

"It means your family really does have a claim on Hengemont. *Your* great-grandfather, Edmund Hatton, was the older brother of *my* great-grandfather."

She couldn't help smiling at the irony of that. They sat in silence for a moment before Lizzie told him that she didn't plan to tell her father of his relationship to the Hattons. He seemed surprised.

"Knowing that they were married doesn't change it?"

"No, why should it? It shows that he had more honor than the rest of his family, but the outcome is no different," she said. "Edmund Hatton was too weak to follow through when she needed him. Elizabeth Manning chose not to tell her son, and I think that her decision has to be honored. My dad is comfortable in his current identity."

"Except that now there is potentially a fortune at stake."

She made a comment that Richard had probably eliminated that factor, which he let pass without comment.

"You really didn't know any of this when you came here?" he asked.

"I came here for what I thought might be an interesting job," Lizzie answered. "And that's all. I didn't know any of the rest of the story until the day after I left Hengemont—though Helen tried to tell me."

"Helen?"

"Mrs. Jeffries. I'm also related to her." She smiled at the thought and explained the rest of the story to Edmund. "I don't want to offend you," she continued softly, "but I feel like I have been living in an anachronistic time warp for the last few weeks. And, not that I haven't enjoyed it, but I'm not comfortable with the idea of where it all originated, or how it has been maintained all this time."

She thought of the young Manning sisters.

"Your family faces no threat from mine," she said finally. "My father will not be charging in to fight a duel with yours."

Her romance with the British aristocracy was finally played out.

Her speech had, however, sounded more caustic than she intended, and she changed the subject by asking for more details about Richard's financial problems. As Edmund explained about his brother's hedge funds, margin trading, and bad investment choices, the enormity of what it meant for George and Edmund hit Lizzie for the first time. She pictured the Gainsborough painting of Francis and Eliza and their brother on the auction block at Sothebey's.

"This must be a blow for you," she said compassionately.

"I don't care about any of it for myself," he said. "You're not the only one who thinks that the time of the landed gentry is over, you know. I've lived on my own income for years. But my dad, this will devastate him."

"He doesn't know yet?"

"No. But he'll have to soon enough. Apparently the news is spreading around London and will be in the papers this week."

She put her arm around him. There were going to be some very unpleasant times ahead for all of the Hattons.

"This business about the belladonna will have to be a secret between us for awhile," she said, "and neither your father nor my husband can know of it."

He groaned. "I didn't think of Martin. Don't you have to tell him?"

"If I tell him now, then I will probably never see you or your father or this house again. Martin will certainly want to see Richard in jail or worse." She thought of their conversation of the night before. She had asked Martin if he would die for her, but not if he would kill for her, and yet she felt that he was very capable of violence if he thought she was threatened.

"But it will help him understand what happened to you."

"He was always more willing to accept the alternative explanations for this episode than either you or I were," she said. "He's all right for now, and I'll tell him all after we get home."

She thought about this a bit more. "The truth is, Edmund, that despite your rational explanation—which satisfies me perfectly, by the way—despite that, I can't help but feel that there are things we cannot explain, as Martin has said often enough." The words came out sounding just as fuzzy as her logic felt.

Edmund leaned over and kissed her gently on the lips.

"Yes there are," he said. "Many things." He touched her face with his fingertips, then stood up and walked over to the Chilkat blanket.

Lizzie went to join him. He handed her the blanket and she fingered the long fringe. "Why did you come to get these things this morning?" she asked.

"Because I feared that once Richard knew we had discovered them he might come down and try to take them."

"For what purpose?"

"I don't know. To sell them, maybe. Or to give them to the British Museum to try to regain his credibility. He's desperate and frightened and I don't know what he's capable of."

"What do you plan to do with them?"

"First to discuss it with my father, and then return them to Alaska." He picked up the box with Eltatsy's remains and Lizzie carried the blanket as they left the church. They walked silently through the gate into the Hengemont garden, and up the slope to the terrace.

George saw them coming from his study, and joined them soon after in the library.

"Are you planning to find a place for those in the cabinet?" George asked with some surprise.

"You know better than that, Dad," Edmund said.

The three of them sat and talked for almost an hour, about all the Hatton ancestors. Lizzie couldn't help wondering why some family stories were hidden as shameful, like that of her great grandmother and her tragic lover, while others were celebrated and romanticized, like that of Elizabeth and John.

"Why did you invite me here?" she finally asked George.

"Because I saw your book and recognized your name," he said simply. "I didn't know if you were actually a descendent of the earlier Elizabeth Manning. It was an impulsive move."

"Were you trying to make amends?"

"In all honesty, I have to say no," George said.

"Did you think she could save Aunt Bette?" Edmund asked.

George looked at him for a moment, then moved his eyes down to stare at his hands. "Not Bette," he said slowly. "If she could save anyone, I thought it might be Lily."

Lizzie wasn't sure if Edmund looked angry or just surprised.

When George spoke again, he addressed Lizzie. "I'm sorry," he said, wiping at the corner of his eye with his fingertips. "I didn't think any of this through. I never acknowledged the danger to you, but I thought you might possibly be someone to stand between Lily and the curse."

"Oh for God's sake!" Edmund said finally. It was now clear that he was angry. "Enough about this damned curse! There is no curse. There is only a long history of people behaving stupidly and of parents failing in their obligation to keep their children safe and look out for their best interests." He stood up and walked to the window and looked out. "Where was your father when Bette was suffering depression as a girl?" he asked George. "And that other Lizzie and Edmund—who gave his parents the right to separate them if they loved each other?" He came back to the table and looked his father in the eye. "Don't lay any of this on Lily, Dad," he said forcefully. "I will decide how and when she learns this particular part of the family story."

"Of course," his father said in a whisper. "Whatever you think is best."

He looked completely defeated and Lizzie could see that Edmund was regretting that he had spoken so harshly to his father. She thought about the additional bad news coming his way and hurried to change the subject.

"George," she said softly, "may I take the poems?"

"You are afraid I'll destroy them, aren't you?" he said, struggling to regain his composure.

"I don't think you need to," she said. "The story has as happy an ending as is possible."

"What will you do with them?"

"I want to encase them in a plastic called mylar, which will preserve them, and seal them behind a new memorial in your family church, if you don't mind."

"It is your church, too," he said, shrugging his shoulders. "You're certainly welcome to put something in it."

"You know that Martin is an artist?" she continued.

"Yes, of course," he said. "He told me about the mural he's going to do in Newcastle."

"I'd like to ask him to design a memorial cenotaph."

He quietly agreed to her request.

Lizzie considered telling him about Bette's diary, but decided that it would be better to just put it with the poems and seal it away.

"Martin has told me that there is a new technology that will allow an engraver to transfer a design from paper to brass, and I'd like him to try to work out the details within the week." She had already asked Martin to design the memorial, and she hoped to see it mounted in the church before she had to leave for Boston.

Edmund spoke for the first time in several minutes. "The memorial is a good idea," he said. "I assume it will be to your great grandmother?"

Lizzie smiled at him. "No, to all those women who died too young. I admire what that woman from the Rossetti painting did. At that time I don't think that the church or the family was ready for anything more elaborate, but I think it's time now to give them a real memorial."

Martin arrived in the middle of the conversation and after a brief exchange of greetings, joined them at the table. "What happens to these now?" he asked, gesturing at the box and the blanket.

Lizzie looked to George to see what he would say, and he was looking back at her as if for advice.

"Now that the heart has been returned to its intended resting place," he said finally, "the corpse of Eltatsy must be returned as well."

"Who is he?" Martin asked.

"He was a Tlingit Indian from the village of Hoonah on the Alaska coast," Lizzie answered. "Francis Hatton, in his collecting zeal, inadvertently stole his corpse from a burial island and now it must go back."

It was clear to her that the return of Eltatsy's remains was just as important as the return of John d'Hautain's heart, and though she had difficulty articulating her thoughts, she knew that each of the three men understood her perfectly.

Edmund asked Lizzie if she knew where it should go, and she told him that she had a good idea from Francis Hatton's journal of the vicinity, if not the specific location, of the island. They should start by making a contact in the Tlingit community, she suggested. Martin volunteered to help with that task; he was active in an organization of Native American artists, and through it knew several Tlingit carvers. He would, he said, make some calls as soon as they got back to London that evening.

It was a good start to the next chapter of the story, Lizzie thought. With two corpses restored to their rightful tomb, only one now remained. Then both Eltatsy and Francis Hatton could rest in peace.

• • • • •

Lizzie spent the next few days in London consolidating her notes about Francis Hatton's voyage, and trying to get ready for her upcoming class at St. Pat's. She had originally planned to be home more than a week before the new term started, but she had changed her ticket in the hopes that she would be able to see the new memorial mounted in the Hatton church before she left England. Martin was working quickly on the design, and had met an artist in Newcastle who could convert his sketch onto a laser-engraved brass plaque.

Tom Clark at the British Museum had strong opinions about the Chilkat blanket and the burial box being returned to an exposed island, and he and Lizzie had a long and heated discussion on the topic.

"Isn't there any way to keep them from going back into the elements?" Tom had asked her. "They are such extraordinary works of art. If the Hattons aren't willing to donate or sell them to us, can't you arrange to get them into a local museum in Alaska?"

A month earlier Lizzie's opinion on the matter would probably have coincided with the curator's. But in the last week she had seen the physical remnants of two Hatton ancestors exhumed and reinterred, and she knew the remains of either would have been welcomed into Tom Clark's museum. Dennis Aiken had wanted to add Elizabeth d'Hautain's corpse to the collection because of the curious nature of her state of preservation. John d'Hautain's heart was contained in a solid gold piece of thirteenth-century craftsmanship, which illustrated the melding styles of the Arab artisan and the European Crusader client. It was an immensely interesting and valuable work of art.

None of the people present at the reburial would have ever entertained a thought of sending the remains to a museum rather than sealing them in the tomb. There was an absolute understanding and acceptance of the right of those two human beings, even so long dead, to be buried in the manner, and in the place, they had chosen for themselves.

She explained this to Tom Clark and asked him what was different about the corpse of Eltatsy, or whoever was in the box. Did the long tradition of disregarding the last wishes of native peoples all around the globe make it more acceptable to treat their remains as legitimate examples of science, art, or commerce?

Tom had a very pragmatic answer. "I think that the interests of the living always outweigh the interests of the dead," he said. "I think science and art and the understanding of culture have a value that is comparable to the spirituality or sentiment, or whatever it is, that makes people want to honor the bodies of dead people–even though they know that everything they treasured in the person is gone and that the corpse is just an empty shell that will eventually disintegrate." He reminded her that she was the one who first brought up the idea that the Hatton ancestors would be as welcome in the museum collection as Eltatsy, then jokingly asked if that possibility was definitely closed.

Lizzie forced a smile. "Would you donate your body to a museum?" she asked.

"If it had some value for science, I would," he insisted.

Lizzie reminded him that Eltatsy's corpse had been stolen from his grave, that Francis Hatton had regretted it, and that if the remains were in an American museum, Federal Law would require their repatriation to the Tlingit.

It was clear that they were not going to resolve the issue except to agree to disagree, which they did. They then turned their attention to another matter, Richard Hatton's financial disaster, which was now widely known in London. His losses were enormous; Lizzie could barely comprehend the figures she was hearing. And he had involved enough people of prominence in his investment schemes to bring down other fortunes besides that of his own family.

"It's pretty unbelievable," Tom Clark told her. "Several people I know have lost huge sums."

"What possessed them to make such risky investments in the first place?"

"They didn't seem so risky at the time. Most of it was high-tech stuff that seemed to hold unlimited potential."

"Still, the amounts they were willing to speculate with—"

"The terrible thing here is that Richard Hatton's firm allowed them to take on risks that were sometimes four times greater than the actual cash they had on hand. When things collapsed, money that had existed only on paper suddenly had to be backed by real property."

"Well, Tom," Lizzie said as she rose to go, "let that be a lesson to us not to get too greedy."

"As long as we stay in our current professions, I think we're safe!" he said.

· · · · ·

Martin also had opinions on Richard Hatton's situation, which he was reading about daily in the *Times*.

"It's too bad about your pal George," he said to Lizzie from behind the newspaper as she dressed one morning. "He seems a good enough guy, and doesn't really deserve to lose everything."

Lizzie agreed.

"On the other hand," Martin continued, "he's always been rich and will probably do all right. The real tragedy here is the working people who are losing pensions." He was stretched out on the bed with the newspaper spread around him and a pot of room-service coffee on a tray nearby. He kept up a running report on what the papers were saying about the Hatton family as Lizzie was preparing to leave.

"Where are you going?" he asked.

"I just have some errands around town before we go. Are you staying in today?"

"By no means," he answered, sweeping the papers aside. "I have to call my friend in Newcastle about the cenotaph. It should be ready today."

Lizzie had been hoping that it would be finished before they left England.

"Any chance we can get it down to Hengemont in the next few days?"

"Every chance, my love. I knew you'd want to see it installed before we go."

She kissed him warmly. "When can I see it?"

"When everyone else does," he answered. "It weighs a ton and the engraver will just load it on his truck and bring it straight to the church."

Lizzie was excited, and said that she would call George Hatton to make the arrangements.

"When we see him, I guess I should return this," Martin said, reaching into his pocket for his wallet and retrieving the paper he had taken from George's document box. He handed it to Lizzie. "I meant to return it, but the time never seemed right."

Lizzie took it from him. "Don't bother," she said. "I'm going to keep it."

Martin's look expressed his astonishment. "Is that the right thing to do?" he asked.

"Yup," she said, finding one of her manila folders and sliding it in. "I'm going to seal it behind the cenotaph with the poems and pictures. It is all part of the story that we are going to put behind us."

"You don't think that someday you or someone in your family might want to legally prove the relationship to the Hattons?"

Lizzie shook her head. "No," she said confidently. "I don't believe that will be necessary. Whatever relationship we will have has to originate in actions, not the law."

He didn't seem to understand her decision, but he accepted it and didn't bring up the topic again while they were in England. Two days later they were back in the church at Hengemont and in a discussion with George and Reverend Moore about where to install the large brass plaque that Martin had created. They decided on the wall above the tomb of Elizabeth and John d'Hautain, where there was an expanse of wall space. Lizzie was pleased with the choice.

The crew who had assembled the week before to open the tomb now reassembled to work with Martin and the engraver to get the cenotaph into place. The stonemason removed a stone from the wall before it was mounted, and into that niche Lizzie placed the package she had created containing the manuscript poems, her photographs and computer files, Bette's diary, and the document acknowledging that in the nineteenth century one Edmund Hatton had fathered the child of one Elizabeth Manning.

"This preserves the story," Lizzie said to George, "but puts it to rest."

As she backed away from the tomb, she saw the completed memorial for the first time. Across the top of the plaque was an engraved chain made of twelve interlinked hearts. Below that Lizzie had asked Martin to include a line from one of the medieval poems: "For love and for honour they did die," which was carved in an Old English script. Ten names with dates were then listed, and then, simply, "Never forgotten." The border was a design of waves woven into the crenellated battlements of the castle tower.

Lizzie looked at Martin with awe. "I love it," she said, giving him a hug. "Thank you. It could not be more perfect."

George was clearly moved and stammered his thanks to

both Martin and the engraver, who was polishing the brass with a soft cloth.

Edmund was standing beside Lizzie. "I see ten names there," he said softly, "though I believe I showed you only nine bricks with women's names."

"I put Rossetti's girlfriend there too," she explained.

"And twelve hearts?" George asked from her other side.

"I thought Bette and I ought to be included some way as well."

They all watched as the brass was affixed to the wall. It was a good choice of material, and it would hang comfortably in the old church for many years to come.

"Martin," George asked, uncomfortably, "may I pay you for the work you've done?"

Martin told him that he had designed the plaque as a gift to Lizzie, and that she had insisted on paying the engraver herself for his time and materials.

George reached into the pocket of his coat and brought out a small package, which he handed to Lizzie. "Perhaps you two will accept this then, as a gift from me," he said.

It was the triptych.

Lizzie was deeply moved by the gesture and Martin, who hadn't seen it before, was speechless at the artistry.

"This is too valuable," he tried to say, but George was insistent.

"I want you to have it," he said. "I'm afraid that many of our paintings are going to have to be sold soon, and I want this to stay in the family."

"It is unbelievably beautiful," Martin said finally.

George was by now fully cognizant of Richard's financial losses, though Lizzie had never spoken to him about it. She looked at Edmund and from his expression knew that it was so, but he gave her a shrug that seemed to indicate that things were going to be all right anyway.

They moved to go. "Poor Uncle Edmund is the only one left with just a brick in the floor," George said. "I'll take care of a new marker for him, and you two must come back to see it."

As they walked back to the house to say their good-byes,

Edmund gently pulled Lizzie aside. George and Martin walked on ahead, the former praising Martin's design, the latter talking enthusiastically about the architecture of the church. Lizzie and Edmund walked more slowly. They hadn't really had a chance to talk again since before she left for London.

Edmund asked her about her plans back in Boston and they talked comfortably for several minutes. Lizzie couldn't help thinking about how much she loved him and suddenly blurted it out.

"I love you."

"I love you too," he answered.

They stopped at the wall leading into the Hengemont grounds and Edmund took her hand and put a small velvet box into it. Inside was a delicate pin, a ruby heart pierced by a golden sword, the Hatton family crest.

She couldn't speak for a long time, then stammered when she told Edmund how beautiful it was.

He took it from the box and pinned it to her coat. "I thought you should have a souvenir of your adventure," he said.

She met his eyes and he kissed her.

"I'm very proud to be related to you," he said.

She couldn't resist wrapping her arms around him. "I'm glad to know that you are in my life, Edmund."

He took her arm and they walked up to the terrace. They reached the door to the library where they found George, Martin, and Lily waiting, and parted without a word.

There was only one bit of business left before Lizzie and Martin flew back to Boston, and that was to plan a rendezvous in Alaska. That done, the time for departure was upon them and Lizzie made a tour of the house, saying goodbye to all her relations upstairs and downstairs, living and dead. She and Helen shared a cup of tea and Lizzie promised to send pictures of all her family when she got home.

It was strange to think of returning home. The last month had been so tumultuous that it seemed like she had been at Hengemont forever.

Chapter 27

Lizzie had lobbied her department for more than two years to let her teach a seminar based on museum collections and had looked forward to it with enthusiasm. Now that she was actually teaching the course, however, she found it hard to concentrate. Her thoughts were often somewhere else, sometimes at Hengemont, staring out through the tall library windows across the terrace to the sea, sometimes on the coast of Alaska as described in Francis Hatton's journal.

Soon after her return to campus she had lunch with Jackie and Kate at Rose Geminiani's restaurant, but Lizzie found herself unable to articulate what had happened to her. She sketched in the straightforward details, including the fact that she was going to have to make a quick trip to Alaska to repatriate the corpse of a Tlingit man from the late eighteenth century, but she couldn't bring herself to tell even these close friends about how she had really felt when she learned of John d'Hautain's missing heart.

She tried to make a joke of it, but felt somehow that to belittle the experience was to betray all those generations of women. She also decided not to tell her friends about her relationship to the Hattons. It was still confusing.

"This seems to have been quite a powerful experience," Kate said as Lizzie fumbled through her narrative.

"And I sense a change in you," Jackie added. She turned to Rose, approaching their table to catch up after the holidays. "Bring the wet noodles, Rose, Lizzie may need that beating after all."

Lizzie was reminded about what she had said to them before she left. Sitting at this very table she had pledged that she would not be altered by the experience. It had been, in fact, a very short time to have been altered so much.

"You liked it, didn't you?" Jackie demanded.

"Liked what?"

"The aristocratic life."

"Of course she did," Rose laughed. "Who wouldn't?" She pulled out a chair and sat down to join them.

"But that doesn't mean she'd change that life for this one," Kate said. "It was just a luxurious interlude.."

"It was more than that," Lizzie admitted. She didn't elaborate.

"Oh no," Jackie gasped in mock seriousness, "I don't believe it. You let those people influence you."

"'Those people' were, in fact, terrific," she said. "You'd like them."

"Never!"

"Why not?"

"Because of what they represent."

"They're perfectly nice."

"How can you say that?"

"Because it's true."

Kate broke into the conversation. "I can't believe that you, Jackie, a champion for the acceptance of all people, without regard to race, creed, color, or sexual orientation, want to condemn these people simply for the accident of their birth."

Rose, ever the good hostess, filled all their glasses. "Yeah, weren't you the one who got in trouble over at St. Pat's last year for supporting same-sex marriages?"

"This is different," Jackie explained. "We're not talking about the victims of society now; these are the victimizers."

"Is this an Irish thing?" Kate asked with pretended innocence.

"Of course not!" Jackie huffed. "It's a *British* thing." More than once in the past Jackie had taunted Kate about her last name, "Wentworth," which to Jackie smacked of the English aristocracy. Everyone at the table had heard Jackie's lecture on the British Empire so many times that Lizzie merely sighed, Kate rolled her eyes, and Rose had long since simply ceased listening whenever Jackie was on the subject.

Lizzie felt it was time to wrestle control of the conversation from Jackie. "Ordinarily, Jackie," she started, "you know that I am in total agreement with you on this topic."

"I know," Jackie said, "that's why I need reassurance that you haven't gone over to the dark side."

"I swear to God," Lizzie responded, "the Hattons are actually nice people. I liked them."

"Do they have servants?"

Lizzie nodded and Jackie gave a loud sigh as if to say, "Well there you have it."

"I think they should sell their house to some Internet millionaire and move into a hovel," Kate said sarcastically. "Then someone who really deserved it would be living in it."

"Oh Kate," Jackie said, shaking her head. "There is something serious here."

Lizzie patted Jackie's arm affectionately. "You're right," she said. "There is something serious here." She looked around the table at her three friends. She regretted that she couldn't tell them everything that had happened. She wasn't even going to tell them about the impending collapse of the Hatton fortune.

"The truth is that I found life at Hengemont very comfortable," she said. "Too comfortable, I guess. I have always felt, like Jackie, that there was something just wrong about the way society was divided into people who were born with wealth and position, and those who had to earn it."

"And those who never have it under any circumstances," Jackie interrupted.

Lizzie smiled at her friend's passion.

"George Hatton," Lizzie continued, "*Sir* George Hatton, was born into a way of life that he simply never questioned. And it wasn't always a life of ease. I can say with confidence that the Hatton family always felt a weight of responsibility that went along with their privileges."

She described the tremendous losses the Hattons had experienced in every English war. Jackie was about to make a comment, but Lizzie held up her hand.

"I know what you're going to say, Jackie," she said, "it's *noblesse oblige*. I fully acknowledge that. And it was a very comfortable way of life, and it exploited the labor of less fortunate people." She paused for a moment and looked at Jackie. "Did I forget anything?"

"That it was originally based on an act of aggression?" Jackie offered with a smile.

"Okay," Lizzie said, "a thousand years ago there was a violent act that brought the Hattons into prominence."

"In all seriousness, Jackie," Kate interjected, "how do you suggest that a family like Lizzie's Hattons make their amends to society?"

Jackie swirled her wine in her glass and took a sip. "Well, that's a problem," she said, "for which I don't have an easy solution. But I guess it would start with giving away large sums of money."

"I think they do that," Lizzie said. "Certainly George's son Edmund lives modestly."

"You never mentioned a son," Rose said. She had been sitting silently, drinking coffee, simultaneously watching her restaurant and listening with half an ear to the conversation. "Now we get to the good stuff. What's the son like?"

Lizzie had not wanted to mention Edmund, but she knew that to avoid describing him now would cause even more curiosity among her friends.

"He's a doctor," she started, "and he has volunteered his services in a number of different countries that Jackie would approve of."

"Is he handsome?" Rose asked.

"Very."

"What does he look like?"

"Tall, well-built, blond hair with a touch of gray, one of those nice trim beards."

"Ooh, I'm shivering," Rose said dramatically. "Handsome, rich, titled, in line to inherit a grand estate. . . ."

Lizzie interrupted her, "Actually, he won't inherit Hengemont. He has an older brother."

"Okay," Rose said, shifting the focus of her fantasy. "What's *he* like?"

Lizzie thought for a moment about Richard. "He is exactly Jackie's model of an aristocrat. Snobbish, grasping, stupid, and an exploiter of the little people."

"Mama mia," Rose said dramatically. "Let's get back to the other brother."

"Yes," Kate said. "This younger son, is he married?"

"Get in line," Rose said, pushing Kate lightly on the shoulder. "You already have a man." Rose turned back to Lizzie. "So, is he married?"

"Divorced, with a nine-year-old daughter."

Rose had been widowed at the age of twenty-nine after only four years of marriage; her two children were now in their teens. She often joked about men with her friends from St. Pat's, but they all knew that her energy was devoted to keeping her restaurant afloat and raising her children. Of the four women, only Lizzie was married. Kate had a serious relationship with a man with whom she had lived for several years, and Jackie was divorced.

"It's too bad I didn't go to England for you," Rose said. "I could use a man like that, and you've already snapped up the best guy I know."

"That's for sure," Jackie added. "What does Martin think of all this?"

Lizzie joked that Martin had pledged to support her in the manner to which she had now become accustomed.

Kate tapped her fork on her glass to get the attention of the others. "We still haven't answered our fundamental question though." The faces around the table turned to her. "Is inherited wealth and position a romantic ideal to which we should all aspire?"

"I vote no," Jackie said.

"I vote no, with tremendous regret," Rose said with a wink.

"I vote no, with somewhat less regret," Kate said, nudging Rose.

They all looked at Lizzie.

"I vote no, of course," Lizzie said with authority. "I have to admit that a life of ease is attractive, but I did not as Jackie feared 'go over to the dark side.' Like you said weeks ago, I would rather earn it than inherit it."

As they left the restaurant to return to campus she thought about Hengemont's beautiful library, and of Helen Jeffries bringing her coffee and pastries as she sat at the table looking across the garden to the Bristol Channel. She loved Hengemont, but she felt in her heart that everything Jackie had said was right.

Despite its fascinating history, she could not regret the fact that when Richard's turn came, Hengemont might be lost to the Hattons.

Chapter 28

When the phone rang the next evening, Lizzie and Martin were lying in bed watching a videotape of *The Black Shield of Falworth*. After what she had recently been through in England, this goofy view of medieval Britain, with its '50s hairdos and bullet bras, was remarkably satisfying, and Martin loved to mimic Tony Curtis's New York accent. "Yondah is da castle of my faddah!" he repeated gleefully.

Lizzie was completely unprepared for the voice at the other end of the line.

"Bad, bad things are going to happen because of you."

She motioned to Martin to turn off the tape.

"Who is this?" she demanded. She knew it was Richard, though his voice was slurred with drink or drugs, but she would not give him the satisfaction of acknowledging him.

A string of violent expletives followed. Lizzie hung up the phone.

It rang again immediately and this time Martin answered.

Lizzie had told her husband about the belladonna only that morning and Martin had been furious that she'd withheld the information about Richard's attack for almost two weeks. The two fought about it all day long, alternating bouts of silence, tears, remonstrance, and invectives until it wore them out. This evening they had begun the process of reconciliation through sex, wine, good food, and an old movie.

Martin was now very ready to transfer his anger from his wife to her assailant. When Richard called back, Martin exploded in a torrent of verbal abuse that far surpassed what Lizzie had heard in the first brief phone call. When he finished, Martin held the receiver away from his ear and she could hear Richard wailing on the other end of the line. It was a horrible sound, like a wild animal caught in a trap.

"What do you want?" Martin asked finally. There was resignation in his tone, but not patience or understanding.

For several minutes the two men talked. Lizzie could hear only Martin's side of the conversation.

"I didn't call the police," he said at one point, adding that he thought Richard deserved jail time and only Lizzie's affection for George had prevented him from calling them. "I don't know," he said repeatedly, answering either the same question over and over, or different questions with the same answer, and then, "No, you can't speak to her."

When he finally hung up the phone, he pulled Lizzie into his arms and the two of them held each other tightly for several minutes. She put her face against his chest and let the tears flow.

"Why did he call?" she whispered. "Is he threatening me?"

Martin shook his head. "I think he's more likely to hurt himself at this point. He sounded desperate."

Lizzie thought about this for awhile. "Did he say the police are after him for poisoning me?"

Martin said that they were.

"Did you call them?" she asked.

"No." His tone was serious. "You made it very clear that you didn't want that, but he'll be arrested anyway. They're giving him a chance to turn himself in tomorrow."

Lizzie never loosened her grip on her husband all that night. The next day was Sunday and she spent most of it sitting in her chair in Martin's studio as he worked on sketches for the Newcastle mural. She didn't feel comfortable that day being more than a few feet away from him. It wasn't that she felt she was in danger, but she was extremely disquieted.

The phone rang again in the late afternoon. Martin answered.

"It's Edmund," he said, handing the phone to Lizzie.

She took it tentatively. "Hello Edmund," she said softly. She waited for the news.

"Richard is dead," he said simply. "I thought you needed to know."

Lizzie reeled a bit from the information. Martin came to stand behind her and she leaned hard against him. She didn't know what to say and for a long time she said nothing.

"How did it happen?" she asked finally, her voice a raspy whisper.

"He killed himself," Edmund answered. "He jumped from the window of his office in London." Lizzie could hear the pain in his voice.

"Oh Edmund," she said, "I'm so sorry." She wasn't sure if she was sorry that Richard was dead, but she was sorry that Edmund was hurting. And George, she thought. A tear slid down her cheek and she reached up to wipe it away. Martin put his arm around her waist. She turned slightly to look up at him as she spoke next.

"Martin didn't call the police," she said. She tried to explain that she hadn't wanted to hurt any of the Hattons. The words came tumbling out somewhat incoherently until Edmund interrupted.

"I know," he said. "I called them."

His explanation was almost as incoherent as Lizzie's. He felt it was his obligation, he said, legally as well as ethically, to report Richard's actions against her. It was a crime, he said. She had been assaulted, and he couldn't, in good conscience, let the fact that the assailant was his brother make him keep the information to himself.

"It's a terrible thing," she stammered, hardly knowing what more to say, but imagining the guilt that Edmund must be feeling. "It's not your fault," she said softly. She wasn't sure he heard her.

"I have to go," he said. "My father needs me."

They mumbled goodbyes and Lizzie collapsed against her husband.

She slept fitfully that night, picturing Richard as he hung up the phone and moved to the window. How long had he stared at the sidewalk below? She remembered with awful vividness how she had felt that night on the roof of Hengemont when she had thought that death would be swift and welcome if she just let herself slip over the edge. It would have been so easy. She shuddered and reached for Martin, who slept soundly beside her. "Damn Richard," she thought. "Damn him."

The next morning Lizzie cancelled her office hours, telling her departmental secretary that there had been a death in her family but not explaining further. She stuck close to Martin for another day. At one point she asked him if he thought they should go to England for the funeral, and was relieved when he assured her it was neither necessary nor expected. She felt like she couldn't make the decision on her own.

It was a painful night and day and another night that followed for Lizzie as she acknowledged, for the first time since it happened, how close she had come to dying. When she thought how incomprehensible it would have been to Martin, to her family, her friends, that she would take her own life, she sobbed uncontrollably. At the time she had been able to distance herself from the seriousness of the event by declaring it to have been a dream, even though she had feared some more sinister, unexplained influence. When she learned from Edmund that Richard had drugged her she was angry, but there was also a certain comfort in being able to rationalize her otherwise unexplainable behavior as drug-induced.

Lizzie had imagined those dead girls before, but never as vividly as she now pictured Richard—or herself if Edmund had not stopped her. Several times in a half-sleep she felt herself falling, saw hard pavement rushing at her like a fast train. She imagined the feeling of smashing into the concrete, and she pictured Richard's handsome face mangled by the impact.

Martin watched helplessly, offering supportive smiles and soft touches through two nights and two days, but not understanding what she was feeling.

"Is all this for Richard?" he asked at one point. As she tried to explain, he realized that the feelings she had repressed in the weeks since her foray to the Hengemont roof were now forcing themselves to the surface. He also knew, in his pragmatic way, that if he waited another day or two the vividness of the pain would pass. Lizzie knew this too and, in time, it did.

• • • • •

To cancel a class would have required explanations that Lizzie did not wish to give, even to her close friends, so on Tuesday she headed to campus and went through the motions of teaching. When she returned home Martin told her that George had called, that he wanted to be sure that Lizzie and Martin were still planning to meet him in Alaska for the repatriation of Eltatsy's remains.

Lizzie hadn't thought of the trip, only two weeks away, since she'd heard the news of Richard's death. Martin insisted that the trip was a good idea and he was glad George felt up to making it.

"How's your new class going?" he asked, changing the subject.

"Oh, I don't know," she answered, sinking into her chair, "my heart's just not in it."

Martin worked the stiff bristles of a paintbrush through his fingers as he dipped it into a pail of water. "Please don't tell me that we're going to have to go off on a trek to find it."

"Good one," Lizzie laughed. "I have to be more careful slinging around those old clichés."

"You were looking forward to this new class," Martin said, coming over to sit on the stool beside her chair and drying his hands on a towel. "I thought you'd be excited to try this new subject matter."

Lizzie shrugged. "When I designed this class, none of this. . . ." She searched for a word, her hand waving in front of her face, "None of this *stuff* had happened. Life is different now."

Martin put his foot onto the arm of Lizzie's chair and leaned back on the stool, his arms folded. "It's hard to come back to regular life after a trip to the edge, isn't it?"

She nodded.

"What can we do to put spice back into your life, my sweet?" he asked gently.

She wished she had an answer. "I'm hoping this trip to Alaska will be a start," she said.

"I hope so too," Martin answered. "But then you are going to need a new project."

She knew it was true, but the bar was now raised so high

that she doubted any research venture could ever compare to
the events of the past month.

• • • • •

Lizzie thought about Martin's suggestion when she went to
St. Pat's early the next morning, and she headed directly to
the library reading room. There were a few students sitting
at widely scattered seats, heads bent and hard at work when
she pulled the door open. She waved at Jackie. There would
be no singing today and it was just as well; there was no song
appropriate to Lizzie's mood on this cold February day. She
plunked her book bag down on one of the long tables and went
over to greet Jackie at her desk.

"Could I see the last few days of the *London Times?*" she
asked.

They were already at hand, a neat pile that Jackie had been
reading as she sat at her elevated perch. Lizzie saw a headline
on the top copy: "Financier Takes Suicide Plunge."

"I assume this is one of your Hattons," Jackie whispered as
she handed the papers to her friend.

Lizzie nodded.

"Sorry," Jackie said. "I know you liked them."

Lizzie smiled ruefully at that. How could she explain that
she had loathed this particular Hatton, just as Jackie thought
she should, and for all the right reasons. Now that he was
dead it didn't seem appropriate to articulate her hatred.

She took the papers back to her desk and began to read
them in chronological order. There was the story of Richard's bad investments, but nothing about herself, or about
Richard's plot against her. He had told Martin that he was
expected to turn himself in; perhaps that meant that they
had not yet filed formal assault charges against him. She was
relieved. She didn't want any of this to be about her.

On an inside page was a picture of Richard's corpse, lying
on a London sidewalk, covered by a sheet and contemplated
by a number of policemen and pedestrians. There was a mention of two divorces and three grown children; Lizzie had
never known about any of them. Despite the horrendous, passionate hatred they had inspired in one another, she had not

known as much about Richard alive as she was now learning about him dead.

The next paper had an editorial about Richard's death that mentioned the suicides that had plagued the Hattons for several generations. The writer knew only enough of the story to make a comparison between the estate at Hengemont and the financial estate that Richard had built, and then to build metaphorical comparisons between the castle tower at Hengemont and the bank tower in London, both of which exploited the labor or capitol of regular people for the benefit of the wealthy.

Lizzie looked up at Jackie as she read this. Had she derived pleasure from reading it, she wondered? Jackie's gaze was firmly directed at the screen of her computer. It must have been devastating for George, Lizzie thought, though surely these hard truths had to be confronted at some point in his life.

What an ending to the story, Lizzie thought as she folded the paper. She sat very still for several minutes, then pushed her chair back from the table and stood up. She went to stand at the window, just as she had done so many times in the Hengemont library. Her breath on the cold glass created a fog of condensation that obscured the world beyond even more than the wavy indistinct glass did. The fact that she couldn't see anything clearly was now an advantage. She contemplated Richard and his awful death. At least he hadn't gone back to kill himself at Hengemont, she thought with some relief.

She touched the cold windowpane with two fingers. Helen would have been left to clean up the mess, she thought. Just like her great-grandmother on that grim and fateful day—the day she had begun her love affair with Edmund Hatton over the corpse of his sister.

Lizzie thought of her great grandmother. They shared the same name and her father had often told her that he thought there was a resemblance between them, of temperament as well as looks. All the horror that Lizzie had felt in the last few days at the manner of Richard's death, that other Lizzie had confronted in flesh and bones and blood on the terrace at Hengemont.

She hadn't fully appreciated this aspect of history before now. The further back the story went, the more possible it was to give it a romantic glow that blurred the edges and made the awful more palatable. Though she had been through all the documents, read the letters and poems, examined the paintings, somehow that was different than the cold, stark, black-and-white typeface with an accompanying photo on page A2.

Lizzie knew that this would change soon enough. More time would pass and the next person to research the Hatton family would pull the newspaper, by then yellowed by time or distanced by the technology of microfilm reader or laser scanner, and Richard would become just another interesting story to tell. His blood and brains on the pavement would add color to the telling. But there would be many things that the next researcher would never know, could never know, because Lizzie was going to make certain that no tangible, document-able evidence survived to tell of her hatred for Richard, or her desire for Edmund, or her conflicting feelings about envying the aristocracy and wanting to be a part of it while simultaneously rejecting all of the attractions that underpinned the wanting. She began to see the difference between *doing* history and *being* history.

The papers behind the cenotaph in the Hatton church nagged at her. She would never have destroyed such valuable historical documents, but she knew that she might as well have put a match to them, for all the use they would be to anyone in the future. She had justified her actions by thinking that this was the Hatton family's business, a small story; it was not like a government rewriting history after a war.

Lizzie felt the chill of the window and took a step back, lost in her thoughts. She knew that individuals tried to manipulate their image all the time—both to present themselves well in their own time and to position themselves for posterity. Politicians, celebrities, businessmen, artists, governments did it all the time. No thinking person could resist the chance to make himself or herself appear more intelligent, benevolent, heroic or romantic, and less dull, dreadful, evil or stupid. The complexities of human beings were the hardest part of any story either to discover or describe, but that was also what made her job interesting.

She smiled to herself. Part of what she must keep in mind in the future was that she would need to outwit people like herself. It was a false rationalization for a historian to say that personal stories were different than public stories. The former made up the latter.

This had been an odd assignment. *Her* story had gotten entangled in history in a way that she had not expected. It could not ever happen again so potently, she thought, as she turned and went back to her seat. She folded her hands in front of her and thought about her job and how in this instance it had turned out to be her life, and how satisfying and disturbing that felt. Everything she had learned about the Hattons had told her something about herself.

How much had the members of this strange family changed over time? There was still madness and confusion, fear and exultation, masters and servants. In some ways it seemed that things had not changed all that much in seven hundred years. But she knew they had. At this moment in time *she* was the ultimate evidence, the document of what the Hattons were and had been and could become. When she was gone, many intangibles would go with her.

She promised herself to try to remember that, to always look beyond the documents of the story to those things that lay unspoken behind them. She did not know yet what the next story would be, but she was certain that it was already headed her way. All she had to do was keep her eyes open for the right manuscript, old book, strange tool, evocative painting, intriguing query. The past was all around her, waiting to be rediscovered.

The newspapers on the table in front of her lay half in and half out of the bright circle of lamplight. Lizzie let her eyes move from the harsh glare of the illuminated paper, past the windows with their beams and patches of cool green light, and up to the dim diffuse gloom of the high ceiling above her. She felt calm, quiet, receptive. She waited.

Epilogue

Through a Tlingit artist, Martin managed to identify a descendent of Eltatsy in Hoonah, Alaska, and Lizzie called him at home one evening to tell him the story of Francis Hatton. Robert Eltatsy was completely surprised by her call. He didn't know the specifics of the incident in which his ancestor's grave had been robbed, but he was happy to learn that the remains were going to be returned. He began immediately to make plans for the arrival of Lizzie and Martin from Boston, and George, Edmund, and Lily from England. They rendezvoused in Juneau in the middle of February and traveled together to Hoonah to meet the Eltatsy family.

Like the Eltatsy described by Francis Hatton, Robert Eltatsy was tall, intelligent, and well-spoken. He had one of those face-transforming smiles that made you like him instantly. He greeted the invading party of the extended Hatton family shyly, but warmly, as they got off the ferry at Hoonah. He introduced his wife, brother, and his daughter Sarah, who was about the same age as Lily.

Robert and his brother helped Martin and Edmund with the crates that contained the burial box and the blanket. Lizzie had sent the dimensions to the British Museum and through Tom Clark had commissioned two traveling cases from their conservation department. Now she watched as the boxes were loaded onto the back of Robert Eltatsy's pickup truck.

George had rented a car in Juneau and taken it on the ferry, and the plan was for Lizzie and Edmund to ride with him and follow Robert to the tribal longhouse. Martin and the two girls climbed into the cab of Robert's pickup, and another truck brought up the rear, filled with goods ordered by George and shipped on the same ferry on which the visitors had arrived.

Lizzie had thought it would be appropriate for George to host a ceremonial potlatch to celebrate the return of the remains of Eltatsy to their burial place, and Robert had been very helpful in handling all the local details. It was customary at such an event to distribute gifts to everyone who attended, and George, with advice from Lizzie, had gone all out. In the truck were two hundred Hudson's Bay Company blankets, two inflatable zodiacs with outboard motors, books for the local library, and five computers for the Hoonah tribal school. There were also crates of oranges, boxes of chocolate, and a number of tins of English tea.

On the ride from the ferry to the longhouse, Lizzie drove George's rental car, being the one most comfortable with the steering wheel on the left. George sat beside her in the front and Edmund sat behind his father. Lizzie caught his eye in the rear view mirror and smiled. The two had had a chance to spend several hours together during the ferry ride, braving the elements on the open deck at the stern of the ship while their companions remained comfortably inside.

Lizzie was glad to have shared that time with Edmund, standing close enough together to keep each other warm as they leaned against the railing of the ship. She had had a chance to see for herself that he was recovering from the blow of his brother's suicide.

When everything had been delivered to the longhouse, Robert and Sarah showed their guests to the only hotel in the village. They had a light supper together and then Robert took his daughter home to change for the potlatch. It was a short walk to the longhouse, and the visitors would meet them there in two hours. George asked Lizzie if she would join him for a cup of coffee in the hotel restaurant and she agreed happily.

"This is a strange culmination to the project for which I hired you, isn't it?" he said, after they had ordered their coffee.

Lizzie laughed. "It is indeed," she said. "You know, George, when I got your letter I was hoping that it would lead to some

sort of wonderful adventurous experience, but you have provided thrills beyond all expectations."

They talked about the process of historical research and
she felt obliged to explain that it didn't always go so quickly.

"Under ordinary circumstances," she said, "I would have
expected it to take several months to lay the groundwork,
search through collections, identify relevant documents, etc."
She took a sip of her coffee. "If you had hired me just to find
the heart," she continued, "I probably would have asked for a
round-trip ticket to the Holy Land as the first step!"

He smiled. "Thank you," he said softly. "Thank you for
everything that you have done." They said nothing of Richard.

The waitress approached to refill their coffee cups and
George and Lizzie were silent for a few minutes. When they
were alone again, he told her that he felt very right about what
they were doing here in Hoonah. She could resist no longer;
she leaned over and kissed him firmly on the cheek.

"There is one other thing," George said, leaning behind
his chair and pulling out a large, flat package. "This evening
many gifts will be exchanged and I want to give the first one
to you now."

They had to stand up to balance the heavy package on a
chair between them and Lizzie stripped off the paper.

It was the Rossetti painting.

She felt the tears well up in her eyes. "Thank you George,"
she said, kissing him again. "It is so valuable though. Are you
sure?"

"Worried about my financial situation?"

Lizzie acknowledged that she was.

"I will get through this," George said. There was no remorse in his voice. "They can't kick me out of my house until
I'm dead, I can still be buried in the family church. And," he
added, winking at her, "before I go I'm committed to giving
away as much stuff as I can to the people I love."

She smiled at him. "Thank you."

"Not a problem," he said. "Are there any other paintings
you'd like to have? Maybe the Gainsborough?"

The both laughed.

"I have a present for you too," she said, pulling a big manila envelope from her bag. "It's my report on Francis Hatton and his collection. I have already anticipated tomorrow's events in it, and it wraps up the whole story very nicely."

He thanked her. "Will you send a copy to Thomas Clark, or should I?"

She answered that, with his permission, she would.

"I've already arranged for him to come to Hengemont to pick up the Pacific collection," George continued. "I'm giving it all to the museum."

Lizzie knew it was the right decision, but hated the thought of it leaving Frank's cabinet in the library. She found herself unable to speak, but nodded to George that she approved of the decision.

"And part of our arrangement," he said, patting the envelope she had given him, "is that this report of yours will be the first thing they publish about it."

Lizzie nodded again. It would be a great career enhancer for her, just as she had always known, only now it didn't seem quite so important.

George walked back with her to the door of her room before going off to his own room to change for the evening's festivities. Lizzie set the painting down against the hallway wall and was struggling with the key when Martin opened the door from inside. He returned to where he had been lying propped up on the bed as Lizzie picked up the painting and brought it into the room. She set it up on the desk and waited for him to notice.

"Is that a Rossetti?" he asked, standing up and crossing the room.

His wife watched as he turned on the light and examined the painting.

"It's a gift from George," she answered. "And look at the subject."

"Elizabeth Wakes from the Dream," he said, reading from the plaque on the frame. He made a whistling sound. "I'll be damned. If this story doesn't just get stranger and stranger."

"She's one of the Hatton girls."

"Obviously."

"Apparently she went and lived with Rossetti in that weird phase after his wife died."

"Before or after he exhumed her corpse?"

"I think before *and* after," Lizzie said, sitting on the bed. "There's some paperwork on the back if you're interested in the details."

"Is she one of the ones who committed suicide?"

"No," she answered, sitting up. "In a strange way I think that she got into Rossetti's bizarre cult of death and left her own behind, but at least she lived to a ripe old age."

Martin came to sit beside her on the bed. "So this thing has really gone on century after century."

She nodded.

"And do you actually think you have broken this spell or whatever it is?"

Lizzie shrugged. "Who knows?" She reached out to touch his hand. "It's not like I'm feeling very powerful."

"You are though," he said, raising her hand to his lips. "Look at what you have made possible here today."

• • • • •

Lizzie had never been to a potlatch but she had read numerous descriptions and she was filled with excitement as they approached the longhouse. There was a good crowd gathering, many dressed in ceremonial clothing. Sarah came out to greet Lily and show her the dancing robe that her mother had made for the occasion. It was a dark blue blanket with a wide border of red, and in the center was the Eltatsy bear crest appliquéd in red and ornamented with mother-of-pearl buttons.

There was plenty of food, followed by a presentation of traditional Tlingit dances and songs, and then a number of people rose to give speeches. The Eltatsys shared the honor of hosting the festivities with George Hatton, but they were also the honored guests. In addition to Robert, his wife Deborah, and Sarah, there were about two dozen members of the family present. Most, like Robert and Deborah, lived in Juneau or Anchorage during the school year, but came back to Hoonah to fish during the summer; many of them had made a special trip this weekend to be here for the potlatch. High-ranking

guests had come from other Tlingit villages as well, including Haines and Chilkat, and there were also visitors from the
Haida village of Masset.

George was clearly nervous when the time came for him to
distribute the gifts. He started with two hundred Canadian
centennial silver dollar coins, many of which had been made
into pendants or brooches. The image on the coin was a totem pole and Lizzie had suggested that they would make good
souvenirs of the occasion. The other gifts followed quickly
and the guests seemed pleased with the selection George and
Lizzie had made.

When there was nothing left on the stage but the two
crates, Martin and Edmund opened them and displayed the
bear-crest blanket and the burial box, as Robert Eltatsy came
forward to receive them from George. It was a very emotional
moment for everyone present.

George then asked Edmund to give him another package,
which he opened carefully. Lizzie was astonished to see that it
contained the bear helmet. George asked Robert if it would be
appropriate for him to read the letter written by Francis Hatton to his sister, in which the circumstances of its acquisition
were described. Robert nodded and George proceeded, in a
soft but clear voice, to read the letter in which Frank Hatton's
fondness for the young chief Eltatsy was so evident. When he
finished, he folded up the letter and handed it, along with the
helmet, to Robert Eltatsy.

"This was first exchanged between our ancestors seven
generations ago," he said, "and we have treasured it since,
but now I would like to return it to you."

Lizzie wasn't sure that Robert, or anyone, would be able
to speak for several minutes, but Sarah was unable to repress
her enthusiasm for the helmet when she saw it.

"That is so cool!" she gasped in a stage whisper to Lily.

The silence broken, Robert and George both laughed.
Robert invited his daughter to hold the helmet while he took
off his ceremonial headpiece. It was made of cedar bark and
feathers, and was fronted by a small stylized bear carving, almost a portrait, with the bear's empty paws held up on either
side of its head. He handed it to George.

"It was an exchange of gifts then," he said, "and it should be again." He then took the bear helmet from his daughter and placed it on his head as the crowd cheered.

"Would it be appropriate for me to wear this here?" George asked Robert, holding up the headdress.

Lizzie was astonished that he would even consider it, but Robert Eltatsy was obviously pleased, and helped him to settle it firmly on his head. Another cheer went up from the crowd.

The final gift of the evening was given by Sarah to Lily. It was a button blanket made by her mother. Appliquéd onto it were two red hearts over rippling water made from mother-of-pearl buttons.

• • • • •

Though Lizzie had worked out the rendezvous in Hoonah based largely on the schedules of the participants, it had not escaped her attention that they would be returning Eltatsy to his gravesite on February 14, the anniversary of the death of Captain Cook. Francis Hatton had been at his lowest moment of despair at that point in the voyage, wishing more than anything that he could return Eltatsy to his resting place. It seemed appropriate that they would finally keep his promise on that day. "Numquam Dediscum," Lizzie thought as she boarded the boat that would take them across Icy Strait.

On one of the Porpoise Islands, a spot chosen by Robert Eltatsy as most appropriate, he and his brother, with help from Martin and Edmund, constructed a grave house from wood they brought with them. Robert invited George to place the burial box inside and the structure was closed with the remaining planks. No one spoke during the whole proceeding. Robert then mounted the blanket on one of the side walls and gestured to Martin to join him at the opposite side. Martin stepped forward and unrolled a mural, painted on sailcloth, which he and Robert nailed securely to the wall of the hut.

Tears rolled down Lizzie's cheeks as she looked at it; Martin had painted it in secret. It depicted the story of the Eltatsys and the Hattons, with the people standing around her incorporated into it. On the left was the rocky coast of Alaska.

From the forest, the Eltatsy bear ancestor emerged to meet his human wife. About them were bears and humans and humans in bear masks and bears in human masks. From the right side came Elizabeth and Jean d'Hautain in medieval garb, looking just as they did in their carved grave image.

Their descendent, Francis Hatton, was shown arriving aboard the ship *Resolution,* met by a number of canoes, in one of which stood Eltatsy, wearing his bear crest blanket and helmet. Martin had used Robert Eltatsy as the model for his ancestor; Frank Hatton looked like his portrait at Hengemont. In the middle of the mural was not only the meeting of the vessels, but beyond them the two tombs—one bearing the familiar Hatton crest, the other the Tlingit grave house, hung with its Chilkat blanket. From them emerged the descendents.

It was signed with Martin's characteristic signature, the date, and the inscription "Never Forgotten."

Lizzie looked around to see that she wasn't the only one in tears. George Hatton wept silently for a few minutes and then grabbed Martin by the arm and held on. Martin smiled at him and gently supported him with his other hand.

"I couldn't have done it without Robert, here," he said. "He provided the design for the blanket and the house, and sent me photographs of his family and this place."

George turned to Robert. "Thank you," he said hoarsely.

Robert Eltatsy reached out his hand to George and they shook hands heartily. "Thank you," Robert said, "for doing the right thing."

"I'm only sorry it took so long to make things right," George said apologetically.

Edmund stood next to Lizzie and she leaned into him with an affectionate poke of her elbow. On her coat she was wearing the pin he had given her, and as he saw it he smiled.

They turned from the burial site at the top of the island and began to make their way cautiously down to the boat. "Icy Bay" had not been misnamed and there was no clear path down the rocks. Martin took Lizzie's hand and Edmund moved back to assist his father and daughter. The Eltatsys remained for several more minutes at the top. Standing at the stern of the boat, Lizzie crossed her arms and concentrated on the nearby shore where the old village of Hoonah had once stood. Bald eagles seemed to be everywhere. Martin touched her back in a gesture that was at once intimate and supportive. When she looked at him his gaze was fixed where hers had been moments before. He turned to her as if sensing her eyes on him and smiled gently. He had, she realized, never been anything but a gentleman.

She thought of Elizabeth Pintard d'Hautain and her great love for her husband John. Had it compared with her own love for Martin? She had asked this question so many times in the last several weeks, and now she felt certain that she knew the answer. The first Elizabeth had been only sixteen when she became a widow. She had known her husband for only a few weeks. They each loved the youthful beauty of their mate and invested in them all the romance of their illusions. Their love had never matured to the point at which the bond had become more than that. John d'Hautain had never really known Elizabeth's intelligence, patience, or honor. She had barely had time to know them herself when she died, and yet her zeal and commitment had carried her quest through twenty-eight generations of descendents over seven hundred years. It was almost as if, not having enjoyed the fruits of a mature love with her husband, she depended on the solidity of their union in death. Lizzie had to admit it was intensely romantic, but there was no reality in it, and nothing to either emulate or envy.

She looked at the Eltatsy family as they came down the rock. Had their ancestors had the same mission? Lizzie thought their quest had as much to do with honor as with love. In order to live among his ancestors, Eltatsy had to rest among them in a manner carefully prescribed by generations of tradition. Francis Hatton had understood that, and everyone here today did as well.

Lizzie thought again about where her own mortal remains should lie. She and Martin had talked about it again after they got home and each had agreed to leave it to the other to decide, according to whatever practice would make the survivor most comfortable. A verse from an Irish emigration song came into her head:

"What matter to me where my bones may be buried,
If in peace and contentment I can live my life."

It had taken her a long time to get to this point, but she suddenly felt an overwhelming sense of peace and contentment. Let others worry about burial practices and ghoulish matters. She was going home where she could be with Martin, to talk and laugh and love and argue. For Lizzie, the romantic did not have to be imagined; it could be felt and appreciated as part of her reality.

Martin slipped his hand into hers and guided her onto a seat on the boat, then sat beside her. She put her arm around his waist, and he put his about her shoulders. Their middle-aged bodies settled comfortably against one another.

"I almost forgot," he whispered, putting his lips against her hair as the boat pulled away from the rocks, "it's Valentine's Day." He reached with his free hand into his coat pocket and pulled out a small envelope. "Here," he said, "this is for you."

She opened the envelope and took out a small paper heart; it was the kind that elementary school kids send to each other.

"My heart belongs to you," it said. On the back Martin had added in his beautiful script: "Literally, to do with as you like."

Lizzie buried her face in his coat so that her laughter would not disturb the reverie of the others on the boat. Eventually she was sobbing loudly, as much with relief as with regret, and when she looked up, she saw that several people on the boat had joined her, either in tears or laughter.

As the island retreated in the distance, they saw a bear amble out of the forest and down to the beach. It paused, stood up to its full height, and looked at the occupants of the boat before dropping back to all fours and returning to the forest with a lumbering gait. Lizzie looked around at Edmund and George and Lily, and each smiled back at her.

She snuggled in against her husband. "I am really looking forward to getting back to my class," she said.

"Home then?" he asked.

She nodded.

"Because you know," Martin continued, "that home is where. . . ."

She put her hand to his lips. "Don't say it," she laughed.

He kissed her fingertips and then moved her hand from his mouth down to lay it upon his chest. "But I believe it," he said.

"I know," Lizzie answered, feeling his heart beating beneath her palm. "Me too."

Acknowledgements

I am grateful to have among my circle of family and friends so many talented writers and perceptive readers who have supported me through the research, writing, and publication of this book. My thanks to Deborah Harrison, Bart St. Armand, Kimberley Davis, Christina Ward, Caroline Preston, Kathleen Quinlivan, Peg Brandon, James McElwain, Gladys Paxton, Juliet Morefield, Pearl Frank, Richard St. Clair, Joost Schokkenbroek, all my sisters, my husband Stuart Frank, and Lisa Graziano.

The Author

Drawing by Wurge

Mary Malloy is the author of four maritime history books, including the award-winning *Devil on the Deep Blue Sea: The Notorious Career of Samuel Hill of Boston*, and *Souvenirs of the Fur Trade: Northwest Coast Indian Art and Artifacts Collected by American Mariners*, published by the Peabody Museum at Harvard. She has a Ph.D. from Brown University and teaches Maritime History at the Sea Education Association in Woods Hole, Mass., and Museum Studies at Harvard University. *The Wandering Heart*, the first of a trilogy, is her first novel.

An Interview with Mary Malloy

· · · · ·

Mary Malloy was interviewed in 2008 by two librarians, Juliet Morefield of the Multnomah County Library in Portland, Oregon, and Kathleen Quinlivan of the University at Buffalo Libraries. Readers' circles might find some interesting points of discussion in their conversation.

Question: This is your first novel, but not your first book. How would you describe the difference between writing nonfiction and fiction?

Answer: There is a real distinction for me between scholarly nonfiction and novel writing in that the former requires that I stick close to my source materials in the conclusions I draw. Many academics who write fiction choose to have it published under a pseudonym, to avoid any confusion in the minds of readers about what information in a book can be documented through background research or personal experience, and what comes from the imagination of the author.

Q: How did you get started on it?

A: I started writing this novel when I was working on my doctoral dissertation at Brown University, in part to allow me to explore the historian's fantasy of having evidence come easily to hand rather than being the result of a methodical and often tedious process. I start the research for every project with some idea about where it is heading, but I am always prepared to let the documents I find change the direction or focus of the work. It can be frustrating when long hours of research do not result in evidence that will support your ideas, so I made it easy for Lizzie to find things by creating the kind of evidence I would love to find myself. All the journal entries, letters, objects, poems and paintings in this book are fictional but I was inspired by historical examples.

Q: It seems that many readers want novels to teach them factual material. Does the novel still reflect historical research?

A: Absolutely. Writing a novel allowed me to stray from the sources, so that I could add new material to existing texts and even invent whole new documents, objects, and works of art, but I still wanted the book to be grounded in the process of historical research, and to introduce readers to how that process works. In order to give Lizzie some veracity as a historian, I gave her my own specialties: maritime history, museums, and Northwest Coast Indian cultural anthropology. But the situations I write about never happened. In the references to Captain James Cook's voyage in the Pacific, for example, I started from Cook's journal but created the characters of Francis Hatton and Eltatsy and all of the scenes in which they appear. I hope that any reader who finds that episode interesting might be inspired to go to the original source, which is terrific reading.

Q: To take another specific example, is the contract between the Templars and Henry III based closely on an actual document?

A: No, I made that one up to serve the plot of the book. There are, however, a surprising number of documents that survive from that period, many of which are now available online through the "Henry III Fine Rolls Project" at http://www.finerollshenry3.org.uk/cocoon/frh3/home.html.

Q: Are there any other places in the book where you would like to make a distinction for readers between fact and fiction?

A: If you go to Salisbury Cathedral you will find the tombs of the William Longespèes (Elder and Younger), which I tried to recreate as I saw them. There is a small tomb adjacent to the effigy of the son that is described as either a boy bishop or a heart burial. The younger Longespèe died at Mansoura in Egypt, and that was what inspired me to send John d'Hautain there too, as his companion. There is absolutely no evidence that Longespèe's corpse was mummified to be returned; that is fiction. I did rather like putting the heart of John d'Hautain in an existing grave and then making the folks in charge of the Cathedral exhume it. You can enjoy a certain power as an author.

Q: Do you think that there will be readers who will challenge your interpretation of history?

A: I do expect that some people will have questions about how I wove past events into the story, and I am prepared to deal with that. The first real critique of the book, and one which I took very seriously, came from one of my professors at Brown University, Barton St. Armand. He wondered "if a family like the Hattons would have been building a new wing on their house in 1650, a year after Charles I had his head chopped off and when Cromwell was in command." I decided I could live with that question since I was wrestling with the overall chronology of the family tree. Bart also commented that "Inigo Jones died in 1652, and I don't really know where he was in 1650, but I doubt he was building in the English countryside." This was another questionable fact that I decided I could keep in the book. Fiction, unlike history, allows us to place characters in places where they never were. If these had been more difficult for me to rationalize I would have changed the timeline in the book to conform to historical events. This is important to me because a glaring historical error can draw the knowledgeable reader out of the book and create doubt about other scenes.

Q: Do you have an example?

A: I love Elizabeth Peters and have read all of her "Amelia

Peabody" novels, but the last one, *Tomb of the Golden Bird*, has a major historical error that really nagged at me. In a very minor reference, Edward II is quoted as the king who precipitated the murder of Thomas Becket by asking if someone could rid him of "this turbulent priest." I happen to be interested in Becket, but I'm certainly not the only reader who knows that it was Henry II with whom Becket had a close and confrontational relationship, and who spoke those famous words. Peters has written novels with themes of English history and that makes this mistake particularly surprising.

Q: What did Professor St. Armand have to say about the poems in the book?

A: He said "a poem written in the fourteenth century would be much closer to Chaucer's Middle English than the version you present, while the 1880s poem would not likely have been in free verse unless the author had been reading Walt Whitman." These were things that I knew. Again, I allowed myself some wiggle room on stylistic decisions.

Q: What books do you acknowledge as having influenced you as you developed the story and the characters?

A: I was a great fan of Jane Austen long before she became a pop-culture icon, and the idea of setting a story in an English manor house clearly came from her novels. One summer when I was in high school I read *Northanger Abbey* and all of the Gothic sources mentioned in it and more. I loved *The Mysteries of Udolpho, The Castle of Otranto,* and *The Monk,* and tried to create in Hengemont a house with a past and with secrets that could be revealed through research. That said, I didn't want there to be a supernatural element in the book. One reviewer describes it as "explained Gothic," and I rather like that idea.

Q: Without some supernatural element, how did the curse pass from generation to generation? You gave clear reasons why Bette and Lizzie were not actually experiencing a curse, but I still want to know about all those other Elizabeths. How did they find out about the heart? How did they ask the same question?

A: I think there is a lot of information that we pick up in ways that can't be specifically pinpointed. In families, this might start when a child overhears conversations of which she is not a part, in whispered exchanges, in discussions that stop when a new person enters the room. Add to that an environment in which paintings of tragic victims are all around, a house where places would be pointed out through generations as having been "the spot" where something important happened, and stories begin to have their own life. I think that you can process a lot of things in this way, not fully conscious of or knowledgeable about details and consequently filling in with imaginative or romantic notions. When heartache or depression enter into the mix I don't think it is beyond the realm of the believable that the Hatton girls would identify with a story of such importance in the family. When I created the Hatton family tree, I tried to make the time between events close enough that there could always be someone in the family who had heard the story within the time span of grandparents or great-grandparents.

Q: What is the role of the dreams?

A: All the information that comes to us in random ways needs to be processed somehow and dreams seem like the way that our subconscious makes that happen. I'm not sure if dreams *actually* do this, but it works as a literary device.

Q: You might have chosen to write a historical novel in which all the action was set in the past. Why didn't you?

A: Mostly because I wanted to describe the historical process, but I also wanted to challenge some of the standard romantic expectations that certain elements of life and character are desirable above all others: wealth, beauty, social position—especially connections to the British aristocracy. It seemed that a modern perspective was required for that. Lizzie's circle of smart and opinionated women friends, especially Jackie, were created to voice some of those ideas. It allowed me to let Lizzie feel the seductive power of Hengemont and the Hattons, but not make moving there the expected happy ending.

Q: When you say you wanted to challenge "standard romantic expectations," do you mean that in social or literary terms?

A: A little of each, I guess. The female characters certainly consider the way that images in the media influence the socialization of girls in America, but I am also interested in the literary conventions and devices that have, for eons, allowed writers to provide a shorthand for character development by describing certain physical traits. For instance, it is not uncommon for heroes to be blonde and blue eyed with fair complexions, while villains are more frequently dark. Lizzie's two potential love interests, Edmund and Martin, represent those two different physical types, but not a good and a bad choice; both are warm-hearted and sexy good guys, which I hope adds complexity to her confusion about being attracted to both of them. They might also be thought of as symbolically representing Old World and New World values, at least in the way those things have been described as literary themes.

Q: Did you base your description of Hengemont on an actual manor house or estate in England?

A: Years ago, when I was driving along the south coast of the Bristol Channel, I saw a big house off in the distance. I was on a fairly high road and the view swept down the hill toward the water. This house was placed in a fabulous position between me and the Channel and when I was considering where to build Hengemont I thought of it, though I never saw the house up close. That region also has a number of the ancient chalk figures on the hillsides, which I decided to reference.

I used several sources in putting together Hengemont and I tried to incorporate architectural details from a number of different eras, and to use architects and landscapers whose work was influential, though I didn't want to just be a name dropper. As with the paintings and other things that filled the house, I chose artists and artisans who would have been hired by people with money and taste. My most important source on the building itself was a series of books called *English Homes* by H. Avray Tipping, published in the 1920s. There are separate volumes for different periods in history, and each has information on architectural styles and garden designs, with excellent illustrations of details. Using those books I drew a pretty detailed floor plan of Hengemont, and referred to it often as I was writing.

Q: There is a lot in this book about corpses and body parts. Did you begin with the idea of making that central to the story, or did it develop as you wrote the book?

A: I have always had a morbid curiosity about relics and the disposition of corpses in the Medieval period. Since 1990 when the U.S. Congress passed the Native American Grave Protection and Repatriation Act, the subject of human remains in museums has also been a topic of keen interest, and much discussed with colleagues and students. The way people view the physical remains of their loved ones (and how dismissive they can be about the remains of strangers) intrigues me. Obviously I am not alone in finding the subject fascinating; all of the descriptions in this book about the multiple burials of body parts of British monarchs are factual.

Q: Near the end of the novel, Lizzie mentions that there is

402 • Mary Malloy

a difference between "doing history" and "being history." Can you elaborate on this statement?

A: Historians are basically nosy about other people's business, but I consider myself a very private person, and so I wondered as I wrote this what it would be like for a researcher to find that she had somehow become part of the story she was telling, as Lizzie did when she realized that the Hattons were her own family. Would you then be willing to obscure evidence, or even destroy it to protect your privacy? I liked giving Lizzie an ethical dilemma about this, so that she didn't destroy all the evidence of the suicides, but just buried it.

Q: At one point, Lizzie promises herself that she will "always look beyond the documents of the story to those things that lie unspoken behind them." What does she mean when she says this?

A: This is closely related to the last question. If clever people obscure or destroy information that they think might reveal too much about themselves or cast them in an unfavorable light, then the curious historian must be even more diligent in ferreting out secrets. This makes the historical process sound a lot like what the tabloid press does, so it also raises some conundrums. Are there some private details that people have a right to keep private? If there are, is it still true if they have chosen to live their life in the public sphere? Is it still true after they are dead? I think anyone who writes about a living person has a responsibility to be judicious and to consider the result of revealing private information, but we are a curious species and prone to gossip. People who lived in the past can provide us with wonderfully interesting and human stories and I'm certainly willing to tell them when they come to my attention. In *Devil on the Deep Blue Sea,* my biography of the Boston sea captain Samuel Hill, I exposed everything about the man I could find and used him as a springboard to talk about really private stuff, including sexual behavior on shipboard, and the awful actions on shore of the young American men who traveled out to the Pacific in the late eighteenth and early nineteenth centuries.

Q: If I were interested in learning more about the Crusades, what do you recommend for Crusades 101?

A: For an overview of the Crusades, *The Oxford Illustrated History of the Crusades* by Jonathan Riley-Smith is excellent, and I recommend two books that have descriptions written by people who were there. *Chronicles of the Crusades* includes accounts by two Europeans, Geoffrey Villehardouin and Jean de Joinville (which I quote from in the book). Amin Maalouf's *The Crusades Through Arab Eyes* gives the perspective of the other side.

Q: And the same question about Captain Cook and his voyages; can you recommend a book or website that would give me some additional information?

A: Cook was a good writer and a perceptive observer and I find his own shipboard journals very compelling. There are several editions of excerpts available, including a paperback Penguin edition. Cook continues to be the subject of much research and discussion. Glyndwr Williams, the preeminent historian of Cook, has a new book out that is very interesting, *The Death of Captain Cook: A Hero Made and Unmade,* and the Mariners' Museum in Newport News, Va., has a good website for looking at Cook's voyages: http://www.mariner.org/educationalad/ageofex/cook.php.

Q: Is Lizzie your alter ego?

A: I am surprised at how many people have asked me this question. When I started writing the book I identified very closely with Lizzie, but the more I wrote the more she evolved in ways that make her very different from me. As time went on over several years of writing I went back and edited out a lot of material that seemed too much like me. I didn't do this out of embarrassment or a need for privacy or anything like that. The character had simply taken on a life of her own and didn't need to be doing things I had done.

Q: Can you give examples?

A: Yes, but frankly they aren't all that interesting. I had a lot of day-to-day episodes that just didn't belong in the novel. In one scene, for instance, Lizzie was grading a pile of papers and I actually wove into it excerpts from papers that I have graded over the years. ("My most favorite thing in the world, after humus with pita bread, is the unknown.") It was probably therapeutic to write, but later, when I was in a strict editing mode, a lot of material like that was cut.

Q: How much did you write that didn't get included in the final book?

A: I think I probably have more than a hundred pages that I wrote but later cut, including a whole scene in which all the characters trooped over to France and met Bette, and another in which Bette came back to England after the heart was reburied. I decided it was better to know Bette through her diary. Managing her to the end of the book would require that I either give her a "miracle cure" for her mental illness (and thereby acknowledge some supernatural element that I was otherwise rejecting), or give poor old George one more burden to bear, which didn't seem quite fair to him under the circumstance.

Q: Would you consider ever making your "deleted scenes" available, like they do on DVDs of movies?

A: No. I have watched those "deleted scenes" and usually understand exactly why the director or editor decided not to include them. Taking those things out is what editing and revision are for. I have preached that mantra to hundreds of students and I absolutely believe it to be true.

Q: Are there other characters in the book that are based on real people?

A: The character of Kate Wentworth is based on my friend Peg Brandon. They aren't actually all that much alike at this point, beyond the facts that they are both sea captains and each has the surname of a Jane Austen hero. Peg accompanied me on a walk across England in 1997, though, and I am currently novelizing that trek to become Lizzie's next adventure, so Kate will play a bigger role in the next book. There were a few other people who I only knew casually or professionally who inspired me, but no character is drawn directly from an actual person.

Q: So we will we be meeting Lizzie again in another book?

A: I'm already at work on a sequel, with plans for a third book in the series. The next book, *Paradise Walk,* takes Lizzie across England looking for evidence that Chaucer based his "Wife of Bath" character in *Canterbury Tales* on an actual woman. I'm working hard to bring the landscape into focus in this book. There will be more descriptions of actual locations, including the great medieval cathedrals at Wells, Glastonbury, Winchester, and Canterbury. Most of the characters from *The Wandering Heart* will be back in the next two books.

Q: Do you still write nonfiction?

A: Yes, I am also working on a history of museums based on a course I teach in the Museum Studies program at the Harvard Extension School. I like to have several projects going and to move between them, so I am simultaneously working on three very different books, including a novel set in thirteenth-century Ireland at the monastic center of Clonmacnoise.

Q: What is the most important piece of advice that you would offer an aspiring writer?

A: The standard advice is to "write what you know," but since I am interested in research I would say "write about something that grabs your curiosity, and learn through the process." Then be prepared to work on it for a long, long time. I think the thing that most people don't understand about writing a novel is how long it can take and how much ideas evolve and change along the way. My motto in teaching is that "writing is a process," and for years I have been telling that to my students.

Q: Do you belong to a reading group?

A: Not currently, but for years I was part of a wonderful group at Brown University that read Medieval texts in modern translation. That sounds very geeky as I say it, but the books were ripping good reading. Being able to discuss books of common interest is very satisfying and I am looking for a new reading group.

Q: Did you read any books in that group that you would recommend to your readers?

A: For anyone who would like to delve into Medieval books, I highly recommend two books to start: *A History of the Franks* by Gregory of Tours, written in the sixth century; and *Heimskringla: History of the Kings of Norway* by Snorri Sturluson, written in the twelfth century. Both authors had the eye of a historian but were close to the subjects about which they were writing, so they have definite political points of view. There is so much love and jealousy and intrigue and grasping for power and violence in these books; the backstabbing is both literal and figural. There is not, however, a sustained narrative, so if plot and character development are what you seek, these books probably aren't for you.

Q: Are you willing to correspond with or visit a group reading *The Wandering Heart?*

A: I would love to be in touch with readers and, if my travel schedule allows, to visit with reading groups. Contact Leapfrog Press for details.

About the Type

This book was set in Plantin, a family of text typefaces inspired by the work of Christophe Plantin (1520-1589.) In 1913, Frank Hinman Pierpont of the English Monotype Corporation directed the Plantin revival. Based on 16th century specimens from the Plantin-Moretus Museum in Antwerp, specifically a type cut by Robert Granjon and a separate cursive Italic, the Plantin typeface was conceived. Plantin was drawn for use in mechanical typesetting on the international publishing markets.

Designed by John Taylor-Convery
Composed at JTC Imagineering, Santa Maria, CA